THE ISLE

JOHN C. FOSTER

GREY MATTER
PRESS

CHICAGO

PRAISE FOR JOHN C. FOSTER AND *THE ISLE*

"Brooding and claustrophobic, one hell of a scary ride. You won't soon forget your visit to *The Isle*."

– **Tom Deady, Bram Stoker Award®-winning author of *Haven***

"If you're the kind of person who seeks out hidden places with awful histories, then *The Isle* is the book is for you. You'll feel the damp and the chill, you'll hear the shrieks and the inhuman mutter, you'll see those children and their awful games. Read it in a safe place."

– **Karen Heuler, author of *The Inner City***

"John Foster masterfully weaves New England folk horror into a hard-boiled murder mystery to form a wholly original and gripping novel that will keep you guessing as the dread builds like a tide rolling over the rocky shore. Strange rituals, hidden histories, and dangerous paranoia intersect on *The Isle* in ways that turn northeastern peculiarity into something uniquely horrific and thoroughly engrossing to read."

– **Ed Kurtz, author of *The Rib from Which I Remake the World* and *Nausea***

"With *The Isle*, John Foster makes a twenty-first century contribution to the tradition of the New England Gothic, taking his lawman protagonist off the coast of the mainland United States to visit a small island in the North Atlantic whose inhabitants might have settled there from one of Nathaniel Hawthorne's Puritan fantasies. Himself riven by guilt over past misdeeds, U.S. Marshall Bone encounters a community on whom the sins of their ancestors continue to exert a very terrible and a very real force. Fast-moving, gripping, it's a tale straight from Old Man Atlantic's barnacled treasure chest.."

– **John Langan, Bram Stoker Award-winning author of *The Fisherman***

"Is it horror? Is it noir? Is it something in-between? Doesn't matter...John Foster crafts lean, mean fiction darker than a serial killer's soul"

– **James Newman, author of *Ugly as Sin***

THE ISLE
ISBN-13: 978-1-940658-51-3
ISBN-10: 1-940658-51-9
Grey Matter Press First Trade Paperback Edition - December 2018

Copyright © 2018 John C. Foster
Cover Image Copyright © 2018 Sabercore Art
Cover Design Copyright © 2018 Grey Matter Press
Book Design Copyright © 2018 Grey Matter Press
Edited by Anthony Rivera

GREY MATTER
P R E S S

CHICAGO

Grey Matter Press
greymatterpress.com

Grey Matter Press on Facebook
facebook.com/greymatterpress

THIS BOOK IS DEDICATED TO DUANE AND CAROL JONES
FOR GIVING ME THE NAMES

THE ISLE

ONE

- 1 -

"I need you to bring back a body."

Bone decided to drive off the end of the pier, but his foot had already slipped from the accelerator to the brake, a betrayal so automatic that the opportunity was missed before he could seize it.

Wind leaned against the hearse, rocking it on its springs as he sat and considered his orders. He considered corpses and the function of the vehicle he drove. He considered the drifting nature of his movements since the accident and slid out of the hearse before the spiral became inescapable, a long man wearing a black raincoat and fresh facial scars.

Dawn was a red rim of anger on the horizon as the storm gathered its strength and the wind tried to rip the door from his grip. Waves detonated against the rocks with loud explosions of white foam, the ocean matching the swirling fury of the storm clouds overhead.

"I need you to bring back a body." Marching orders. He looked away from the hearse, remembering the last time he had seen such a car, freshly waxed and gleaming in the October sun. This one was dirt-streaked and hunched against November. He thought it more appropriate to its function. The Atlantic beckoned to him, and he touched the change in his pocket, thinking about coins for the ferryman.

- 2 -

"Some sonofabitch is standing out on North Pier," old Vic said from the window inside the cramped Dock Office. His big-knuckled, arthritic hands were holding a bulky pair of binoculars he had owned since his time in Vietnam, and he adjusted the focus to see better.

"Yep," the dock boss said from his perch at the rickety metal desk. The white paint was mostly gone and salt air had rusted the legs, but it held his ledger, dock schedule and overstuffed ticket book—he was a demon for writing tickets—and worked "well enough" as he liked to say about anything that didn't need change. "Bastid asked to charter a boat out to the Isle."

Vic turned away from the window with its view of fishing boats bobbing at anchor in the small bay. "Ain't no one fool enough to run 'im out there," he said.

The dock boss leaned over and spit a mass of phlegm and tobacco juice into the Folger's can he kept on the floor for just that purpose.

"Could be I mentioned that, and could be that's why he's standin' over there on North Pier waitin' on the Isle boat herself."

Vic returned to looking out the window at the slim, black figure waiting alone. "Well I'll be. Is that his hearse parked out there?"

The front door banged open just then and two fishermen bundled inside. "Gonna get big weather today," a bearded fisherman in a thick sweater said as he headed over to the coffee pot and poured dubious-looking sludge into a Styrofoam cup.

"What you looking at?" the other newcomer asked, nicknamed Babyface for the obvious reason.

"Fella wants to charter a boat out to the Isle."

Babyface and his partner exchanged looks.

"Isle folk are awfully jealous about their waters," the bearded man said.

"Ain't no one fool enough to run him out there," Babyface said.

"If another body repeats that phrase, I believe I will shoot him," the dock boss said, spitting a wad that rocked the Folger's can. The bearded fisherman glanced in the can and gave the dock boss a nod of respect before taking a sip of coffee.

"Jesus Christ, this is awful," he said, frowning at his cup.

"Second pot," Vic said, and the other man nodded. The dock boss was in the habit of using coffee grounds at least twice to save money.

"Say," Vic said as Babyface held out a hand for the binoculars. "What'd he want out there?"

The dock boss shrugged. "Didn't rightly say, but he showed me a badge. A Federal badge no less."

"FBI, DEA?" the bearded man asked as he put on a new pot of coffee. The dock boss ignored him.

"So you get a man with a Federal badge, which means he's carryin' a Federal gun, and he shows up drivin' a hearse. Ain't too hard to jump to a certain conclusion," the dock boss said, not entirely sure what that conclusion was but enjoying the expressions on the faces of the two younger men.

"If Old Jenny gets her teeth into him, this Federal man might be finding himself in the back of that hearse on the return trip, badge or no badge," Vic said.

"Yep," the dock boss said.

"Yep," the bearded man said.

Babyface surrendered the binoculars and echoed the common wisdom. Hell, *everybody* knew to avoid that stretch of the Atlantic. Boats that didn't had a habit of not returning to port.

"Yep."

TWO

- 1 -

YESTERDAY

An empty coffee cup jittered on the dashboard as Bone piloted his Ford down a county road, the dirt frozen into jagged ruts by November's foreplay with winter. Fallow fields stretched off to either side, grass and broken cornstalks white with frost.

He finished his second coffee and tossed the cup into the passenger footwell when a phone rang in the glove compartment.

Julia's phone.

He didn't understand why he hadn't thrown it out. He didn't understand why he had plugged it into a recharger in the first place instead of letting the battery wind down and…

die.

He carefully pulled to the side of the road until it stopped ringing.

Who called?

The muffled beep of a new voicemail came from the glove compartment.

Bone pulled back onto the road.

- 2 -

Headquarters was in a low, brick building the cops imaginatively nicknamed The Brick. The town, which paid the bills and had reluctantly designated it the combined task force command center, still called it the Kittery Elementary School. It was central, it had enough space, and it was visible enough to let the public know *Something is Being Done.*

Bone parked in the visitor's lot and tried not to notice the marshals and state police smoking and bullshitting around an old swing set. A month ago he would have stopped to cadge a smoke and trade insults.

He grabbed the door handle and snuck a quick glance to see if they had noticed him. They had not. Somehow that felt worse.

- 3 -

Chief Inspector Roland's office was at the end of a hallway and had once been a third grade classroom. Rows of diminutive desks had been replaced with metal file cabinets, and muddy boot prints marred the tiles.

Chief Roland himself sat at the teacher's desk, a big man permanently mired in the final stages of exhaustion. Fluorescent lighting gleamed off his sweaty forehead and his left eye twitched in time with its ragged buzzing.

Case photos were taped around the walls, staring down at Roland with an almost physical pressure. He had put them there to remind him at every moment that they were real people, criminals and victims both. Now he looked down at his desk, avoiding them.

Bone sat across from Roland for nearly a minute before the chief looked up. "Cigarette?" he asked.

"What?" Bone said.

"Do you have one? I've been meaning to get a new pack since yesterday."

"I don't smoke any more." Bone paused to assess the chief. The room. The tension. "I was told to see you."

No response.

"For an assignment," Bone continued.

Roland looked at Bone and finally seemed to focus, bring himself back. "You sober, Virgil?"

Bone refused to flinch and said, "Of course." He ignored the flash of skepticism on Roland's face.

"You've lost weight," the chief said. "Damn clothes are swimming on you."

Bone grunted. When he dressed in the morning it looked like he was donning another man's suit, maybe his father's.

"Your pysch leave is over," Roland said. "I need you to bring back a body. It's not part of this." He gestured at the photos on the walls. "I don't have anyone else to do it."

Bone shifted in his seat. "You can use locals for that."

"Actually, I can't," Roland said. "This guy's name is Richard Slocum. Still a federal fugitive until we bring him in."

"He's dead?"

"He's not dead until a federal or state ME officially says he's dead," Roland said.

"Then send state."

"I can't. The Isle is technically only a territory. Not part of Maine. It's eighty-two miles off the coast. Isolated. Only about three hundred people living there. The only regular transport back and forth is a boat that delivers lobster and fish and picks up supplies. This needs a federal officer."

"The Isle authorities can't—"

Roland's bark of laughter cut Bone off.

"There's only a local constable and he's a right sonofabitch. He said... Shit, I wrote it down because I loved it so much." Roland fished out a Post-It from the piles on his desk. "'There's three ways you can do this, I can stick the body in the boneyard here' – that's how he said it, *boneyard* – 'or two, I can stuff him in a Hefty and float his dead self back to you, or three, you can fetch him.'"

Roland tossed the note back and picked up a file folder, handing it to Bone. "Isle boat won't dock 'til tomorrow. Here's a little background on where you're going." He sat back and deflated. "That's it. Get outta here. Bring me that fucking body."

Bone rose, but paused at the door. "How did Slocum die?"

"Accident. Not your problem. You're just the UPS man."

- 4 -

Bone was nearly to the front doors of The Brick when he heard his name called out behind him. He turned as Roland trotted after him, face purpling with effort.

Roland held out an envelope.

"What's this?" Bone asked, wondering if the heart attack would let a stroke kill the chief first.

"You know what it is," Roland said.

Bone slit the envelope with his thumb and slid out a sheet of paper as Roland's breathing provided sound effects. NOTICE OF HEARING was printed at the top. His stomach twisted, and it must have shown on his face.

"You knew it was coming," Roland said.

Purple and black emotions twined about each other in Bone's gut and he had to make his voice quiet to keep them at bay.

"So I'm done?" Bone said.

Roland's eyelid twitched, a bubble of humanity breaching the surface. "Do this thing, all right? Maybe it will help."

"You think?"

"We'll deal with it when you get back."

Bone pushed through the doors and his feet grew roots into the black-top as he watched a group of agents hurry to a van. He reached into a pocket before he remembered he had no cigarettes. Giving them up was part of his twenty-eight days following the accident. He hadn't truly accepted that he was a non-smoker, but he hadn't bought himself a pack either.

When he eventually moved, it was because he could determine no other course than to attend to the duty at hand. He walked woodenly towards his parked car, only pausing to open the folder of background material when he was settled behind the wheel.

He felt a sudden drop as one more degree of his reality slipped away.

The top sheet was a report on the last Federal visit to the Isle. A census taker named Tate who went out there nearly a decade ago. Following the visit he was reported lost at sea and only recovered after several weeks adrift.

On his return, Tate was committed to an insane asylum.

THREE

- 1 -

Bone saw it.

A speck grew on the horizon, a black clot against the blood red sky of the east, growing in size as if arising from the sea. It was a perfectly outlined shadow devoid of details, a boat-shaped hole punched into the dawn. Strange arachnoid arms reached up and out to either side, dangling long lines, looking to Bone like the claws of a massive lobster raised in warning, trailing lengths of seaweed.

Blue-black clouds belched from its main stack, and Bone heard an aggressive, repetitive chuffing, animal in nature. The fishing trawler was ancient and ungainly, its bloated hull pebbled like the hide of something that swims below sight, covered in a wet blanket of glistening barnacles like the armor of a Mesozoic crustacean. A son of New England, Bone thought it was the most repulsive-looking boat he had ever seen.

A medusa's slurry of thick ropes floated around it, coated with fluttering green seaweed in the rainbow slick of oil that surrounded the boat. The choking odor of burning oil swept in from the water, smothering the organic smell of the coast.

Wind and waves slapped against the vessel as if to push it aside, and Bone felt a palpable sense of unwelcome rise as it plodded dully through the resistance.

He could see no sailors on deck and no movement behind the filthy glass of the pilot's cabin, a poor man's Mary Celeste, unguided by human hands. Faded lettering in archaic script on the bow gave the ugly craft a name.

Leviathan.

- 2 -

Tension rose in Samuel Weeks as *Leviathan* came closer to the mainland. The pilot disliked the coastal waves and the wind that tried to push *Leviathan* off course. He eased the throttle up a notch and the comforting chuff of the engine increased in speed.

He looked through the smeared windows at the figure standing on the pier and said something that sounded like, "What's this whale shit?" his tongue pushing at the gaps in his teeth.

He leaned away from the large, wooden wheel and raked a grimy fingernail across the row of black and green lobster claws that hung like chimes in the window. Smooth sea pebbles inside of each rattled with a sound like bones.

Weeks looked back at the man on the pier and watched the wind yank at him, quietly urging it to pitch the man in the water.

"Mainlanders swarmin' like flies," he said, thinking of the trouble the last one had brought. His accent was such as to render the word "accent" meaningless. Rather, it was like the steel in a well-forged sword, folded over and over a hundred times and pounded down into a density that made it something wholly apart from the original materials.

He walked back out of the door to a main deck stained white with seagull shit and crouched over the wooden hatch set in the floor. The shrill cries of the birds overhead grated on him like beggars asking for his last dime. He gave the door a pounding with bony knuckles and then headed aft to a cleaning table, stepping around stacked lobster traps and navigating dangerous lines and cables with the ease of long experience.

"C'mon down you beauties. Breakfast time," he called up to the noisy clutch of birds as he reached into a cooler beneath the table and grabbed a handful of fish guts, tossing the wet pile onto the table and wiping his hand on his shirt. He grinned through his black teeth as the birds darted lower, competing for the entrails. The garbage eaters that died over the water from eating the poisoned slop he counted as God's work well done. The ones that fell dead on his deck he counted as God's work very well done and gave back to the sea by cutting them up for bait on the return trip.

A wooden *boom!* behind him caused him to turn, and he saw the hatch in the floor was open. He felt the chill roll outward from the ice hold and smelled the sweet smell of their catch as he approached it.

"Almost there," he said down into the black hole. "Mainlander waitin' for us. Fella as looks like he got a purpose."

The darkness shifted in the unlit hold, and the pilot saw two flashes of white set close together. Eyes.

"'E make 'e self scarce," he shouted before lifting the hatch and dropping it back down so it slammed closed with another hollow *boom!*

- 3 -

Bone felt the shock through his feet as the trawler bumped into the wooden pier, old rubber tires hung over the side of the craft absorbing the impact. He hopped on the rail and grabbed a rope, returning to the pier and tying it off on a rusted cleat. When he turned back again he was ready to call out a greeting.

Leviathan's deck was empty.

Bone stepped back onto the rail of the boat and hopped down, his foot nearly landing on the splayed body of a seagull.

"What the hell?" he said, crouching down. The bird twitched, one wing flopping weakly against the peeling deck boards. Instinct insisted he do something about it but he had no idea what.

"Huh," he said and stood, looking around.

The smell of dead fish and decay assaulted his nostrils as he took in the peeling paint and rusting metal of the boat. White stripes of guano had dried over every surface. He thought of the well-scrubbed working boats he had seen earlier in the harbor. It was no wonder the old dock master had no truck with *Leviathan*. It would be like stabling a diseased pig among thoroughbred horses.

"Hello?" Bone said, just shy of shouting.

Nothing stirred on the boat.

Bone felt the alienness of the vessel through his feet. A clear sense that he did not belong. He suppressed the urge to open his coat and unsnap the safety strap on his hip holster.

"Hello!" A shout this time. "Federal agent!" He moved carefully across the slippery deck to the pilot house and tried peering through the muck-spat-tered porthole on the door. He grabbed the handle and slid the door open, eliciting a screech as it fought the rusting track.

Stink rolled outward from the small cabin, a mélange of man and fish. Rattling drew his gaze and Bone saw a string of lobster claws hung like Christmas ornaments on a length of fishing line. A small cross made of sea shells hung from the fishing line, wrapped in wet lengths of seaweed, and Bone, who had last been to church at the time of his wedding, still felt a subtle dissonance.

He stepped through the cabin and out the port side door, ducking against the spray as a wave slammed against the hull. Grabbing the slick railing, he moved carefully aft, regretting his slick-soled shoes.

The rear of the boat was a large, open deck with lobster cages and equipment lashed down along the rails. Bone slip-stepped across the wood, splashing through puddles and cursing as he felt the chill wetness soak through his shoes and into the tips of his socks.

"Hello!" he said, dropping to one knee—seawater instantly soaking through his slacks—and pounding on the rear hatch with the side of his fist.

Something heavy shifted below and Bone leaned over the hatch, steadying himself on his hands as he brought his ear close to the wood.

There was a brief sensation of air pushing at him and a smell, a strong smell, in the split second before a large metal hook slammed into the hatch mere inches from his nose.

"Hey!" Bone shouted, moving away with a sudden push-up and slip-scrambling backwards until he skidded across the deck on the seat of his pants.

A bent figure in fisherman's oilskins and a long, draping hat wrenched at the long handle of a boathook, pulling it free from the hatch. He wheeled on Bone, bulging eyes fixed and furious, lips pulled back over gapped and blackened teeth.

"What are you doing on my boat?" The fisherman yelled, lumbering forward with the boathook raised threateningly.

"Hey, Goddammit, stop!" Bone shouted, balancing on his ass as he reached under his coat and jerked out the Glock. "Stop right there. I'm a Federal agent!"

The fisherman's fleshy lips froze in mid-snarl and his thick-soled boots planted themselves, but he didn't lower the hook. Bone carefully slid one knee under him, keeping the Glock trained on the fisherman's chest.

"Step back right the fuck now! Step back and drop the hook," Bone said, fighting the surge of adrenaline trying to turn his startled fear into anger. He felt his throat tighten and his vision narrow as biology kicked in.

De-escalate this.

"Who are you?" Bone asked. He kept his voice low.

"I'm the pilot of this here boat," Samuel Weeks said.

Bone patted the air with his free hand before reaching under his coat again. "I'm going to show you my badge, and you're going to lower the hook."

The pilot grunted and Bone fished out his badge case, flicking it open.

"See that there bit o' shine," Weeks said, holding out one wide-palmed hand. Bone stood and extended it, and the other man inched closer, squinting. "Federal marshal, eh?" he said, lips peeling back in what might be a grin. "Thought you was a thief."

The pilot strode to the side of the boat and pointed south at the harbor. "Bad enough the coast-hugging bastards try to thief our traps and channels at sea without 'em coming onto *Leviathan* when she's in dock."

He turned back, smiling awfully at Bone. "I didn't mean nothing by it." He glanced at the hook in his hand with something like surprise before setting it back in its clamps beneath the rail.

Bone holstered his weapon and slid his badge case back into its pocket. "I need a ride out to the Isle on your return leg."

"*Leviathan* ain't no cruise ship."

Bone ignored the statement. "I'm told you'll be sailing back to the Isle before nightfall."

"'Fore nightfall? 'Fore lunch, if 'e delivery boys ain't late with their truck," the pilot said, then spat over the side. He glanced up at Bone slyly. "You're after the cawpse."

"The marshal's office called ahead?"

The pilot laughed derisively. "Ain't no phone out to the Isle after October. Line went down for the season last week."

Bone heard a coughing rumble and looked inland to see a heavy delivery truck making its way towards the pier.

"Mainlanders are like bugs that leave tracks, if one comes out, more follow," the pilot said. "'Sides, you're driving a hearse."

Weeks threw back his head and laughed at his own deductive capabilities, his Adam's apple bobbing visibly. "Come, come. You wait inside the cabin while we transfer the catch and goods for the return leg."

He patted Bone on the shoulder, guiding him. Bone was struck by a memory from early in his career when he was briefly stationed in a correctional facility. Prison trustees, jailbirds with enough status to perform menial jobs and earn small amounts of responsibility. Ingratiating.

"You just stay out of the way here," the pilot said as Bone stepped into the cabin. "We'll get you out to your dead fella presently."

As the pilot lumbered away, oilskins making *swish-swish* sounds, Bone remembered something else about trustees.

It paid to never turn your back on them.

FOUR

- 1 -

Leviathan's engine made an oily, slamming sound as it pushed the blunt boat through the heavy swells, and Bone watched the coast recede behind him with a strange feeling of relief.

He wandered back to the boxes of supplies the boat was carrying to the Isle. A stack of newspapers was bound by blue cord, and Bone read the topmost page.

RED RIVER STRANGLER TAKES ANOTHER was the headline. Below it was information on the task force he was no longer a part of.

Bone turned away and grasped the handle on the sliding door of the main cabin, wrestling it open against the rust, and stepped outside into the spray.

The last of the white seagulls leapt up from the rail and Bone watched it fly back toward the mainland. He moved to the bow and leaned into the wind and foam, letting the cold needles cut through his personal fog.

- 2 -

TWO WEEKS AGO

The office was dark and somehow unfriendly. Bone's eyes remained fixed and unblinking on the man in the brown wool jacket.

"You understand that I'm not here on your behalf, although I can refer you to a colleague if you wish," Dr. Kleer said.

Bone sat like a statue, a white bandage taped over the angry scarring on his face.

"I'm here on behalf of the marshal's service as part of the inquiry surrounding your…the incident," Kleer continued.

The cigarette dangling from between two of Bone's fingers was a grey length of smoldering ash. He watched the shrink's eyes dip to it and waited for the rebuke.

The psychologist cleared his throat. "Mr. Bone, what happened to your wife?"

"She died," he said.

Kleer looked away from Bone's eyes. "She died in a car accident. She was pregnant, yes?"

Bone's flat stare was unwavering.

"Your wife died in an accident in which you were at the wheel. Prior to which you had been drinking?"

Bone stared. Kleer looked away again.

"Your reaction is puzzling. And perhaps the reason I was asked to speak with you."

Dr. Kleer rose and began to pace.

"Do you believe that the eyes are the windows to the soul, Mr. Bone?" Kleer asked.

Bone was laying on the hood of his car, the rain pounding down, staring back through the windshield into his wife's eyes as life leaked from her. She was saying something, but he couldn't hear her.

"Because I didn't see anything in yours when you told me your wife had died."

Bone's head swiveled to track the pacing doctor.

"Mr. Bone, your wife was having an affair, wasn't she?"

Bone looked at the ash on his cigarette.

"Mr. Bone?"

He ignored the shrink, watching as the ash collapsed. Solid one moment, falling to dust the next.

"Mr. Bone?"

- 3 -

ONE MONTH AGO

"You…"

Bone heard it over the roaring of his own blood and the droning liturgy of the priest. They were outdoors and the day was dead. The trees had lost their leaves. The grass, no longer watered as autumn tightened its grip, was yellow. The ground itself was cold and hard.

He was on furlough from rehab, aware that he had spoken and been spoken to, hands had been shaken, commiserations shared. He retained none of it. His pain medication had worn off, and he was more aware of his own knitting flesh than anything around him.

"Yooouuu…"

He glanced down the row of mourners in black standing on the hillside. Julia's family was clustered around her parents. All eyes were on the priest where he stood at the head of the oak-and-brass coffin.

He noted the veiled face turned his way, hate-filled eyes glittering behind black gauze. He realized he had been hearing the muttered word, the *accusation*, for quite some time now. A sudden wind blew dead leaves in a crackling swirl across the freshly dug grave, depositing several inside. Bone fought back a shiver.

"You…" Louder now. The ranks of mourners began to shuffle, muttering.

"…senseless and preventable tragedy." The priest continued, his eyes flicking worriedly from his text to the disturbance in the flock.

"You!" Full-voiced now and hoarse with emotion. Julia's mother stepped from the row and turned to face him directly, a bony, quivering finger leveled at him.

"Mama," one of Julia's stocky, Italian brothers put a hand on his mother's shoulders and she shook it off. The family was a swirl of black around the old woman, and Bone was abruptly aware of how alone he stood beside his wife's grave.

"Drunk! Liar! Killer!" the old woman shrieked, steaming towards him, her thick legs churning under the heavy black dress. Bone's jaw unhinged and his mouth hung slackly open. The roaring filled his ears and his vision narrowed to a tiny black tunnel focused on his mother-in-law.

"Everyone—" the priest said and was drowned out by the erupting crowd.

The old woman's first blow thudded into his chest, and Bone took a step back, seeing but not believing as the second blow arced up towards his face, rocking his head to the side as it glanced off his cheekbone. Then the swirl of black was between them, brothers, cousins, friends, enfolding the old woman in a myriad of shifting hugs and bulling him backward through sheer mass.

"Hey!" Bone finally said, still in shock. A broad hand planted itself on his chest and shoved. Bone staggered and almost fell.

"Get outta here," Lou said. Julia's younger brother, already balding and thick through the chest and shoulders.

"You!" The shouts from Julia's mother were frightening now. "You!" The word scraped out over raw vocal cords. "You!" Bone heard madness in the metronomic vitriol.

"Get outta here! You're not wanted, you fucking sonofabitch!" Lou said, spitting anger in Bone's face.

"I—" Bone tried to say something, but the rush of blood in his ears drowned out his ability to think.

"Yoooouuuuuuu!"

Bone turned and walked away, legs stiff, as if he had no knee joints. He shoved his hands in his pockets, feeling the wind pluck his tie free from its clasp and whip it around his face and shoulders.

Behind him, the shouts and cries continued.

- 4 -

Bone watched with his hands in his front pockets as the two gravediggers filled in the rectangular hole, dirt bouncing and scraping across the coffin resting at the bottom.

"Can I buy a cigarette off you?" Bone asked when one of the men paused and pulled out a pack of Camels. He was a rangy guy with a handlebar mustache and a Harley-Davidson T-shirt under his dirty coveralls.

"No," the man said, stabbing his shovel into the dirt pile and giving the head a stomp to make sure it stuck. "But you can have one."

He produced a pack, tapped it once and slid out a white cigarette. Bone stuck it between his teeth and leaned forward as the digger flicked a lighter.

"Thanks," Bone said, smoke streaming from his mouth with the word. He watched as the other digger kept working steadily, earphones blocking out the world.

"Heard there was a bit of a rumble at the service," the digger said, gesturing with his cigarette at the discoloration on Bone's cheek. "You there?"

Bone nodded. "Lot of emotion. The mother." He shrugged and the digger nodded.

"You close to her?" The digger jabbed his cigarette at the headstone.

Bone shook his head, feeling the smoke scratch its way deep into his lungs. Feeling. Just glad to be feeling something. He stared at the headstone. At the engraving on it. He thought he should be angry that Julia's family had chosen the inscription without consulting him. Thought it but didn't feel it.

Smoke leaked out the side of his mouth.

What are you doing? What's going to happen if you keep standing here?

"You know who she was?" the digger asked as he field-stripped his cigarette and stuck the paper in a pocket. Bone thought about flicking his own cigarette butt into the open grave and decided that was just...

"Yeah," he said. "She was my wife."

FIVE

- 1 -

Bone heard the beeping again, muffled by the crash of the waves and stuttering bump of the engine. He reached into his pocket and pulled out two phones, his own and Julia's.

Why did I bring...?

He had no recollection of taking her phone from the glove compartment of his car. Then again, he had no recollection of *not* taking the phone either.

Strangely, the idea of sleepwalking through portions of his life did not frighten him. Maybe it was the cool salt spray wetting his face, or the steady wind that blew the pollution from *Leviathan's* stack behind him. The air he breathed came from three thousand miles of Atlantic untroubled by men and filled his lungs the way the leaden air of Maine did not.

His phone beeped again and he glanced down at the screen to see the last signal bar flicker and die.

A moment later his wife's phone beeped as well, clinging stubbornly to the signal for several minutes longer than his own device. Eventually it too jettisoned its electronic tie to the mainland, and he began to slide both phones back into his pocket when an idea struck him. He plucked his wife's phone back out and threw it hard. It spun and flashed in the air, catching the sun, before splashing into the sea. Bone fixed the spot with his eyes, smiling faintly at the absurdity of what he had just done as the boat sailed over the spot where the phone had been eaten by the waves.

Let it go, he thought, closing his eyes.

When his pocket beeped again, he pulled out the phone, staring in shock at the name on the screen as it relentlessly attempted to reacquire a signal.

He'd thrown away the wrong phone.

- 2 -

"Why have we stopped?" Bone asked, pulling open the door to the cabin and stepping inside. The rank air seemed, if anything, to have increased in offensiveness after several hours of sailing.

"Oh did 'e not get the schedule?" the pilot said. He slid open the opposite door and headed out on deck, pulling on his heavy coat.

Bone stepped back out on his side and walked carefully on the slick wood until he reached the bow, where the pilot was releasing a heavy lever of iron and wood. A splash came from in front of the boat, and a geyser of water plumed upward as a massive pile of anchor chain began uncoiling, shooting through a wide hole beneath the railing.

"You're setting anchor?" Bone said.

The pilot gave him a grimace, and Bone saw naked contempt before the grizzled sailor pushed past him and made his way to the broad rear deck.

Bone stared out at the empty sea, lit orange by the setting sun. Whitecaps roiled across the vast expanse of water, broken only by a single, rocky spire covered in green seaweed and white stripes of bird shit.

He heard a splash from the rear of the boat and the rattle of uncoiling chain. Bone made his way aft, slipping twice in his haste.

"What are you doing?"

The pilot looked at him, one eye squinting nearly shut, and Bone imagined him sighting down a rifle.

"We anchor here for the night," Weeks said.

Bone shook his head. "I need to get to the Isle tonight."

"Then swim, 'e bloody idiot," the pilot snarled. "Fancy bit o'shine may mean somethin' standing on shore, but it means nothin' out here. There is one captain of *Leviathan*. One!" He slammed his clenched fist against his chest, then pointed at the spire of rock rising from the unruly waves. "The Finger tells us we're at shallow water, shallow enough to anchor. Even *Leviathan* will not run the Teeth in dark of night. We wait 'til morning, when one hour's sailing puts us in dock."

Bone studied the man.

"The Teeth," Bone said. "Jenny Green Teeth?"

"She'll savage any vessel foolish enough to tempt her at night."

- 3 -

"That there's why we don't fish at Jenny Green Teeth, nor drop our lobster pots," he said after finding Bone at the bow. Once again, the pilot's mood had reversed completely and Bone wondered about the stability of the man's mind.

"See it at the base there," he continued.

As the sun set, Jenny glinted green in the fading light, and Bone noticed a thick chain wrapped around the spire of rock right at the water line. It was black with rust and hairy with seaweed.

"'Twas nigh on thirty years ago that the last man of the Isle came here to fish," he said. "A sturdy trawler named *Luck o' the Day*, she was called, crewed by two brothers name of Fetchwater."

Bone settled in on the gunwale opposite, suppressing by force of will the urge to look behind him at the roiling water.

Weeks lit a bent cigarette, and the wind blew a fleeting scent of smoke to Bone.

"'E don't mind, do yeah?" he asked, then continued on without waiting for a response. "Call comes in, broken up though the skies were clear. Distress call for sure, but naught else could be made out. My father was first mate on *White Clouds,* and they set out immediately for old Jenny, speculating on what might've happened. Sharkin', they thought. One of the brothers hooked a big one and went over."

He turned and lifted a long-handled boathook from its rack, giving Bone his trustee's smile.

"See, in those days, *Luck* didn't have a crane, so when you went sharkin', you caught the fish on a heavy line and reeled her in by sweat and muscle. When she got close to the surface, your mate did this."

The pilot turned and jammed the toe of one boot hard into the tiny drain hole set in the gunwale at deck level.

"And then 'e did *this*," he said, abruptly doubling over the gunwale so his upper body disappeared from view, and Bone heard a splash as the boathook ripped into the sea. The only thing keeping him from upending completely and going over was the toe of one boot.

After a minute of slashing at imaginary sharks, the pilot jackknifed up and spun about, boathook held across his body like a rifle at port arms, his chin whiskers dripping with water.

"Aye, 'e get right down there and stick your face in it to hook the shark until 'e can drag it into the boat and stave in its skull." He grinned at Bone, rivulets of water framing his teeth. "If the man on the line, the more experienced man always, but if that man made a mistake about the size of the fish he was pullin' up, the hookman might find himself grin-to-grin with a great white."

Bone heard the slap of waves against the boat and flinched at the touch of cold droplets on the back of his neck. The pilot held his grin, his great white's grin, for a moment longer.

The grin slowly faded.

"When my father arrived aboard *White Clouds*, he an' the captain found a sea empty of buoys. 'Twas as if none had ever been planted, though they both knew there were at least twenty seeded around old Jenny."

He picked up his cigarette from the railing and suckled greedily.

"They heard the crashing and bashing of wood on rock, a terrible sound at sea, long before they saw *Luck*," the pilot said, gesturing to the rock. "She was bound to the Teeth by her bow anchor chain, only there weren't no anchor at the end of the chain. The aft anchor had been dropped though, and *Luck* was bucking against the rock. 'Get aboard there boy,' the captain said to my father, 'and untie her from the rocks before she's smashed to pieces.' So they pull up close and my father jumps from railing to railing, near to falling in himself. He ran through the boat shouting for the Fetchwaters, but neither brother was to be seen. So he set to releasing the bow anchor chain but couldn't get it free from Jenny's bite by himself. 'Cut her loose,' the captain shouted at him, and my father released the bow chain from the boat with fingers gone dumb from the fear that gripped him. See, Mr. Bone, men are lost at sea all the time, and my father was an experienced fisherman before he was eighteen, 'But something was wrong on that boat,' he told me when I was still a boy. 'The Fetchwaters were cool as cucumbers and able seamen both, but tying off to Jenny was the act of a man panicked into foolishness.'"

He pitched the cigarette over the side as if the taste disgusted him.

"Captain of *White Clouds* told my father to bring *Luck* back to the Isle himself. And my father, he set to pulling up the aft anchor, the *Luck* now swinging away from Jenny… But at any moment she could swing back and smash hard, dropping my father into the drink. He told me that he did not want to go into that water there around old Jenny, and he a man who swam like a fish when he was only three. In fact, he told me once after he had finished his whiskey, that if he had hit that water, he thought he would scream."

Weeks squinted one eye and lowered his voice.

"But the aft anchor, she wouldn't come up more than a crank or two. My father was certain she was not hooked onto the bottom, but was being held by something. 'Captain,' he shouted to the other boat, 'Anchor's bein' held by a shark!' The captain heard panic creeping into my father's voice and told him to set sail, so my father did as he was told and cranked the engine over until black smoke poured from her stack. Whatever it was held onto *Luck* for a moment…then another moment…and my father was ready to call *White Clouds* alongside so he could abandon *Luck* to whatever wanted to keep her…and then she pulled free. My father set her course and ran aft, working the crank to pull up the chain. It looped around and around the spindle and stopped before the anchor was fully up, but my father thought it was high enough not to catch on any rocks if he were careful approaching the Isle port."

The old fisherman pulled another cigarette from his pack and lit it with a match that trembled slightly.

"A good sailor, my father, and he brought that battered *Luck* back to port dragging the anchor. The captain of *White Clouds* came aboard to help, and while my father tied the bow off with a fresh line waiting on the dock, the captain went aft to secure the stern. My father went after him to help and found the captain starin' over the side at the anchor chain. He jumped when my father put a hand on his shoulder and straightened up, his face white as a sheet. Without sayin' a word 'e pointed over the side and my father leaned over to take a look. 'It was a claw,' my father told me, and his voice was a whisper. 'A severed lobster's claw over a foot and a half long and black as night, still clinging to the anchor chain and preventin' her from retracting fully.'

"A foot and a half long?" Bone said, snorting. "Bullshit."

The pilot straightened up from his storyteller's hunch and laughed, as if caught in a whopper of a tale. "Aye, 'tis hard to believe. How old would such a beast be? But 'tis a fact and recorded history of the Isle that more boats went out to look for the brothers and found not a sign of them."

He turned and started back towards the pilot house, then stopped with one last bit to say. "But we don't fish or set pots out around Jenny Green Teeth anymore, even though these waters used to be rich fishing. She seems content to let us anchor here as long as we keep away from her bounty."

Bone shook his head and automatically reached up to his pocket for the cigarettes he no longer smoked.

"But if 'e be thinking of taking a midnight dip." The pilot glanced at Jenny Green Teeth before grinning back at Bone. "Give a thought to why the sharks don't swim around Jenny anymore, even at this hour when the light goes and the dark rolls in. Give it a thought."

The man entered the pilot house, trailing laughter. Bone succumbed to the urge to turn and look out over the black waves hiding their secrets. He thought about two brothers named Fetchwater and wondered about jealous seas.

- 4 -

Bone's right rear pocket was wet. Not his left, just the right. He squirmed under the blanket and reached back, pulling out his wallet and stuffing it into a coat pocket. When he settled back down his left rear pocket soaked up frigid water.

Oh good, he thought.

Even wedged against the solid wood of the gunwale, Bone felt terribly exposed. It wasn't the cold wind that cut through his blanket as if it were cobwebs. It wasn't the vast expanse of starry sky overhead. It wasn't even thoughts of trouble from the increasingly disturbing boat pilot.

It was the water.

He could hear it sloshing directly beneath him. He could feel the vibration as waves struck the hull and sporadic wetness gusted in through the anchor ports. It rolled the boat, shifting contents around in the hold with erratic thumps.

Black water. Deep water. Hiding God knew what. Kept at bay by insignificant inches of old wood.

He closed his eyes and leaned back against heavy coils of damp hawser, pulling the blanket up to his chin. The thick, scratchy rope tickled the bare skin on the back of his neck and he shifted, unable to find a comfortable position.

Eventually the effect of not seeing the water became too much and he kicked off his blankets. Leaning on the coil of hawser to climb to his feet, he braced his hands on the gunwale and looked out.

It was endless. Not endless in the manner of night skies overhead, which pulled at Bone, insisting he was missing something incredible by not soaring among the stars. The sea was *terrifyingly* endless. It dwarfed him. It told him in no uncertain terms that he was too small. His boat was too small. He might as well be riding on a floating leaf for all the safety the boat could offer.

Whitecaps glowed briefly atop oily blackness, blackness without end. The pilot had said the spire—The Finger, he called it—marked shallow water, but Bone knew differently. He knew that to fall into the grip of the sea was to sink forever.

Something broke the surface in front of the boat and was gone before Bone could react. He shivered with the knowledge of what swam below the surface, below the boat itself. The fear was deep, curling around his guts. Race memory. A wave slapped against the boat and drops of seawater struck his face, the ocean's smell pressing itself into his nostrils, invading him. Threatening.

Something thumped. He felt the vibration in his feet, unsure if it was shifting cargo in the hold or something vast beneath them, probing at the barnacle-clad keel.

The boat rocked once, violently. *A wave?* Bone was unsure, and the lack of certainty was fraying his self-control. He stared down into the depths, caught by the growing urge to throw himself into the deep. If there was to be confrontation, then bring it immediately. *Bring an end*—

"Shit, get a grip, asshole," Bone said aloud. He hawked and spat over the side in an effort to take some sort of action. To repudiate the pull of the deep.

He glanced back at the cabin, expecting the jeering face of the pilot to be pressed against the glass. But the cabin was dark.

"Well fuck you too," Bone said to the empty windows.

He forced himself to sit down, back against the pile of hawser, and untangled the blanket before pulling it over his legs. "Son of a fucking bitch," he muttered, reaching for his briefcase, wiping a scrim of wetness from its sides with the blade of his hand.

He pulled out the file folder, flipping quickly past several articles, the plastic pages crackling. He didn't need to read about missing trawlers and shipwrecks. He slid Julia's phone from his pocket and hit the button, casting light from the screen on the snippets of unhinged Tate's own writing.

> *What strange evolution must have taken place in those deep spaces? Some break in the assault of other sea creatures had allowed the crustacean to take hold and dominate. "Locusta" in the Latin. Unchallenged and grown huge, aggressive, cannibalistic in a closed ecological system. We trod across empty claws and hollowed tails, the chitin crunching beneath our feet. At one point we were forced to turn back and skirt wide around the edge of a cave, around water so full of lobsters that they crawled over each other like enormous ants as their horrible warbling beat against our eardrums.*

"Jesus." Bone tore his eyes away from the printed words as if they might leak a contagion madness.

A slip of newspaper fell out and Bone caught it before it see-sawed its way to the damp wood of the deck. RECORD LOBSTER CAUGHT OFF NEW-FOUNDLAND COAST the article said, with a picture of a fisherman reclining on the deck of a boat not dissimilar to the one Bone was on. An enormous black lobster, easily three feet long, was stretched out next to the grinning fisherman. Someone had outlined the lobster on the newsprint with a blue pen, increasing the size of it. The words MUCH OLDER were written next to the outline with a question mark.

Great claws waving from dark water, Tate had written. Another line leapt off the page, *I ate my fingers because I was terribly hungry, adrift at sea. I understand that now.* The account was jumbled, and Bone wasn't sure if the man had visited the Isle or not and wondered why Roland had seen fit to share the file at all.

He fought the urge to again look over the side of the boat. Instead, he stuffed the folder into his briefcase.

Christ, I could use a drink, he thought. He imagined the bloom of heat in his chest, the burn in his throat. He imagined being able to unmoor his mind, to stop chewing on problems, to float.

Waving from dark water.

"Shit."

He closed his briefcase and looked up at the sky. Trying to remember the name of a particular star when, incredibly, sleep crept up on him and wrapped him in its embrace.

- 5 -

Bone's sleep was fragmented and crawling with dreams. Without alcohol to dampen his thoughts, his mind gnawed at him, his id unfettered and given row upon row of teeth.

He heard the great lobster pulling itself across the boat's deck towards him. Its heavy shell was draped with seaweed and it scraped its belly over the wood, demanding he open his eyes.

Bone refused.

It drew closer and Bone heard a gurgling sound, as if the huge carapace of the thing were filled with roiling liquid. He instinctively began to pull his feet in.

He could feel himself rising towards consciousness, as if an inflatable device were dragging him up towards the surface of a deep sea.

"Shut up," he slurred, rolling over on his side. He slid his hand under the pile of extra blankets next to him, vaguely confused but unsure why.

His hand sought out warmth until his fingers moved over something bristling with short hair. A mouth opened against his knuckles and thick lips wrapped around the meat at the edge of his palm. He felt the momentary heat of a wet tongue running over his skin before teeth closed on his hand.

- 6 -

Bone surged up in an explosion of lobster crates, tripping backwards even as he reached for the weapon in his shoulder holster—

Empty!

—and crashed back into the gunwale.

Boom! A hollow sound echoed over the crashing sea, and Bone had a split second to wonder if something had hit the boat when the deck lurched at precisely the wrong moment, the railing behind him dipping towards the water.

Time stretched as he arched backwards into an eagerly reaching wave, black foam filling his nose and mouth even as the sheer watery weight of pure terror galvanized him to kick and swing his arms wildly. He was helpless. A toad stabbed with electrical current. Consumed with doom. Unable to comprehend what was happening as forces so much bigger dragged it beneath—

His foot caught in a trap, the trap caught in the anchor chain, and Bone's plunge into the sea halted. The shock of the stoppage slammed him backwards across the wooden gunwale, his back stretched painfully as *Leviathan* lurched back in the other direction. Bone desperately wrenched away from the water in a full-body sit-up, flinging himself face forward onto the deck, splinters driving into hands thrown out to break his fall. He landed badly, feet still tangled, and his chin impacted the deck planks, snapping his teeth closed with a painful clack.

He pushed up onto his hands and knees, scrambling and kicking to free his shoes from the traps and ropes.

My gun.

He lunged at the matte black shape of the Glock and misjudged the grab. The weapon pinwheeled across the deck and Bone looked up, casting about wildly. The deck was empty, lit by the pale green glow from Jenny. It was an ugly color. Seasickness made visible on the light spectrum.

Bone sat on his haunches, wiping the wet hair from his eyes and coughing up more seawater. Shooting pain lanced from his back into the top of his hips and up to his shoulder blades. Stiffness would follow.

You motherfucker.

He crawled to his pistol and picked it up, racking the slide to chamber a .40-caliber bullet. He stood carefully on the pitching deck, and the winds bashed at him, whipping his jacket up until it flared like a cape.

Sick fury coiled in his guts. *Violation.* He eyed the dark windows of the pilot house and started forward without hesitation, shoes sliding on the wet deck. His right foot shot out from under him and he went down to one knee. Pushed himself up. Grabbed the door handle to the cabin in his free hand and lifted the Glock to a ready position beside his right cheek.

One, two...

He slid the door open and swung inside, the Glock held out before him.

- 7 -

Bone stood over the snoring pilot, gun barrel wavering as it pointed down at the man's florid face.

"Get up," he said.

Weeks failed to register the command.

"Get up right now, you sick sack of shit," Bone said, kicking the pilot in the leg.

The sleeping man grunted and shifted slightly. An airy belch slid from his half-open mouth.

Bone stepped back, face wrinkling in disgust. The air was dense with the smell of the man, and Bone knew that Weeks had not been out on deck. He slid his pistol back in the holster before backing out and pulling the door closed. In the sick light from the deadly rock formation, Bone felt doubt. The eerie unreality began working on his memory.

What the hell happened?

- 8 -

The blue of a morning sky held quiet conference with the green morning sea, and the only sound was the lap of waves against the boat.

Bone rubbed the cut on his chin as the pilot deftly removed two small lobsters from an ice chest and set them in the boiling water.

"Nerve system is so primitive they don't even feel it," the fisherman said.

The lobsters' armor and claws scraped against the inside of the pot, and Bone thought they were feeling something.

"Now try that other one there. Just use your hands," Weeks said. "Should be cool enough."

Bone twisted the still-warm shell of the lobster in both fists and heard a crack. A mouth-watering smell burst from the break in the carapace and a spray of warm water ran over his knuckles.

"Don't just tickle 'er, twist, like 'e was breaking a man's neck," he said from his position on the other side of the metal pot of boiling water. The grizzled lobsterman matched actions to words and twisted sharply, yanking the tail free from the bright red torso. He lifted the tail and sucked the fluids from it, juice running over his face and wetting his beard.

The two men squatted on their haunches on the deck, each on opposite sides of the pot. The pot itself was placed atop a hotplate connected by a long black cord to a plug inside the pilot house. Inside the lobsters bobbed and bubbled in boiling seawater, shells going from green to red in minutes.

Bone snapped the large, left claw free from the body and worked against the joint until he could break the shell open. He sucked at the exposed bit of white meat until he could get his teeth into it. He pulled back gently and nearly the entire section of claw meat slipped free. Juice ran from the corners of his mouth and he let it, focusing on the taste.

"We won't never go hungry," the pilot said, grinning through white flecks of flesh as he tossed the empty tail carapace over the side.

Bone held up the teeth of the big claw next to the crescent of angry red marks on his hand.

"'Twas a lobster, or more like a crab that got 'e," he said, eager to cut off the line of thought.

Bone eyed him, surprised at how capable he was, considering the drunken stupor of the night before.

"Something happened last night," Bone said.

"Aye," the pilot said. "Something bit your hand and startled you so bad you nearly went over the side. It's no wonder, sleeping out under the stars, in ol' Jenny's glow." He paused. "Here, have a second lobster and then we'll weigh anchor."

The pilot grabbed another from the pot with a pair of metal tongs and set it on the deck next to Bone before returning to his own side of the pot.

"Hot now, give her a second," he said.

Bone eyed the red crustacean, watching the water run off and drain into a crack in the decking. Something clicked in his memory and he rose, knees popping with the effort.

"What's wrong?" the pilot asked.

Bone moved to the cabin as the pilot twisted around in his sitting position to follow with his eyes.

"'Ere now, what do you need?"

Bone grabbed the latch of the door to the pilot house in one hand and jerked it up, wrenching the door open with a rusty squeal until it banged into the wall.

"Hey, what are you doing?"

"Testing a theory," he said, mentally comparing this sound to the hollow booming he'd heard the night before.

There was not enough time for Weeks to have attacked him and made it back to the cabin before Bone saw him. He had known that even as...

"Tell me," Bone said to the pilot as he walked across the rocking deck to the locked hatch. "Who else is on this boat?"

- 9 -

Bone dropped through the black hatchway, knees bent to absorb the shock, but still surprised when his feet hit something unyielding and slick. He was struck immediately by sensations of impenetrable blackness and a chill that lanced through his wet clothes so quickly it felt like heat.

He lost neither the grip on his pistol nor his mini-flashlight.

Bone activated the light and pivoted in a circle. The tiny beam flickered across surfaces too fast to give anything but snap impressions. Peeling wooden walls crowding close. Doors. A rack of equipment and netting.

He was alone in a small room.

"Get down here," Bone shouted up to the blue square of daylight over his head. He aimed the gun straight up at the decking where he heard the pilot's stomping gate. *This was the moment...*

"My knees cannot handle the drop. Can 'e lift the ladder?"

Bone spotted the wooden ladder laying down against a wall. A grunt escaped as he hauled it into place.

"Careful now, careful," the pilot said as he climbed haltingly down the ladder. His voice had taken on a whining quality.

Bone flicked off the light and the two men were plunged into darkness. He could feel the closeness of the other man and knew the pilot could feel his proximity.

"Got a cigarette?" Bone asked

"What?"

"I said, got a cigarette?"

Bone heard fumbling and clothes rustling and a match flared. Bone could see the offered hand-rolled cigarette in the yellow circle made by the match flame and took it, leaning in close to light it. He sucked in the smoke, enjoying the scratching heat of it clawing down into his lungs.

"I thought 'e didn't smoke?"

"Sometimes I lie," Bone said and blew the match out. "Don't light another one."

In the darkness he racked the slide on his Glock and heard the pilot gasp.

"What are 'e doing?"

"Tell me, have you ever been incarcerated?"

"Been who?"

"In prison." Bone aimed the light at the man's face and flicked it on.

"Not me, no."

"What happened last night?"

"I don't know," he stammered. "I shouldn't have been telling 'e stories. I don't—"

"Who else is on the boat?"

"Not another soul, I swear."

"What happened to my hand?"

"I tell 'e I don't know, but a crab could'a been lurking in the lines—"

Bone waved his hand, and the pilot shut up in mid-sentence.

"Why is the ladder down here? How did you plan to get back down when we dock?"

"I dropped it, that's all," the pilot said, looking around. "We should be quick. You'll catch a chill in them wet things down here."

"I'll be fine," Bone said. "Which way?"

"Here, here," the man said, sidling around Bone to get at the door leading forward.

Bone stepped to the door on the wall leading aft and grabbed the handle.

"No!" the pilot shouted when the marshal opened the door. A frozen spill of ice chips flooded out to pool around their ankles.

Bone flashed the thin beam of light onto a slithering pile of ice that rose to his waist and stepped inside, bulling through. His breath fogged around his head as he made out haunches of meat hanging from hooks in the ceiling and plastic-wrapped bundles buried throughout the ice.

He stepped in further, struggling to keep his footing. "Follow me," he said.

"Just the ice rooms in here," the pilot said behind him as Bone stuck the light in his teeth and punched his fist into the freezing drifts, pulling up a plastic package of chicken legs. He tossed it aside and pushed forward more, slipping once and the ice came to his chest until he pushed up again.

Shimmering crystals floated in the air, catching the beam of his flashlight as he played it around the ice room. A faint mist rose from the ice surrounding his thighs, casting an odd luminescence over everything. The vapor from his breath was already freezing on his eyelashes and his feet felt detached, buried in cold.

The pilot whined as he struggled in pursuit. "We'll freeze," he said.

"What's through there?" Bone pointed at a door across the room.

- 10 -

Trouble, the pilot thought to himself. *You're in trouble with this boy.* There was a red bulb flashing in his head, like a collision alarm from an old submarine movie he'd seen long ago.

He dripped and shivered, closing the ice room door behind him to cut off the chill as he watched the back of the federal lawman digging through the dry goods. The gun dangled from the marshal's right hand as naturally as a long tooth from a dog's mouth.

"Just the dry goods here, food, newspapers and mail," Weeks said, blushing beneath his blue chill at the wheedling sound in his voice.

"Who else is on the boat?" the lawman asked casually over his shoulder, the question lobbed again and again like Chinese water torture.

"Two souls, you and m'self," he said, a bubble of anger in his belly at his own cowardice.

Oh aye, 'e misjudged this one, 'e fool, and now he could undo every damn thing.

But the lawman had been so distant and oddly unsettled. *Lost at sea,* as it were. And so he had pushed him, grinning at the unease in the man's eyes while he unspooled the story of ol' Jenny and the missing Fetchwater lads.

"Open the door. We're going back up front now," the lawman said, his eyes flat despite the blue in his lips and the chattering of his teeth.

The pilot opened the door and pushed a path into the ice room, breaking through the already freezing crust forming over the trail they'd made on their first trip through. The skin between his shoulder blades crawled, and he thought of the black, futuristic looking gun the lawman carried.

They reached the ladder room, and the lawman shut the door behind him, kicking aside valuable ice where it would melt into the floor. A package of pork chops in plastic lay near his foot, looking like three, ear-shaped hunks of gray flesh. *Wasting them!* But the pilot said nothing.

"Am I going to find anything through that door there?" the lawman asked.

"Generator and gear."

"Where's the engine?"

The pilot scuffed a frozen boot along the floorboards. "Beneath us. 'E can get to what 'e need to get to, at sea mind you, 'e can get to that from the generator room."

The lawman moved past him, and the pilot leaned aside to make way. The bubble of anger stirred a stomach already uneasy from last night's whiskey.

"Am I going to find someone in here?" the man asked, thin lips smiling. But not a friendly smile, a contemptuous smile.

"Not another soul, I swear it." The words crawled out over his bottom lip like so many beetles eager to serve.

"Not one of the Fetchwater brothers?" The smile widened, but the eyes stayed flat.

Oh 'e misjudged this one, you fool, the pilot thought as he shook his head, unable to hold the lawman's stare.

Bone lifted his matte black pistol up beside his cheek and nodded, friendly like, then jerked open the door and stepped inside while the pilot stood rooted in place. The thump of the generator growled through the open doorway, and the ozone smell of electricity reached the pilot. A moment later the lawman was back out, cutting off the noise as he shut the door.

"All right then. Let's get underway." He clambered up the ladder without another word. "Come on," the lawman called down from above, and the pilot heard his steps overhead as the man walked to the pilot house.

Only then did Weeks move, stepping aside and glancing down at the thing hidden beneath his boot.

"God have mercy," he thought, seeing the gold glint of the marshal's star on the floor. He kicked it carefully under the piled netting and hurried up the ladder, much faster than he had descended.

He was in a rush to get topside and close the hatch behind him.

- 11 -

"There she is," the pilot said as *Leviathan* chugged towards the great, gray hulk of its mother.

The sky overhead threatened a darker turn, and the green and brown of the trees lining the island's humped shape were leached of color, as were the few visible buildings and bulges of old stone. At the nearest peak, a dark steeple scraped aggressively at the gathering weather, and in the distance, the defiant, white shape of a tower was just visible above a curve of land. A lighthouse with no light, yet tall and straight in stark contrast to the island's aspect of lowered brow and brutish forehead. For an instant Bone beheld the enormity of an ancient, horned giant on its hands and knees in the Atlantic, bent under the weight of eons, battered by wind and waves, but still very much aware.

Fishing craft bobbed near a long pier, weathered but well maintained and no kin to the grotesque vessel on which he sailed.

He wiped sea spray from his eyes and made out a large man waiting at the end of the pier, stoic as gusting winds attempted to snatch his fisherman's slicker. His hard features told Bone this was the constable, the man he would be dealing with, and he felt weary.

As they docked, Bone clambered up to the pier without helping to tie off because the constable had not moved to assist. His mouth still tasted of lobster as he said, "Constable." And the constable replied, "Marshal."

A land breeze fluttered down the slope and past Bone, blowing his hood back, and the pilot said, "She kissed 'e." Neither lawman acknowledged him.

"Well, take me to him," Bone said, noting that the constable's eyes revealed all the emotion of a lizard.

"Not until you turn over your firearm," he said.

"The hell you say."

"Isle ordinance. There is no bend or give to it."

Bone glanced up at the dark Isle and spit the taste of lobster into the sea.

SIX

- 1 -

Beneath an arch of intertwined branches, Burden Ipswich angled the baby carriage along a faint trail, wincing at the rusty squeak a rear wheel made on each rotation. The carriage was spindly and black, a pen-and-ink drawing of a Victorian conveyance with a dark lace covering pulled over the cradle itself. The old typewriter nestled inside rang faintly each time he bumped over a rock or a rut.

It was long past time he moved out of town. And thinking that, his eyelids grew thick and his eyes hot.

It will give me time to write, he thought.

A collection of toadstools clustered together in his path, flesh-colored and thick. Concave half-disks of various sizes bulging up from the moss like so many ears, as if the ground itself were listening to his passage.

And thinking of listening, he heard singing.

Littles, he thought as the high-pitched warbling wove its way through the trees.

He left the trail and pushed through thick bracken, branches slapping harmlessly against his heavy rain slicker, occasionally ducking his head to take a jabbing branch off his hood, protecting his eyes.

He had once volunteered to assist in teaching the Littles, assuming that his height would mean less in that setting. Memory of the laughter still stung.

"Nephew can you see, one two three," the Littles sang as he pushed aside a pine bough with a stubby fingered hand to see the circle of children dancing in a ring, holding hands and skipping.

"Nephew look at this, four five six," the children sang.

He looked about the clearing, surrounded by a mix of pines and bent crabapple trees, their fallen leaves forming a moldering carpet churned by the boots of the Littles. Scarves bounced, and here and there a hat had fallen off a curly-haired head, but he saw no adult in attendance.

No wonder they're singing the song.

"Nephew am I fine? Seven eight, nine," the song continued. He saw the child in the middle of the ring, holding up his pink fingers as they counted. He was maybe five or six, old enough to get it right, so the ring continued moving around him. Bright spots of color rode his cheeks, excitement visible as the ring danced faster and faster.

Where is the teacher? he thought. The Littles were far from town, too close to the waterfront.

"Children?" he said, pushing the baby carriage into the clearing.

The reaction was instantaneous. The circle broke as the children shrieked, the sound carrying an equal measure of fear and glee.

"It's Gentle Annie!"

"Gentle Annie! Gentle Annie!"

He ducked as an apple arced from the children huddling on the opposite side of the clearing.

"Wait! Wait!" He threw his arms out, palms forward in a calming gesture. "It's only—"

Another apple struck him over the right eye and he gasped, more in surprise than pain.

"What are 'e doing!?!" a shrill voice called from the far side of the clearing and a bony woman pushed from the trees. The whites of her eyes were huge, and her pupils had contracted to black pinpoints even as the pock scars on her face caught the shadows, giving her cheeks another dozen pupils with which to glare at him.

"He came to steal us in the baby carriage!" one young girl shouted, pointing a chubby finger at him.

"What?" he said, overcome by the surprise turn of events. "No, no—"

"What are 'e doing!?! Why are 'e bothering the children?" Her lips were stretched thin, a tiny bead of spittle catching the sunlight as she challenged him, and the children clustered around her, clutching at her long woolen coat.

"I wasn't. There was no teacher so I thought—"

"Thought what, dwarf?" she asked, eyes narrowing. He flashed back to his own childhood, when both she and he were counted among the Littles. He remembered that she hadn't thrown apples when they were younger. Mary Nutter threw stones.

"You know my name, Mary," he said, the sense of despair covering the bubbling acid in his stomach like a blanket, smothering the spark of anger. "I didn't see a teacher with the Littles, so I was concerned—"

"'E were *concerned*," Mary said, mocking his clean speech, deepening the thick stew of her own accent as if to emphasize the difference. "And what are 'e doing with the carriage?"

He stood on his tiptoes and pulled aside the blanket as Mary strode over, towering over him to look inside. She laughed once. "Get 'e self gone, Burden Ipswich, 'ere I tell the constable."

- 2 -

The carriage wheel squeaked and the typewriter chimed as it bumped over every obstructing root. The air smelled wet and moldy. The dirt itself vaguely fecal.

"Why am I talkin' to you?" the outlander Richard Slocum had said one evening over beers. "You're the only one here ain't talkin' like he's got a mouthful of chowder."

Burden pushed the carriage, accepting the absurd image he presented. A crumpled tree stump of a man, fully of age, yet wearing a child's cast-off trousers. His steps were a slip-slide, left leg angled slightly forward because his right leg was two inches longer.

"Like a crab," his mother had once told him.

"Like a fighter," Slocum had said. "You move like a boxer, left foot forward, left shoulder forward.

He had missed the gleam in Slocum's eye as the man from Detroit pumped him for information on the Isle. Or perhaps he had seen it and dismissed it. Regular, extended conversation was so rare for Burden that he threw himself in wholeheartedly, surprising himself with the details of the Isle he was able to conjure forth.

"If you're ever in Detroit…" Slocum had said, as if their plans were set and visiting Detroit was something that might actually happen. Later, when their empty mugs filled the corner table, Slocum had said, "You're gonna tell somebody. It's human nature. So you gotta find the right person you can tell, see?"

A crow cawed overhead, and a branch snapped deeper in the woods, falling with a clatter.

"You're gonna tell somebody," Slocum had said.

Burden supposed he would. After all, Slocum had told him.

- 3 -

The waterfront, Burden thought, and a macabre chill raced down his spine.

The abandoned settlement gave the impression of jumbled straws from a distance, the low roofline broken by a tangle of chimneys and tilted widow's walks, none seeming to point uniformly skyward.

Closer still, the dead village was a crowded mess of crumbling foundations and winding alleys, the interior structures sagging inward under the slow chewing of wind, salt and water.

The alleyways were cracked stone pulled up from the skeleton of the Isle itself, as were the two- and three-story buildings. The windows were gaping and empty, crossed sticks of rotting wood devoid of glass.

It was a place that did not want to be lived in. Not anymore. And no one did. If it was a home to anything it was to the crows and the rats. Every flat surface bore some remnant of their morbid feasts, partial and even whole crab shells of various sizes littered by the score, with the occasional living cannibal scuttling among them. Rotting mackerel heads picked free of meat and the drying membranes of codfish tails blew along like so many dead leaves, contributing a powerful undersmell to the salty air.

It was a place best forgotten, collective will reducing it to a path not traveled, never traveled, not existing.

Burden's footsteps scraped along a narrow alley, crunching crab shells underneath, his human sounds eagerly consumed by the rotting remnants of habitation. A murder of crows took flight to fill the air with their ugly cries. Grey rats flowed towards the walls clutching crab claws, bits of watery meat, and even dragging entire carapaces across the rocks before they disappeared amongst invisible crevices like streaks of filthy water. The houses, looking down slyly from the empty sockets of second-story windows, heard things spoken as well as unspoken. Burden had a natural quality of lurking, of instinctively moving close to a building, seeming always to find shadows to stand in. His frequent visits to the waterfront only added to his oddness in the eyes of the other Isle folk, and the affinity of the local crows spurred the occasional dark whisper, but Burden found solace in its strange geometries and crumbling order. He sensed that the place welcomed him for his own twisted form.

Up ahead were the six bastions: crumbling stone foundations holding the remains of rotting timbers. The Littles told stories about those timbers, back in older days, and what had hung from them—

Stop it, he told himself, ducking his head and passing between two bastions until he realized he was standing in shadow.

Looming over him, massive and pale, was the old lighthouse with its crown of thorns.

A beach of crushed shells sloped down towards the greenish water, waves slapping against the shore and exploding in a white spray from the rocky island a mere twenty yards offshore. The lighthouse was weathered, rock seams burned away by wind and time, the stone itself pocked by a thousand insults. Jagged spires of rusting iron thrust violently from the top, all that was left of the great beacon. Only a fool would call it home.

It should be noted that the Gods of the Sea are aware of all in their presence, but they are not kind, they are not soft and they have no patience for things that scuttle, flap and crawl. Old Man Atlantic is colder than most, perhaps because he is most familiar with men, present at their earliest great voyages, drowning pauper and prince alike. But even Old Man Atlantic knows that to draw men to him, he must offer hope. Hope with danger, surely. Opportunity with destruction.

It could also be said by a fool—*only* a fool would presume to know the mind of that hoary old spirit in his ancient, wet hall buttressed by the ribs of rotting shipwrecks—that Old Man Atlantic is lonely with his chosen companions, dead as they are. And being lonely he calls to those who crawl along his shoreline. Unable to resist drowning those that come to him, unable to resist calling to still more.

To reach the tower required crossing a bridge of stone beneath the waves, topped with waving tendrils of seaweed. Hidden even at low tide by a swirl of water and buried beneath icy fathoms at high tide.

Burden turned away from the solace of the tower and eyed the sprawling settlement.

"Exodus twelve, eleven, thirteen," he muttered to himself, remembering Slocum's cryptic statement. "'The Israelites marked their doors with the blood of a spring lamb.'"

Burden paused at a wooden door hanging crookedly in its frame, the doorknob nearly level with his head. The brown stain on the door had dried but was recent nonetheless. Burden scraped it with a thick fingernail and blood flakes fell away.

"Good Lord," he muttered, his sense of rebellion, of adventure, vanishing with a near audible sound. Unease crept into its place.

This...something...is really happening.

Burden pushed open the door with a rusty squeal of hinges.

The room inside was dark until he fished out a fat storm candle and lit it with a match.

Cobwebs dangled from the rafters, swaying in breezes that swirled through the windows and down the staircase from the second floor. It was as if a giant hag was sleeping on the floor upstairs, having been still so long her hair grew down through the cracks to hang into the room below. The disturbance of his entry set everything to shifting, a colony reacting to intrusion. A trill of unease rippled down his spine.

"Stop it," he scolded himself.

Burden set his candle in a crack between the floorboards amidst the rotted remains of furniture and broken crockery. He pushed back his hood. Brown hair stood up in tufts over a broad, flat forehead, the features beneath blunt and clenched like a fist, gathered together too close as if afraid to expand and make full use of the face.

Gathering his courage, he climbed the staircase carefully, the wooden boards shaking beneath his feet and loosing a cascade of dust.

Soon Burden stood in the black of the upstairs hallway in the tiny shelter of light provided by the storm candle. No giant woman lay asleep or dead on the floor, though more lengths of dusty filth hung from the low ceiling overhead.

Perhaps she's up on the roof, he thought.

Heavy, rotting things that had evolved under the influence of rain and years into something other than curtains still covered the small window at one end and denied entry to light. Cracks in the roofing overhead allowed thin slivers access, daytime scouts that were quickly surrounded and ambushed by the dark, a warning to future mornings that they were not welcome.

Burden wondered at how many years, decades even, had passed since someone had last drawn aside the curtains and let in the day. He was tempted to march down the hall and do it himself, but the idea of touching them, the anticipation of their slick and slimy texture, stayed his approach.

Besides, he needed to remain unseen.

He wondered at the hidden things in this moldering place and realized his mind was dark even before ascending the rickety stairs. He was contemplating the continuation of something—*blackmail*—that had resulted in the death of his friend.

Was he your friend?

Burden lifted the candle high and stomped forward, the floor creaking mightily beneath him as he approached a closed door and pushed it open.

There was an immediate sensation of movement at the corners of the room in the split second before the wind of the opening portal sucked the candle flame to a length of several bright inches and it went out.

"Shit!" Burden said.

He fumbled at the matches in his pocket, keeping his eyes focused intently on the red glow of at the tip of the candle wick, afraid to move lest another bit of hag's hair reach out for him and make him scream.

"Nothing has happened. There's nothing here," Burden whispered. But there had been movement.

He let a pent-up breath escape as the candle flared to life again and moved more cautiously into the room, wary of hanging things, only gradually aware that a thin gray light was seeping through holes and cracks in the decaying shutters. He followed his flame around the small bedroom, past descending streaks of brown and growing circles of whitish-green mold on the walls. A composting pile of something unidentifiable humped in the corner and continued to trick Burden with hints of movement seen from the corner of his eye. It was big enough that a person could be curled beneath it, slumbering.

The decaying remains of a seaman's chest occupied another corner and Burden made his way to it, lowering the candle in an effort to peer through cracks in the lid. He knelt and held the light close to the lock, but inspection revealed it to be a single mass of rust. Slocum had not opened it.

Burden wedged his candle carefully into a knothole in the wall and pressed a shoulder to the chest. He grunted and pushed. The thing imploded under his shoulder and he crashed into its middle, shattering three of the four sides. He immediately pushed back, paddling with his hands at the thought of white grubs and fat spiders lurking inside, but succeeded only in disturbing fat splinters, turgid with sea moisture. Overhead the filaments danced, the close air upset at his disturbance. He heard a scuttling sound and whipped about to look at the pile in the corner, but his candlelight refused to show him what had moved.

The hag moves.

Burden pushed back onto his knees and wrapped his fingers around the fat candle, a waxy talisman of little comfort.

The house was upset.

Nonsense!

"Slocum was here and him not even an Isle man," Burden asserted. *Slocum died,* answered a damnable voice.

It was only then that Burden noticed marks on the floor and placed his feet against the corner of the sea chest, bracing his hands. He pushed and it slid aside before the remaining structure collapsed.

Wind howled and shook the house.

Burden's heart leapt into his throat, but he fought back the urge to flee and ran his hands over the exposed floor where the chest had stood, oblivious to splinters and the sharp pain in his fingernails as he jammed his stubby digits between two loose boards and yanked upward with too much force.

The boards clattered apart, and he heard a scuffle in the hall and a wet slap from the far corner of the room. Clammy sweat ran down Burden's face as he thrust a hand into the gap in the floor, pushing through mushrooms and crushing their pulpy flesh until his fingers closed over something wide and flat. He glanced up as dirt rattled down from above. It seemed as if the ceiling was dancing as he reared back and clutched the prize to his chest.

The air was utterly still. It did not become still. It simply *was* still. The air of a tomb unopened in a century.

Burden placed his find on the floor and lifted the storm candle closer, eliciting muddy reflections on the surface of his discovery.

It was a book.

- 4 -

The staircase wobbled and shook beneath his descent as he peered into the downstairs. That he saw nothing did not ease his mind. The old waterfront was a living ghost story.

A glance at the closed door showed daylight still creeping in around the edges. He had determined before setting out that he would exercise an overabundance of caution. More caution than Slocum, at any rate. He would not transport his discovery home until after dark and the low tide that would allow him to cross the bridge.

The downstairs was dank and unappealing. Still, the upstairs was too unnerving, too active to remain in for any longer than necessary, so he took a seat next to the old baby carriage, trying and failing to find a comfortable position. A cloud of grit hung in the air, mold and dirt stirred by the increasing wind pushing through gaps in the walls. Burden coughed and leaned back with the book on his lap, mouth twisting with distaste.

"Let's have a look at you, beauty," he whispered.

The book had a shine to it, the wet gleam of garbage too long in a ditch. He ran a finger down the spine and shivered, turning the book to look, tapping a cracked fingernail against it. Overlapping black plates of mottled green, furred with mold. He felt queasy on touching them, but even a pariah of the Isle knew lobster's armor when he saw it.

What the hell is this?

It was a large tome roughly the size of a Bible, and ornate carvings in the peeled leather and wood of its cover were occupied by the fuzz of white fungus.

He pulled the candle from its spot and held it close to the book's cover, cursing when a drip of liquid wax struck the leather. With a fingernail he engaged in the distasteful task of scraping fungus from a delicate tracery.

SOLEMNITATEM CULPAM

He struggled to recall his Latin, thankful for the pretentions that had caused him to study it in the first place. "Guilt?"

He tilted the book and blew across it, sending fungal blossoms across his legs. Then rested it across his thighs and carefully opened it, wincing at the creaking spine.

The pages were yellowed and cracked and did not bend in the way of paper. He cursed his clumsy fingers as a small fissure appeared in the edge of the first page and leaned over to see wavering rows of black spiders, words barely decipherable as such often hidden behind splotches of faded ink. The book was decrepit with age and his unease returned. This thing had been bound long before he was born, yet he had never seen it, never even heard rumor of it.

Delicately he began lifting the pages, noting that they were supported, each of them, with crosses made from dried wood. And despite this, the tome did not feel in the least bit holy.

There were not nearly as many pages as he had first thought, and soon the spidery script gave way to uneven rows of names and numbers, written in a variety of hands. The ink was often smeared in the latter pages, and Burden could clearly make out where drops of water had distorted the writing.

He lifted the candle close to the page, cupping his free hand to catch falling wax. There were more than a dozen entries, for lack of a better term, in *blue* ink.

A hot splash struck his palm and he hissed.

Solemnitatem Culpam. He gently closed the book and stared at the cover. There weren't many people on the Isle who possessed any Latin at all. A few of the older folks. The reverend. Himself of course. Hazel had none and, off hand, he couldn't think of anyone else. Not even that pious bitch Mary Nutter.

"Feast of Guilt," he said aloud, wishing he had his Latin texts close to hand. But they were in his tower, and he was being a cautious dwarf.

Like curtains parting on a stage of bone, his lips peeled back from his teeth.

Burden opened the book again and let his eyes adjust as best they could to the crabbed writing. He sneezed and turned his head aside to spit, working his tongue around his mouth, letting the translation take shape.

"In the year of our Lord 1687, the black ship rode the wind to our shores."

SEVEN

- 1 -

A thin branch whipped across Hazel's cheek and she finally slowed, placing two fingers against the line of heat on her face. She lifted her fingers up before her eyes and saw tiny beads of red blood.

Her chest rose and fell, breasts pushing against her white blouse, the lungs beneath them coal-hot with the heat of exertion, the back of her neck wet with perspiration. She reached up and pulled a tangled twig from her hair, feeling the sharp pain as a long, black strand pulled free with it, the wood unwilling to give up its prize.

The camera on the strap around her shoulder bounced against her hip, and she recalled, vaguely, the discomfiting whack of it as she ran through the woods.

Sensations. Perhaps this was what she sought. Flight into feeling.

She turned quite deliberately and stepped off the worn path, pushing through the underbrush that plucked at her long skirt. Deliberately stepping off the path but not, perhaps, deliberately choosing a destination. It occurred to her that bringing her camera had been an excuse, a ruse to get her moving away from town and the fugue she walked in. But distance had not done it—or had it?—and running had not done it—or had it?—only the sudden pain in her cheek and the sight of her own blood, bright in the gloaming beneath the trees, had awakened her.

Even in her fugue she had felt change in the town, and while she had wondered if her sight had been skewed by her own despair, she thought now that the ugliness was not emerging from inside her but was instead growing on its own, moss-like, to cover the community.

She had seen it clearly in the public house the night before. The nose on old Zachariah Beech had grown fatter, more turnip-like, and that of

Hatevil Nutter had grown longer even as his eyes grew deeper and his Adam's apple more prominent. The hump of Oram Fetchwater had thickened and lowered, and Annabelle Corn's cough had grown wetter, her spitting more frequent. Men's beards grew denser as shaving grew more erratic. Women's voices became shrewish, their invective more cutting.

"Will you be back for services?" someone had asked. A woman. She couldn't remember what her own response had been, only the clear feeling of revulsion at the thought of sitting in the midst of them, shoulder to shoulder on stern wooden pews as they sang, revealing teeth grown long in receding gums.

She had run west because Burden was going east, moving into his tower at the edge of everything. When they were young they had joked about making their own house along the waterfront one day, those musings accompanied by terrified giggles at the thought of living in that seaside mausoleum. And she had the hint of a recollection that Burden might have said something recently while she walked in fog, perhaps after he had drunk too much beer. Something about a house of their own down by the waterfront, something that left him embarrassed and withdrawn.

She was standing still on the edge of a deep slope. A cold wind blew and her skirt pressed around her legs. She scratched a nail along her cheek and felt the newborn scab give way, a tiny trickle of warmth running down until it reached her jaw and dripped.

She stepped down carefully, grabbing a bush for balance, enjoying the hot burn as the thin branches pulled across her palm and leaves fluttered free. Black water burbled along the bottom of the streambed, littered with stones and broken branches. Hazel followed the watery voice, no longer wrapped in fugue, but not entirely free.

- 2 -

It was an old stone bridge deep in the woods, and the arched opening was a black mouth. Above it the woods had thickened into old growth, dense and unplundered, nearly impassable.

Hazel picked her way down to the sluggish creek bed where cool air slowly pushed its way out of the dark archway, as if the bridge itself were breathing.

The creek was narrower but deeper under the bridge. Chill water slopped over the tops of her low boots and her feet were already going numb. It was impenetrably dark and overhung with vines. She lifted her skirt above her knees to keep it out of the water, and goosebumps broke out on her shins.

Hazel fired the camera's flash, illuminating a split-second image full of branches and detritus. She stepped forward on feet gone wooden with cold, working her way beneath the bridge and taking photos. Each camera flash froze a moment in time and she froze with it, only advancing again when the darkness returned.

The pain was sudden and she recoiled, an electric bolt of fear sizzling through her nervous system as a giant hand clutched at her leg. The camera flash fired as if on its own, and she saw the spindly wooden fingers of a fallen tree limb thrusting up from the water, their broken tips like jagged claws.

Hazel backed carefully away and out from under the archway, lifting the hem of her skirt until she could see the narrow gash in her thigh. She stepped to the creek's bank and placed her boot firmly on shore, baring her leg nearly to the waist. The red was deep in color, nearly black against the paleness of her skin. The wound not deep, but...

Hazel pressed her leg and blood seeped out in tiny lines, almost like writing. She watched the lines as their message grew increasingly coherent across the white roundness of her thigh. When she was certain she would not interrupt them, she aimed her camera down at the wound and waited.

- 3 -

"Did anything come out?" Hazel imagined Burden asking, and since she was imagining, he called her Witch-Hazel as he had when they were children.

"Just me." she would say, seeing her bare leg and running wound depicted in stark black and white through the lens of her camera.

- 4 -

A gust of wind sighed through the trees, gaining moderate force as it pushed down the gully, tugging at her hair and skirt. She freed a few loose strands from the sticky cut on her cheek and dropped them into the flowing water, watching them swirl and vanish.

"Hello?" she said to the breeze, which chose that moment to quiet. The *pock* of a pine nut falling came from deeper in the trees, no doubt dislodged by a squirrel.

"Hello?"

She reminded herself that there were no truly threatening animals on the Isle, unlike the surrounding waters.

Enough, she thought, moving on until she found the long, sliding marks her boots had made in her descent down the bank. She tightened the camera strap and used her hands to pull herself up, digging the tips of her boots into the soft dirt and bracing them on exposed roots when they availed themselves.

"Hazel Milk," the deep voice said, utterly flat.

Hazel almost slipped back down the slope, glancing up to see muddy boots and then further up at the man waiting for her.

She looked aside, blushing as adrenaline hit her system. The man's enormous erection was clearly visible through his khaki work pants.

A wide, leathery hand reached down and caught her wrist, nearly pulling her to the top of the gully. She helped automatically, pushing with her feet and reaching up to grab one of his boots with her free hand before she could think to do otherwise. When she rose, gravity swung her close to him, and she brushed up along thighs like stone and over the bulge at his crotch, the man making no particular effort to move back and give her space.

"Constable," she said, her voice thready.

Still, he made no effort to step away, and she sidled to her right, kicking a small rain of dirt and pebbles down behind her, the feeling of unease grown coherent and very much present.

She was no virgin but the bold display, the disinclination to turn away or conceal, was unsettling.

How long was he watching me at the bridge?

She forced herself to raise her gaze, looking into the too-small eyes of the big man who always reminded her of a whiskey barrel on legs. A barrel in which the contents had gone sour.

"That camera take pictures in the dark?" the constable asked.

"Ah, I have a better one for genuinely dark—"

"Get it," he said. "You're needed at the bone yard."

He reached down and shifted his engorged cock inside his pants, eyes on her, expression impassive, then turned and strode back through the underbrush towards the path.

She waited for several minutes, until the *swish-thwack* of brush against his khakis faded to nothing. Her chest was tight and she sipped at the air, her nerves stretched taut as she realized that somehow, for some reason, she had just experienced a genuine threat.

EIGHT

- 1 -

The graveyard was hidden in a hollow surrounded by a rusting iron fence, and Hazel leaned back against the barrier, careful not to let her camera bag bang against it. The grass was untended and grew high, the gravestones jutting up like uneven teeth. A single tree loomed in the center of the hollow, skeletal branches reaching out over the dead.

Kerosene lamps had been hung in the wind-blown branches of the tree and threw four writhing shadows across the ground. A pair of gravediggers leaned on their shovels, breath fogging in the cold.

They hadn't seen her yet, and Hazel circled through the outer ring of headstones until she paused at a familiar marker and rested her hand on it in the same place she always did. There was a time that the press of her warm flesh against the cool stone would bring tears, but lately the contact was as natural and commonplace as drawing her first breath in the morning. She hated the healing power of time, hated that she was moving on, even as she thanked God the knife no longer cut so deeply.

The stranger was immediately recognizable as such: a tall, painfully thin scarecrow of a man with a face not so much shaped but inspired by hunting knives and flint. The kerosene lanterns drew his features with shifting black shadows, and his cheekbones looked sharp enough to cut. His long black raincoat, not Isle made, fluttered in the wind, *fwip-fwip-fwip*.

The constable stood off by himself, a silent bulk in the dark. She pushed aside the instant flash of cold she felt at the sight of him, suppressing the sense memory of brushing past his erection. The air was fairly crackling with electricity and not only from the coming storm. She could feel bands of tension between the constable and the gaunt newcomer.

"Hazel," the constable said and pointed at the newcomer.

"You're Mr. Bone?" Hazel asked, and the man turned to face her. His eyes locked on hers, deep-set pools of exhaustion in that angular face, half bathed in light from the lamps in the tree, and half in shadow.

There was something else, something unsettling. She might not have had the thought if he wasn't in the constable's company, but she couldn't help but contrast him against the constable's physical presence and its perpetually implied threat. *This man from the mainland would threaten silently*, she thought. *This man would threaten silently and you might never know it until he carried out his threat.*

"Miss Milk," Bone said. "What were you doing back there?"

And just like that, the man from the mainland was quietly attacking, pressing her to explain herself.

"I was talking to my husband," she said.

Bone glanced into the dark where her husband's gravestone stood, and she saw the long scars that violated the side of his face. She wondered at the cause and the pain of it.

He looked back at her and nodded at the fresh grave in front of him.

"I need you to make a photographic record of the entire process," he said. "This will serve as a legal record of the exhumation."

Hazel glanced at the constable and unlimbered her camera. "When should I start?"

"Now," Bone said.

"But they're not doing anything."

"Exactly."

Hazel snapped a picture and the flash lit up the hollow.

"You really want to do this." the constable said.

"Yes," Bone said.

The constable nodded to the gravediggers. "Dig 'm up."

The two men shrugged and one planted his shovel blade, bracing a boot against it just as lightning and thunder cracked overhead and the storm finally hit. One moment there was no rain, the next moment it was falling in sheets.

"Storm's after us like a fat woman on hot biscuits," the first digger said.

Bone pulled a hood over his head and bundled his coat closed. Hazel noticed he wore a holster beneath the coat and that it was empty.

"Gonna get 'im wet," the second digger said.

"I don't think he'll mind," Bone said, and the diggers cackled.

Hazel snapped another picture and edged closer to the grave.

"What will… What can we expect? I mean…" Hazel said.

"Slocum has been buried for a week?" Bone said.

"Yes."

His shrug was almost imperceptible. She could feel his lack of engagement with her. His brutal honesty.

"It will be grotesque," he said. "The ugliest thing you have ever seen."

Hazel felt her stomach twist.

The kerosene lanterns sputtered out one by one and darkness enveloped the graveyard.

"Oh, that's just peaches," a digger said, looking around warily.

The camera flashed and they were all lit up for a brief moment, frozen in time. The diggers working, the constable glaring, and Bone uncaring.

"If something grabs my ankle I will scream holy hell," the second digger said, and their laughter floated out of the darkness.

"You boys cut the grab ass," the constable said. A flashlight retrieved from his pocket panned over the diggers. "This is no place to be and the Devil's work we're doin'."

The beam moved over to shine against Bone's head. He turned to look directly into the light.

Electricity in the air.

Scars.

- 2 -

Bone stepped to the edge of the open rectangle in the sod. The bottom of the hole was a stew of mud and cracked pine boards. And an arm.

"Get this," Bone said.

Hazel stepped forward and snapped a picture. The ground shifted and she started to slip, but Bone steadied her arm.

"Thank you," she said.

The constable glanced back and forth between them.

"We need to get him up," Bone said.

"Pine box has come apart," the first digger said, arms and legs coated with black mud. "I'll fetch 'e a giant stew ladle."

The diggers climbed down gingerly and pulled up the broken coffin lid. "Jesus wept."

"This is an obscenity," the constable said.

The two men in the hole used shovels to lever up the body with a wet squelch. It was bloated and horribly twisted.

"Oh, God." Hazel covered her mouth with one hand.

"Steady," Bone said. "Shoot it."

Hazel snapped a picture but winced away from the flash.

The diggers had nearly raised the corpse when one pierced the swollen abdomen with his shovel. A rush of gas escaped, and everyone but the constable was driven back.

"Aww, Christ!"

"My God!"

Bone covered his nose and mouth and knelt by the body. "Hazel!"

Hazel tried to focus the camera with her eyes closed, and so it was that when she opened them, the image of the body was magnified through the lens.

"Oh, my God!" Hazel shrieked and backpedaled. The camera snapped a blurry shot of sky and the flash startled everyone.

"What is it?" Bone grabbed her arm.

"He…he moved!"

"What?" Bone let go of her and strode to the edge of the grave, the constable rushing to stand at the opposite edge. At first the two men saw no motion but the cratering strikes of raindrops in the muddy cauldron, then something white shifted beneath the water, appearing and disappearing too quickly to comprehend.

"What the hell was that?" Bone asked.

"Holy mother." The constable fought the urge to cross himself.

As if the invocations of Heaven and Hell were a summoning, the water began to boil. Bone's eyes widened, but he stood in place as if he'd put down roots.

Bone's jaw unhinged as he searched for a frame of reference to describe what he was seeing, the white suggestion of thin bones waving from the water.

Then they came to the surface.

"Christ."

The twisted corpse vomited forth crabs. Hundreds of small, white crustaceans scrambling through the water and mud. Someone retched behind Bone and the words "crab boil" escaped his lips a moment before he knew what he was saying, and he covered his own mouth to hold back the contents of his stomach.

He tried three times before he could express a controlled, coherent sentence. "It's only crabs. Somehow crabs got in there. Get him up."

- 3 -

It was indecent, the exposure of the body. Torn and muddy, the bloated abdomen rent open and collapsed like a puff pastry. The grey meat of it was chewed in every conceivable way, with fingers missing, eyes hollow caverns that were somehow *too large*, and Bone looked into those tunnels to witness hints of movement suggesting that new residents resided within Slocum's hollowed-out skull, eating new rooms into their palace with every day. He leaned back in sudden, irrational alarm. Afraid something even more hideous, something *incomprehensible*, would churn up those dark tunnels and snatch him down inside.

No one would stand near the disgusting pile of former human, so it was up to Bone to flick away the occasional crab that still surfaced like an armored blister.

A real assessment of the body was impossible. It had no nose left, no lips. But even with the mud, Bone could see the skull had been caved in.

He stood slowly, making sure his legs would hold him, and backed away from the thing as if some more horrible event would occur the minute he turned his back.

He stopped when he and the constable stood side by side, neither looking at the other, both fixated on the gruesome tableau.

"He fell?" Bone asked.

"He fell," the constable said.

"How the hell did crabs get in there like that? Did he spend time in the water first?"

"We're closer to the shore than you think. Old waterfront town's just over that way."

"Crabs came from the beach and burrowed?" Incredulity dripped in time with the rain from Bone's hood.

Bone felt the constable shrug before the big man spoke. "You don't know too much about things out here."

Bone met the constable's eyes, but the big man seemed as untroubled by his stare as he was by the rain drumming against his hat.

"Bag him," Bone said to the diggers.

"You'll want to be leaving immediately," the constable said. He walked away, saying over his shoulder, "I'll meet you at the boat with your weapon."

NINE

- 1 -

Bone hunched in his coat and slogged along a dirt track churned into mud by the rain. His feet slid over grit inside his shoes, socks soaked, toes long since gone numb. He felt fatigue like a pressing weight against his ability to think, and rather than resist the feeling, he accepted it.

A reflexive thought, *remember details to share with Julia*. He shook his head, banishing it. Vaguely upset. He hadn't made that mistake in at least a month.

"Come on 'e stubborn beast." The words rolled back to Bone from the murk up ahead.

The two diggers led a mule-drawn cart carrying the blanket-wrapped corpse of Richard Slocum. A glass lantern hung from an elevated spar on the cart, casting a bouncing, jittering glow over the march. The conveyance made a surprising racket, even over the sound-smothering rain. Wheels creaked, the mule's hooves splashed, and the entire contraption rattled.

Bone held a borrowed flashlight and panned it ineffectually along the wall of trees on either side. He had asked for another casket and had been told there was none ready. He had asked for plastic bags, Hefty bags, and been told they had none. The body, already grossly violated, would suffer more from the soaking.

He was the UPS man. The state of Richard Slocum's remains was not his concern. Even the temporary surrender of his pistol to the constable barely registered. His weariness mattered. His upcoming hearing mattered. He wished he had a cigarette and a drink. He felt less involved in the entire effort than the mule.

"Lord 'e is a stinker," one of the Isle men said. Bone missed the other's response but caught the quiet chuckle.

Trees whipped on either side of the narrow road, frenzied in the storm. Sideways gusts began to blow his coat out so that it flared around his waist, his legs splashed with rain and mud.

The woman trudged along beside him. Hazel. He could feel her curiosity about him but found it hard to reciprocate. In a matter of hours, a day at most, he would be home, and this remote place and all of its people would matter not at all.

"How do you do this?" Hazel asked.

Bone glanced at her, rain sluicing off of his hood. She was covering her nose and mouth against Slocum's aroma.

"Do what?"

Hazel waved vaguely at the body in the cart. "This. You were right. It's the most horrible thing I've ever seen."

"Or smelled," one of the diggers cackled.

"Is it always like this?" Hazel asked.

"This is a first," Bone said. "Sometimes it's worse."

"'E don't say?" came a question from near the mule's head.

"What could be worse than this pile of rotten meat?" The other digger said.

Bone stopped, glancing about at the wet darkness. "Got a cigarette?"

"Whoa," the man with the mule said, guiding the animal to a halt. Both men walked back to where Bone and Hazel were braced against the weather. "That 'e do," said one, elbowing the other.

Bone took the offered cigarette, noting an expert hand roll, and leaned forward to take the light. A match scraped against a thick thumbnail and Bone drew in greedily, feeling the burn of smoke in his lungs and a brief surge of energy as the nicotine struck his system.

"Keep walking." Bone gestured with the cigarette. "Was a guy we were looking for," he said, smoke trickling out with his words. "Mortician."

"Aye?"

Bone nodded. "Believed in the seven sins."

"Wrath, greed, sloth, pride," one digger said.

"Gluttony, envy and lust," the other man added, eager to be a part. "We know our sins."

"Committed every one," the first digger said and both laughed.

"Right," Bone said. "Had a tendency to express his belief on the bodies of the people that passed through his funeral home. Place in northern New Hampshire."

"Express his beliefs?" Hazel asked.

Bone eyed her, wondering how much she wanted to hear, how much he wanted to tell. "He disappeared after being questioned by local police. Year or so later, reports came in of mutilations connected to a funeral parlor in upstate New York."

"What sort of mutilations are 'e talkin' about?" asked the man with the cigarettes, lighting one himself.

Bone let smoke stream out his nose, hot and scratchy.

"They matched our fugitive from New Hampshire."

- 2 -

SEVERAL YEARS AGO

It was a small house and smelled faintly of cabbage and something spoiled.

"I don't know what you're talking about!" the portly man screamed from the living room.

"Sir, just sit there on the couch," a marshal said.

"Stay out of my things! Stay out of my bedroom!"

Bone walked carefully down a narrow hallway, his shoes noisy on the sticky linoleum. The Glock .40 was held up by his cheekbone.

"Is there anybody in the kitchen?" Bone called back.

"Stay out of my kitchen, you Gestapo! You fascist!"

"I'll put a spit shield on you, sir, if you don't—"

Bone tuned out the argument in the other room and focused his listening forward, around the corner.

"United States—"

He cut himself off in mid-sentence as he swiveled into the small room and saw it was empty.

Quick. Efficient. He pulled open cabinets over the sink. Cupboards down low. Canned goods. Two dozen boxes of Kraft Macaroni and Cheese. Had the thought, *guy probably hasn't eaten a vegetable in two years*, in the moment before he opened the refrigerator.

"Oh, fuck me."

He felt a flash of heat in his face even as a roar filled his ears. He closed his eyes and stepped back, heard the squeak of the door swinging shut and stuck out his foot blindly, batting it back open.

"Ahh, hey," he called out, voice weak. He steadied himself and opened his eyes, looking at the sealed jars lining the shelves.

"In here!" he shouted, pulling in air from his diaphragm.

He heard movement in the house. Shoes pounding towards the kitchen. He was fixated on a poorly wrapped, half stick of butter. An open container of milk. You needed those things to make macaroni and cheese.

How could anyone keep open dairy in a fridge full of…

"What do we got?" a marshal named Sands asked behind him.

"In the fridge," Bone nodded towards the glass jars.

"Oh you're fucking kidding me. Is that some guy's dick?" Sands asked.

Bone nodded. The roaring sound was receding, but he didn't want to take any chances.

"What the… What's that?" Sands asked.

Bone shrugged. "Stomach?"

"Stay out of my refrigerator," the mutilator whimpered from the living room.

"What do we got?" the marshal in the front room called.

"This is our guy," Bone called back.

Sands closed the fridge and shook his head, face dead white beneath a spray of freckles. "You check the freezer?"

"You check the fucking freezer." Bone dragged the back of a wrist across his mouth as he walked past the now pleading fat man on the couch in the living room.

He stepped outside and breathed the fresh air, trying to banish the scent memory of rotting butter.

He fished out a pack of cigarettes and lipped one free, lighting it with a disposable job he'd picked up at a gas station off I-95.

It's blue, he thought, looking at the lighter as he pulled out his phone and thumbed a button.

"Hello?" Her voice.

"Hey, it's me."

"That's horrible," Hazel said.

Bone fought the urge to pull out his phone, the urge inspired by his memory. Remembered it wasn't his phone, it was Julia's.

"It was really his Johnson?" one of the gleefully horrified diggers asked.

Bone nodded, tapping the ash free from the end of his cigarette. "A penis, stomach, breast, several fingers. The freezer had more, and there were signs of eating."

"Stop, no more, stop." Hazel stepped away from the group and picked up her pace.

Bone watched her boots splash in the flowing stream on the side of the road. He felt cheap. Tossed his cigarette away.

They were traveling down now, the descent perceptible. Bone had to dig in with his heels to avoid slipping. The trees were opening up, disbanding from a solid wall on either side to scattered squads of leafless oaks and stunted pines. Here and there a white birch glimmered as they passed.

A howl was perceptible over the hiss of the rain.

"What was that?" Bone asked.

Hazel froze in the road, waiting for the group to catch up with her. She pulled a small flashlight from her bulky camera bag, and a thin beam shot out from it, pointed resolutely at the mud at her feet.

Another howl echoed across the hillside.

"What was that?" Bone repeated.

Hazel opened her mouth. Shut it. The two diggers glanced at each other uneasily.

"Nothing to worry about, Mr. Bone. Whale song comin' off the water, maybe."

Bone realized he could see shifting planes of white up ahead. The frothy tips of waves against a black sea. His stomach curled in upon itself at the thought of setting sail. He looked down at his feet to mind his footing, but not before he noticed Hazel's reaction at the mention of whale song.

- 4 -

The dock building smelled like fish stew and body odor, and fat drops of rainwater dripped from cracks in the often repaired but never replaced ceiling. A thousand drummers beat their sticks against the roof as Hazel huddled closer to the crackling warmth of the fireplace, and a bubbling pot hung on an iron rod over the flames.

"'E cannot set out in this weather, Mr. Bone," Samuel Weeks said.

Hazel watched as the lawman from the mainland argued with the odious pilot of *Leviathan*, who seemed to enjoy having nature to back him in thwarting the marshal's will. The flickering light from the fireplace cast their faces into cartoonish masks, enhancing the core of each man.

The pilot, leering.

Marshal Bone, blazing.

The pilot, crouched.

Bone, looming.

The pilot, defiant.

Bone, passing judgment.

"Obstruction of justice is a serious offense."

"So is drowning, 'e fool."

Hazel wasn't sure if she was disappointed, but she was surprised. She had carried a secret suspicion that the men of the mainland were New Testament in their ideas, but found the stark lines of Bone's face drawn straight from the older book. It was not hard to imagine his eyes burning above his thin slash of a mouth as he spoke the word, "Heretic."

"...the ice hold on *Leviathan*," Bone was saying.

"You'll do no such thing! That filthy corpse will corrupt the hold. Make it unclean."

Bone seemed to draw shadows into himself and grew taller in his black coat. "Put the goddamned body in the ice hold. That's not a request."

Firelight glinted in his eyes and Hazel saw, physically, as the pilot surrendered the argument. A tiny green crab scuttled in the corner of the room, and the pilot stomped a heavy boot on it, reducing it to a shiny smear.

- 5 -

Outside the haphazard dock house, the falling rain pressed against Bone's shoulders, tapping against his hood, fraying concentration. He aimed his flashlight at the dock and grunted at the futility. He might as well have shined his beam through hanging laundry for all he saw. The rain falling in sheets lit up white and blinded his sight to all but a heaving, mocking shape riding the sea where *Leviathan* was tied.

His twisting stomach echoed the truth of the pilot's words. There would be no sailing until the storm ceased.

Not returning to the mainland. His will stretched and the weather poured through the gaps, chilling him.

Where is the constable?

Where is my gun?

A trill of worry, the holster for his Glock suddenly weighted down by its emptiness, made important by its temporary lack of purpose.

Shit. It was fatigue. Fatigue had always made him despondent, negative, irritable. It was hunger that did it for Julia, made her snappish. For Bone it was fatigue.

Words came to him from the local woman. The camera woman. Some part of him was listening and may have responded.

- 6 -

The muddy track had become a swift flowing stream, and his feet quickly lost all feeling. Bone picked his way along the side of the trail, out of the water, calves and thighs aching with the effort.

His flashlight was useless, his visibility reduced to feet by shiny strands of liquid that seemed to move sideways and up as much as it fell down. It crowded in on Bone. The upcoming hearing. The hissing voice of the rain. He remembered a snow globe given to him as a child, cheaply made by other children in a country on the far side of the world. Too much snow had been included, and when he shook the globe nothing could be seen but swirling white.

He thought of his absent pistol and realized his sense of unease came from his lack of a sense of place. Where the hell was he? Arriving at night he had no sense of the Isle as a whole, and realized he had already formed a picture of it in his mind, an image he could neither confirm nor correct. The Isle was a series of unpleasant vignettes. The constable on the dock when he arrived. The graveyard lit by hanging lanterns. A narrow mud track closed in by trees and rain.

After the wide open expanse of starry sky at sea, the Isle crowded him. A cheap and leaking snow globe.

He waved his flashlight along the tree line to the right and staggered to a stop as the beam pushed into a clearing, illuminating a towering figure in black, indistinct in the downpour.

Bone stumbled backwards into the flowing stream and his foot skidded, dropping him to one knee. He fumbled to bring the light to bear again on the looming figure, which twisted and shivered in place even as a pair of eyes flashed in his light.

"Hey!" Bone shouted. The glowing eyes vanished but the figure remained, watching him. He glanced about for Hazel and realized he was alone.

"Who are you?" he called out as sharp claws of panic grabbed for his lungs. He shook them off as a light bobbed towards him from the other direction, the splashing shape of Hazel Milk crossing from the far side of the track.

"There's someone over there," Bone said as he painted the figure with his light. "His eyes glowed."

He caught a quick flash of her teeth, maybe a grin. She made her way into the clearing towards the dark figure and he called out, "Wait!" But she beckoned and he had no choice but to follow.

"Watch your step," Hazel said, and Bone picked his way amidst tangled vines and round humps. His shoe came down on something unseen that gave way with a meaty crack, and he was struck with a mealy, vegetative stink. He aimed his light at his foot as he withdrew it from the pebbled husk of a pumpkin. Wet things flew free as he stomped in disgust.

"Look," Hazel said, panning her light up and down the scarecrow in its fluttering black rain slicker and wide Quaker hat atop a round, pumpkin head. It was a disagreeable thing to see on a rainswept night, for all its inanimate nature.

"I'd swear it was moving when I saw it. And those eyes."

"Likely a feral cat, Mr. Bone, maybe nested inside the hollow pumpkin. Cats, rats, crows and crabs live on the Isle. The Littles sing a song about it."

"Scared the shit out of me."

"He's doing his job then, eh?"

"Yeah." Bone held the circle of his light on the pumpkin head with its empty, triangle eyes. "Where'd you go?"

"Right on the other side of the path," Hazel said, holding her flashlight up under her chin. "You didn't seem much interested in talk."

He didn't like being surprised and decided to push her a bit. "That wasn't whale song earlier, was it, that sound we heard."

The grin was gone from her voice when she answered, "No."

"What was it?"

"We should hurry before the storm gets worse," Hazel said and splashed up the track.

TEN

- 1 -

The woman lay restless on sweat-stained sheets, the dark room thick with the smell of blood and tissue.

"Do you not know that your body is a temple of the Holy Spirit, who is in you, whom you have received from God?"

Was the voice speaking in the room, or in her head? Where was Jeremiah?

"You are not your own; you were bought at a price. Therefore honor God with your body."

Hot. Stifling. Her hair hung in greasy tangles. Water, she needed water. Something was missing.

"Jeremiah?" she croaked.

"Hush," a shadow said, moving in the room.

Her abdomen throbbed with pain, great waves rolling up her body. She felt torn.

"Where is Jeremiah?"

A small cup of water was brought to her lips and she sipped, rivulets running down her face and neck.

For a moment, clarity.

"I heard him cry," the woman said.

"Hush, Mrs. Pruitt," the shadow replied.

- 2 -

The man was bent beneath the downpour, sodden shirt and pants clinging to his wiry frame. His wet hair hung in his eyes and he made awful sounds, ignoring the Word.

"'I prayed for this child, and the Lord has granted me what I asked of him.'" Words audible from inside the old church.

Light in warm hues of red and gold streamed from its stained-glass windows, offering warmth, welcome, sanctuary.

The man, Jeremiah, took three steps in the muddy street and stopped, unaware that he was standing in a deep puddle.

"This...this..." Jeremiah said.

He looked up at the sky and the rain pounded into his open eyes, blinding him. Jeremiah could hear the rhythm from inside the church. He knew the Book of Samuel and muttered in time.

"'So now I give him to the Lord. For his whole life he will be given over to the Lord.'"

"I don't like this," he added in the tiny voice of a child.

"Jeremiah, come in out of the rain," two men said as they splashed up the muddy street to bundle him in a raincoat.

"No," he said, pulling back from them. "I should... I need to speak to the reverend." He jerked away from the two men, and the coat slipped free as he mounted the stone steps leading to the great double doors. Water from a bent gutter sluiced directly down onto him, plastering his hair to his head.

"Jeremiah Pruitt," a voice barked. The constable's bulky form materialized out of the rain. Jeremiah turned.

"But I need to speak to the reverend," he said.

The constable was a figure carved of stone and authority, as uncaring of Jeremiah's need as he was of the falling rain. Jeremiah blinked repeatedly against the water and the constable's flat stare.

"You need to speak to your wife," the two townsmen said, slipping the coat back around his shoulders and herding him away from the church. "She needs you now."

"I don't like this," he said as the three of them made their way back towards home. Behind him he felt the words continuing inside the church as his child was baptized.

"'And he worshiped the Lord there'," Jeremiah said, finishing that bit of Samuel.

- 3 -

The baptismal bowl was larger than a punchbowl and made of smooth stone. Still water reflected the light of a hundred candles. Rain pattered against the stained-glass windows, and Reverend Ambrose Tinker liked to think it soothed the child.

"For I am convinced that neither death nor life, neither angels nor demons, neither the present nor the future'…"

His voice was oddly high-pitched and strained, though the words were rote.

"Nor any powers, neither height nor depth, nor anything else in all creation'…"

He liked to finish these sad baptisms with Romans. The phrases comforted him, guiding his thinking into well-worn ruts. It was no easy task, what he did for the community.

"Will be able to separate us from the love of God that is in Christ Jesus our Lord'," he wheezed to a finish.

A tiny foot, oddly shaped and toeless, broke the surface of the water. A long finger with a yellowed nail gently pressed it back.

The reverend looked down inside the bowl, uncertain if he was looking into the reflection of his own eyes. He searched for meaning in his confusion.

A tiny bubble rose to the surface of the water and floated for a moment before breaking.

"Amen," the reverend said.

ELEVEN

- 1 -

There were two kinds of laws, according to the constable. God's law and man's law, and any law decided by men that wasn't based on God's law was worth less than a pound of lobster shit. The fact that the constable actively engaged this thought at least once each day said something about him. The fact that everyone knew how he thought without him ever expressing his feelings on the matter said something about his effect on the community as a whole.

Lobster shit, a pound, he thought.

His boots splashed heavily in mud puddles as he passed among the dark humps of houses in the center of town. Somewhere an unlocked door whacked and thudded for attention and didn't get any. The constable shook his head.

Lantern light glowed behind shutters, but he made no effort to get in out of the rain. Nor did he make an effort to avoid the puddles. He'd heard that no-good Daniel Woodhouse liked to joke that he left straight trails when he walked in the woods and the trees just stepped out of his way, that's how the Isle got its pathways. Daniel Woodhouse never made a joke about him when he was in the room, though, which said a little bit more about the constable.

The sound of laughter rolled out of the public house, and he could smell both woodstove and pipe smoke on the air. He expected the mainlander marshal was staying the night in the big, stone building with its back to the cliff. He considered walking into the room, waiting until every jackdaw in there, drunk or sober, shut the hell up, so he could look that marshal in the eye and ask him how much a law not based on scripture was worth.

As if in answer, another wave of laughter rolled from the place and he scowled, walking past. *Not so important without your gun*, he thought.

A weird cry carried to him on a gust of wind and he paused, cocking his head to listen. *Goddamn Enoch Weeks. Freak should be locked up.*

A narrow road opened to his left and he took it without much conscious thought, as he had been doing more and more often lately.

- 2 -

Hazel Milk's house stood aloof at the end of a small lane, a two-story built four generations before as a one-story stone affair. Hazel's father had added a second floor of wood and a sharply peaked roof that made the constable think of unhappy spinsters.

He felt his crotch swell under the chafing trousers as he pictured Hazel down by the bridge, shooting her strange photographs.

No lights shone from the windows, but he stepped up onto the front porch anyway, the wood complaining under his weight. Once before he had gone inside when she was out and just sat in her front room in the dark, enjoying the way a house smells when a woman took care of it.

"Constable," a voice said, and he jumped, completely caught up in his reverie.

"Who is it?" he asked, barking the words.

A shadow stirred on the two-person swing, and he heard it creak as a small shape slipped off. Shoes thudded against the porch.

"Burden Ipswich," the shadow replied.

The constable undid his coat enough to pull the flashlight from his belt and shine the beam on the deformed face of the dwarf. Burden turned away but didn't retreat.

"What the hell are you doing here?" the constable said. "Lurking around the town after dark, houses where no one is home?"

"I'm waiting for Hazel, Constable," Burden said. "What are you doing here, around houses where no one is home?"

The constable was actually stunned into silence for a beat. The tree stump was questioning him? He took a step forward, boots clomping on the porch floor, then hesitated and switched off his flashlight, conscious that it was the only bright illumination at the end of the road.

"Come to sit in the dark?" Burden asked, and the constable flinched as the dwarf picked his recent memory from the air. "Come to warm the wid—"

The constable's hand swung in a tight, invisible arc, and his palm cracked across the dwarf's temple. As the little man spun into the side of the house the constable moved again, speed unexpected in such a big man, and threw Burden off the porch to land with a splash in the yard.

Burden had pushed himself up to his hands and knees, struggling to get air back into his lungs, when the constable's heavy boot pressed between his shoulder blades and drove his face down into the sopping grass.

"You'd best spend more time in your tower where you belong, living alongside bad memories and crabs," the constable said, fighting down the anger that pricked and boiled under his skin.

Burden thrashed, his breath bubbling in the thick water. The constable ground the toe of his boot into the little man's spine before stepping back. He was well versed in administering private corrections, and the resulting black eyes and bruises were inevitably written off as accidents by those who sported them.

"Go," the constable said, wiping his hands in the rain as the dwarf splashed away from Hazel's house.

- 3 -

The bathtub was an old claw-foot affair of cracked white porcelain. A narrow V of rust marred the white beneath the faucet, but it was otherwise immaculate, the way women kept such things. The water gurgling into it soothed him. The rising steam enticed him.

He dropped his gun belt to the floor, the clatter loud on the tiles. His clothes were wet and chafing, and he had begun to strip them off in Hazel's living room. His coat was back there somewhere, a soaked pile in the dark. His shoes were there as well, and his socks.

A glance down at his thick toes, white from immersion. *Boots are leaking.* An absent thought masking the deeper realization that he had not only crossed an invisible line, he was practically whistling as he did so.

The constable offered an actual whistle, a windy and weak sound. He grinned and looked at himself in the mirror as he stripped off his shirt.

His eyes caught the flickering light of the single candle he allowed himself. Candles were romantic.

The hair on his chest glistened with damp, black curls in a line down the hard swell of his gut and disappeared into the waistband of his pants. He sucked his stomach in, seeing the size of his arms, the breadth of his shoulders.

He unbuttoned his pants and slid them down, freeing the near-erection he had been walking around with for hours. She would appreciate it, he thought. Hazel was—had been—a married woman. She was no virgin. And once a woman got a taste of what a man carried between his legs, she wanted more. Needed more.

He gripped the side of the tub and stepped in carefully, lowering his buttocks almost daintily into the hot water.

"Aaaaah," the sound came out unbidden, but that was all right. The entire evening was all right. He thought of words he had written on paper every night, only to burn them in his wood stove. Letters to Hazel.

The muscles in his stomach bunched, and he stretched forward to turn off the flow of hot water. Leaned back and let his eyes drift shut.

The brassieres he had found upstairs in her bedroom were amazing. That was the word for them. Full and soft and smelling faintly of something pleasant as he pressed his nose into them. He imagined what her breasts would look like as they lay round and heavy in his hands. He imagined tearing her blouse open. Imagined her saying, "Yes."

The pictures of her husband, of the two of them together, had made him uneasy, and he considered laying them face down on the dresser or hiding them in a drawer. Was still considering the pictures when he had lain back on the bed and noted the rise of dust. The general mustiness of the room. His policeman's mind made a connection with a blanket and pillow neatly folded at the edge of her living room couch and wondered how long it had been since she slept in the bedroom.

Muscles unknotted as the hot water worked its will on his body, and he tried to recall if Hazel had ever said his name, or had she always called him Constable as everyone else did, as he often did inside his own mind, the job fusing seamlessly into his identity.

The constable opened his eyes, looking at the candle. The flame leaned over sideways and then stood back up even as he felt a light eddy of cooler air.

Someone else was in the house.

"Hazel?" Best to let her know he was there.

He braced his hands on either side of the tub and pushed himself up, water sluicing down his body, his skin red from the warmth.

He stopped. Stared.

A lobsterman leaned against the bathroom doorway. The corners of his mouth twitched up. She had snuck in, had seen him lying there and…

Tension he didn't know he was holding eased out of his body.

She wanted to play a game.

The constable stepped out of the tub, dripping across the tiled floor. He walked naked to the doorway, letting himself be seen if she was watching, and picked up the lobsterman. His grin faltered a bit.

Blasphemous it was, a tiny Christ made of shells, with spiny lobster legs splayed out to either side representing the Lord's arms. It was crucified to a cross made of wet sticks.

But the rock rattled inside the barrel of the carapace and the constable's lips twitched up in a smile again. It was naughty. Mischievous. He felt his cock swell as he shook the rattle. Once. Twice.

After a moment he heard an answering rattle from inside the house.

He stepped out of the bathroom, guessing where she would be going. "Ready or not, here I come," he said. When he reached the bottom of the staircase, he shook the rattle again, three times. He cocked his head and waited for the answering sound from the bedroom.

A tiny rock struck shell three times and he turned, confused. He padded towards the dark living room and his damp feet sounded like wet tape peeling off of the cold floor. A chill wind brushed him as he stepped into the wide space. Goosebumps rose on his exposed skin even as he felt his scrotum tighten. He had a brief concern that his cock would shrink and become laughable.

"You left the door open," he said to the dark, waiting for his eyes to adjust. When they didn't, he moved cautiously across the floor until his toes touched the wet pile of his raincoat. He crouched and fumbled to find the flashlight in the coat pocket. Came up empty.

Damn it, he thought as he stood and shook the rattle four times. If he didn't find her on that round, he was allowed one more attempt, five shakes of his rattle. Would she stay if he didn't find her?

"Hazel?" he said.

Four distinctly paced shakes of a rattle sounded from the bathroom and the constable grinned in relief. He thought of her already in the tub, and his shrinking reversed course so that his cock bounced comically in front of him as he hurried across the floor, feet slapping against the smooth wood.

Christ, she might be naked already. His throat felt full and tight and his breath grew quick.

"Are you surprised to see me?" he asked as he stepped into the warm glow of the candlelit bathroom and skidded to a halt, heel slipping on the wet tiles.

The constable had trouble finding his voice. "You're not Hazel."

Metal gleamed.

"No, I'm not."

TWELVE

- 1 -

"I need a room," Bone said.

Julia had taken him to see a play in Boston once.

"Can I speak to the innkeeper?" he asked.

It was very *avante garde*, faces pressing from behind a thin white sheet, spouting nonsense dialogue.

"And I need someone to find the constable."

The crowd that formed around him the instant he entered the pub was something like that. It was a dark, smoky space with low ceilings, lit by lanterns and a fireplace. The two diggers were there, telling stories already, and the crowd of men in wool sweaters and fisherman's caps was on him immediately, hungry for contact with the stranger.

"Sit down here."

"Like a drink?"

"Wet as Moses outside."

Bone sat, pushed by hands. "I need to speak to the innkeeper."

"Eaton Fenn the innkeeper, hah! Ol' Fenn puttin' on airs."

"Heard the cawpse came outta the ground like stew meat!"

"Was there really a cut up Johnson in a refrigerator?"

Except it wasn't faces pressing against a white screen, it was features. All Bone could make out were features pressing into the sphere of light thrown by the small lantern on the wooden table beside him. "Is the constable here? He was supposed to meet me at the boat."

A ship's prow of a nose: "What kind of lawman are you?"

A porcupine bristle of facial hair: "What other parts you find in that fridge?"

A liver spotted dome gleaming in the orange light: "Have a drink."

A tumbler of rough cut glass slid into his palm, and he sipped the amber liquid in reflex, startled as the fire rushed down his throat. A flash of guilt, overwhelmed by the human tide. "Look, I need the constable. He has my—"

"That fella Slocum, he put those bodies in the freezer?" Thick finger thudding down on the table.

"Eat and get some warm in 'e." Bobbing Adam's apple.

"Not so much excitement since that census fella wanted to count us." Red-veined mushroom of a nose.

"What was that? Who said that?" Bone said, thinking *Tate*.

A wooden bowl of fish stew clattered onto the table, steam redolent of cod and clam rising to Bone's nose. His senses swam. His stomach grumbled. "Oh, shit," he might have said, and downed the rest of the whiskey in his glass.

"There once was a lady from Ghent!" a high-pitched voice cried out and the men shouted the barroom poet down.

"Shut up 'e freak."

"You're drunk, Burden Ipswich."

Bone rode the wave of relaxation that swam into the stream of his fatigue. "I really need a room." He was speaking to turned backs obscuring some sort of commotion.

"Where's the lawman?"

"Need to find the lawman. Is he here?"

"He's here, he's here."

Bone wasn't looking, was in fact dipping a chunk of fresh bread into the stew and placing it on his tongue. Rich flavor suffused him, and he thought of how long it had been since he had a drink. Christ he was hungry. He dipped the bread into the stew again and was lifting it to his lips when he paused and looked up, mouth still open.

Belt buckles.

Wet coats.

Burning eyes over bristling beards.

"'E need to come with us right now."

"Get your coat."

"There's been some trouble."

Bone had to lean back to meet their eyes. Shook his head.

"I have no jurisdiction for local crimes. You need the constable."

The tall figure in the middle leaned down, water running from his hat to patter on the table. Lantern light shimmered off raindrops in his beard and it looked like the hair was woven with jewels.

"That's just it, Mr. Bone. It *is* the constable."

Bone stood up, pushing back the wooden chair with his legs as he rose. He slid into his dripping coat, and the crowd pulled back. The air was expectant. Still hungry. So was Bone.

"I still need a room."

- 2 -

The entire pub crowded out after, some running back inside for coats when the weather hit them.

"'E folk stay here," one of the tall men barked, before leading his fellows and Bone to splash their way up the street.

Since then, they hadn't said a thing.

Shapes lurked on either side of the road, more visible by the nimbus of exploding raindrops hitting roofs than by anything else. An undercurrent of wood smoke tickled the wet air. Bone's gaze lingered on thin lines of light framing wooden shutters until a sideways gust of rain slashed across his face and he ducked into his hood.

They walked single file, body language alone telling him this was a task and not social. An unpleasant task at that. Twice the leader had turned to say something to the man behind him, who in turn spoke to the third man in line. Both times that man had reflexively turned to Bone but pivoted forward before saying anything. They acted as if they expected to have a fourth man other than Bone along with them.

A terrible gust shoved them off balance, and the file staggered to the left.

"Hey," Bone called out. "Where the hell are we going?"

Either the last man in line didn't hear or was ignoring him, but Bone was in danger of being left behind so he hurried after them, shoes slipping and sliding on the mud, cold wetness creeping up to his knees.

"Your island sucks," he said in a conversational tone to the back of the man in front of him.

- 3 -

The house had a cobbled-together but not unattractive appearance. The shutters were not drawn, and he could see the dim glow of candlelight from somewhere inside.

The elements were having their way with the open front door. As Bone approached, the door swung partially closed and then, gripped by an invisible fist, was thrown wide to bang against the wall.

"Inside, Mr. Bone."

All three men were in between him and the house, turned to look at him with unreadable expressions. The door slammed shut behind them and the men flinched. It was painted some dark color Bone couldn't make out in the poor light.

"The hell you say," Bone said. "I'm not going in there."

CRASH! The door was open, a black mouth hungry and waiting. Bone had no idea what was going on. It felt outside of his frame of reference, a twisted hazing or initiation.

"I'm not moving until you bring me the constable," Bone said.

"That's just it," the leader said. "He's inside."

The second man said something Bone didn't catch, and the three Isle men trooped up the steps onto the porch and slogged inside. Bone noted they made no effort to wipe off their boots or shake the water from their jackets.

He waited until they were out of sight and slipped a stiletto from the small of his back, holding it in his fist as he slid that hand into the appropriate coat pocket.

Lightning flashed overhead, and the house and trees were lit in black and white. Thunder crashed and hurled darkness back across the tableau.

BANG! The door slammed shut, mocking him. Something was making him uneasy. Tickling at his brain. Something besides the cheap Hollywood horror movie he had walked into.

The steps boomed resentfully under his shoes, and the boards of the porch creaked even over the storm. He waited a beat to see if the angry door would take a swipe at him.

When that didn't happen he grabbed the worn metal knob and twisted it, bracing for what was to come as he pulled the door open.

- 4 -

The air was heavy with cigarette smoke and death. Bone felt the world slide beneath him.

"Ain't never gonna forget this," a dark shape spoke dully from a couch, located by the orange tip of a lit cigarette. "Ain't never gonna forget this."

Bone knew he had been saying the same thing for a long time, a machine winding down.

"Who are you?" the automaton on the couch asked.

Bone shook his head as his eyes adjusted and he made out the shape of a banister, heading towards it.

"Mr. Bone," a voice said, and he paused with his foot on the first step.

"What?" Bone asked.

"In here, sir."

Lightning flashed through the windows, and he saw the bony angles of the three men who had brought him.

"He's...ah...in here," one said.

"I ain't gonna forget this," the man on the couch muttered.

Thunder shook the house.

- 5 -

A hundred fingers tapped against the window as the storm typed up its report. The bathroom smelled like he had torn open a dog's belly and pressed his face deep inside the carcass. Someone had placed a storm lamp on the white sink so Bone could see.

There was blood covering everything.

Red runnels flowed down the walls, and the floor was a tacky patchwork of pools and smears. Dripping circles even marred the ceiling.

"Whoa," Bone muttered to himself. He had expected something, but not *this*. He glanced around, deliberately avoiding the red to look for the black and gray scorch marks indicating some type of blast. There was that much blood.

No black marks. If not a bomb then some sort of industrial accident, some sort of massive machine meant to grind rocks or shred tree trunks.

"How many people have been in here?" Bone asked over his shoulder. He heard gagging noises. The sound of men struggling to breathe.

"We thought...Jesus and Mary...he might be in the tub."

The claw-foot tub, normally white like everything else, was a gory work by Pollock with a thickening pool of roux filling the bottom. A chocolate treacle with hints of red. A molé sauce perhaps, chocolate seasoned with chili peppers.

Bone fought down his own gorge and ruthlessly reigned in his imagination. Sweat beaded his forehead.

"Blood's four inches deep," Bone said, scorn riding his words. "How the hell could the constable be in that?"

His panning gaze took in the crumpled pile of clothes. Those on the bottom were sodden and black, but those on top...

He pulled out the stiletto and pressed a button with his thumb. Six inches of shining steel sprang free and caught the lantern light.

Footsteps backing off hurriedly behind him. "Lord!"

"You got a pig farm on this island?" Bone said.

"Yeah...ah...we do," came the response. "Nutter's."

"You sure this isn't a prank? Maybe for you? Maybe for me?" Bone said. His throat tightened with the surge of adrenaline, adding snap to each word he spoke.

"Mary, mother of God, no sir," said a voice.

Another voice, quieter and farther away. "Can't you feel it?"

Bone stepped carefully inside the bathroom, the tacky blood was slippery and he didn't want to fall. The room was already contaminated as a crime scene, assuming this wasn't pig's blood. But he didn't want to go down and end up covered in the stuff no matter what kind of blood it was. He crouched, carefully maintaining his balance, and used the tip of his weapon to lift a bit of shirt from the top of the pile. Damp, but not with blood.

Clothes were taken off before this happened, he thought.

He backed out and wiped his shoes uselessly in the hall.

"The constable's clothes?"

"Yessir," one of the men said.

"No gun," Bone noted. He remembered the constable's belt, the brass shells winking from loops.

"You check upstairs?" Bone asked, carefully pressing the point of the stiletto against the wall and pushing the blade back into the smooth black hilt until he heard the snick of the locking mechanism. He ran a finger over the dimple it left in the wood.

"We did, after John Wallis came and got us."

"John Wallis," Bone said, glancing at the muttering shadow on the couch. "The guy who discovered this?"

"He is."

Bone crossed to the seated man and noticed, for the first time, he had something in his hands that Bone at first took to be a child's doll. Wallis was turning it over and over, something inside rattling as it revolved.

"What's that?" Bone asked.

Wallis stopped as if he had heard the question shouted from far away and wasn't sure it was for him.

"You find that here?" Bone asked and Wallis nodded, holding the object up to Bone.

"Shit," Bone said, stepping back from the lobsterman crucified to crossed sticks. One claw had been cracked. "What is that?"

"Lobsterman," Wallis said, clearing his throat and focusing on Bone. "I stepped on it when I came in."

"Was it Hazel's?" Bone asked and Wallis shrugged.

"It's a toy the Littles make," Mather said from behind him. "I had one when I was a boy."

Bone took the thing, knowing there would be no usable prints. He stared down into the vertical slit of the mouth, an alien parody of a human face. "They always crucified?"

"No," Mather said. "This is a blasphemy."

Bone tilted the lobsterman upside down and shook it until the rattling object inside danced towards the broken claw. He was hoping for a class ring the murderer accidentally left behind, the gallows humor kicking in a bit. Standard armor for the cop's soul.

He finally worried the object free and it fell into his cupped palm. He leaned closer, squinting. "What the hell is this?"

Mather made an uncomfortable sound and shifted his feet. "It's a tooth. Custom tells the Littles to put a baby tooth inside for good luck."

Bone studied the small, brownish tooth, the twin roots unmistakable.

He felt his skin crawl and pushed the tooth back inside the broken claw with his thumb, tossing the toy onto the couch and wiping his hand against his wet coat.

"You need to consider this place a crime scene. Close it off," Bone said. "Someone in authority here who can do that?"

The three men glanced at each other and Bone noticed, for the first time really, how similar they looked. Not identical, but all tall men with bony noses, cheeks covered in spiky bushes of white and gray.

"We can," said the one with the whitest beard. Great curling hairs that sprouted in all directions

"And who are you?" Bone asked, pulling out a small notebook from an inside pocket.

"What are 'e doing?" one of them asked.

"I need your names, gentlemen," Bone said.

"But we didn't see anything."

Bone gestured with the notebook. "You saw this."

The white beard held up a hand to the other men and turned back to Bone. "I'm the first selectman, name of Increase Mather. These other fellas are the rest of the town selectmen, Eldred Smith and John Wallis. Nutter ain't here."

Bone shook his head, realizing he'd ignored an obvious question. "Who lives here?"

It was Wallis, the man who found a bloody bathroom with no body to claim the blood, who answered. "This house? You've met her."

"I have?" Bone said.

"It's Hazel Milk's house," Wallis said. "And we have no idea where she is."

- 6 -

In the recesses of his mind, Bone detected the shape of possibility. An opportunity that might halt his downward plunge. Machinery grown rusty since the death of his wife stirred slowly to life. Fresh current coursed along old, dry lines.

He reached out for it like a drowning man.

Bone was staring out a dark window smeared with rain. He didn't remember crossing to it and had the sense that conversation had continued while his mind took a smoke break.

"We need to get out there and find that Jezebel," a hard voice said, and Bone turned to look at Eldred Smith. His eyes were coals set deep in the seams of his face.

"That who?" Bone asked.

"Woman who killed the constable," Smith said. "Hazel Milk."

Bone looked him up and down as the first trickle of adrenaline entered his bloodstream, and the sounds of the storm faded. "Was the constable a tough man, in your opinion?"

"As nails," Smith said.

"Then how do you think she managed to kill him? He was in the bathtub from what I can see, so she didn't hit him with a rock while he was asleep. Besides, let's say for some reason," Bone let the suggestiveness into his voice, "the constable was asleep upstairs. I wonder, having met her and being able to take a stab at her weight and muscle tone, how would she move him into the bathroom? Drag him? Really? He's a big guy. Let alone lift him up into the tub."

"Now there, Marshal—" Mather began but stopped at Bone's raised hand.

"There is no evidence that the constable was shot with his own pistol, which to my understanding is the only firearm on the Isle other than my own," he said, eyes holding Smith's. "And while a .38 round might not go through a body that big, it probably would."

"Constable was a self-loader, and he loaded hot rounds," Wallis interjected, but looked down at Smith's withering glare. Bone too looked at Wallis.

"Mr. Wallis, where were you around dinner time?" Bone asked.

"Me?"

"Yes, at dinner time."

"Eatin' dinner. At home, I mean. But after I brought that over." Wallis pointed to a covered basket made of tan wicker. "Missus asked me to share some of the muffins. Hazel doesn't bake anymore since her husband..."

Bone was nodding. "You're a big man, Mr. Wallis. Not as big as the constable but pretty big. Work the boats all your life?"

"Of course."

"Strong guy like you pulling ropes and nets all his life could haul even the constable's weight. Maybe haul him right out of here."

"'E are insane," Smith said, and Bone fixed him with a look. The air between them was heated near to sparking.

"And maybe you had help moving the body, Wallis," Bone said, his eyes still on Eldred Smith's.

"Marshal," Mather said, "none of us had anything to do with this crime. We're the *selectmen*."

Bone looked away from Smith and strolled around the room, hands in his coat pockets. He let the tension simmer a bit before glancing at Mather.

"Don't jump to conclusions, gentlemen," he said, playing with the watch around his wrist, letting the band stretch and snap. Mather and Wallis both had their eyes on his watch soon enough, but Smith kept his stare on Bone. "Everyone is a suspect. Hazel Milk is, even though I can't see the how of it yet. You gentlemen are... Hell, how do I know Mr. Wallis found the house in the present state?" He strolled over to the bathroom doorway and kept his voice steady with a slight effort as he felt the confrontation pass.

Once again the house uttered its muffled groans under the lashing of the wind as the rain pecked and pattered on the glass windowpanes.

"Mr. Bone, what are we supposed to do?" Mather asked as he saw the tension leach away from the marshal.

"We should still get a search party going, look for the constable and Hazel," Wallis said from behind Bone.

"Gentlemen," Bone said quietly, stopping the bullshit with his watch and turning to face them. The Isle men moved up closer. "Who would want to kill the constable?"

A silence drew out, and Bone looked over the bent forms of the men, hooded in shadows.

"Have 'e ever seen a tree growing out of a hillside of pure rock?" Mather asked.

Bone nodded.

"It starts small, it does. A seedling lands in a clump of dirt stuck in a natural fissure. Like most small things, it will likely die on its own, ground away by time," Mather said.

The door bucked in its frame behind Bone, the wind giving it a good kick. Rain drummed against the windows, uncountable watery kamikazes smashing themselves to atoms against a barrier they could never breach. Bone felt the branch of opportunity gaining shape as the old selectman spoke and he tightened his grip upon it. He need not return home as the unwanted errand boy ripe for dismissal. He could return as a pivotal figure. Needed.

"Other times, maybe one in a thousand," Mather said.

"One in a million," Wallis said quietly, and Mather nodded, glancing back as the shaken selectman joined them.

"One in a million, maybe, like John says," Mather continued. "That time the seedling takes root and grows. In time the roots dig deeper, weakening that mass of solid stone. The bole of the tree doesn't just reach out for light and air, it grows thicker, it pushes the rock itself apart. Again, rocky hillside, it can usually absorb the change. It's big, it's old. But maybe one time…"

"One in a million," Wallis offered.

Mather nodded and placed a comforting hand on Wallis' shoulder. "That one time there was already a weakness, an old insult to the stone. When this new thing presses and pushes and digs, the whole hillside breaks and slides down to crash into rubble."

"Do you think that's what happened here?" Bone said.

"This is an old place, Mr. Bone," Mather said. "An old place where small cracks can grow wide."

Bone played his flashlight beam around the bathroom. He could feel the violence in the room, a psychic stink in the air. He was, by training, a hunter, not a crime scene investigator. But he had worked with homicide detectives over the years and been on scene more times than he could count. They talked about it, a smell that wasn't a smell, a scent invisible, undetectable to the nose, but discovered by some deeper organ. Something, perhaps, older.

"Gentlemen," he said, turning to look at the tall shadows. Wind howled and shook the house, then subsided. "My concern is that what happened here, this event, is exactly what it might appear to be. Not a killing caused by sudden emotion or alcohol or an argument that escalated out of control. But something involving sickness."

"You mean disease?" Mather said.

"Not of the body," Bone said, panning his beam of light around the neat room. He saw the pillow and folded blanket at one end of the couch and felt a tiny spark of connection to Hazel Milk. His own bed at home was a bed of nails after Julia's passing, and he slept on the sofa.

"The scene suggests violence of an extreme order of magnitude. Yet organized. There is no body. No sign of struggle. The blood is contained in the bathroom, yet no effort was made to clean it up. On the contrary, it has the feeling of a display."

"A display?" one of the shadows asked. Bone thought it was Smith.

"A message," Bone said. Thunder rumbled assent overhead.

"Saying what?"

Bone shook his head. "I don't know exactly. But I can guess at part of it."

"What?" Mather asked.

Bone let his light wander around the bathroom again, panning across the dark spots on the ceiling, steadying on the thickening pool of blood in the claw-foot tub.

"Psychosis," Bone said.

- 8 -

"We will need a crime scene crew from the mainland to come out here and work the house," Bone said. "We need a quick sweep tonight to make sure that neither the constable or Hazel Milk are nearby. We should also have people check every house in the vicinity."

"Right," Mather said. "I can get volunteers."

"Have the men work in groups. We don't want individuals wandering off and getting lost. Then we'll have to find them as well."

"Right. Ain't going to find much in this here soup, not at night."

Bone nodded. "We'll need to block access to the house and photograph the scene."

"I can stay here tonight, keep people out," Wallis said.

"You sure?" Bone asked. "No shame in wanting to step out, after what you've seen tonight."

Wallis nodded.

"Mr. Bone," Wallis said. "Where do you think Hazel Milk is?"

Bone shook his head.

"Do you think she was involved in...this?" Mather asked.

"We just need to find her," Bone said.

"I'll run home and tell m'wife where I'm staying tonight, then be right back," Wallis said, moving for the door with Smith on his heels. Lightning flashed as the door opened, and for a moment Bone saw Wallis as a black silhouette, the cutout of a man. The door banged shut before the thunder boomed.

"Sweet Mary, mother of God," Mather said, glancing about the dark downstairs now that only he and Bone remained.

"Who did it, Mr. Mather?" Bone asked. "The fact of the matter is this: you know the person who did it."

"What are 'e saying?" Mather said, aghast.

Bone smiled. "Only that the population here isn't very large, and I suspect you know everyone as first selectman, right?"

"Right."

"Which means one of these folks you know is a murderer," Bone said, nodding at Mathers' reaction. "Think hard. This is a tight community. Who did it?"

Mather's mouth opened and closed silently, a fish trying to breathe air. "Nothing like this has ever happened before."

"Except Slocum. Richard Slocum died here just recently."

"But that was an accident," Mather said after a long look at Bone, who returned the gaze until the other man looked away.

Interesting.

"Let's go," Bone said. He pulled the door open. The storm bullied its way in and his coat flapped against his body. He looked back.

Hazel.

- 9 -

Bone stood on the porch for a moment, allowing his eyes to readjust to the impenetrable nature of the stormy night, and his body to the grasping chill. The yard was black before him, the narrow walkway disappearing mere feet from the front steps.

Bone felt the glimmer of opportunity again. The dusty knock of purpose at his door. If that glimmer was the color of blood, so be it.

Lightning squirted in jags across the sky and filled the air with ozone. The yard was abruptly full of men staring up at him on the porch, their appearance so jarring they seemed conjured or, considering the smell, somehow flash-baked into existence.

The night pressed back down and Bone blinked away the afterimage as voices came to him over the thunder.

"Something happen to Hazel Milk?"

"There a killin', Marshal?"

"We heard there was blood everywhere!"

A chorus of voices shouting different words but asking the same thing.

He walked down the steps, pulling his hood up, able to make the men out as shapes in the darkness now that he knew where they were.

"Gentlemen, there appears to have been a crime of some significance. We are concerned that the constable is missing and maybe injured. Hazel Milk is also missing, and we need to find her."

He turned to see Increase Mather standing tall on the steps. "Get 'em moving, Mr. Mather," he called out before pushing his way through the milling crowd.

"Where are you going, Marshal?" Mather shouted back.

"To get my gun," he said. "Someone show me to the constable's office."

THIRTEEN

- 1 -

She staggered through the rain, skirt and blouse plastered to her body. The muscles at the back of her jaw flexed and spasmed, her teeth slamming together in machine-gun chatter that was near to driving her mad.

If she wasn't there already.

She tore away the bloody blouse and screamed in revulsion. Hooked her fingers into claws and ran it through her tangled hair to remove clots of blood, imagined or otherwise she didn't know.

Couldn't focus.

Lightning flashed and she saw the clumps of hair caught in her fingers, held her hands out before herself and wept. Her long hair. Her proud hair. The sob overcome by a shudder that drove her to her knees.

Horror.

She thought only of succor. Of her husband. Realized as she staggered into the fence surrounding the graveyard that he was dead. Dead. Dead.

Her pale fingers wrapped around iron bars as she sagged, knees watery.

"Hazel Milk!"

She was on her knees, still holding the fence. Her head rolled around on her neck and she looked up from beneath sopping tangles.

"Hazel, my God!"

A distorted figure emerged out of the murk, great geysers of water splashing up from running feet.

She felt the raincoat wrapped around her body, and her eyes were closing, closing. She fought the pull but even the horrid chill was growing warm.

"What happened?" Worried eyes staring down.

"The constable is dead, Burden," she said, slurring. "He's so incredibly dead."

- 2 -

Mary Nutter knelt within her prayer closet, the hardwood floor cruel to her bony knees. Her hands were clasped and her head bowed, her eyes closed against the dark. The air was stifling and only the tiniest light slithered in through cracks. It was so narrow a space that Mary could scarcely pull the door shut behind her, and she took care when standing up so as not to crack her head on the low ceiling. The closet had been a punishment, a purification, when she was a child. As she grew older, cloistering herself in the closet became refuge when father boiled into one of his furies, particularly after mother passed away.

This night the storm itself might as well have been powered by father's emotion, and she entered her closet immediately after clearing the dinner table. He eventually slammed his way outside to deal with the sick chickens. Father was a most pious man and would not let even his great anger interrupt the solemnity of his daughter's prayer.

She heard a pounding outside and flinched before realizing it was coming from the front of the house. A great clatter came to her ears and she heard a raised voice.

"Nutter!" A man's muffled shout. "Wickedness afoot tonight. Nutter!"

Mary pushed backwards out of her closet and stumbled. Increase Mather twitched back in alarm at the woman who seemed to materialize from the kitchen wall.

"What 'e saying, Increase?" Mary asked, enjoying his startled expression.

"Your father, where is he?"

"What happened?"

"We need him, now."

- 3 -

The flat metal blade of the shovel cut into the mud beneath the bloody, feather-strewn offal. Rain pocked and pinged off the blade as the shovel was expertly flicked and the mud and guts went into the hole. The pervasive stink of pigs was leavened by the sharp odor of fresh blood.

Folks said the hole had once been a spring, but nothing of use had come from it since Hatevil Nutter had first seen it. Only thing to ever come out besides a stench was an upward boil of crabs, spreading over the ground as if a giant blister had burst and spewed forth the white scuttling mass that set his pigs to squealing.

Now things went *into* the black maw: uneaten slops, garbage, pig shit and, tonight, the remains of a dozen dead chickens he fed to the pigs when they came down sick. He had built a fence around the hole years back after a new piglet slid into it and cost him money. No one knew how deep it went, and it could smell something awful in the summer heat, but Hatevil didn't care.

"Get back, you," Hatevil said, swinging the shovel in a short, vicious arc. The metal flat smacked against the boar's shoulder and it recoiled, squealing. Hell-begotten pigs were mean animals, and it paid to remind them of their place.

He was a tall, rawboned man, and his too-long arms were corded with sinew, his hands wide and almost distorted by bony knuckles. Hatevil was a man with an aggressively prominent nose, rain dripping off of it as he worked to clean up the dead chickens as Holy God cleansed his world.

He wore no coat, letting the rain soak him through and paint his wool shirt to his body, making his brown pants dark, washing away his personal filth. Mary had been a particular bother at dinner, and it was all he could do to storm outside and not lay his hands on her. His brows were black and tufted over yellow eyes, angled like a horned owl's and giving his mien an appearance of never-ending anger. That he existed in a perpetually simmering state was beside the point. He knew folks on the Isle had on occasion mocked his name, calling him Hate-Everything Nutter. He took satisfaction in the fact that no one had ever said it in his presence.

The back door of the house banged open and his daughter, Mary, came outside, holding her coat over her head and shoulders to ward off the rain. A tall man hurried behind her, and Hatevil had to wipe the rain from his eyes before he could make the man out.

"What do you want?" Hatevil asked, water trickling into his mouth as he spoke.

Lightning flashed and thunder cracked overhead, drowning out the newcomer's words.

"What?" Hatevil said.

"Been a killing," Increase Mather said.

"It was the slattern!" Mary crowed, eyes flashing.

"Shut your mouth, girl," Hatevil said and Mary flinched.

Increase pulled off his hat and wrung it out in his hands as the rain plastered his hair to his round skull. "Happened at the Milk house."

"Who died?"

"Constable's been murdered."

- 4 -

"Look, it's bleeding!" Woody said, backing up. "How can it bleed?"

Something struck the backs of his thighs and he whirled wildly in the dark office, swinging the flashlight through empty space and nearly tripping over a guest chair.

"Stop!" the marshal shouted, but Woody was too far downstream on a torrent of adrenaline and whiskey. He rushed for the doorway and bounced off the frame, jarring the flashlight from his grip. The staircase rocked and shuddered as he pounded up out of the basement, and for one terrifying instant thought the entire construction would collapse, hurling him back down into the dark. An animal sound, high and pig-like, followed him as he sprinted along the dark hallway for the open front door where he tripped on the threshold to sprawl headlong into the muddy street.

The icy rain jolted him upright, and he struggled into a mud-splattering sprint, abandoning the scarred lawman to the horror of the constable's office. The squealing sound followed him, and Woody was struck by the realization that the noise was coming from his own mouth.

The fun was gone. The sense of adventure was gone. And Woody wished he had never met the hooded marshal in a black graveyard where he had committed sin at the lawman's request, unearthing a body already committed to Almighty God.

- 5 -

"Sonofabitch," Bone said, aiming Woody's discarded flashlight up the staircase and holding one hand over his face. The stench of old sweat and ancient shit was a palpable force in the basement, seeping out from behind a heavy, locked door.

"Holding cell," Woody had told him with a shudder, when they first descended into the basement of the municipal building. "Ol' TB," Woody called it. "Town building."

Bone panned his flashlight back towards the open doorway to the constable's office, dust and fragments of cobweb glowing in the bright beam. He'd picked the old man to serve as native guide because he recognized him from the exhumation, not realizing how drunk the erstwhile digger was until they were well away from the crowd of townsfolk.

"Sonofabitch," he said again, reluctantly making his way back past the cell towards the office. The walls of the hallway were cut stone and clammy to the touch, green with mold where it hadn't been scraped away. The revelation into the constable's character was unsettling. Buttoned-up authority in public but moldering in his private domain.

They had been standing in this spot when he'd asked Woody the question. "You've been around forever and know everyone. I'll bet you hear more than people think. Who do you think killed the constable?"

"What?" Woody asked and, after Bone repeated the question, paused to think. Bone could hear the wheels turning, waterwheels in a river of whiskey. "I think it was that fella Slocum," Woody said, fixing a bleary eye on Bone. "We dug'm up and freed him to get revenge."

Bone let out a pent-up breath and dragged the bright circle of his flashlight away from the chaotic desk to the square metal plate of the wall safe.

It *was* bleeding.

Black trickles made their serpentine way to the floor where a thickening puddle had formed. A small shadow shifted and eyes glowed as a tiny cat hissed, then returned to lapping at the thick blood.

"Get out of here," Bone said, lashing out with a foot. The cat darted around the walls of the room until it disappeared through the door.

Bone wriggled his left hand until he had a portion of the cuff clutched in his fingers, then used that to grasp the short handle on the safe. He jerked it sharply down and stepped back, letting his weight pull open the door. A small tide of red cascaded out, painting a broad swath down the wall. Bone shuffled back to avoid getting it on his shoes.

"God," Bone muttered. "What the…"

He shined the beam into the cramped interior of the safe.

Something fleshy and deflated rested where he had hoped to find his pistol. It was pink and lined with purple veins, an organ of some kind.

Bone shook his head and backed away. "What the hell is going on?"

The bloody patter eventually gave way and became the tapping of the rain against window glass.

- 6 -

Woody could hear the rumble of voices inside the public house as he slogged towards the front door. He paused to wipe wet hair back from his forehead before leaning a shoulder into the door and pushing it open, already dragging an arm across his mouth in anticipation of whiskey's coarse burn. The last time he'd walked with the marshal his stories had been good enough for several rounds, and after regaining his composure on the wet hike back, he realized he had a real thumper to share.

"You'll never believe…"

The seething anger in the room shocked Woody into silence. Everyone was speaking at once, some yelling. Loudest of all was the booming voice of Hatevil Nutter, waving his frayed Bible over his head.

Woody grabbed Arn Corn by the arm. "What the hell happened?"

Arn whirled, wide-eyed. He had a bottle in one hand and a flashlight in the other. "That Hazel Milk is holed up with the dwarf down in the old tower." He jerked his arm free and lifted the bottle, amber liquid spilling from the corner of his mouth.

Woody backed away and looked all around the room. The place was charged, the men vibrating like inebriated electrons.

Something slammed into his hand and he grabbed it, hoping it was a bottle in the split second before he felt rough wood and realized he was holding a torch.

"Gonna go fetch her back," Arn shouted over the din, spittle striking Woody's cheek.

Woody snatched the bottle out of Arn's hand and upended it, thankful for the fiery liquid burn. He was fairly certain he did not want to be sober for what came next.

Was that shouting outside?

Honor Pruitt wiped sweaty strands of hair from her eyes, blinking in the dark room and searching for the sound. She tried to sit up and felt the enormous emptiness in her middle, the feeling of being scoured all through her insides.

As she awoke in her bed, in her bedroom, she thought the sobbing was her own. As her mind cleared, she realized it was not.

"Jeremiah?" she called out. She pursed her lips, sucking moisture from her cheeks to wet her throat. "Jeremiah, is that you?"

The doorway filled with a warm glow as her husband entered with a glass lamp holding a single candle. The weak light carved cruel lines in his face and rendered his eyes into deep pools gleaming with water. His long, strong, net-thrower's arms dangled as if they had no joints, and his shoulders were stooped with more than fatigue.

"Oh...come here," Honor said and her husband sat on the edge of the bed, her gentle husband.

"I'm so sorry," he choked out, shoulders heaving as he fought to stay silent against the tears.

She placed a warm hand over his bony knuckles and squeezed.

"I went to the church..."

She squeezed tighter, her own pain so present, her own heart so freshly torn open. She realized that she had had time to think while Jeremiah barged out of the house to do God knew what. That she was already accepting in a way that he had not—

Something banged against the door in the front room, and a muffled voice shouted, "Jeremiah Pruitt, come on!"

She could hear it now, through the thin glass of the window. A great racket and clamor of voices. A shrill woman's screech rose above the others. "Slattern!"

"What's that noise?" she asked.

"Terrible things have happened this night, terrible things even beyond the loss of our own son," Jeremiah said, choking on the words. "The constable has been killed, murdered. They say his severed head was found in the bed of Hazel Milk."

"What?" Honor asked, sitting halfway up in surprise before pain gripped her middle and shoved her back down.

Jeremiah's hands fluttered ineffectually over her.

"I'm all right," she said when she could finally draw air into her lungs. "What has Hazel Milk got to do with this?"

Jeremiah shook his head, and she could see the long fringe around his bald spot sticking every which way in spikes.

"She's disappeared," Jeremiah said. "There's word she's down at the old waterfront, in the lighthouse with the dwarf."

"Burden Ipswich?" Honor Pruitt believed in using a name once it was given.

A great shout erupted outside, many voices in unison. Lights bobbed and danced beyond the windowpanes.

"John Wallis is staying at the Milk house in case Hazel comes back, but Hatevil Nutter is leading a group of men down to the lighthouse."

"And those are Mary Nutter's dulcet tones I hear outside?"

"Yes, she's come out with her father."

"And what do they mean to do?"

Jeremiah shook his head.

"Has there been drink?" Honor asked.

"I suspect so."

Honor closed her eyes and drew in a breath, slowly sneaking it past the places that hurt. When she opened her eyes they were clear and held her husband's gaze.

"I don't like the sound of this," Honor said. And Jeremiah looked up at the window, his face drawn with guilt.

That wouldn't do.

"You're a good man, Jeremiah Pruitt," Honor said. "I trust you'll do the right thing. You always do."

Honor closed her eyes and let her breaths lengthen, releasing her grip on his hand. It was a good minute before Jeremiah carefully slid his hand from beneath hers. Hands so big and bony and surprising in their gentleness.

She waited until she could no longer see the glow of the candle through her eyelids and opened her eyes.

"God guide my dearest love," she said to the empty room.

FOURTEEN

A circle of light jagged and bobbed across the ground as Bone made his careful way down the muddy track towards the lighthouse. It was churned up as if by the passage of a small army.

Or a lynch mob.

He thought about the mouth-twisting taste as warm liquid left a trail of embers down his throat until it bloomed in the hearth of his stomach.

Goddammit.

A fucking murder scene. Constable likely dead. A woman missing. A mob of drunken men. His weapon missing and a bloody *something* left in its place.

The memory of whiskey slid down his throat, the liquid conjuring a host of memories laid to rest long before this night.

Enough.

He could not afford a relapse now. He could not afford to go into a black hole, dragging a bottle behind him. Not with the hearing coming up so quickly, his future hanging in the balance.

Something grabbed his leg, cupping his heel in a stiff hand and he stumbled off balance into the teeth of the torrent, his heels shooting out from under him. He landed on his back with teeth-jarring force. In an instant he was covered in ice water. Beyond soaked, he was bathing in it. Something else struck him then, and a round object tumbled by even as a broad-brimmed hat skated past on the water.

Bone sat up, biting back a scream against the burning ice as a bent stick jabbed his back and he lashed out reflexively, lifting it.

An arm wearing a checkered sleeve.

An animal sound escaped him and he surged up in an explosion of water, staggering towards the edge and shining his light on what he held.

It was an arm in a shirtsleeve. A severed arm. An arm made of wood.

He sagged, shoulders slumping, and so cold he was not yet shivering. *Second time you got me*, he thought towards the distant scarecrow. Must have fallen in the storm and been caught in the downward flow. He staggered forward to snatch the scarecrow's hat up off of a broken tree limb.

But it was so far from the track, how— he thought before a convulsive bout of shivering took hold. He stumbled upright and looked downhill. He saw lights in the distance and a deeper color, a vastness that could only be the sea.

A wail erupted from the woods so suddenly that Bone staggered off the bank and back into the running water. He was fighting for footing when the sky broke open and light washed over everything.

The figure waiting on the track ahead of him was a moving series of impressions, indefinite and formless. Matted hair sprouting leaves and nettles, a gaping mouth, rag-wrapped arms and legs with bent branches for fingers. It looked at him, pinning him in place with the force of its mad eyes.

As inky night rushed back in to steal his sight, Bone lifted his flashlight a moment too late. There was a sensation of movement, of underbrush beside the track snapping back into position.

Bone sucked in great gasps of air, adrenaline narrowing his vision to points.

"Holy shit."

He pivoted in a slow circle, carefully working his light around until he faced toward the distant shore, and saw a glitter beneath the flowing rainwater.

He splashed towards it and shoved back his hood, slapping the hat on his head instinctively before crouching and reaching into the stream. His fingers went numb. Still he felt the sharp bite of metal and carefully lifted the bit o' shine into the beam of his flashlight. A star within a metal ring, the words UNITED STATES MARSHALS embedded into it.

Bone slid the badge into his pocket, and he knew that he had encountered the apparition before.

On *Leviathan*.

FIFTEEN

- 1 -

"The tower moves," Hazel said, running one hand along the stone wall to feel the thrum of the storm outside. "It looks so solid, I never thought you could actually feel it move."

The crows Huginn and Muninn shifted and fluttered atop their respective bookshelves. Muninn let out a hoarse sound and Hazel glanced at the crow. Burden's cheeks flushed with embarrassment.

"The tower is safe," he said, placing a metal pot under a leak. The spatter of water on the stone floor became a loud clangor as fat drops struck the pot. Every candle he possessed was lit, as were the lanterns.

"There are fireflies on the beach," Hazel said, continuing her circle of the top room in the tower, pausing at each window to peer out. "Fireflies running around in the rain."

Burden sat in the chair at his desk and watched her, the warm light painting her like a dream he had tried to forget. She looked absurd in his largest sweater and her hair was a hag's tangle, but still…

He tore his eyes away from the sight of her bare legs.

"This is the first time you've been here since I moved in," Burden said, wishing he could bite the words even as he spoke them.

She nodded and circled around to the side facing the sea, touching titles on the bookcase he had dragged laboriously up the staircase by himself.

"Your tower at the edge of everything," she said. "You're not frightened by the old waterfront?"

"What happened, Hazel?" Burden swiveled the chair as she continued around. He sensed she was still in a state of shock.

"He's been following me, the constable," Hazel said. "Since…since my husband died, he's been around, very close. Too close."

A clamor arose outside and Burden heard his own name called. Hazel flinched away from the window.

"They can't cross the bridge until low tide," he said. "They won't dare falling in that water."

"He was in my house when I got home," Hazel said, and it was Burden's turn to flinch. She looked at him, actually looked at him for perhaps the first time that night. "What happened to your eye?"

He turned away to hide the swelling. "Nothing."

"You said you had something to tell me, earlier," Hazel said. "Something important."

Burden slid off the chair and waved a dismissive hand as he crossed to the beachfront windows, aware of his odd, crablike movement and disgusted by it.

"Those fools," he said, standing on a stack of books to peer outside.

"What?"

"They're getting ropes."

"So much for superstition." Hazel stood behind him. He could feel her warmth blazing along his back. "We could shoot them. We could shoot them from up here and scare them away."

"What?" Burden asked, turning, aware of her proximity.

Hazel fished in the deep pocket of her ruined skirt where it hung in a futile effort to dry. She struggled to pull something free but it caught on fabric.

"What is it?" Burden asked.

Hazel finally produced the object. It gleamed with oil in the candlelight.

"Is that the constable's?"

"Yes," Hazel nodded, holding the .38 revolver awkwardly in both hands. "It was right there and I was frightened." She shrugged.

"Is it loaded?" Burden asked.

"I think so."

"My, God. We have to hide that." Burden hopped down from his vantage at the window and hurried to her. "If they see you with that, they'll be convinced you killed him."

Hazel put the gun on Burden's kitchen table and walked away, head lowered. How many times had he imagined her visiting his new home, his tower?

"Hazel," Burden said, "Did you—"

"There's something happening outside."

- 2 -

"Hey, would 'e listen to me?" Jeremiah asked, crunching over wet stones and shells as he ran up the beach towards the slick, moving mass of men standing in the surf. "Listen!"

As he trotted with his sure-footed Isle man's gate to the old waterfront, he envisioned every scenario and braced himself for the confrontation. Unpleasant frescoes of David and Goliath danced through his imagination, and he began to feel foolish as well as scared, truth be told. But he ran on, boots splashing and sliding, breath whistling in and out of his lungs, until he saw the mob of men with flashlights and lanterns and honest-to-God torches howling at the old lighthouse.

There was in him a sense of failure from the events earlier in the night, and a need to *do something*.

Jeremiah could see lights glowing from the top room of the tower, and he wondered at the fear his wife's friend Hazel must be feeling, with nothing but the dwarf to protect her.

"Hey!" he shouted, skidding to a stop. One thing he had not expected was to be completely ignored.

"In the water!"

"Steady now, give 'em slack!"

He made out commands coming from the tall form of Increase Mather and saw a man bundled head-to-toe in thick weather-gear stepping into the surf with a rope tied around his waist.

"Are you insane?" Jeremiah shouted, pushing and sliding through the crowd. Even over the smell of sea and storm he choked at the stink of whiskey riding the panting breaths of his fellow Isle men. He felt a flash of gratitude that Honor was not here to see such a thing, a thing to challenge her belief in the goodness of folk.

The man at the end of the rope held his arms out wide, legs spread for balance as he struggled forward, the water surging from his knees to his waist. There was a guide rope on the bridge, Jeremiah knew, but he couldn't see it in the dark.

"Pull him back, for Christ's sake!" Jeremiah shouted, pushing into the front rank, the surf foaming up over the top of his boots.

"Hazel Milk is in the tower!" Someone shouted.

"You get back, Jeremiah Pruitt." Hatevil Nutter loomed over him.

Despite his fear of the big man, Jeremiah stood his ground. "This is wrong!"

Nutter snatched at Jeremiah's shirt, and the smaller man batted his hand away.

"By God I'll—"

Jeremiah stepped into Hatevil Nutter and shouted up into Nutter's yellowed teeth. "By God you'll leave that woman alone!"

Men around the confrontation were stunned at the sight of a man signing his own death sentence. Hell, stepping into it eagerly. Veins bulged on Nutter's forehead and tendons writhed under the skin at his neck.

Unnoticed for a moment, the man on the bridge stumbled to one knee as a wave broke completely over him. A sudden cry and Mather's warning drew everyone's attention, and they spun to see the tethered man struggling.

Jeremiah moved without hesitation, as would any man who grew up on the boats. He grabbed the thick, slippery rope in both hands and heaved back with all of the strength of his arms and back. "We need to get him—"

He was in mid-shout, fighting to drag the man from the mighty pull of the sea, when something struck his back. His feet slid and he overbalanced forward, given a brief moment to discern the deliberateness of the impact, before he stumbled deeper into the surf, missing the submerged bridge completely.

Jeremiah Pruitt disappeared beneath the waves.

- 3 -

"Man in the water!" Increase Mather shouted, his long fingers wrapped around the rope, his beard bristling as they dragged back the man he had sent onto the bridge while the others peeled away to aid Pruitt.

Another rope was rushed to the surf and the floatation ring at the end fluttered out against the wind and back towards them.

"I need a sinker," a brawny man shouted, gripping the rope in bulging forearms and slashing through it with one stroke of an inwardly curved knife.

"Jon Tuttle!" a voice shouted in the big man's ear.

The experienced men worked together like a single organism, and a heavy sinker was waiting when the big man, Jon Tuttle, thrust his hand out for it. In moments he had the rope through the sinker's iron loop and was tightening a sailor's knot.

Tuttle stepped into the surf, ignoring the cries to hold back. Rope burned hot against his calloused palm as he swung it through two circles by his side while eyeing a spot in the raging sea just beyond the last sighting of his friend.

"God guide my throw!" he shouted. "Ha!" The sinker flew out in an arc, the rope snaking behind it.

A dozen men surged to the rope and dug their heels into the rocky beach, heaving in ferocious unison. It was instinct for men raised on the sea.

"Pull for Jeremiah Pruitt!" Jon Tuttle bellowed over the storm.

"Pull, you godless bastards!" a fisherman shouted.

Increase Mather felt ice in his belly when Pruitt's name was called out, but he couldn't falter in front of the men.

"The sinker's caught!" Mather shouted as the rope went taught.

Tuttle screamed at the sky. "Why won't he move?"

- 4 -

The rope burned through Jeremiah's failing grip as his struggles weakened. Something had hold of his ankle and was crushing the bones.

He thought he could see lights up above and realized that less than a man's length separated him from the surface.

A stream of tiny bubbles rose from his nose despite his best effort, and he felt command of his arms and legs fade. He looked down into the inky dark that held his foot and terror filled him.

Jeremiah screamed out the last of his breath into the sea.

- 5 -

A pale white form darted towards Jeremiah in a trail of luminescent bubbles.

A bright light cut through the ocean dark, and he felt hands on his body. Then he was rising.

- 6 -

The crowd pulled back as the blue-white man stumbled out of the surf dragging the limp form of Jeremiah Pruitt.

A devil from the court of Old Man Atlantic himself, thought Increase Mather as he gave way with the rest.

The naked man threw Jeremiah roughly down onto his back and dropped hard to his knees beside the unbreathing form. He grasped Jeremiah's head and tilted it, opening his mouth and running a finger inside with quick professionalism, and then bent over to place his open mouth over that of Jeremiah and blow two hard breaths.

He tore open Jeremiah's shirt, buttons popping free like shrapnel. "Is there an AED in town?" he growled.

"What?" Increase said.

"Is there an—" The naked man's eyes blazed and he jabbed a finger at a big man. "You, is there an automated external defibrillator in town?"

"No, sir," Jon Tuttle said.

"Is there a doctor? Get me the fucking doctor, right now!"

Tuttle pushed through the crowd, breaking into a heavy run, even as the unclothed rescuer turned back to Jeremiah and placed the heel of his left hand over Jeremiah's heart, pressing his right hand down on top of the first. Questions erupted from the men and were ignored as the man settled into a rhythm of rapid chest compressions.

"That's the lawman," someone said.

Bone glanced up, fixing Increase with his eyes. "I need," he paused, timing words to compressions. "I need...a coat over me...before...I freeze..."

A man beside Increase slipped out of his own coat and draped it over Bone's pistoning form. He knelt beside Bone, and Increase saw but could not hear the exchange.

"Dry clothes! We need dry clothes for Jeremiah and the marshal," the man shouted as he rose.

"What's his name?" Bone asked without stopping.

"Jeremiah Pruitt," Increase said.

Bone stopped compressions and grabbed Jeremiah's jaw, pressing his mouth down again to repeat the breaths.

"Come on, Jeremiah," Bone said, placing his hand flat on the unbreathing man's chest and pounding his fist down twice on top of it. "Come on!"

Jeremiah twitched and his back arched as water belched forth from between his lips. He began hacking, struggling to breath, and Bone slid hands beneath his shoulders to roll him over.

"Onto his left side. That's it," Bone said as Increase knelt to help him. Jeremiah vomited a thin stream of seawater and bile and began shivering violently.

Bone stood and wrapped the long coat around himself, feeling the chill air scrape along his ribs and legs even as his arms throbbed with the fire of exertion. His balls had shrunk to painful tightness, and his breath was a whistling rasp as he turned to spit the salty taste of Jeremiah from his lips.

The pile of his clothes waited where he had left it and he pulled them on clumsily with dead fingers, underwear and pants and shirt. He stepped into his clammy shoes without socks and slung his long raincoat around his shoulders, picking up the Quaker hat that had somehow become a part of his wardrobe.

He settled it on his head and walked back to the recovering Pruitt on the ground. He knelt as others approached with dry clothes.

"How you feeling?" Bone asked, noticing for the first time that Jeremiah wore only a single boot, blood oozing like black beads from the white skin of the bare foot.

Jeremiah looked up at Bone, the marshal's face half in shadow, half a pale blur. "Did you see it?"

"We need to get him home and dry," Increase said.

The first selectman and several others picked up Jeremiah under each arm and led him away from the crashing surf.

A tall man with anger spiking from him glared at Bone, but Bone was too cold too care. He walked to the edge of the beach, staying clear of the waves. He stared up at the lighthouse and could see two silhouettes in a window.

"Hazel Milk! Are you all right?" he shouted, cupping his hands around his mouth.

"Yes, Mr. Bone! Yes I am!" Hazel's voice floated down from above.

"You stay put tonight with Mr. Ipswich," Bone shouted back. "I'll come for you in the morning!"

Bone turned back to the remaining men on the beach. "You men cool off and sober up."

Bone stalked away from the beach, ignoring the calls behind him. Unsure if they had even paid attention to his order. He clenched and unclenched his hands trying to get the blood moving. His toes felt as if they were simply gone.

- 7 -

Hazel stood at the window long after the men had left, and Burden sat at his desk, rhythmically tapping the N key on his typewriter.

"He was pushed, wasn't he?" Hazel asked.

Burden grunted and stood up from his desk, walking to the table with its neat stacks of books and flowers of white wax left by candles burning night after night. He traced one blunt finger over the grains until it touched the constable's pistol. He picked it up, examining it.

"Burden?"

Burden muttered something and looked up at Hazel standing by the window. "Maybe it's a good thing you brought this here, Hazel."

"Why?" she asked, eyeing her friend. He seemed to thicken somehow, drawing a darker mien around himself. It occurred to her how little she had seen of him of late. How little she really knew about him now that she was a widow and he a hermit alone in his tower at the edge.

The gun clicked against Burden's belt as he slid it beneath the buckle. It was a distinct sound, Hazel realized. Quite specifically the sound a gun makes striking a belt buckle. She watched as Burden crossed to the ladder that led up to the ceiling.

"Would you like to know a secret?"

He climbed the splintery ladder to the dripping hatch in the ceiling and looked down as Hazel hesitated at its foot.

"Is this what you wanted to tell me earlier?" Hazel asked.

"Come on," he said, wrenching at the lock bar in rusty brackets. He blinked and shook his head to avoid the falling brown flakes and slid the lock open.

- 8 -

The upper deck of the lighthouse had been ravaged by years of Atlantic weather, the great panes of glass reduced to memories, the iron framework only pitted spikes thrusting up from the perimeter to form a spiny crown. The wooden roof was long since eroded and an unrecognizable metal mount, rusted into immobility, was the only remnant of the great light that had once warned boats away from the rocky shoals.

Burden stood with one hand on the ancient light-mount, his hair whipping in the wind, squinting against the slashing rain. The crash of the sea all around was terrifying, and Hazel crouched in the hatchway, afraid that the wind would pluck her from the tower and dash her on the rocks below.

"Come!" Burden shouted over the wind, extending a hand.

Hazel moved quickly to the mount, her hands white-knuckled against the slimy metal. Her hair blew out straight and she shook it out of her eyes as Burden closed the hatch with a wicked grin.

"Richard Slocum was the only one to really talk to me since you got married," Burden said. "It almost made me feel like a man, just having a conversation. Pathetic, eh?"

Hazel was struck by his ugliness, his deformity, and wondered how it was that she had been blind to it for so many years. *But were you blind, Hazel?*

"I know why he was killed, Hazel," Burden said, the grin seeping from his face. "I know it all, now."

Hazel clung to the mount as the wind tried to pry her free. She stared at the pain in her old friend's face, wondering if he meant to kill her.

- 9 -

The night was finally empty of living voices and only the whistling howl of the gale echoed in the crumbling streets of the old waterfront.

A shrouded form was bent against the wind as it stood at the ragged stone lip of an old well. He looked carefully towards the distant lighthouse. The gathering of torches at its base was breaking up, but none of the townsmen would venture through the abandoned village. Not on such a grim night. Not on any night.

When he was certain he was alone, he spoke.

"Merciful God, we have sinned in what we have thought and said, in the wrong we have done and in the good we have not done. We have sinned in ignorance, we have sinned in weakness, we have sinned through our own deliberate fault. We are truly sorry. We repent and turn to you. Forgive us, for our Savior Christ's sake, and renew our lives to the glory of your name."

A bundle wrapped in dark strips of cloth was lifted over the dark hole.

"Look ye at the mark of our sin, oh Lord, and deliver us from evil."

The bundle was dropped into the well.

A sudden crunch and scrape of shells announced someone approaching, and the shrouded form shrank back into an open doorway. *Was he seen?* No, the man staggering through the waterfront had his head bent as if pushing into a mighty wind. His feet dragged like anchors, pushing up a bow wave of rainwater and crab shells. Even so, the noise of the storm had covered his approach until it was almost too late.

It was the lawman.

SIXTEEN

- 1 -

"I'm in trouble," Bone mumbled through numb lips.

He should have stayed with the crowd on the beach.

Lost and without his flashlight, he had eventually headed towards the silhouettes of man-made structures but was completely turned around, his inner compass spinning freely.

He seemed to still be on a road of some sort and occasionally bumped off of surfaces that he believed had him moving in the same direction. He noticed he was no longer cold. Was in fact warm, which seemed as if it should be odd.

Right foot. Left foot.

He was so completely wet he felt as if he were still deep in the surf, diving after the drowning man.

"Mebbe you are," his voice bubbled.

A hand flapped back behind him for his hood but couldn't locate it. He gave up trying and accepted the pounding deluge from the sky.

He croaked something intended as a laugh. "Mebbe he's still holding you down there under the sea."

Right foot. Left foot. His left foot caught on something and he fell hard to his knees, the sound of his teeth clacking together, something he felt through the bones of his skull rather than heard over the incredible drum corps.

He looked up and gagged as water filled his mouth. He was so numb he hadn't even felt it hitting his tongue. Coughed and felt a distant pain as something tried to tear lose inside. Damage signals sent by telegram.

"Fuck."

A moment of bright light washed over everything and Bone could see buildings collapsed on either side, their doors empty, windows black holes. It didn't make any sense. He hadn't seen anything like it, a completely dead place. A town that used to be.

Night closed its fist over the scene.

He was on his feet and moving, the diminishing spark in his brain firing its few remaining command options.

Right. Left.

He walked into a graveyard fence and clutched it in cement hands. He pulled himself around the iron bars, not remembering the fence at Julia's funeral, but he had been distracted. He staggered into the cemetery to look for his wife's grave.

"Something is wrong."

Why was it night? Where were the mourners? Her family?"

He stepped into open air as lightning bloomed over his head like the world's biggest halo.

"Julia?" Bone asked as he toppled into an open grave.

- 2 -

Hands pulled at Bone. Yanked his coat. His hair. He coughed and gagged as muddy liquid vomited from his mouth, and he was lifted, his torso slapping against the squishy lip of the grave. He flung out his hands, fingers ripping across wet grass but he was sliding and had no strength, going back into the pit as a form vaulted up beside him and caught him with no care for niceties. He screamed and batted about as another voice and horrible breath wailed into his face. His knees slid up over the edge of the grave and the grip on Bone shifted, catching him under the arms and dragging him fully onto the grass to flip him over so he blinked and coughed up into the falling rain.

The wild tangle of hair triggered recognition but the man disappeared before Bone could speak.

"Hey...help," Bone said, the cry stepped on by the weather. "Julia," he said, and he was crying then, truly crying because he was so warm and wet and right beside her grave. "Julia!"

"I've got you, friend, I've got you," a new voice said. Bone opened his eyes as a man in a hood knelt over him, a scarf covering his lower face.

"I need her," Bone said.

"You are dying right this moment, do you understand?" The voice, a man's voice, warm and rolling, pushed through the storm in his brain. "I have to get you inside and dry right now. I'm going to drag you."

Strong hands grabbed him under the arms and Bone tried to shake them off, confused. Where was the man with the wild hair? Where was—

"Don't fight me. You need to be inside now!"

And Bone felt the world sliding beneath his body, as if he were on a greased conveyor belt. The idea of seeing Julia was already fading back into the madness of a dying brain and left him only with longing for something he knew not what. The sun collapsed in on itself and a black hole consumed everything.

SEVENTEEN

- 1 -

Prickles of sensation sparked along Bone's skin, flesh pulling tightly across his face, the backs of his hands and his thighs.

He remembered.

Cold. Wet. Trapped.

He remembered the wild man pulling him free and the hooded man carrying him and then he could remember no more.

- 2 -

Bone sat up abruptly and felt a wash of heat across his dry skin, eyes opening on darkness as circles of purple and green flashed across his vision.

A sound. He collapsed back onto his right elbow to see a man silhouetted before the fireplace, rising and rising until he towered over Bone.

"Who is Julia?" a voice asked.

"She's dead." Bone responded.

A large blanket was held up and blocked out Bone's site. It descended across him in a smothering wave as his eyes, and then his mind, went black.

- 3 -

"Drink," the voice said and something ceramic pressed against his lips. "A small sip."

The cup tilted and warm, tangy liquid splashed against his teeth. He opened his mouth and let the wet heat of it roll across his tongue, lemon and honey and brandy all striking their own chords of recognition.

He was supported, nerve endings belatedly relaying the attentions of a splayed hand held under his shoulders.

"Where?" he asked, voice hoarse and cracking.

"Open your eyes if you can."

Bone hadn't realized they were closed and sent a muddy command to optical control. Lids slid up, feeling as if they scraped their way across sandstone orbs.

He groaned and the cup was against his lips again. He sipped without being told to, enjoying the warm rush of flavor.

"Where?" he asked. "I was in a dead place where the ruins stared..."

"You're at the inn, a room I asked Mr. Fenn to prepare for you," the voice said. It was gentle and somehow teasing. Not particularly remarkable, but it might have been kind. "You had a close call there, Mr. Bone. Do you remember what happened?"

Bone shuddered, remembered walking, his thoughts growing confused as his strength fled. Falling into Julia's grave. Struggling.

"I can't thank you enough for what you did, going into the water after Jeremiah. I thank God we didn't lose you both."

Did you see it? Bone shivered at the remembered question.

"I fell into a grave," Bone said, trying to order his thoughts.

"The grave of the late Mr. Slocum," the voice responded. "That hole would have been your grave if you hadn't been discovered."

Bone let his eyes slide shut, parted his lips as the cup touched them and he heard, "Drink."

- 4 -

Flickering orange light bathed the room, built high in a brick fireplace with a brass screen. Bone found it bright enough to study his benefactor.

He was a short man, but broad, sitting in a chair by the fireplace, wearing reading glasses and holding a book. His hair was thinning and of indeterminate color. He wore a rough suit of dark wool.

The room itself was small and square, with a single, closed door and a single small window covered by wooden shutters. His bed was narrow but deep, the mattress soft with an ornately stitched quilt draped over his body. Bone discovered he was wearing some sort of oversized nightshirt of white cotton.

He set his ceramic cup on the spare nightstand.

"I have to use the bathroom." Bone tried to push himself fully upright and found his head swimming at the effort as weakness flooded his limbs.

"Here, let me help you," the man said, hurrying over from his seat by the fireplace. "It's in the hall, I'm afraid."

"That's all right," Bone waved him off.

"I don't plan to hold it for you, sir, just help you to the door," the man said, looking pained.

Bone was surprised into laughing and he fell back onto the soft pillows. After a moment, the other's laughter joined his.

- 5 -

The man helped Bone into the bed and he sank back gratefully, weaker than he had imagined.

"Hypothermia is no laughing matter," the man said as if reading Bone's thoughts. He pulled Bone's cover up, tucking the quilt under his chin. "The water out here will kill a man, especially where you went for your swim."

Bone nodded thanks as the man refilled his mug from a metal pot hung on a hook over the fire.

Bone sipped. A *hot toddy* the man had called it. *Isle remedy.*

"Now listen, from what you've told me and what I've heard from Increase Mather, we need to get you well enough to sail to the mainland in the morning and bring back a team of investigators."

Bone nodded. "Whoever killed the constable is bad news, especially on an island this small." *And he has my gun.*

"Then it's important for you to get some sleep. In spite of the cliché, it is the body's best mechanism for healing."

"I don't think I can," Bone said.

"Nonsense," the man said, holding his own mug. "Lay back and close your eyes. I'll tell you a ghost story."

"A ghost story?" Bone asked, laughing again.

"It's a sure tonic for sleep if anything is. Whenever I have the Littles over for lessons, I tell them a story at bedtime and they drop off immediately." A pained note crept into his voice. "It bodes ill for my dreams of vaudeville stardom, but it has its uses."

"You don't sound like the other folk here. Not just the accent. Who are you?"

"Ambrose Tinker, at your service." He man smiled and removed his glasses, folding them carefully and sliding them down into an inside pocket.

"As a lad I watched old black-and-white Cary Grant movies on the one VCR we had in town. It was my great secret," he said, a smile in his voice. "I planned to visit the great cities on the mainland and didn't want to be taken for a rube, so I listened to the man speak over and over until I sounded, if not like Cary Grant, then not like a fisherman."

"What happened?"

"I found my calling here. Now lay back and close your eyes, my story-telling will have you out in no time."

Bone's face twisted into a smirk but he lay back and closed his eyes. Warmth suffused him.

"Ask me again about the place you wandered through, the ruins with empty eyes."

Bone suppressed a shiver but decided to play along.

"All right," Bone said. "Why is that place down at the waterfront abandoned? The location seems perfect, so why is it empty?"

Bone breathed in through his nose and let it trickle out between his teeth. After several long, slow breaths, he began to wonder if the old man was asleep. Just as Bone was about to open his eyes, he heard a stirring.

"After the events of 1687, people began to drift away. No one could live there."

"Why?"

"Because it is cursed."

EIGHTEEN

- 1 -

The Year of Our Lord Sixteen Hundred and Eighty-Seven

A stomach cramp doubled her over and she fell, bare knees crunching colorful shells into shards that tore skin and scored bone. The incredible pain of starvation, however, occupied every pew in the temple of her body, and she didn't even notice.

Isabelle was eight years old.

The surf rolled in, white foam stopping far short of her kneeling form before receding. Isabelle watched this for some time, eyes wide and round, mouth slack, a shimmering strand of drool connecting her bottom lip to the torn collar of her Sunday dress.

The footprint was still there.

Another, less severe cramp struck her and the beach echoed with her animal mewling. She pushed back upright, sitting on her heels in the manner of a monk, if monks wore muddy Sunday dresses and were children.

Absently she wiped the grains of sand from the grey piece of meat clutched in her fist. It had been pink and hot when she picked it up. Now it was grey, but it didn't stink yet, and she thought it was still all right.

The wind was blowing in over the ocean, sweeping away the stink of what had happened. Lord how it stank, yes it did. "Stank to high Heaven," is what her ma would have said. *Belle*—her ma called her Belle—wasn't sure if Heaven had any part in things, despite what the reverend had said.

She looked back at the deep divot left by the heel of Reverend Ezekial Healy when he stepped from the prow of the longboat and landed on their beach, impossibly tall in his black coat and flowing cape, eyes lost in the shadow of a broad-brimmed hat with a buckle that caught the sun. His face was so white it was nearly bone.

How could a footprint remain on the beach for seven days? Maybe it wasn't his footprint. Maybe this wasn't even where he first alighted from the boat, but she thought it was. Something squirted and burbled in her middle and Belle whimpered, fearing another cramp. The more she looked at the footprint, the more she thought it was really only just a dent left by the reverend's boot heel. Because a man couldn't leave a print in the shape of a hoof, right?

More boats had scraped up onto the beach after the reverend's, and Belle had fussed as her ma dressed her in her Sunday best. Visitors were a rare thing on the Isle and she was excited.

"I want to go closer, Ma," Belle said.

"You'll ruin your Sunday dress. Now quiet, child."

The Isle men made as if to help pull the boats up onto the beach before they backed away, milling in a group. She was confused and asked her ma, but Ma said nothing, just watched with a hand held across her brow to block the sun.

The reverend was a sight indeed, towering darkly over everyone, even the men splashing ashore with muskets in their hands.

"Good Lord, no," Ma said.

"What is it?" Belle asked and was shushed for her efforts. But she remembered the crawling sensation, as if a crab were making its way down her spine, sharp feet dimpling the flesh as it passed.

The reverend unbuttoned his coat and pulled a heavy, black book from inside, holding it up over his head. The ocean breeze stole most of his words, but she could still hear the shrill note of command.

"Belle, mind me now," Ma said.

"What—"

There was a loud crack on the beach and a white cloud of smoke rose into the air. One of her father's friends emitted a womanish shriek and staggered into the surf holding his belly. Before Belle could finish her question, her ma crouched in front of her, clutching her shoulders with fingers like steel.

"You run, Belle. Run and don't stop," she said.

"Ma—"

Ma slapped her then, a thing she never did, and Belle stumbled back, holding a hand to her burning cheek.

"Run and hide, Belle, run and hide in the woods until they leave!" she said, shoving her back toward town. "I said run!"

Belle was so startled by the pop-eyed, thin-lipped thing that had replaced her mother that she ran from the beach without a second thought. She didn't understand what was happening. Didn't understand why her ma had screamed and slapped her and told her to go into the woods in her beautiful Sunday dress, the prettiest thing she owned. She cried and ran and didn't understand at all.

Seven days later she was much older.

- 2 -

The looking glass showed him skin like milk and strong teeth the color of honey. A glance at the thumb wrapped around the mirror's handle showed a long, healthy nail of that same honeyed appearance.

"Grace of God," Ezekial Healy said quietly, staring into the reflected depths of his own dark eyes. His black Bible slid across the desktop as the ship tilted to port, and he caught it before it could fall.

"For you shall know them by their twisted ugliness, sin doth defile the flesh," he continued, readying himself for the task ahead. His skin pebbled in anticipation of his plunge into this isolated pool of filth, too long away from the stern eye of the Lord. Even as he readied himself in the loneliness of his cabin aboard the good ship *Purity*, he felt the serpent winding its way across dark waters to evoke that first sin, that first concession of will to temptation. He shifted uncomfortably on his wooden stool.

"Away with ye, wicked tempter, for I come armored in the Will of Chastity," he whispered.

At a knock on the door Ezekial slipped the mirror into a drawer in the tiny desk and picked up the worn black Bible that was his ticket of entry anywhere in the colonies.

"Reverend Healy, sir, land ho," a sailor relayed through the cracked open door, then quickly pulled it shut.

The Reverend Ezekial Healy stood but kept his head bowed, both in piety and to avoid knocking his skull on the low beams. He stuffed black gloves of soft kid through his wide belt and picked up the broad-brimmed hat even as the first orange glimmer of dawn sent its soothing rays through the tiny panes of the cabin's windows.

"Your will, my Lord," he said to God above and reached for the door with a hand of milk tipped by nails of honey.

- 3 -

Belle stood on the beach in the pale moonlight and stared up at the soles of a woman's feet. There were curls of callous at the ball and heel of the left foot, though the right was covered in an old wool sock with a hole at the big toe. Belle circled in time with the rotation of the woman, concerned with where the woman's shoes had gone off to.

The woman had been hung by the neck from a rope attached to a broad wooden crossbar, which in turn was attached to a mast that stuck into a stone bastion right next to Belle. She was not yet aware of the word *gallows*.

Five more such contraptions, as yet unoccupied, stretched away down the beach.

Belle stepped back, wincing at the crackle of small shells under her feet. The surf itself was a quiet rustle, the white edges of waves glowing as they lapped up onto shore, delivering a clean, ocean smell. Once or twice on a quiet night like this her pa had taken her outside and dared her to jump in the water. She never had and her ma had protested—though she was laughing—when pa broke the night with his shout as he hit the cold waves.

Belle was like a sailor washed ashore in a land that conformed to no recognizable natural laws. After two nights without food in the woods, huddled in the embrace of moss-covered tree roots, she had set out for home.

She had already wet herself while looking at the hanged woman and was weeping silent tears, her thin chest hitching under her filthy dress. It was if some small part of her brain had redirected awareness to only that which she could handle. It was an incredible mental task and to be lauded, a feat of mental prestidigitation that only the most capable soldiers and sailors could accomplish. Belle's river of horror had been reduced to a trickle she could understand. She had ruined her dress. She was cold and very hungry. She missed her folks.

Belle looked up from her new perspective and saw the back of the woman, her long, plain dress, the knot of an apron still visible. Belle thought she might have been collecting clams when the black ship came.

"I like clams," Belle whispered.

The woman's hair was a long tangle, hanging more to the left shoulder than down her back because of the way the head was leaning over.

The rope creaked as the woman turned.

Belle herself turned and looked at the small town, a quiet, church-going girl, well-behaved, in a piss-stained dress with spiders in her hair. Her town a few days ago but already an alien landscape that might as well have held castle walls and minarets flying banners in strange languages.

Not many windows were lit, but there were a few. Not many chimneys smoked, but there were a few. A low rustle of voices came to her, almost like the tide, but moving out instead of in. None of the men with muskets were visible, and Belle kept a special watch out for the tall man with the white face and black hat.

As for the hanging woman, Belle knew she was dead.

Please don't be Ma.

The dead woman's face was more melon than skull, an unrecognizable bloat of black skin with bulging, dead eyes and a fat tongue bursting from compressed lips. Wisps of oily hair flitted and blew in and out of her eyes, sticking to the surface of the unseeing orbs.

Belle stared into the eyes in the dark pumpkin face and wanted nothing so much as to pluck the hairs free.

After what seemed like months, Belle stood up, though she didn't remember falling down. Her eyes remained fixed on the dead woman's own, and she did not yell. Did not scream.

She howled in confusion and fear and pain. Her jaws stretched wide enough that she felt the pop behind her ears, a tiny girl with fists clenched at her side, rising up on her toes to unleash the pent-up tidal wave of emotion.

Shouts echoed from the town and Belle heard doors slamming.

She bolted down the beach on the balls of her feet, fleet as a deer, a ghost girl in the pale moonlight sobbing as she ran and trailing a wake of tears.

A light rain fell against his cape, darkening it still further, and grey mud stained his clean boots. Still, Ezekial Healy marched back and forth before the windows with their shutters thrown wide, his eyes digging, his words pulling.

"And ye have nothing to fear if thou art true Christians, for God roots out the wicked through me, his instrument, but also exalts the chaste and true," Ezekial said.

The cramped and stinking crowd of islanders in the dark storeroom shifted, their beady eyes lowered to avoid his stare, their mouths shut so they would not betray themselves. The thatch-roofed building was built of stone quarried on the Isle itself and had been used for storing foodstuffs. The food had been removed and placed safely aboard the *Purity*, though on the first day of confinement the hunger-inducing scents had remained, speeding the captives' awareness of their empty bellies, as Ezekial had hoped.

"And ye who are true but have not come forward have nothing to fear, for the Devil did put a veil over your eyes as the filth lived among ye, so that the wickedness of their features was hidden and made normal, long noses shrunk and blemishes concealed. They that have looked to you like neighbors are not."

Ezekial stopped and leaned in a window, wrinkling his nose at the sour smell. They shifted as they could to move away from him, and in an instant he understood why. Even as he had spoken the last words, it was if they had pulled down the veil of lies to reveal straight teeth twisting like old gravestones, noses grown thick like potatoes with pores like eyes. Even worse were the hips of the women, which grew pronounced under their deceptively simple garments.

Ezekial hissed and stepped away, closing his eyes and composing his thoughts into a straight line of righteous speaking.

"Good friends, speak now to me of the liars and cheats among you, the wanton and wicked. The veil is gone. I can see it here before me," he said. "Point them out to me and you are free, having proved yourself just. Look about you and point them out. *POINT THEM OUT!*"

The last repetition emerged in a cloud of spittle, and they flinched back as one body.

But did not speak.

Ezekial's lips stretched into a thin line and he stepped back, gesturing to the waiting soldiers, their muskets covered in sacking to keep powder dry.

"Hunger will sharpen their vision, and thirst will loosen their tongues," he said. "Fetch me only when they give up the wicked among their number."

He wheeled, the elevated heel of his boot squelching in the mud, and marched back to the large house he had selected for his own. Though the brim of his hat had kept most of the rain at bay, some drops had snuck through and streaked the powder on his cheeks.

The sobs and cries behind him where muffled as the soldiers closed the wooden shutters.

- 5 -

Hadley saw the ghost girl on the path and fled, her childish cackles audible over the thunder of his boots as he raced between the boney clusters of white birches and back into the waterfront village. Blood suffused his unshaven face, and he turned back to the woods, hefting his heavy musket. The solid *thunk* of wooden stock into the meat of his shoulder and the smell of iron and black powder never failed to fill him with red strength, even more so than the reverend's preaching, if truth be told. Hadley was a man who never closed his eyes, as many did, when the weapon bucked and spit fire, billowing clouds of smoke. But when he made out the pale shape floating along the ground among the trees, he closed his eyes and prayed through clenched teeth.

A sing-song stream of nonsense words drifted from the rapidly darkening woods, and Hadley ducked into a low and recessed doorway, his powder horn clanking against the wood. He had heard the speaking in tongues of the holiest parishioners as they danced between spare wooden pews, but this was an older sound, more horrifying. A language from mankind's darkest days. Something deeper than his righteous appreciation for the

Lord God recognized the tongue and issued rapid commands. The guard glanced back and forth between the dark tree line and the lighted waterfront and realized he would be flogged if he returned. But if the Reverend Healy spoke truth about the Isle as a haven for witchcraft, something infinitely more terrible might happen if he re-entered the woods and resumed his post. He spun quickly and tried the door. Finding it unlocked, he ducked inside and crouched beneath a window with no plan beyond waiting for dawn.

Five days of hunger and solitude had transformed Belle into a feral thing. Her dress was a filthy mess of mud and effluence, and her once-beautiful hair was a petri dish of local fauna and flora, with birch branches and oak leaves, strands of spider web and honest Isle dirt.

Like an animal, she recognized the howling cries of her own kind and wandered straight into the village, her bare and bloody feet silent on the cobblestones. Her head was light with lack of nourishment, and she muttered and sang as little girls were wont to do, a stream of nonsense sounds that kept her company.

She wandered past the hidden guard—who covered his ears when he heard the terrible language fused and hammered together out of spare parts in the insane foundry of her mind—and even past the storage building where the starving population of the Isle was held. She cocked her head towards the cries. They sounded like wounded dogs.

Lights drew Belle. Flickering, orange, beautiful lights. There were torches and lanterns and even a large bonfire on the beach. She thought of the great Christmas tree the adults erected in the center of town every year. Her mouth watered and she drooled as sense memory fed her the smells of roasting pig and fish and chestnuts.

The many soldiers had their backs to her, black silhouettes watching the goings on before them. Belle noted the three bodies now hanging from the gallows, but her eyes were drawn to the long trench dug into the beach.

She saw bare toes wiggling up from inside the hole, and also a flailing hand. The horrible man in black with his giant hat crouched next to the trench and the pile of rocks visible inside it.

Belle wanted to hear what the dark man was saying and stopped her mad speech. She stepped forward until she was within touching distance of the guards and heard the words, "Confess and we will remove the weight." They were kind words. Pleading almost. But the man lying in the trench did not comply.

"Another stone," the black-clad figure said, and a soldier picked up a rock and added it to the pile. A quiet groan emerged from the trench.

Belle might have wandered between them, brushing past frayed coat hems and cloth sacks jostling with musket balls, might have wandered right up to the trench if not for the closer inspection of the bare feet, both in view now. She could clearly see the black crust of dirt at ball and heel, but she was at the wrong angle to see if the toenails were clipped. What caught her attention, however, what rooted her own tiny bare feet to the earth was that the left foot, the one newly visible, had only one toe, the smallest toe, wiggling from its end.

Belle did not scream.

She turned and walked back into town, away from the light and the things she knew. Silent tears carved white lines across the geometry of her face and she felt unaccountably weary.

She recognized the foot, the toes of which had been removed years before to prevent gangrene.

Her father's.

- 6 -

"For mine eyes do see the sin, harlot," he said as he snatched the stained front of the woman's blouse and tore it downward so that her breasts tumbled free, round and burnished in gold by the light of the several lanterns he had lit.

The woman cried out but could not speak through the gag tied around her mouth, parting lips overripe and shouting silently of wicked purpose.

He struck her across the face with his kid gloves, and she made the sound of a cur as he took one breast in his long-fingered hand.

"Seek ye to tempt me with thy breasts as yet untested by milking?" He squeezed and her knees buckled, but he caught her and pushed her back into the table, which skidded loudly across the floor. An ornately carved chair crashed over, and he sneered at the lush tastes of the sinner who owned the home he had commandeered. *Mayor, they called him. Sinner, say I.* "For you have been denounced by good women who bear children as the Lord demands, and thy un-sagging teats do concur."

Her hands were bound behind her, and the woman would have fallen if an instinct of pity had not caused Ezekial to catch her, but she pressed her thighs against him, warm even through her woolen skirt, and he released her to fall on her knees.

"And why are ye not yet wed? Seek ye to keep thy temple a place of sin?"

She looked up at him and tears streaked through the grime, splashing to the floor as she shook her head. Her eyes grew even wider still, a feat he had not thought possible, when he produced the long-bladed knife. He caught her hair and pulled it into his fist until she uttered her cur's whine, then deftly slipped the blade down alongside her cheek and cut the gag free.

"Sir," she tried to say, coughing, but was silenced when the clean length of his fingers caught her jaw and squeezed.

"Aye, Jezebel, I know the ways of your master, placing you here to put me to the test," Ezekial said, his voice hoarse as he fought the tendrils of dark will that sought his undoing. He glanced up and saw that the embroidered curtains were drawn across the study's only window, then looked down at her upturned face. "One word only, harlot. Thy name."

"Agatha," she said, her voice catching.

"Such an innocent name, Agatha," he said, grinning. "Does it work, this neatly scented trap?"

He squeezed her jaw before she could speak and she made a low sound.

"Open thy mouth but do not speak, witch. I have not fetched thee forth from gaol to bandy words."

He released her and stepped back with a flourish and she sagged, but her eyes never left the bright blade in his fist. Not until he slid the dagger back into its plain sheath and drew the flintlock pistol from beneath his cape at the small of his back.

"Please…" she whispered, and he cocked the weapon with his thumb.

"Not one more word or I blow your black soul from its mortal coil straight back into the arms of Satan," Ezekial hissed, glancing again at the curtained window. The door behind him was locked, a possibility he had been pleased to note when he took the house.

He doffed his hat with his free hand and tossed it down behind him before unfastening a single button on his trousers and stepping towards the kneeling Agatha.

"I," he began, but paused to clear his throat. "I am the better of thee, servant of flies."

- 7 -

The two men who stood outside the front door of the great house were older than most of the crew, scarred, silver-haired men who had sailed with the reverend to bring the Glory of the Lord to many dark places. They had been with him during the Campaign of the Northern Coast as it was later called, striking settlements up and down the shore with the swiftness of Viking raiders.

They had wintered with the reverend at a harbor village, the only members of the current crew still sailing aboard *Purity* after that season of harsh testing, and so they did not unshoulder their muskets at the sound of screaming from within the house. Nor did they rush inside when they heard the sharp report of a pistol.

The man to the left of the door withdrew a leather flask and pulled the stopper with his teeth, offering it to his companion first. The companion sipped before handing it back.

The beach fire was lit. It drew their eyes and they each said, in their own way, a prayer of thanks that they had survived the frozen horror of the northern coastal campaign and would survive this one as well.

- 8 -

There were lights on in the large house owned by Mr. Bierce, the merchant who snuck sweets to the children when their mothers were not looking, and who once delivered into Belle's tiny hands a small meat pie with the command that she was, "Absolutely not to share it." She remembered hiding behind the stone well where she had eaten the entire pastry herself in between fits of mischievous giggling.

She followed the scent of food into a room with tumbled furniture and very nice rugs from India. There was a fallen lady next to the tipped table and a platter of bread and cheese scattered across the floor.

Belle picked up a wedge of yellow cheese with only a touch of mold and took a bite, looking down at the room's other occupant as saliva filled her mouth, and she swallowed the chunk.

"Your blouse has torn, ma'am," Belle said in a cracked voice before taking another bite, larger than the first. Her stomach contracted painfully, but Belle was only dimly aware of it as she continued to chew her way through the wedge.

The lady had not much head remaining, but Belle was glad for some company and was so very tired. She lay down next to the woman, uncaring of the sticky floor. After sleeping in the roots of a tree, she found even the tacky carpet as soft as a thick mattress. One hand snaked across the floor and her fingers wrapped around a small loaf of sugared bread. She hugged it to her chest as if it were a comforting animal of cloth and filling, curling around it and her cramping gut.

- 9 -

The Reverend Ezekial Healy looked at his reflection in the mirror and thought that something had gone subtly wrong. He had placed a candelabra made of silver and containing five fat candles on the vanity in the master bedroom and was addressing his powder when he felt a chill, as if a centipede were crawling down his spine beneath his shirt. The feeling was so vivid that he removed his vest and white shirt, twisting and craning his neck to glance in the mirror as he turned his back towards it. He saw nothing but the shadowy valley of his own spinal column and felt goosebumps arise across his unblemished skin.

"Damnable draft," he cursed quietly, allowing himself the coarse language because he was alone. He slipped the vest on over his shoulders and hurried to check each room for open windows, the bare skin of his hairless chest pebbled from more than the temperature.

The damned deserter, he thought as he returned to the master bedroom, having examined all chambers save the study in which the harlot's body lay. He had resisted her wanton temptation but had no wish to see her physical ruination. "That whore-begotten coward," he cursed again.

Discovered asleep in a house by the sergeant of the watch, the deserter Hadley had expressed only relief that he was to be taken back to the ship, and him in irons with a bloody flogging in his immediate future. "I saw a ghost in the woods," Hadley had said. "And her speech was madness and witchcraft, a rim of ice along my very soul."

The story moved quickly among the men. Hadley's ghost was made of snow or made from parts of trees. It was a singing child and a wailing banshee. No two versions reflected the same details save one.

"The ghost walked among us last night as we purified the wicked by stone and rope," Ezekial muttered. "And none but the guard had seen her."

Ezekial glanced into the mirror, and the shadows drew lines on his body, drawing his ribs from his flesh so they protruded like a corpse. The candles popped and sizzled with fat, and he stretched wide his lips, leaning close to see that his eye teeth had grown in length, as if his very skull was pushing its way forward and through his face.

"No," he shuddered, turning away from the mirror and stalking to the window. He drew aside the heavy drapes and saw the torch of a guard on patrol. Laying his cheek against the chilly glass, he could just make out the glow from the bow and stern lanterns of a boat returning from *Purity*, where it had deposited another load of supplies from the village. The view faded and went white, and he pulled back in alarm until his rational mind told him it was only the fog of his own breath.

"To bed," he said aloud, finding some comfort in the sound.

He approached the canopied bed with its double curtains and climbed into the embroidered cave, taking solace in the shield of draperies, thin things to keep out mosquitoes in warm weather backed by thicker hangings to contain warmth.

He pulled back the handmade quilt, proof again he was in the house of a wealthy man, the very type Jesus had cast out of the temple. He kicked off his shoes and slid into the bed wearing only a nightshirt, certain he would be too cold to sleep. Too awake.

But the candlelight was blocked by the heavy curtain at the foot of his bed, and he was warm enough and tired enough. His mind soon wandered into a world of half-dreams, and so it was that the gentle glow at the corners of the curtains simply flowed into the stream of images: candlelight on the bared breasts of the woman Agatha, the collection of quilts he had already transported back to the ship, his anticipated return to Massachusetts. He stirred and murmured when the heavy curtain at the foot was pushed aside and the glow of the candelabra came close to the thin curtain that remained drawn.

His eyes flickered open and he was confused at the soft glow that filled his bower, five flickering points of light that he gradually understood must be the candle flames.

When four tiny dimples appeared in the white veil and dragged across it to make it shimmer with ripples, Ezekial recognized the indentation of fingertips. He clapped a hand over his mouth and sat up, feeling the tiny hairs raise along the back of his neck.

A face pressed against the white curtain, slowly pushing into the sanctuary of the bower, and he remembered his earlier horror at the idea that his own skull was emerging, eager to be out of his skin and visible to every eye.

He opened his mouth to speak, perhaps a prayer, perhaps a query, when the veil caught fire and began to smolder. All Ezekial could manage by way of speech was a dry click in the depths of his palate. Tiny flames raced towards one another and spread outward in a circle, as if a thin tissue covering the world of men and ships and handmade quilts was peeling back to reveal the darker and more frightening realm beyond, opening a portal to reveal the bizarre visage staring in at him.

Hadley's ghost! he thought, and only the rigid tension of his body prevented him from releasing the contents of his bladder.

The face was lit from the side by the candelabra, a dark countenance covered in strange white lines that he thought—with mounting horror—were runes, heathen writing of the wicked. The tiny mouth whispered a continuous stream of unintelligible words, and Ezekial shrunk back against the headboard, certain he would crawl through the wood itself if it were possible.

Prayer, prayer for salvation against incantations, he thought, but all knowledge of the good book was flushed from his brain when the burning circle, having grown by several feet, smoldered to a stop, it's edges limned in red as if it were the gateway to Hell itself.

The gateway through which Hadley's ghost would pass.

Ezekial shrieked, high and womanish, as the form slithered up into the hole and perched on the footboard of the bed like an unholy bird, candelabra held before it in rude mockery of a cross. The charnel stench of the grave entered the bower with the ghost, and Ezekial could make out the filth and dirt, the sticks and webbing in its wild explosion of hair, as if it had only recently clawed its way up through pine boards and six feet of churned earth.

"Oh, God," Ezekial said, his voice not the thunderous oration of the witch hunter, but the mewling of an urchin.

The ghost twitched and its head tilted to regard him, almost as if it were seeing the cowering reverend for the first time. He covered his eyes with his hands, but parted his fingers as he realized it was not a crone's face but an awful parody of childhood.

"Know you no decency?" he tried to shout, though he barely managed a whisper.

At his words the thing's awful whispering stopped, and the wet runes carved through the grave dirt on its face writhed in the flickering glow.

"What do you want?" Ezekial asked.

"Get out," a girl's voice said from the mouth of Hadley's ghost. "GET OUT!"

Ezekial screamed and pawed the air as the ghost stood and balanced on the footboard, thrusting the living flame into dry fabric only too happy to embrace it. The white veil burned once more and flaming lines raced up towards the high canopy overhead.

Then the candelabra was flying at him trailing five tiny comets, and he swung a hand but missed, the metal thing striking him over the eye.

He pulled the covers over his face, but the acrid stink of burning cloth sent him scurrying out from the bed, and he saw that the canopy was rapidly being consumed by a crackling blaze. He threw an arm over his eyes to protect them from the light and falling embers and looked at Hadley's ghost.

But it had vanished.

There was a crash below as a door was broken in and a deep voice called out, "Reverend! The house is afire!"

- 10 -

The longboat banged against the side of the ship as if the ocean itself were reacting to their fear. The reverend grasped the webbed climbing ropes that draped the side and was slammed against the slimy wood, his wrist laid open as it dragged across masses of sharp barnacles that suckled his blood like so many tiny mouths. He felt the terrible animus of the water below him, sloshing with the sound of a great beast licking its lips. He feared this terrible place would not let him go.

"Take my hand," a sailor said. Ezekial grasped the tattooed forearm and scaled the webbed climbing ropes, pulled over *Purity's* gunwale by another crewman in a blue-striped shirt.

Men stood around him with hanging jaws and wide-eyed stares, so sudden had been their call to retreat.

"It were the ghost," he heard more than one sailor say, for Hadley had continued his lurid tale even after he was placed in irons.

Confused commands were issued by various men, and a winch-hauled crate of goods tumbled over the side to splash irretrievably into the water. The panic was a living thing, an animal racing among the crew devouring order and shitting entropy. Ezekial knew he had only moments to regain control, for sullen eyes were already turning his way.

Ezekial pulled the Bible from inside his hastily buttoned coat and stepped up onto the gunwale, a sudden gust flaring his black cape out dramatically.

"I am the Reverend Ezekial Healy!" he shouted at the island. "You are accursed in the eyes of God." He gestured dramatically at his men. "Make sail, honest men of Massachusetts! Make sail before the Lord of Hosts does send down his wrath and render this Hellish Isle into a new Sodom!"

"They're coming!" a nameless sailor shouted. Like wasps boiling from a hive, the captive islanders were rushing towards the beach, fanning out in great numbers.

"Portside guns, fire!" Ezekial shouted, casting about among the mass of crewmen crowding the rails. Bright flame belched forth in a ragged volley, the last clumsy shot fired a full minute after the first of the portside cannons had delivered its deadly load. Billows of white smoke obscured the island as the round cannon shot skipped across the water to send up geysers of sand from the beach, or blasted random buildings to splinters in the already burning town.

Ezekial wrenched a brass spyglass from a startled sailor and returned to the gunwale, extending the instrument and placing it to his right eye.

"Horror," he whispered as the grotesquerie on the beach came into focus.

Flapping revenants in tattered rags staggered through the ugly black smoke of the bonfire, their incoherent moans and cries drifting across the water to wound ears and shrivel courage. But they did not charge the waterline. Instead, they fell upon the bonfire itself, maddened beyond fear by starvation. In a howling pack they pulled the bodies of their dead kin from the flames.

"They eat…" Ezekial said, and his words were repeated by the frightened crew.

The villagers were fighting among themselves, crazed, pulling at legs and arms, the victorious lurching or crawling away with hunks of blackened meat. Even more horrid were those that simply dropped to their knees and pressed their faces into the corpses, asses high like wild animals as they devoured their feast of carrion.

"Set sail from this accursed island at once!" Ezekial said, making a panicked leap to the deck where he stumbled to his knees, hat tumbling from his head. "Set sail at once before those demons dine on us!"

- 11 -

Belle walked away from the black smoke and the burning town.

She walked along the shoreline, watching the black ship as it faded into a small speck on the horizon, occasionally stopping to whimper as pain struck her middle.

She sat down at one point and fell asleep, unaware of this transitory consciousness until she awoke, cradled in someone's arms. The night sky overhead glittered with a million bright stars.

She was set down beside a group of ragged people squatting in a circle, the red glow of embers all that remained of the bonfire not far beyond them. Inland, their homes still burned.

"Eat child," the one who carried her said, squatting heavily with a sigh and crackle of knee joints.

Belle looked up to see kindly Mr. Bierce, but he was a Mr. Bierce she had never before known. He glistened with grease, white teeth gleaming in bright contrast to a face painted dark by soot and blood. Belle glanced around the group—so few left, so few—and saw them painted like the savage red men of the mainland.

"Eat, dear Isabelle," Mr. Bierce said, and Belle shook her head.

"Ma and Pa?" she asked, dropping her gaze when he told her what her heart already knew.

"She has to eat," old Mrs. Drood said, words whistling past missing teeth. Belle could barely recognize the old woman with half of her hair singed off and her face pinched with desperation. "We all have to eat now," Mrs. Drood continued.

Mr. Bierce held out an unidentifiable piece of charred meat in the palm of his big hand. The porcine smell made her stomach gurgle enough that the surrounding people stirred in understanding.

"What is your favorite part of the Christmas Day feast?" Mr. Bierce asked.

Belle lifted her head and wiped straggles of oily hair from her eyes. "Pa said when I'm ten I can have a turkey leg for myself."

Murmurs of agreement rumbled around the group and Mrs. Drood said, "That's good, child. That's good." Someone wept.

"I think, and I think everyone else thinks, that you're quite old enough right now to have your very own turkey leg," Mr. Bierce said quietly, his white smile widening. "But only if you promise to eat it all, Isabelle."

Belle reached for the piece of meat in his hand. It was still warm, and succulent juices ran down her wrist to her elbow. She rubbed her thumb in a small circle and a scale of black skin slid aside to display the bright pink of a rare steak.

"Turkey," a woman said reverently.

"With bread and chestnut stuffing," a man added.

Strained chuckles rounded the circle.

"Will you eat it all, Isabelle?" Mr. Bierce asked.

"Yes sir," she said quietly.

Belle lifted the meat to her lips and bit. An incredible flood of taste and energy surged across her tongue, and her jaws actually ached with the pain of her flaring taste buds. It was tough and she pulled with her hand, leaning her head back until a piece stretched and tore free.

A sigh of relief drifted from the group as eight-year-old Belle chewed and swallowed, wondering which of her kin or neighbors she was eating, and hoping it wasn't her parents.

NINETEEN

- 1 -

The red light of an Atlantic dawn stretched through the tower windows to patiently erase the darkness, but had not yet reached Burden, who sat on a wooden stool in the shadows.

He was turning the constable's pistol over and over in his hands. A clarity had come to him, perhaps beaten into shape by the intensity of the previous night.

When he spoke to Slocum, he had toyed with the idea of leaving the Isle. His move to the edge of everything had been a half measure taken to appease the inner longing he did not want to articulate because he wasn't sure he could face the idea of it being untrue.

He did not belong on the Isle. He did not belong to the community. The thought of the years ahead spent in isolation brought wetness to his eyes.

And so he considered the weapon in his hand. One of two such on the Isle, the other belonging to the tall lawman. He considered the many doors such a key might open.

The gun presented him with two options. The first depended on the lawman and his ability to take him back to the mainland as part of a solution to the recent murders. But if this hope was as worthy of ridicule as the dark voices in his head suggested, the gun was the key to another path, one both fatal and final.

A caw announced Huginn's arrival as the crow landed on the ledge of an open window. Backlit, the carrion bird was an indistinct black shape outlined in red, a featureless representation of a bird seeking to satisfy itself with dead flesh.

Burden took it as an omen and rose to find his boots.

He tucked the .38 revolver and its six deadly loads into his pack. Huginn cawed and dropped something red and wet onto the floor. "Thank you, my friend," Burden said through a chipped smile.

- 2 -

Bone wished the old man had stayed the night, but he had awakened alone, the fire dimmed to embers.

He poured water from the pitcher on the nightstand into his cupped palm and splashed his face, rubbing away the aftertaste, smell and feel of the night before. Even with the shutters thrown wide and the crisp morning light flooding the room, he could not shake off the nightmares, the most vivid he had ever experienced. He wondered if he had been hallucinating from his exposure to the frigid waters. He wondered what the difference was between a hallucination and a dream and if it mattered.

He glanced at the bed, his black coat and purloined hat resting across the ornate quilt where they ate the morning light. He shuddered and pressed his palms against the top of the dresser, leaning in and taking the weight as he examined his face in the mirror, his eyes dark against the unhealthy pallor of his skin. The scarring on his face took on the appearance of writing, and he closed his eyes before he could read what it said.

"Shit."

He scooped up the coat and hat without looking at them and left his room, clunking heavily down the steps as if he were used to a different body.

It smelled of cooking bacon downstairs, and Bone heard the popping fat of it as he entered the main room where two men sat alone at a table, plates smothered in grease and yellow egg yolks dripping from their beards and mustaches. A metal fork dragging its tines across a plate was a thought-crumbling shriek in his ears. A heavy knife cutting into bacon that looked like a strip of fried skin made him close his eyes, but he could still see every individual drop of liquefied fat—

Blood.

—bubbling up as the blade sawed it in half. His senses had become acute, bionic even, and he could not shut out their maddening input. He opened his eyes and saw every detail of the diners' yellowed teeth, the bits of gristle jammed into gaps, turgid tongues pushing at them, bloated and fat.

"Breakfast, Marshal?" Fenn the innkeeper asked as he pushed through the swinging door from the kitchen, rubbing his hands briskly with a dish towel. "Good to see you up and about after those sad doings last night, but we need to get something hot and warm in you."

Bone saw a smoking bonfire on the beach overlaid with the image of the thickset proprietor. He dragged a hand over his eyes and nose, making an inadvertent smacking sound when it slid over his lips. He could feel the whiskers growing in the valleys and ridges of his face.

"Thick cut bacon from Nutter's pigs," Fenn said, grinning with the grotesque glee of a morning person. "Nutter's bacon is the best bacon on the Isle."

"Nutter's bacon is the only bacon on the Isle," one of the two men said and barked a single syllable of laughter, scattering bits of white and yellow across his table. The other man made a point of ignoring Bone, and he wondered how people felt in the aftermath of mob violence, whether it made them ashamed or angry.

"I'll take a rain check on the bacon, Mr. Fenn," Bone said, forcing steadiness into his words.

Fenn laughed and planted himself in Bone's path. "I was told 'e were not to leave until 'e had something hot in your guts."

Bone was charmed in spite of himself. "Some bread would be good. Something to settle my stomach."

"Then sit 'e down and I'll be right out with this morning's baking," he said, pulling out a roughhewn chair and bustling back into the kitchen.

"You leaving this morning with the cawpse?" the spitter of eggs asked as Bone sat, more or less equidistant between the two diners.

He nodded. "But I'll be back with a crew as fast as *Leviathan* can make the trip."

The other diner grunted something.

"What was that?" Bone asked.

The grunter glanced back at him, one eye gleaming beneath a spiky mess of self-cut hair. He looked back down at his plate and mopped at the gelatinous mess with a heel of bread and grunted again.

Bone stood as Fenn returned with a half loaf of homemade bread and a thick pat of butter. "I'll take it with me," he said.

Fenn wrapped the bread in several napkins, and Bone wedged it into a coat pocket. The words he thought he heard as he hit the street sounded suspiciously like, "Don't let the door hit 'e ass on the way out."

The wind blew strands of Bone's hair against his forehead where they had escaped the hat's embrace. He reached back in his mind for the feeling of certitude that had bloomed the night before, the opportunity presented by these new crimes, the chance to prove himself and regain at least a portion of his old life. That such potent emotions could now crumble to dust was unnerving. He felt out of balance and very, very alone.

A rooster crowed somewhere nearby, and Bone glanced up to see a tall steeple rising over the nineteenth-century village. The dislocating sense of walking out the door into the wrong era was powerful, and he imagined a dingy theme park without any rides. A historical village to which bored school children were no longer taken on field trips, continuing to exist without purpose. He realized he was actually seeing a few thatched roofs among the more traditional shingled tops and saw straw tips quivering in the wind. He thought, oddly, of a cat purring and glanced up again at white cotton balls scudding across the blue sky-sea overhead.

Balls. He focused on the anachronisms within his sight. A phone line sagging between two houses. Scattered electric light posts. A modern wheelbarrow at rest in the mud, filled with brown water.

He lowered his head and raised his shoulders as if the sky were still pouring down torrents instead of sunshine and set out for the pier, eager to get off the Isle.

TWENTY

- 1 -

"It was right here," Samuel Meeks said, bracing one hand on the bulkhead as *Leviathan* rocked violently on the swells.

Bone struggled to keep his balance as melting ice sloshed about the hold. He saw something in the beam of his flashlight and kicked a path over to it, hooking a dripping black length of plastic in his free hand.

"Here's one of the trash bags you put it in," Bone said, tossing it down in disgust. The pilot flinched away as Bone raked the flashlight beam across his eyes. "Where the hell is the body?"

Something thudded heavily against the outer hull and both men jumped.

"It ain't on the boat," Meeks said. The two men struggled out of the hold, Bone shouldering the door shut behind him and cutting off the flow of ice. The pilot immediately clambered up the ladder as Bone waited.

Leviathan tilted and Bone slammed into the ladder, face barking painfully off the wood. He tasted copper pennies and touched a finger to his lip, then looked at the bright bead of blood on his fingertip.

- 2 -

Clothes were hung about the dock house and steam filled the air, warmed by a blazing fire in the fireplace.

Bone sat on a splintered stool before the fire and set down the radio handset again. Isle phones couldn't reach the mainland and he was out of marine radio range. He had hoped to at least reach a lobsterman, but all he caught were the ghosts of Maine fishermen, static-laden.

At least his teeth were no longer chattering from the search through the ice hold.

"I told 'e," Weeks said.

The pilot, in all his rancid glory, was playing nursemaid, holding out a cup of hot tea. Bone took the cup with a nod and set it down on a counter littered with empty bottles and soup cans. He handed the pilot a hastily written note.

"Lord but 'e write like 'e got palsy," the pilot said, squinting at the paper.

Passing fucking notes in class. That was the technology Bone was reduced to. "Just read the goddamned note."

The pilot waved a hand in a calming gesture without looking up, then shook his head. "'E won't listen to the likes of me," he said, slapping his own chest.

"They'll pay attention to that letter," Bone said, taking another sip of the tea laced with brandy as a gust of cold swirled through the room and he heard a door slam. "They'll send a team."

Would they? To a barely legible, handwritten note on a piece of stained paper delivered by a strange fisherman demanding they go haring off across the water on the say so of a disgraced marshal?

That's what he was thinking but he asked, "What happened?"

"I don't know," the pilot said, his expression without guile. "I was asleep, hard asleep, and noticed nothing out of place until 'e roused me to board *Leviathan*. The body were wrapped in plastic and stuffed in the ice hold as 'e told me to keep him."

The pilot swigged his own spiked tea and grimaced, belching slightly and rubbing a sour stomach.

"I'll tell 'e one thing," Weeks said, grimacing at the taste of the belch. "Richard Slocum didn't get up and walk away himself."

Bone nodded and considered more of the tea, but he needed a clear head. The pilot pointed at the star pinned to his shirt.

"You found this, eh?"

Bone touched it. "Yes, in the water. The water on the track, I mean."

He followed the pilot with his gaze as the man looked out the rain-streaked window.

"See anyone, did 'e?"

"I…" He remembered the apparition. "I saw something."

Weeks mumbled something like, "He wanted you to have it back," but Bone wasn't certain. The pilot turned, eyes wanting.

"'E won't give him trouble, will 'e? The boy doesn't mean anything by it," the pilot said, tapping his head with one crooked finger. "It were just shiny is all. Something he ain't never seen before."

"Is he the one who screams at night?" Bone asked, surprised by the tenderness he saw creep over the man's homely face.

The pilot nodded. "He is afraid of the lightning and thunder and gets confused."

"Who is he?"

"My brother, Enoch," he said, head dropping as if ashamed.

"Where does he live? Here on the boat?"

It was as if a film slid over the pilot's eyes and Bone felt the lie. "'E does."

Bone looked back into the dancing flames in the fireplace and squeezed the star in his palm as he thought about psychosis.

"You're sure they will listen to me?" the pilot said. "Sure 'e shouldn't go back to the mainland as 'e planned?"

"I can't go back without the body."

The pilot cocked his head and asked with a rare display of intelligence, "Do 'e think whoever took the cawpse knew it'd make you stay?"

"I don't know."

TWENTY-ONE

- 1 -

The surf crashed to Bone's right, jagged rocks gleaming black in the morning sun as they reached up from the sea in ominous warning.

To his left the Isle loomed above him, and in the pall of his nightmares and the reality of the missing dead man it rose in a manner equally ominous, the spire of the church a barely visible threat to dirigibles and hope.

The trail of his march was lined with divots in the sand and sea-tossed debris in such obvious metaphor that his lip curled in derision.

He was a boat at sea, adrift and spinning.

Ahead: laughter, brass chimes high and tinkling. Children.

"How many legs does it have?" A woman's voice.

"Eight! Just like a spider!" A small child's voice. A summer brook running over smooth stones.

Bone walked up a hump in the earth tufted with long seagrass and the salt smell of things redoubled, collected in the flora. His ruined shoes disturbed small, scuttling things, lopsided with oversized claws to the dexter.

Fiddler crabs. He remembered catching them at the beach as a kid and putting them in his sandcastle to fight like armored warriors. Instead they flowed away, a spill of rice he could not contain.

A dozen children and a single adult had gathered below around an object in the sand, prodding it with sticks.

The children wore rough hand-me-downs and were of a single make if various years. Light-skinned and exploding with freckles, great shocks of brown and red hair dancing in the offshore breeze like so many escapees from the id of Norman Rockwell.

The woman: "God made horseshoe crabs so perfectly that they are unchanged even after millions of years. See the armor 'e carries? It looks like what?"

"Dinosaurs!" This from several of the younger children. None was older than eleven or twelve. It occurred to Bone that these were the first kids he had seen and wondered about their lives.

"What do they eat?" a small child asked, creeping closer.

"Littles!" the woman said, giving him a goose.

The group exploded in laughter. Wind chimes in a gale.

Bone's shadow stretched towards the group, and it was the woman who noticed him first, squinting in alarm at his shape in silhouette.

"Marshal," she said after a moment.

"Ma'am," he said. The quiet stretched as the woman weighed the necessity of manners.

"Mary Nutter," she said, choosing a middle path. The children had all looked up at him, faces wide with open curiosity. One child looked frightened. "Littles," Mary continued. "This is Marshal Bone."

The Littles regarded the shadow man on the hill and he regarded them.

"Good morning," he said, descending the rise in long strides and walking past. He heard the rustle of their clothes and the windy whisper of children asking secret questions.

He glanced back once after passing, and the kids were still watching him, holding their sticks. He noticed the domed shape of a large horseshoe crab flipped onto its back, its legs still moving.

- 2 -

Hazel crushed dried mint leaves in her fist and then relaxed her grip, letting the fragrant pieces tumble into a steaming mug of hot water. Absently, and out of habit, she lifted her palm to her nose and inhaled the clean scent of the "Isle Flower," as it was sometimes called, its blossom invisible to the eye but detectable by the nose. The mint was hardy and grew wild all across the island. As a child she delighted in finding patches of it in the woods and rolling about if no one was around to see her.

Hazel thought of these things and of burning books.

She sipped at her mint tea and glanced about Burden's tower, feeling his defiance in the choice of dwelling, seeing the loneliness in the typewriter and the stack of pages piled beside it. She had ignored the remark he made about her first visit, easy enough to do with the frightening mob onshore. But even if it had been a quiet afternoon she would have ignored the observation and knew that, just as he had done last night, Burden would have let her.

She set down her tea and slipped his old sweater over her head, crossing the stone floor in bare feet as the cool sea air raised goose pimples across her naked torso. Hanging in front of the fire, her blouse was dry and stiff, as were her underclothes. She stripped completely and dressed, folding the sweater he had lent her and placing it on a low stool.

She thought of Burden's increasingly obvious feelings for her and also of drowning books, but was afraid the cold Atlantic would conspire against her. She thought of burying books but that had already been tried. She thought of casting torn pages into the wind and dismissed it as folly. The pages, if left intact, would be found.

"You want to be found," she said.

Idly, her fingers riffled the edges of Burden's writing, and she tried to convince herself that what she had seen was a fiction he had concocted to make himself seem important.

"It's true, isn't it, Burden?" she asked in a low voice. One of the crows squawked and shifted atop a bookshelf, eyeing her balefully. Huginn or Muninn, she could never tell which. Named after a pagan God's companions or some such. Burden lending himself an air of the exotic.

But if it was true, if all of it was true, then the worst of it was true as well, and the proof was in the dead man from the mainland. Slocum.

And Burden had proof he undoubtedly thought would enable him to escape the Isle.

Hazel thought the Isle would kill him first.

She would burn the book and drown it, scattering its ashes across the white-capped waves. The thought was action, and she was at the base of the ladder before she knew it, clambering up until she could unfasten the hatch above her head and push it open.

The wind caught her as she pulled herself up into sunshine, and she paused to find her balance, her hair blowing wildly around her head. The sun was glorious and bright, but cold pools of water still littered the roof, and she stepped around them until she found the place he had hidden the old book.

A happenstance glance at the shoreline as she reached down caused her to freeze in place. A tall man in black was striding down the beach towards the tower, his face obscured by a wide hat, coat billowing behind him.

She stood and stared as the marshal stopped in his approach and lifted his face, staring right back.

- 3 -

Bone halted in mid-step at the sight of Hazel atop the white tower, the stone itself shining in the sunlight. Her hair blew in towards the Isle, waving like a banner in the wind, her tall form regal. It was an image out of fantasy, somehow otherworldly, a thing that spoke of queens and honor and haunted fortresses. If it were the cover of a book, the book would be entitled *The Lady in the Tower*.

He had no idea what expression was on his face—in fact, it was dead flat—but worried that he might look foolish. Why he should care about that never crossed his mind.

After an interminable amount of time, he lifted his right hand high overhead. The waves lapped beside him, and he had indeed begun to feel foolish when Hazel raised her own.

- 4 -

She crushed dried mint leaves in her hand as he looked out at the ruins of the waterfront village. He shuddered, remembering his dreams.

"No one goes there," Hazel said, appearing at his side with a cup of tea. He took it as she added, "Except Burden, rooting around for lost things."

"Did you kill the constable?" Bone asked, and she shook her head. She smelled faintly of sea salt and her own perspiration, but it wasn't unpleasant.

"That was something you did last night, going into the water," she said. "Burden thinks Jeremiah was pushed."

"Who pushed him?"

"Burden wasn't sure, and I didn't see."

Bone glanced at her, eyebrow raised. "Where is Mr. Ipswich?"

"Out there, looking for you."

"Why is he looking for me?"

Hazel shrugged and walked away. The crows stirred and Bone glanced at them.

"Huginn and Muninn," Hazel said. "Or Muninn and Huginn. I get them confused. Burden found them when they were chicks and took care of them."

"And the cats downstairs?"

"Burden feeds them bits of cooked crab and they stay around," Hazel said. "Otherwise he'd have rats. He hates rats."

Bone crossed to the desk and the two crow heads swiveled to track him, four beady eyes reflecting miniature versions of himself. He flipped through a few exposed pages, feeling slightly invasive, like a party guest rifling the host's medicine cabinet. He picked up a sheet and read aloud but quietly, "Thin and sharp, reaching to the sky, cold wind blows down from on high. Not a leaf, no shade of green. An absence of life to be seen."

He set the page back carefully. "Sad."

Hazel nodded. "He intended the poem to be a song, but when he tried to pluck it out on a guitar," she held up her hands and scrunched them, "he just couldn't pluck the strings. So he finished it as a poem."

Bone leaned out the open window and looked down at the bridge, a shallow wave breaking across it. A wooden rowboat with a square prow was pulled up on shore and roped to a metal stake. "Mr. Ipswich likes his privacy?" Bone asked, but instead of answering Hazel fixed him with a stare.

"I thought you were leaving this morning," Hazel said.

"I'm staying."

"I'm afraid to go to my house. Am I allowed to go to my house?"

"Can you stay here?"

"Burden should have his privacy," Hazel said, and she glanced down as if lying, but Bone let it pass.

"Stay at the inn until the crime scene crew comes back from the mainland," Bone said, and she looked away, back at the ruins.

"What's wrong?" he asked.

"This place is small and it talks."

"Let it talk."

"All right."

TWENTY-TWO

- 1 -

"I'm afraid to go inside," Hazel said, stopping on the path.

He had walked up two steps and halted, turning to look at her, but her wide eyes were focused on her house.

Without thinking he reached out a hand and she took it. "Come on," Bone said. "I need your eyes, and I want to see the place in daylight."

They mounted the steps and only then did Hazel seem to realize she was holding his hand. She slid her hand free as he knocked on the door.

"Wallis?" Bone called out. He turned to Hazel, "I left him to watch the place last night." When there was no answer, he knocked again, then tried the door. "I don't suppose you have a key?"

Hazel shrugged. "I never lock it."

Bone slipped his stiletto free and flicked out the blade.

"Mr. Bone?"

"I'll just be a minute." He slid the narrow blade between the door and the jamb and worked the simple lock on Hazel Milk's front door. It was painted red, a bright, almost garish color compared to the doors in the center of town.

He felt the tension in the lock release and opened the door, calling out, "Hello?" His voice echoed in the empty space. "John Wallis?"

"Stay behind me," he said without looking back at Hazel and entered, closing the blade and replacing it in his pocket. The front room was open and should have been airy, but a meat store smell thickened the atmosphere.

"Oh," Hazel said, covering her nose.

"Breathe through your mouth. Tell me what looks wrong."

In daylight Bone saw a neat space furnished comfortably, if sparsely, with chairs and tables that would fetch a pretty penny in a Maine antique store.

"Someone has disturbed my blankets," Hazel said, pointing at the couch. "I haven't been able to sleep in my bed for some time, but I fold them every morning."

"Good, but it was Wallis, I think. What else?"

The walls were lined with warm hangings and, in a slight dissonance, framed black-and-white photographs. The floor creaked as he moved closer, stepping over throw rugs he suspected were made locally. He studied a row of pictures depicting smooth, rounded forms that he finally determined were shots of the human anatomy, but taken so close as to transform them into landscapes.

"Huh," he said, thinking that should tell him something about Hazel but not sure what. "Are these yours?"

"Yes," Hazel said, standing next to him.

"They're beautiful, but I can't quite tell what they are."

"They're mostly me," she said, and he suddenly beheld a landscape of hips and calves and gentle skin. He was very aware of the warmth of her at his shoulder.

"And what about this one?" he asked, pointing at a smashed frame and scattering of broken glass.

"Trees," she said, oddly controlled.

He slipped his pocket notebook out automatically and wandered over to a desk, stealing a pen. Wrote: NO DRAG MARKS. NO RUGS DISTURBED.

So either someone had cleaned up after removing the body, or the body had not been dragged out. Wrote: SOMEONE BIG TO CARRY BODY. The constable had been a big man and would be even heavier dead. Hazel wasn't big enough to move him without leaving a mess.

"So what looks wrong? Out of place?" he asked.

"Nothing. That broken picture and the couch, and the thing in the bathroom, but nothing else."

"Why would they break that picture, only that one?"

"Maybe they thought it was bad."

"Who killed him, Hazel?"

"I don't know."

This was the third time he had asked her, the first time being when she had offered him mint tea inside the tower. The second while they walked into town.

"Did you kill him?" Bone asked.

"No," Hazel said, unperturbed. "Do you think I killed him?"

Bone glanced at a photograph depicting the smooth planes of what might be her belly. "No."

The air grew noticeably thicker as he walked towards the bathroom, unconsciously quiet in his movements as if unwilling to disturb the stillness in the house. "You'd best not come over here," he said, standing back as he poked his head through the doorway and grimaced.

The blood had dried to blackened smears, and Bone decided the constable had been exsanguinated in the room. He wrote that down, then glanced at the pile of the constable's clothes. Noted the absence of gun and gun belt, then looked into the claw-foot tub.

The blood at the bottom had congealed, thickening into a hard pudding that was beginning to crack on the surface. The sides of the tub were surprisingly clean, slick enough that the blood had run down into the bottom. He stared close, noticing several nicks and divots in the porcelain that had been invisible by candlelight.

He carefully drew a representation of the tub, turning to brace the notebook against the door frame. He glanced back and marked the spots where there was the most noticeable damage to the porcelain, then decided his drawing didn't actually look like anything, so he added arrows and wrote *nick* next to each. He had an idea of what had occurred in the tub but didn't note it yet, trying to keep his mind open. He briefly thought of noting what he knew had been touched by others since the murder, but wrote that off as an impossible task. Crime Scene would bitch, but there wasn't a damn thing to be done about it.

He left the bathroom and walked to the kitchen, an obviously well-used but orderly space.

"Well, shit."

He placed the notebook on the counter and sketched the wooden knife block, writing, *Big knife, little knife, cleaver?* next to the empty slots. Glanced at the drawing and observed it was even worse than the tub. Still, it helped him fix the details in his mind, and he planned to borrow a camera from Hazel to shoot some photos.

He flipped the notebook closed with a snap and replaced it in his pocket, deciding to keep the pen. Glanced around the downstairs from his new perspective.

The house was isolated enough and the storm bad enough that a pitched battle could have been fought with none of the neighbors the wiser. He suspected the constable was a man capable of mussing someone's hair, but aside from the bathroom, damn it if the place wasn't ready to be a showroom in *Yankee Magazine*.

He pulled out his notebook and wrote: THERE WAS NO FIGHT. Thought about it a moment and added a question mark.

"Just one more minute," he called out towards the front, then headed for the staircase.

"I'll wait for you on the porch," Hazel said, and he heard her footsteps crossing the hardwood floor.

- 2 -

The second story was narrower than the first, and contained two rooms. Bone walked to a closed door and opened it to find a small, empty space, the walls rough, unfinished wood.

He walked through the open doorway opposite and into the master bedroom. The space was dominated by a large, quilt-covered bed, neatly made though sprinkled with discarded clothes. Rays of morning sunshine streamed in through the single window, carrying a squadron of dust motes. Bone crossed to the window and looked outside at the nearby trees, leafless and dark from the rain, but beautiful in their stark way. A widow's view.

He glanced casually into a standing wardrobe and found men's clothes hanging inside. Rough work shirts, green work pants. The air smelled musty, as if it had remained shut away for some time. Bone felt a slight frisson of connection and shrugged it off to remain clear-headed. A closet held blouses and dresses, while a low dresser held drawers full of folded nightgowns and underthings.

He turned back to the closet and reached out, letting his fingers trail over the clothes, ignoring the chiding rattle of the hangers.

- 3 -

It had been surreal, choosing the last dress his wife would ever wear. He had opened her side of the closet and ran his fingers along the fabric of several hanging dresses and blouses. His fingers reported back an amazing array of sensations: smooth, soft, gauzy, heavy.

It had been two days since he last saw Julia.

He stepped back from the closet in confusion and sat on the bed, as if distance would improve his perspective. He felt incapable of retaining the information provided by his senses.

The room already smelled different. The shower unused for several days by Julia, so that the floral scents of her soaps were no longer present.

"Oh, dammit," he said. Even his sorrow was fatigued, his emotional centers pumping at a low ebb.

He stood, remembering something Julia had read aloud from a magazine about jewelry making the outfit. He couldn't remember if she had been approving or if a note of derision laced the comment, a note he had become increasingly attuned to in the last year of their marriage. Still, it gave him a plan.

"Jewelry."

As he crossed to her low dresser and opened the jewelry box, he worried that there had been a note of derision. The only time Julia read women's magazines was when she was struck by a desire to tease and amuse. *Secrets of the Ten-Minute Orgasm* she would read to him. *Twenty-one Ways to Make Him Yours in (and out) of Bed.* She'd needle him with it when they stood in the checkout line. She had a tendency to pick something deliberately absurd and repeat it endlessly until he no longer found it entertaining, which made it truly amusing for her.

"Jewelry," he said again. His fingers sifted through pearl earrings. A necklace. Some large silver hoops he couldn't remember her wearing. He selected a pearl necklace and the pearl earrings with the notion they were the most expensive and they matched.

He wished there was someone to talk to about this, about how stupidly surreal it was to sift through your dead wife's things to dress her corpse. He knew it had been done in the past by other people, thousands and millions of times. Why didn't anyone talk about it? What the hell was he supposed to do?

Jesus. He wished he could break down and weep, but was incapable. His emotions were wrapped in cotton.

Bone glanced at the narrow drawers and dragged a finger along the gentle curve, pausing to flip the brass handle on one, creating what was easily the loudest sound in the house.

He tugged open the drawer, just to do something, and stared down at the neatly folded pairs of underwear. Does she need underwear? The funeral home hadn't told him. It seemed asinine. She was dead. But still, to lie forever with no underwear? He wondered where the dignity was in this criminally stupid moment.

He picked up a pair, dropped them. They were filmy and he couldn't remember the last time she had worn them. His emotions began to color with purple streaks. He felt guilty, dirty, rooting through her underwear drawer.

And underneath, deep beneath the muffling cotton encasing his emotions...

Anger. A liquid thing stirring the acid in his gut.

"Grow up," he said, grabbing underwear and a bra and tossing them vaguely in the direction of the bed.

He glanced over his shoulder to see if his aim had been any good, and it occurred to him that Julia would never sleep in the bed again. He imagined a picture he wished he could unsee.

- 4 -

"This way, Mr. Bone," the police officer said. Not *Marshal.* Mister. Bone felt the hand on his triceps and let himself be guided, his movements stiff, sharp pains shooting through his body. The side of his face was covered in a giant mound of white bandages and felt numb, more than numb, as if that side of his face simply weren't there. He smelled like iodine.

"Stand here," the police officer said.

Bone saw his reflection in the large window, the bulge of the bandages, the odd way he held himself.

"It's a formality," he had been told because Julia wasn't carrying any identification.

The folded curtain behind the window slid aside with a mechanical whir and Bone was looking into a room that seemed entirely composed in blue-gray shades. The floor, the walls, the dull metal of the table, the sheet-covered body atop the table.

An attendant in hospital scrubs entered the room and stepped to the table, not looking up at Bone behind the window. He lifted the top of the sheet without any fanfare and folded it back so that Bone could see the face. Her skin was bluish-white and subtle bulges of bone were incorrectly placed.

"That's her," he said in a voice that beamed in from thousands of miles away. "That's my wife."

The sheet was folded back into position over Julia's face, and the curtain behind the window whirred closed.

- 5 -

Bone was sitting in the small chair in front of Hazel Milk's vanity table. He glanced at his watch, but the ticking hand meant nothing to him. A doctor had called these periods fugues. Not catatonia, but a near-complete state of inaction, of disassociation. "Completely normal after a traumatic incident," the doctor had said.

Bone stood up, the chair scraping on the floor loudly in the quiet house. He slid it back in and coughed into his fist, deliberately pulling himself back into the present.

He glanced back at the bed. At the scattered bras and panties, all of them white and a bit out of style. The untidiness was at odds with the way Hazel kept the rest of the house. He picked up a bra and glanced at the doorway to make sure Hazel hadn't materialized, then gave it a quick sniff. It smelled clean, faintly of detergent. He tossed it down and started to write, then decided he'd just keep the note mentally. *Underclothes on bed, unworn.*

Bone had been with several women before marrying and had determined that they came in two types. Stereotypically neat women, everything put away in its place, and slobs who left their dirty clothes lying around like they lived in a sorority. The thing was, the sloppy girls were sloppy everywhere, dishes in the sink, toilet grungy, cigarette ashes on the coffee table. Hazel seemed pretty visually focused, taking into account the photographs downstairs. And everything else in the house was well ordered.

He glanced at the things littering the bed and thought about Hazel Milk being an attractive woman. Pictured another man in her bedroom thinking about how attractive she was and remembered his own automatic flash of guilt when he picked up the bra.

"Huh," he said.

- 6 -

"Why was the constable at your house?"

Hazel was sitting on the porch with her back to him and Bone didn't notice the tension. Her voice was distant.

"He's been making his interest known since Frank…" Hazel trailed off as Bone sat beside her, careful not to get a splinter in the seat of his pants. He opened his mouth to ask, "Did his interest make anyone jealous?" when he noticed the silver streaks of tears down her cheeks. She turned to look at him and her words came out hollow, as if projected from another person and not from this weeping widow.

"I looked into the bathroom while you were upstairs," Hazel said as a fresh tear welled into a pool along the bottom of her right eye until it splashed its way free. "I saw Frank lying in the tub."

Her eyelids lowered slowly. Curtains on a stage. "I asked you about the worst thing you'd ever seen, do you remember?"

Bone nodded and then realized she couldn't see him. "Yes," he said.

"Was that thing, that refrigerator thing, the worst thing you've ever seen?" Hazel asked.

"No."

Her eyes opened and Bone knew she was seeing into another plane. "The worst thing I ever saw was my husband when they brought him back to shore," she said. "They told me not to look, but I ignored them because I just…I didn't believe. I wanted to hold his hand and make it not be."

"How did he die?"

"He drowned. A hook caught his arm and pulled him overboard. He was a good swimmer, but they think he just couldn't get the hook out of his arm and eventually he gave up. Inhaled the black."

Hazel focused on him, as if to drive home a message. "What came back wasn't him. I snuck into the church and lifted the lid on his coffin.

I thought I had prepared myself, that I knew he would look different, but..."

She looked forward and her voice cracked. "It wasn't him. It was this bloated, fat-faced thing made of white dough with black holes where his eyes had been eaten out. And that...*thing* took his place in my memories. That goddamned swollen thing is all I can remember. I looked in the bathtub and saw him lying there in the blood and—"

She dropped her face into her hands and her shoulders shook, though Bone could hear no sobs. He placed a gentle hand on her arm, just to share contact.

"The worst thing I ever saw was in my apartment. Worse even than when I had to identify my wife's body in the morgue because I was prepared for that."

He let the words sit there as her shoulders stopped shaking, letting the breeze and sunlight work whatever calm they could. At first he didn't hear her question, it was so quiet.

"What happened?" she asked.

He told her about the apartment and, finding himself unable to stop, told her more. Hazel thought of photographing the wound on her thigh, of the need to see what was inside herself, and hoped he was helping himself.

When his eyes gleamed with a wet sheen, Hazel Milk said nothing, knew silence would help him to see.

- 7 -

TEN HOURS BEFORE JULIA DIED

Bone could feel the tension as soon as he opened the cheap door, a current of emotion that rode along with the normal fast food and flatulence miasma of a surveillance.

"What?" he asked the two guys sitting at a card table in the dark studio apartment with the shades drawn. A camera with a bulky telephoto lens stood on a tripod near the windows. Only a small table lamp was lit, but he could see enough to recognize a marshal he knew named Simon and another guy he didn't know. A badge glinted on the other guy's chest as he turned in the folding chair to face the doorway, and Bone asked again, "What?"

"Hey, c'mon," McKinnon said behind him in his strained voice. *Jaw tension* was what McKinnon said made him sound so funny.

Bone stepped in and set down the bag of coffees on a chipped kitchen counter as he heard the front door click shut, and the room darkened another shade. He felt pretty foolish all of a sudden in his sneakers and shorts, just a seven shot .380 clipped under the long tail of his Red Sox jersey.

"Hey, Virgil," Simon said, waving a hand at another chair at the table. There was a game set up with cards scattered around. "Siddown," Simon added.

Bone scuffed across the cheap rug and shocked himself when he grabbed the metal back of a chair. "Shit."

"Hey, I saw that," McKinnon said, taking the fourth chair. "A blue spark."

"No shit?" Simon said.

"A fucking blue spark," McKinnon said, his voice cracking.

Simon leaned over and tapped the table in front of the uniformed cop, who was watching Bone and not smiling.

"Listen to this," Simon said, turning to McKinnon. "Say, 'Freeze motherfucker'."

"Screw you." McKinnon shoved some cards out of the way and dropped a sack of donuts and breakfast wraps on the table. The smell was immediate and seductive, and Simon reached for the bag.

Bone picked up a card and squinted to read it. "Who was the only American member of the Monty Python troupe?"

"Terry Gilliam," McKinnon piped in immediately.

"How the hell— You been reading the cards?" Simon asked.

Bone flipped the card on the table and looked at the cop. "Who the hell is this?"

"C'mon, Virge," McKinnon started, and Bone raised a hand.

"You said we were just gonna stop by, surprise Simon with some snacks and coffee," Bone said. "But this guy's here for me, right?" In the low light he could make out the word OGUNQUIT on the police badge.

Simon and McKinnon exchanged glances and the cop spoke up. "Maybe this isn't such a good idea."

"Sure it is," Simon said, waving him back into his seat. "Virgil's just a bit on edge lately. Right, Mick?"

"Yep, always an asshole lately."

"I meant about being on edge lately," Simon said.

"Cut the shit," Bone interrupted. His stomach was bloated with acid.

"We actually, uh, met a couple times before," the cop said. "Bill Graham, like the TV preacher," he added, holding out his hand. Virgil shook it out of reflex as Graham continued, "Last couple years at the firefighter and police picnic down at Kittery with our wives and stuff."

Bone nodded vaguely, remembering the smell of barbecues and the hot sweaty summer fun of Frisbees and kids running around everywhere. "Right, I remember," Bone said, not remembering the cop.

"So, anyway…" Graham looked up at Simon.

"Look, Virge, it's not exactly a secret that things at home aren't, you know, perfect right now, right?" Simon said.

Bone felt the acid in his stomach churn into his throat and fought back an urge to cough. He grabbed the bag of food and pulled out a plain donut, picking at it with his fingers. He said, "In front of this guy?"

McKinnon leaned his elbows on the table. "Graham's a good guy and owes me one. He came here because I asked him. As a friend. He's a good guy." He reached and patted Bone's shoulder.

Bone felt the pat as a distant thing. He had the sudden urge to leave and resisted, sticking a piece of donut into his mouth instead.

"Look, I…uh… I wouldn't say anything because it's none of my business, but I remember you were a nice enough guy and Mick here is a buddy and, well, my lieutenant is a real prick," Graham said.

"Cut to the chase," Simon said.

"So…uh…I was driving past the Sea View Motel on—"

"I know where it is," Bone said.

"Right," Graham said. His shoulders dropped and he leaned back in his chair. "I saw Lieutenant Lapierre coming out of a room, in his civvies, and coming out right behind him was your wife."

Bone couldn't hear the next words over the hollow roaring sound in his ears. He could see the bright blue doors of the motel, the cars parked in diagonal slots in front with sun glinting off chrome bumpers.

"Bone? Virgil?" McKinnon was saying, a hand gripping his shoulder.

"You all right?"

"I'm sorry. Maybe I shouldn't have said anything," Graham said, rising.

"No, no, you did the right thing," Simon said. "Virge, buddy, you okay?"

"We wanted to tell you here man because you gotta right to know. But we didn't want you to do something stupid and go off half-cocked," McKinnon said.

"Right. Let's sit here and shoot the shit," Simon said. "I got some Rolling Rocks in the trunk."

"C'mon, Virgil," McKinnon said, patting Bone's shoulder. "You okay?"

"I thought you should know," Graham said.

They stopped talking, waiting for Bone to say something, but he couldn't. The piece of donut in his mouth was unswallowable, and he couldn't summon up enough saliva to break it up. Finally he choked it down and coughed into his fist.

He leaned forward, not looking at the other guys and braced his elbows on his thighs, hands dangling loosely from his wrists. "So all I can think is, the other day I was supposed to bring home some stuff from the supermarket, and I didn't write it down. So I get home and the only thing I bought that was on the imaginary list was a jar of pickles. I mean, I figured I'd just run back out when Julia told me what she wanted, but she starts laughing instead. Really laughing and I'm like 'What?' And she says, 'This is so you. Of all the things you could get at the store you bring home pickles. It's always like that. You're the guy who doesn't think to grab milk or eggs or bread, you bring home pickles. The pickle guy.' And she's laughing and it isn't really mean, you know, just sort of funny because it's true. So you've been telling me what you told me, and I'm thinking about the pickle thing and how here she is laughing about it like I'm so cute and meanwhile she's fucking a lieutenant in Ogunquit."

- 8 -

He wasn't sure when the soft-spoken voices of NPR decided to abandon him, but he sat up with a start when an ungodly instrument he couldn't identify filled his car with eerie wailing. *Iraqi fusion jazz* he remembered hearing.

"Jesus," he said as he stabbed a button with his finger and the radio died. He reached with the same hand for the paper bag on the seat next to him, yanked the paper down from the bottle and took a throat-searing swig of Cutty Sark, cursing under his breath at the taste. He bought it because he hated it and he was in a mood for hate.

Mostly, though, he just felt the wind whistling through the empty space where his middle used to be.

He propped the bottle back against the passenger seat of the Buick and patted around with his hand until he felt the cold metal of the .380. He picked it up and thumbed off the safety, then thumbed it back on.

He was parked in front of an empty house, watching a driveway maybe three houses up the street. Not big houses, but a little nicer than his. Good lawns. The one he was parked nearest had a freestanding basketball hoop set to one side of the driveway.

If the wrong cop came by he'd toss the bottle and pistol into the footwell in back to disappear amidst the mess of Dunkin' Donuts cups and McDonald's wrappers. Flash his badge. Drive away.

If the right cop came by he'd slip out of the car and stroll up as close as he could. If he was outside twenty-five yards he planned to fire for center mass and knock Lapierre down even if he was wearing a vest, then run up and empty the gun into the lieutenant's head. If he was closer than twenty-five yards he'd go straight for the head shot. Lapierre would be tired and might not even see him coming. Then again, Bone could feel he was past the buzzed stage and striding purposefully towards drunk, so maybe it was a fair fight.

He thumbed the release and the clip slid out into his cupped left palm. Bone counted the winking tips of seven .380 hollow points. He slid the clip back in with the heel of his hand and racked the slide.

"The fuck are you doing?"

The voice was slurred and he looked up before realizing it was his own.

He glanced into the rearview mirror and saw the red blood vessels in his eyes. He looked like he'd been crying, which he hadn't, or sitting in a car drinking Cutty and waiting to murder a town cop in his driveway, which was a pretty accurate assessment.

"What the fuck," he said, pausing to lick his lips and wipe the slur out of his voice, "are you doing?"

He turned to his left and spit out the window, the taste in his mouth abruptly overwhelming.

"Fuck!" he shouted, banging the steering wheel with his left hand. He dropped the pistol on the seat and it bounced down into the passenger footwell as he keyed the ignition. He stomped the gas and the engine nearly flooded, then roared painfully, the automatic shift not keeping pace as he jerked forward, swerving to straighten as he left long black streaks of rubber in the road right past Lapierre's driveway.

- 9 -

The TV was on with the volume off as Bone wandered through the house, trying to figure out which things belonged to Julia and which things belonged to him.

"How can this be happening?" He thought he said it out loud.

He ran his finger along the spines of books on a shelf and tugged it free if he thought the book was hers. They fell haphazardly and in spine-damaging fashion, bouncing off his feet. He really didn't give a fuck about art books and theater books and couldn't fathom why their tumbling descent from his life was causing his breath to come in short hiccups.

He spun, stumbling a bit, and looked at the things on the walls. Black-and-white photographs from her trip to Istanbul. Posters from the shows she'd seen in the West End as a college student. He began pulling them off the wall where they fell, some surviving, others shattering in an explosion of glass shards, bright sparkles hidden in the soft rug, eager to taste bare feet.

"It's fucking barren," he said, looking at the empty squares where her pictures had hung, the paint a bit lighter in color. He was stunned at how little of him was on the walls with Julia removed.

He pressed the heels of his hands to his eyes and marched stiff-legged into the kitchen, looking for a beer. When his white-knuckled hand closed over the jar of pickles, he threw it into the sink without hesitation, juice splattering the wall and winking off the sharp hunks of the broken jar as the pickles lay like so many dead things amidst the wreckage.

A glimpse in the bathroom mirror convinced him to change his clothes, but opening the closet to reveal the sight and smell of his wife's wardrobe was too much, and he closed the door without choosing any-thing for himself.

"Where the hell are you, Julia?"

He kept checking the time and forgetting what he saw the instant he looked away. He thought it might be best if he called somebody, maybe just left and got himself a hotel room. But he wanted to talk with her. It wasn't real, it couldn't be real, not with the bright sunlight streaming in through the windows, green leaves on the branches touching the glass.

"Oh, no." The words rode out on a gulping sound.

His marriage was over. Forget the arguments, the increasing amount of time he spent away from home on the job. Forget the number of times she had taken off her ring and stormed out of the house and, if he was being honest—*and why not?*—he had pulled the ring stunt as well. Now it was here. It was happening.

The roaring would not leave his ears.

"Shit, I don't like this."

He was bouncing the keys to the Buick in his palm when he noticed his cell phone vibrating on the coffee table. He picked it up, saw her name and the notation of six missed calls.

"Sorry, I had the ringer off," he said, trying not to slur and knowing she would hear the effort.

"Oh, God, where have you been?" Julia's voice came through with mi-nor distractions from static and cars in the background.

"What do you need?" he asked.

"I… The Camry broke down and I'm stuck at Dr. Martin's office. I need you to pick me up?"

"Why are you at Dr. Martin's office?"

"Look, just come get me and I'll tell—"

"Tell me now, Julia," he said, feeling the reins on his temper fray a bit. Instead of snapping back, her voice quieted, and he had to strain to hear her response.

"I want to tell you in person."

"Tell me now. I'm on my way."

"I'm pregnant," she said. A long, crackling silence followed. He could hear her breathing. It was thick, as if she had a cold. *Or was crying*, he thought.

The roaring filled his ears, or maybe it came through the phone connection, but the sound and the wind blowing straight through him was carrying him away from the moment in which he existed.

"I'll be right there," he said.

TWENTY-THREE

- 1 -

Reverend Ambrose Tinker awoke before the old rooster offended the morning with his horrendous noises, but didn't actually rise until he heard the sound. It had become his habit after many years, to rise at the crowing and make his morning coffee, sipping it while he walked around to the yard behind the church to scatter corn for the still spry but admittedly mangy bird, its once bright feathers a dull red and muddy blue.

"Two old bachelors," he said, as he did most mornings. The rooster, called Crab Apple because he held court beneath a tree of that type, ignored Ambrose as the old man in his thick robe sat on a seat made from a stump, clutching the hot mug in both hands and enjoying the steam as it rose to his nostrils and awakened his senses. That he looked ridiculous with thick sailor socks pulled nearly up to his knobby knees mattered not at all, and if it did, it was only to give him a tinkle of amusement.

The sky was bright and blue and though the air was crisp, he could see the wet of last night's terrible rain stretching up from the ground in a mist like gossamer fingers, the bright jewels of pooled water on the red and gold leaves around him lifting until they broke their adhesive relationship and rose back towards the home of their maker.

These mornings belonged to Ambrose and Ambrose alone—well, maybe Crab Apple as well—in a way that no other time of the day was his. And while he was no preacher of austerity, he still relished the indulgence of his private moments enough to do it in the depths of winter, out in his robe with his coffee, even if he had to hide a sweater beneath it and wear heavy boots on his feet. Deep winter had its beauty too. All of the seasons and all of the weather did, although last night it had been more challenging to find it.

"But it's our job to look, eh?" he said to Crab Apple, who wandered under the tree and pecked at a fallen fruit, the skin grown tight and pulled into a wrinkled old face. Ambrose was reminded that he needed to gather the best of them from the tree so the Littles could make *Themselves*, tiny figures dressed in clothes from the early days of the Isle. It was a simple way to teach them about the people that celebrated Feast Day in years past, and why they celebrated the end of the famine that had decimated the settlement centuries before. The Littles, of course, were more interested in making the wizened features of the crab apple children as distinctive as possible so they could be placed around the great tables to mark their chosen seats. In thanks for the children, their parents allowed them to choose any seat they wanted on Feast Day.

He sipped again, wishing the caffeine would do more to push sleep back into its box for another day. The incidents of the night before had been a trial, and staying up with Marshal Bone meant that by the time he returned to the church, Ambrose himself only managed a few hours of sleep. He was unsure about the best way to proceed with a funeral service and burial for the constable since there was no body. Perhaps the remains would be found today by a search party that prized sobriety, at least before five o'clock.

He thought of the marshal again, of how professional training would help in the search, but knew the lawman was heading home this very morning. *And that's for the best*, he thought.

He smiled a bit at the memory of his storytelling, knocking the man out with impressive speed, and oh how the marshal's snores cut the air.

The Lord gave Moses the power to part seas with a word and me the power to put children and tired men to sleep with mine.

"Here we go," he said, and his knees popped like rifle shots as he rose, startling Crab Apple into a bouncing run around the far side of the tree.

Ambrose was still smiling as he returned to the dim sanctuary and closed the door behind him, blessed by visible rays of many hues that streamed across the simple wooden pews with glowing motes of gold and red and blue flickering into existence as they entered the light.

Motion at the edge of his vision caused him to raise his head and his lips went slack, his smile sliding into the void.

Hung from the rafters overhead and swaying as if it had only just been lowered was a small bundle wrapped in ragged cloth, moving in the beautiful beams of light. Ambrose felt himself pulled towards it, the object hanging at head height. He reached up with a trembling, old man's hand and tugged at an exposed corner of cloth.

The breath exploded out of him in one great wheeze and Ambrose stumbled back until he fell jarringly to sit in a pew.

Staring back from the bundle was the bright eye of an infant.

- 2 -

Beads of liquid formed on the cherubic face and ran like wax across its cheeks.

Not like wax. Like plastic, Ambrose thought.

Beneath the milk-white infant skin was material the color of terra cotta. Heat and distortion of the orbital section of the head caused one of the eyes to roll free. It bounced through the grate and onto the floor. Ambrose reached down and caught it before it could roll past. An automatic reflex he regretted when the hot marble burned his fingers.

He bit back a curse and tossed it aside, listening as it bounced off the wall and rolled to a stop beneath his bed.

My God, they were in the church while I was outside with my morning coffee, he thought. *They were watching me.*

The infant hanging in the sanctuary was a doll. Or at least part of one.

The round head had been affixed atop the black shell of a lobster mottled with green smears of algae, the claws held open in a pose of deliberate blasphemy by a stick. White liquid leaked from cracks in the carapace as the meat inside was charbroiled, and Ambrose was angered by the small insult in causing him to recoil from a smell he normally loved. A smell that meant home and industry and lobster pot feasts with friends.

"This is sick," he muttered from his perch on the stool before the bedroom fireplace. As if in agreement, one quarter of the skull thinned and dimpled inward.

The door leading into his outer room rattled under someone's knock, and Ambrose jerked around, breath catching.

"Who is it?" he asked, rising as the stool clattered onto its side.

"Increase Mather," came a voice and Ambrose unlocked the door, pulling the solid panel open with a squeak of hinges. "Came to talk about getting together a search party."

The tall forms of Mather, Wallis and Eldred Smith entered in single file.

"This was in the church this morning," Ambrose said without preamble, pointing with a wavering finger.

"Good Lord," Wallis said, eyes widening above his bristling face as he spied the thing in the fire.

"Where is Nutter?" Ambrose asked, slipping his woolen jacket on and picking up the white length of his clerical collar.

"He said his pigs was acting funny," Eldred Smith said.

Ambrose looked back into the fireplace and saw half a dozen cornflower blue flames sprouting from the pocked and separating doll's head, roughly of a size with those beautiful and delicate flowers in nature. Black tendrils drifted through the apartment, the acrid stench made visible.

"Open a window but close the door," Ambrose said.

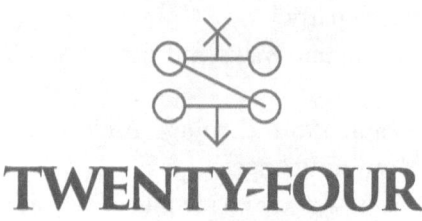

TWENTY-FOUR

- 1 -

The narrow track wound its way towards the center of the village and Bone caught occasional whiffs of wood smoke and baking bread filtering through the trees. He glanced at the woman walking by his side, her face shifting and altering as she moved through the mottled sunlight. He would see an eye, then her mouth, then her cheekbone, each feature existing perfectly in solitude. Mud squelched and a few fallen sticks cracked beneath their steps, but otherwise the woods were quiet, save for the trills of morning birds he could not see. They walked side by side and close together, occasionally brushing shoulders due to the narrowness of the track. These contacts where met with a quiet "Excuse me," or "Sorry," but neither made an effort to walk ahead or behind.

It was a good feeling. He was so unused to such a sensation in recent months, maybe years, that it was certainly an *odd* feeling. But he decided that all things being equal, he was all right with odd for a change.

"What are you smiling at?" Hazel asked.

He said, "Pretty," and then shook his head, trying not to see—yet pleased by—the pink on her cheeks as she looked around them.

"It can be beautiful here, Marshal Bone."

"Virgil."

"All right then, Virgil."

She glanced up at him, and now it was Bone who looked ahead, enjoying the golden light through a patch of yellow leaves, illuminating the floating bits of forest that had shrunk small enough to lift into the air. The shafts of light created a strange pattern of horizontal shadows on the ground, and it took him a moment to see the small trap made out of sticks.

"What's that?" Bone asked.

Hazel followed his pointing finger and grimaced. "It's a trap for feral cats." She did stride ahead of him then, and he was caught by the dark swing of her hair against her back when she surprised him by kicking the trap into pieces. She spun back to face him and lifted her chin, looking satisfied.

"I'll huff and I'll puff," he said because she seemed to expect some acknowledgement.

"You're not far off," she said as they resumed walking. "It is because of an old story, a stupid story. Gentle Annie."

"Sounds like the madam of a Boston brothel," he said, aiming for clever and not sure if he succeeded. "Wait, isn't it a song?"

"I don't know about that," she said. "But on the Isle it's an old tale, told when I was a Little and when my mother before me was a Little. Gentle Annie is an old woman who lives in the woods. She sneaks into houses at night and steals the children right out from their beds, and their parents never find out until morning, when it's too late.

She drags the children deep into the heart of the forest where she lives in a terrible old house and turns them into wicked creatures that make their mothers weep."

"Is that a real thing?" Bone asked.

"A real thing? No, but, oh, if you mean is it a real myth or whatever, then yes. It's from Scotland I think, and centuries old. She was also known as Black Annis and was quite fearsome."

Bone waved back behind them. "And the cat thing?"

Hazel shook her head and pressed praying hands together against her lips in an unconscious gesture as she thought. "The story has it that the only way to protect the children is to drag a dead cat through town on the night she plans to visit. It's unfortunately become something of a rite of passage for some Littles once they reach a certain age."

"That's awful."

"I know. That's why…" And she kicked at the air as she walked, wobbling into him. "Sorry."

"You have a lot of stories here," he said, then took off his hat and scratched his hair. "I mean, you folks tell a lot of stories."

"We're out here all alone, Mr. Bone—"

He held up a hand to stop her, and she pressed it down with her own. "*Virgil.* We have no proper television and phones that are out half of the year," she said, taking in the surrounding terrain with a gesture. "Campfire stories when we're young, tall tales in the pub when we're older. It's how we pass the time."

She elbowed him in the arm. "No doubt that disgusting story you told about the refrigerator has been traded for a dozen beers already by Woody Smalls and Arn Corn." When he looked at her blankly she added, "The men who took Slocum's body down to *Leviathan.*"

"A lot of drinking here?" he asked.

She shrugged. "It passes the time."

- 2 -

They were in the clearing where a restored scarecrow stood guard over a field of black and liquefying pumpkins

"You again," Bone said. Hazel chuckled, and he smiled to cover the faint queasiness that stole over him. He was relieved when she fell into the role of local guide, pointing out the tall spire of the church in town, the direction to the main pier, and inland where she often walked in a spring-fed river to take pictures.

"It's very cold water, but it focuses me," she said.

"Hazel?"

"Yes?"

"Why didn't you tell me what was screaming in the night? Remember when I asked?"

Her eyes narrowed, considering. "Because then you were Marshal Bone, not Virgil."

"And now?"

"It's a local embarrassment."

"Embarrassment?"

She nodded. "His name is Enoch Weeks, and he is a madman. He is physically deformed. He's been terribly treated his entire life by people who think he's a punishment on us. The rest are ashamed that we've done nothing to stop that ugliness, or really help him, but...he's unpleasant to be around. Hideous. That makes me sound terribly shallow but it's true."

Hazel paused, then added something after a moment's thought. "Burden has talked to him near the lighthouse. Tried to talk to him but said Enoch really couldn't. He goes to the old waterfront town because no one else does."

"Burden or Enoch?"

Hazel shrugged. "Both, I guess.

"Is Enoch dangerous? Has he ever hurt anyone?"

"Never. Not even when he was teased as a kid," she said, and her expression changed so that Bone wondered if *teased* was the right word for what had happened.

"Does he live on the boat with his brother?"

She tilted her head in appraisal, as if remembering the nature of his profession. "He lives with his mother in a small house in the woods. She lives off of what passes for public assistance here. Food donations."

He forced a smile. "Sounds like that Gentle Annie person."

"I know."

- 3 -

Two old women with shawls around their shoulders and heavy rubber boots on their feet dragged wooden rakes up Main Street, smoothing out the ruts before the mud hardened in the sun. They were a matched set, bookends even: bent backs, knobby hands, their iron gray hair pulled back into buns. They lived side by side and had met every day for coffee since their husbands died, sitting in near toothless silence but with the comfort of companionship. On the day before Feast Day, it had become tradition for them to take out the rakes and smooth out the street, making it a suitable dirt floor for the celebration. On this day, as they walked side by side, they spoke nearly non-stop, squishy syllables from liverish lips regaling each other with stories of former happiness. And if the stories were more or less the same each year, that was okay because neither one of them remembered very well. And if the sharing of their most protected hearts made them glow a bit and gave them strength to celebrate on the morrow when the town came out, that was okay as well. They deserved it.

They were the only two who did not react as Bone and Hazel emerged from the track onto the main drag, he a scarecrow in black that seemed to elicit almost a race-memory of fear in the Isle folk. She with her pale skin and dark hair, eliciting too many other feelings to count.

The women parted and raked long lines in the mud around the younger pair, so that Bone felt as if he had been trapped between musical scales on which notes had yet to be written. He shared his thought aloud and Hazel smiled, which made such a foolish statement worth the risk.

"I would not have expected such an odd thought from you yesterday," Hazel said.

"And today?" he said.

"Today I think more of you," she said and their smiles were easier.

Up ahead, Bone made out a number of people setting trestle tables in a long line down the center of the road. It was an odd sight and strangely medieval, as was the sight of the houses themselves in daylight and under clear sky, where the carved wood and the shapes suggested a European influence.

Several of the workers stared openly in surprise as they passed. Bone nodded at a few and saw a mixture of confusion and something less friendly.

"…the tables are for Feast Day tomorrow, really the biggest holiday of the year for us," Hazel said. She hunched over comically and tilted her head, pitching her voice into a thick Isle accent. "Big Eats Day, don't 'e know?" Her hand hooked into an arthritic claw.

She laughed but stopped and straightened when she saw his expression. She glanced around and seemed to shrink in on herself.

"I should have stayed at the tower," she said.

"I don't think it's you. I think it's me."

The church loomed before them, and this was the first time Bone was able to take in its full measure. It was a tall building of Isle stone, narrow for its height and reeking of age. A spire jutted up from the peak to scratch at the vulnerable underbelly of the sky, as if waiting to catch an unwary cloud. It was so high, in fact, that Bone was certain it could be seen over the horizon even before a sailor spotted the Isle itself. It made the building feel top-heavy, as if at any moment—or on a whim—it would roll on its side like a great beast and crush the houses around it. It was different from the rest of the village, almost as if it had been built in another time with a purpose other than ministry, but a town had sprung up around it nonetheless. It cast a literal shadow over the community and, like a sundial, held every part of the town in a moment of darkness every day there was light.

The front doors of the church swung wide and men emerged from the murky depths of the interior. A cluster of faces Bone recognized looked up in surprise upon seeing him. From the lowering brows and thinning lips it was not a pleasant surprise.

Bone saw the short form of Ambrose Tinker, still wearing the same woolen suit. He stepped towards the group automatically before realizing Hazel wasn't with him. But he continued after an awkward pause with his hand outstretched. "Hello, I wanted to thank you again for last night..." His eyes caught the white clerical collar and the word rose to his lips unbidden. "...Reverend." The jolt he felt at the word was small, but it was certainly there.

Ambrose shook his hand but looked a question at him.

"There was a problem down at *Leviathan*," Bone said. "I sent the pilot on ahead with a note to return with the team. I will stay in the meantime." He noticed Increase Mather staring at Hazel and continued. "Miss Milk will be staying at the inn where I can make sure she is safe."

"*Mrs.* Milk," Eldred Smith said, and Bone met his glare.

"I was under the impression she is a widow," Bone said.

"Some folks won't be happy to hear she's at the inn with you," Mather said with a suggestion of impropriety in his tone.

Bone stepped back a bit and raked his eyes over the group. "Let me make something clear. There will be no repeat of last night's behavior."

"'E think so?" Smith asked and stepped forward to make his point. His chin was up and he moved on the balls of his feet in the manner of a shorter man, though he was as much a beanpole as the others.

Bone stepped close enough to smell the smoked fish on Smith's breath. "There's a standing reservation at the Cumberland County Jail for anyone who hassles me."

"Gentlemen," Ambrose said, putting a hand on Eldred Smith's shoulder until the taller man stepped back. "Allow the marshal to go about his business. I didn't stay up all night playing Florence Nightingale so you could brawl in the mud."

He fixed a hard look at Smith, then at Bone. Then to Bone's surprise he winked. Coiled with tension, Bone couldn't catch a sharp laugh before it escaped.

"Off with you now, Marshal," Ambrose said. "We all have work to do and none of it will get done on the front steps of the church."

Bone tipped his hat and returned to Hazel. A quick glance around revealed the number of people who had stopped to watch the confrontation. As he looked at them, they ducked their heads and returned to work.

"C'mon," Bone said, and Hazel followed him past the empty tables, not meeting her neighbors' eyes.

"'E walk funny, Marshal," Bone heard behind him and looked over his shoulder to see Eldred Smith standing in the street, bony fists planted on his hips. "As if 'e miss the weight of a pistol."

Bone touched his fingers to his lips and blew the man a kiss, walking on with a satisfied step at the confused twist of Smith's features. Someone laughed.

"Hazel Milk!" A strong female voice cut through the air and Bone saw a woman emerging from a house. One hand was held to her belly as if in pain, but her chin was up and her eyes bright as she closed the weathered green door behind her.

Bone made to step between them when Hazel said, "Honor, what are you doing out of bed?" The two women embraced warmly and exchanged words rapidly, too quiet for Bone to hear. He glanced around and could feel tension leaking out of the surrounding townsfolk.

"And you, sir, you," Honor said, striding purposefully to Bone, who was almost bowled back by the bow wave of her presence. She was a bony woman with unusually bright eyes, chips of ice on a winter day. Not pretty but not unattractive in a rough-hewn way. She looked to be about Hazel's age, but dark smudges marred the skin beneath her eyes, her cheeks drawn tight with exhaustion.

"You are the lawman Bone?" she asked.

He nodded. Without warning she pulled him into a powerful hug, wrapping both arms around him and kissing him firmly on the cheek. He was still trying to figure out if he should hug her in return when she stepped back and held him at arm's length. She looked him up and down, as if inspecting a new purchase and *hmmphed*, looking into his eyes. He was surprised to see that tears were running freely from hers.

"You saved my heart, Mr. Bone," Honor said. "That man is my life, and if you hadn't pulled him out from that evil water..." Her voice cracked and she wiped an arm across her eyes, which did nothing more than smear the wetness across her face. "Thank you, Mr. Bone, thank you for saving my Jeremiah."

Stunned, Bone realized who the woman was just as her face twisted and she pressed both hands to her stomach.

"Let's get you back in bed," Hazel said, and walked Honor back into her house, leaving Bone alone. The door closed behind them, and he stood staring stupidly at the fading green of it.

"Lost her newborn last night," a voice said at his side, and he turned to see a young woman of around the same age as Hazel and Honor. "If 'e hadn't gone into the water, that poor woman would have lost her husband too."

The woman picked up the wooden chair she had set down in the road and carried it away to slide into place at the table. "I'll walk Hazel over to the inn when she comes out," she called to Bone, and he nodded at her, then made his way up to the inn, a refuge from scrutiny.

He pushed in the front door and the bell overhead gave a metallic *clack*, too rusted to tinkle. He scraped the mud off his shoes on a metal bar on the step as he had seen other men do and walked inside.

"Mr. Fenn?" he called out, thinking to rustle up lunch and determine his next steps. But there was no one in the main room, only empty tables and chairs awaiting the evening's guests. He noticed there was a dirty spoon on one table next to a half-full mug of ale, and a ghostly twist of cigarette smoke drifted up from a crushed butt in an ashtray.

When no one emerged from the kitchen he walked upstairs, shrugging off his coat as he creaked up the risers.

The day before had been an escalating series of disasters. Pure reaction to events, leading up to and ending with the mob scene on the beach and the near death of Jeremiah Pruitt. Scratch that, with his *own* near death from hypothermia.

Bone fought back a shudder and paused on the steps with his coat dangling from his left arm, fumbling out his notebook and flipping it to a new page.

SEAL OFF MILK HOUSE

Seal off constable's ofc.

Preserve organ in safe

He had to see if Fenn would be able to provide securable freezer space. He had to take at least informal depositions, maybe starting with the selectmen and Hazel Milk and… And he had no goddamned idea beyond that, so he would start there. The reverend seemed sharp and reasonable, unlike the testy selectmen, so maybe he could pick the man's brain for an interim constable, someone to liaise with locally.

Bone stuck the notebook between his teeth and was still shaking the sleeve off of his left arm as he turned the rusty doorknob to his room and heard the latch click, giving the wood a bump with his shoulder to open it.

His nostrils flared at the acrid tang of cigarette smoke, and his head lifted of its own accord. The notebook tumbled from between his teeth, and he forgot about the sleeve and everything else as he stared down the yawning black barrel of a gun.

TWENTY-FIVE

- 1 -

Mary Nutter's buoyant mood lasted all the way home after teaching the Littles to smoke fish. Even the odor, which she knew would take several washes to remove from her clothes and hair, didn't bother her. The evil weather had broken and the Lord's sunshine washed the world in Grace. The Littles reminded her of all that was best on the Isle with their excitement and curiosity about things to which she had long since become jaded.

They are our treasure. Truly our treasure.

Not even gossip about the slattern shacking up with that horrid scarecrow from the mainland in Eaton Fenn's booze hall broke through the armor she wore.

The buoyancy lasted until the moment she opened the door of her home, bathed in its invisible aura of pig-stink. A lobsterman rested on the table and she shivered. Her father tolerated no such foolishness, not even if one of the Littles had left it on his teacher's doorstep. She picked the ugly thing up and heard the rattle of a stone within. *A child's tooth was supposed to go inside,* she remembered. She closed her eyes at the sound of her father cursing outside and a great clatter from the hog pen.

Like any experienced survivor, a mechanism in her subconscious interpreted the data and immediately dumped the armor as too clumsy for a time when invisibility was needed. Her balance changed, her actual walk changed, feet coming down quietly on the outside edge and rolling to flat, stepping as Algonquin hunters in long ago times, slinking through the forest like ghosts.

She made her way to mother's room and immediately knelt, whispered prayers spiraling up from her vast repertoire with no need for conscious thought, wrapping her in a cloud of untouchability even as her secret mind committed energy to hearing, listening to the ruckus.

After several minutes there arose a great clamor and the sound of wood on wood. She heard a violent yell, and then all was quiet.

Too quiet, her subconscious reported. *This is not patterned behavior.*

The great quiet continued, and the prayers were no longer wrapping her in untouchability. She wasn't aware of leaking a small sob as she decided that not checking on the hog pen was a riskier choice than rising to check it. She wasn't even aware she still held the rattling lobsterman in one, white-knuckled hand.

She moved on Indian feet until her hearing would relate a recognizable pattern but encountered only silence.

She glanced through the panes of glass set high in the back door and not only failed to see her father, she failed to see any pigs.

Her heart stuttered as her protective systems recognized the potential for catastrophe. Catastrophe would result in one ultimate end, no matter its particular route.

Another leaked sob.

She twisted the knob in her bony hand and quietly pulled open the door, Indian quiet, and stepped into the humid stink of churned mud and manure where the wet glop gleamed like spilled wine in too many places and an outer fence had been splintered.

Her boot squelched down into the filth, muck rising up to her ankle as she held up the hem of her long skirt, and she noticed that the boar's pen had been violently breached.

Good Lord, the boar broke loose.

She glanced at the outer fence and joined this discovery with her father's abrupt absence.

Father is chasing the boar. He will be furious.

She spied the oddly pallid shape of a plucked chicken leg freshly broken from the carcass and squelched over to it, hesitating before she bent to pick it up in two fingers, holding it out at arm's length to examine it. Blood still dripped from the thing, and it only took her a moment to decide it was actually the leg of a suckling pig, broken free and left in the filth.

Mary Nutter knew how to work with hogs, and this was not it. She was an expert at curing bacon—*best bacon on the Isle*—as well as making sausage from the leavings. Her pork shoulder—*a perennial favorite that would be represented at Big Eats*—quite literally fell apart to the touch, and she prepared thick chops and succulent ribs with equal dexterity. She was, all other qualities aside, a master chef when it came to pork.

"This is not how you handle a suckling pig," she said, pocketing the tiny leg for cleaning and inclusion in the sausage. *Waste not, want not,* was a favorite saying in the Nutter household.

She turned in a circle, taking tiny steps and peering intently for signs of the pursuit, but she could see nothing. She opened her mouth to call out. She would have to help capture the boar, but her teeth clacked shut when she made out something near the awful hole at the far side of the pen. Her hem dragged through the mud as she approached, and she stared down at the unexpected object for some time before finally picking it up in two fingers and examining it at arm's length.

Her jaw unhinged slowly and a bray of laughter emerged like an unexpected bubble of gas. Indian quiet went out the window and thoughts of invisibility vanished as Mad Mary, Thrower of Rocks and Shrieker at Slatterns, erupted forth in a rolling barrage of laughter seasoned with coughs and hiccups. The lobsterman fell from her fingers, no longer a source of concern. She was still laughing when she brought the odd find inside, tracking muck through the house until she collapsed into a kitchen chair.

- 2 -

Hedde Smith and Reliance Wallis stopped their chatter at the same time without conscious thought as they entered the invisible bubble surrounding Hatevil Nutter's house. Their ears perked up and listened for the thunder and racket that always followed the elder Nutter like a dust cloud. Hearing no noise, they pushed open the gate on its rusting hinges, wincing at the sound and simultaneously executing a well-choreographed, if infinitesimal, pause. Two matrons of a particular age and shape, their graying hair in the same tightly pulled bun, their heads tilting in the same way.

"Hello?" Hedde said, knocking lightly on the glass panes in the door. "Are you in, Mary?"

Reliance turned the knob and gave the door a push, and the two women followed its swing as if sucked inside by the door's draft. "We're here about 'e wonderful pulled pork for Big Eats tomorrow," she called out to the empty room, wrinkling her nose at the smell of pigs.

A chair had been tipped and that just wouldn't do. Hedde bent, one hand pressed to the small of her back, and righted it.

"Mar—" Hedde stopped at the sight of her friend's white face.

"Hedde," Reliance said in a breathy whisper, raising one arm and extending a finger to point.

Hedde followed her friend's arthritic digit and felt a sudden dizziness and heard a rush like waves crashing on the beach.

"Daddy?" Hedde asked, reading what had been finger-painted in foothigh letters across the wall.

"The rest, Hedde, the rest."

"Is…" Hedde read aloud, her head continuing its eon long swivel on a neck made of petrified oak, "…in…"

Black motes danced across the tiny window of sight left to Hedde and she collapsed backwards into the chair she had just righted, exhaling with a low, moaning her husband would never have recognized.

"Oh, my Lord," Reliance said, her voice breaking. "What is this, Hedde? What is this?"

Hedde put both hands against the side of her head and pressed hard against the gray on her temples to keep her sanity in place.

Reliance, however, let her mind slip free, and she bolted from the living room, slamming into the door before she thought to tear it open and run outside.

Hedde was a fisherman's wife and had stitched and bandaged any number of wounds over the years. Fishhooks had a particular hunger for a man's flesh, and if a squid got its tentacles wrapped around an arm, skin would come free when the squid did. So she was well aware the color blood turned when it had been left to dry for a bit, and she had a pretty good inkling of whose blood it was that had been used to finger-paint the walls.

DADDY IS IN HELL the words said when you made that thousand-year turn of the head and strung the ugly things together. DADDY IS IN HELL written over and over around the room. It was work done eagerly and with passion.

"Mary?" Hedde said, calling out for the girl. "Mary, are you all right?"

Steeling herself, Hedde placed a hand against the trim of an open doorway and leaned forward to peer inside the bedroom.

"Oh, God in Heaven," she said, falling to her knees in a boneless heap at the sight of Mary Nutter.

"Hello, Hedde!" Mary said, her pocked faced stretched taut by something that had begun as a grin but evolved into a thing much larger. Mary's eyes were fever-bright and they looked at Hedde, but the older woman would swear they were staring straight into another plane.

"No need for Indian quiet anymore!" Mary said, releasing a peal of laughter. Her small and dangling breasts wobbled as she rocked, cupped but not supported by handprints of the same brownish ink. Mary reached down and scratched her crotch through her bloomers, the only garment she still had on, and gestured wildly with both hands. She had been busy in the prayer room, tearing down the framed pictures of Jesus and the crosses of every size. They lay piled and broken in a corner beneath the freshly graffitied walls. This work, much newer, still ran in burgundy streaks.

Hedde closed her eyes against the sight of Mary's bobbling breasts and muttered a silent plea for strength.

"What happened, child?" she whispered.

"What happened?" Mary asked, spinning gaily away from Hedde, who let out a shriek at the outline of the severed hand jammed down the back of Mary's bloomers where it cupped one, spindly buttock. The wrist itself was a near unrecognizable protrusion from the frayed waistline of the garment.

"What happened is," Mary said, her tone thick with the glorious secret she had to share, "Daddy's in Hell, and there's no need for us to be Indian quiet anymore!"

Mad Mary Nutter spun around, smile vanishing as she heard the elephantine thunder of Hedde Smith's clumsy flight. She ran after her with light, athletic strides and saw the older woman bang out the front door.

A terrified Reliance waited near the gate for her friend and embraced Hedde as the older woman ran to her, weeping. Reliance looked up over Hedde's plump shoulder as Mary filled the doorway in all her savage glory and peeled her lips back to reveal teeth jutting every which way like shattered ruins in a post-apocalyptic smile.

"Pigs are gone, ladies," Mary said, her visible ribs expanding and contracting as she panted, hanging onto the top of the door frame and leaning out as far as her body could stretch. "'E are shit outta luck if 'e want pulled pork."

- 3 -

"Would you like some more tea?" Mary asked, pausing in her work at the counter.

Ambrose Tinker leaned back, feeling the pleasant warmth of the oven and basking, to his surprise, in the rich aroma of apples and onions roasting in bacon fat. "I'll get some for both of us," he said, rising from the kitchen table.

"Aren't 'e a dear," Mary Nutter said, flashing greasy hands, a gobbet of something pale clinging to her right thumb. "I'm all covered in grue."

Ambrose stepped past her to set the kettle on the stovetop. It was a house he had been in many times and, rooting in the cupboard with the smell of dinner preparations tickling his appetite, it was almost as if his hostess wasn't naked save for brown patches of dried blood on her drooping breasts and a pair of muddy bloomers. Her legs were caked up to the shin in dried muck from the pigpen, and something had hardened in her hair, giving it a frightful stiffness.

He took his time getting the cups ready and was rewarded with a whistle from the teapot.

"The trick with this cut is to debone it without removing the skin. Without skin 'e ain't got a lick of cracklin' and I love cracklin'. Don't you, Reverend?"

"That I do, Mary," he said as he set her cup near her, careful not to look at the cutting board where she worked with an array of knives. Her heard the *plink* of a small bone landing in a metal bowl. "Planning to make some broth?" he asked, willing his eyes to unfocus as his gaze slid across the horrible accusations written on the walls in blood.

"I am," she said as another small bone *plinked* into the bowl. "I'm behind on doing my part for the Big Eats tomorrow, and you can't go wrong with a good pork stock."

She dropped the meat and nicked her finger. "Shitfire," she said and then giggled at Ambrose. "Sorry, Reverend."

He waved it away as she sucked on the wounded digit and washed down the blood with a sip of tea. He wondered if he should be forcing himself to consume every detail of the experience, or if he should continue his formerly unconscious but now quite conscious effort to deny what was happening in the Nutter household.

"All right then," Mary said, her rump thrust towards Ambrose as she bent to remove the pan of apples and onions from the oven. She sipped her tea again and then placed the deboned meat into the pan. "Smells good, too bad 'e ain't got more meat on it."

"Smells delicious, Mary," Ambrose said as she slid the pan back into the oven and carried her tea over to the table. Her breasts jiggled as she sat across from him, her bright eyes drooping a bit.

"Sure is nice of you to stop by, Reverend," she said, sipping. Her cup sloshed when it rapped against the tabletop. The smell of cooking pork was already seeping into the kitchen. "Say, would you mind checking on it in a few minutes?" she asked, blinking.

"I'd be happy to." Ambrose slid back his chair and stood as her chin dipped lower. He stepped past her and froze when she muttered what might have been, "Indian quiet," then had the oven door open and the pan on the counter.

Reverend Ambrose Tinker glanced back once to make sure the sleeping powder he had placed in her tea was doing its job, then snatched up a pair of kitchen tongs to lift Hatevil Nutter's boneless hand from the pan and onto the counter. Garlic cloves popped from slits that drooled pink juices, and it was all he could do not to retch.

The fingers had already started to bloat in the heat, and the fingernails had a swollen quality to them. One of them burst with an audible *pop!*, the nail sliding free on a spread of yellowish liquid. Ambrose was just quick enough to make it to the bathroom before vomiting a thin stream into the toilet. A cruel eddy of wind brought the smell of roasted apples to him, and he dropped to his knees, gut cramping.

It was several minutes before he was able to step outside to the crowd of waiting neighbors and enlist their help.

TWENTY-SIX

- 1 -

Three hours of tramping through the sodden woods, whipped by wet branches and stumbling into mudholes, and the whereabouts of Hatevil Nutter remained a mystery.

But Bone discovered plenty.

- 2 -

"Did you kill the constable?" Bone had asked the dwarf sitting on his bed aiming the gun.

"Is that your investigative technique? No magnifying glass or deerstalker cap?" Burden Ipswich asked with mock horror, then explained why he had the gun and handed it inexpertly over to Bone, who emptied the shells into his coat pocket and stuck the weapon in his holster.

"Why shouldn't I arrest you right here?"

"Because you're not a stupid man and I know why—"

Shouting from the street interrupted Burden.

Bone slammed downstairs and found a search party gathering. Burden was quick on his heels.

The cluster of men hurried in a disorganized mass to the Nutter house where a rotund woman refused to let Bone inside.

"Mary has just quieted after a sleeping draught, and you men will have to wait," Hedde said as three older women appeared in the doorway behind her.

"Shit," Bone said, deciding the search was more urgent. "But I'll be back."

The gathered Isle men kept their distance as the searchers began beating the woods and calling Nutter's name. Soon Bone and Burden were out of sight of the group.

"I know why Slocum was killed," Burden said.

"Then it wasn't an accident."

Burden shook his head and gestured at the revolver Bone now carried. "I brought that to demonstrate some credibility."

"Three deaths in such a short period of time, assuming Nutter is dead."

"Four deaths, actually."

"Who else?" Bone asked.

"The Pruitt baby."

"Are they related?"

"You need to come back to my tower and read a book."

"I'm not a fan of games."

"Nor of coincidences, I imagine," Burden said, then told him about finding the book where Slocum had hidden it, hinting at the guardian rats and stopping as Bone's expression changed. "No one knows I have it except you and Hazel. I need to keep it that way."

"Stop fucking around, Burden," Bone said, pushing a little hardness into his voice. "Who killed Slocum and the constable?"

"I don't know who did it," he said, holding up a hand to stop Bone's interruption. "I think I understand why, if the book is to be believed." Burden felt Bone's belief slipping. "Tonight at nine o'clock, we'll meet at Fenn's."

"So I can read a book?"

Burden shook his head. "So I can show you something else you need to see."

"What does this have to do with the deaths?"

Burden offered a tight grin. "You're the detective."

"Bring me this book," he said, and Burden shook his head violently.

"The hell I will. Someone killed Slocum for it and I won't be next."

- 3 -

"Tell me about Enoch Weeks running around the woods at night," Bone said, nursing a welt on his cheek, courtesy of an unfriendly branch.

Burden shook his head. "A sad story."

"Where does he live? Can you show me?"

"Of course. But it's a waste of time."

"What happened to the constable could be the work of a psychotic."

"Enoch is psychotic but not dangerous."

"What?"

"That poor man is so afraid of people, he's even afraid of me," Burden said, aware he was either stretching or shrinking the truth, depending on perspective.

- 4 -

Heading back to Nutter's house, the search party kept their distance and Bone heard mutters.

"I feel like I crashed a party," Bone said.

"Walk a mile in my shoes," Burden said and caught Bone's reflexive glimpse at his limping gait. "Don't say it," he added, and Bone felt the surprising urge to smile.

"What's their problem?" Bone asked, waving at the men visible through the trees.

"You were supposed to leave."

Burden stumbled headlong into a puddle covered with leaves and arose soaking. "Oh, dammit."

Bone helped him up and Burden wiped muddy leaves from his face and hair.

"Why do you want to help me when no one else does?" Bone asked.

"The good of mankind?"

"I read some of your poetry. I wouldn't have expected such positive outlook behind those words."

"Then maybe this is my penance," the little man said, kicking a clump of mud from his shoe.

- 5 -

Bone shouldered through the crowd circling the hole in Nutter's pigpen. He covered his nose at the stench. "What the hell is down there?" he asked.

"Shit and bones," Eldred Smith said.

"We're going to rig a block and tackle—" Increase Mather began.

"It's too small for anyone of us to go down there," Bone interrupted.

"Not for the dwarf," Eldred Smith said.

"The hell I'm going down there," Burden said.

"Coward," Smith said.

"Enough of that," Bone said, pointing at Eldred. "Cause another disturbance and you're going into a cell."

"I'd like to see you try," Smith said, teeth bared in a vicious grin.

Men pressed in on Bone, who held his ground and threw the left side of his long coat back. The crowding stopped as they saw the constable's pistol jammed into the holster. Bone fixed each man in turn with a flat, cop look while wondering quietly why the hell he had emptied out the shells.

"Where did 'e get that?" Increase asked.

"Investigating, that's where," Bone snapped, staring until Mather dropped his eyes. "We can rig a rope and lower a video camera," he said, looking around at bristling beards and furrowed brows. "If someone has a camera."

"Hazel has an old video model with a light," Burden said.

"Get it." Bone pushed through the men to follow Burden for a few steps so they could speak quietly. "You never did say where you were the night the constable disappeared."

"You never asked."

"Where were you the night the constable disappeared?"

"At Hazel's house waiting for her on the porch, but I left before she got home."

"Why did you leave?"

Burden smiled as if he were delivering a punchline. "The constable struck me and threw me off the porch."

"He did?"

"Oh, it's worse than that. He ground me into the mud with his boot. Humiliating. I felt like a worm."

"And you didn't kill him?"

"I am very wee, Master Bone," Burden said, face solemn. "Also, I did not yet have that fine revolver." He stepped back then pointed a crooked finger at the marshal. "Nine o'clock at Fenn's."

Bone nodded his head and looked back at the file of men watching him with dull eyes. He let his coat open so the gun and the badge, the symbols of his authority, were clearly visible.

"Gentlemen, I know you are angry and even afraid. You should be. Something terrible has happened, not once but twice in your community. A very close-knit community as I have come to learn. But we must work together to determine what happened. Who did what to who. *Leviathan* is on her way back to the mainland and will return with a crime scene crew, so I must ask that you stay out of Hazel Milk's house, the constable's house and office, and except for those of you involved in putting a camera down in that hole, out of the Nutter house as well. I am an outsider, and I know my presence rankles some of you, but we need to work together."

Bone stopped and looked at the men, waiting for some response.

"'E don't know nothing." It wasn't even an angry statement, just a plain statement of fact.

Bone glanced at Eldred Smith but saw he hadn't spoken. Looked at Mather. Wasn't him.

"The body of Richard Slocum was stolen from the ice hold of *Leviathan* last night," he said, his eyes darting from face to face. "If anyone has information, please come see me at the public house."

Not a flinch from any of them, but Eldred Smith took a half step forward. "Why would we know anything about that, Lawman Bone? It goes missing and you stay. We want 'e gone," he said, showing his teeth in a grin. "Like a fart in a high wind. A bad memory we'll laugh about later."

"At the public house," Bone repeated, letting his eyes roam over the group before mucking his way up to the Nutter house and past Hedde and the other women watching from the doorway.

The women bustled outside and he was left alone to study the walls. There was an eager passion to the work, and he crossed to a small bedroom where Mary was asleep with the blanket clutched to her neck like a child. One hand was heavily bandaged, soaked through with red.

He left her to sleep, and he read about Daddy and Hell and wondered if she killed her father.

TWENTY-SEVEN

- 1 -

"Don't break it," Hazel Milk said to the men wrapping black electrical tape around her Magnavox camcorder. It was a big machine in grey plastic that recorded on full-size VHS tapes. They were affixing a flashlight to the side.

Lit by several lanterns placed around the area, the three men huddled about the camera, which they had already attached to a rope, which was itself run over a hastily rigged winch. The idea, as Hazel understood it, was to lower her camera into the hole in Nutter's pigpen and see if Hatevil himself was down there.

Hazel had no special desire to step in the effluence of hogs and stood several feet away outside the broken fence and made an effort to breathe through her nose.

"Turn on the light," Increase Mather said.

"'E taped over the switch," Eldred Smith grumbled, peeling back the tape and turning on the flashlight so the beam of illumination flitted wildly about the place as the rigged contraption swung on the rope. John Wallis, who quietly thought Hatevil Nutter was destined to descend much farther than a mudhole after his death, twisted the light until it more or less lined up with the camera lens.

"Do we need to focus it or anything?" Wallis asked.

Hazel's headshake was a barely visible ripple. "Just turn it on when you want to record and turn it off when you're done."

"Thank you, Mrs. Milk," Mather said. "We'll bring the camera back when we're done."

"You have the use of my first name, Increase Mather," Hazel said.

"That what he calls you?" Eldred Smith asked, teeth visible through his beard.

"Who?" she asked, feeling the twist in her middle.

"'E know who. Ain't decent, a married woman winkin' and twinklin' with some mainlander."

The air around Hazel dropped twenty degrees.

"My husband is dead, Eldred," she said conversationally. "Perhaps you heard?"

She stepped into the muck of the pigpen, lifting her skirt to keep the hem from dragging. Her head tilted as she looked up at Eldred, stepping well within his personal space. "Oh Eldred," she said in tones gravid with concern. She stroked his cheek with her fingertips, letting her nails run through his greasy whiskers. "Did you think it would be you?"

He twitched back as if her touch was acid, and she twirled away, long hair tossing as she stepped with a royal lightness from the gluey mud.

The three older men watched her fade into the evening and endured a long silence.

"Cruel woman," Smith said at last.

- 2 -

The men were used to dropping lines, and they worked smoothly to lower the camera, straddling the hole, feet dug into the mud.

"Let her twist," Smith said, relaxing his grip as the rope rotated in his hand. "We'll see more." Smith felt slack in the line a moment later. "Hit the bottom," he said, noting the marks on the rope. "Thirty-two feet and change."

Mather and Wallis traded glances. It was good to put a number on the unknown, but...

"Awfully deep," Wallis said for them all as he cranked the winch back a few feet.

Smith twisted the rope so the camera would swing about and give them a good look at the bottom. "Bring her up?" he asked, looking at Mather who nodded as he carried a lantern around to the far side to even out the light.

Wallis cranked the winch and Smith let the rope slide through his palm, enjoying the faint burn of it as the rough hemp dug at his calluses. "Wait," he said, jerking the rope once, sharply. "Okay then. 'E were stuck on something."

When the camera emerged from the hole, Mather leaned over and snagged it in both hands. "Wet," he noted.

"It's a mudhole," Smith said.

The next words came from Wallis after they had figured out how to rewind the tape and leaned in to watch it on the tiny view screen.

"Is that human?" he asked, wiping his eyes as if to rub the image away.

- 3 -

The hollow shell of the constable's house was once again warmed by life, if only for a moment. He had possessed one of the only video players in town, and when a white-faced Increase Mather handed Ambrose Tinker the videotape, the preacher knew it was the only place he could watch it in privacy.

The camera swung wildly, sickeningly, the spinning flashlight beam doing more to disorient Ambrose than illuminate what he was seeing. He had turned on no lamps in the house, and the flickering light from the screen made him blink and squint.

He heard a creak downstairs and straightened where he sat on the edge of the dead man's bed, his thumb pressing the PAUSE button.

"Hello?" he called out, but there was no answer.

He shifted and disturbed the scents in the room. The entire house was so devoid of adornment that he expected it to smell of sawdust, but it still carried the slightly rank and musky odor of the constable, particularly in the bedroom. The kitchen was neat but smelled of beans and burned toast, a bachelor's odor ingrained into the wood. There was a small table with one straight-backed chair of local make. Taken *in toto* the house reflected almost no personality at all or, more worrying, a personality of such barren rigidity that even in solitude there was no room for indulgence.

What would wrapping oneself in such tight restraints do to a man? But he knew. Dishonesty to self was something that Ambrose avoided, and he knew what it did. It created a man like the late constable, and the Isle had needed someone like the constable, more controlled than Nutter or Smith, to keep order.

He wondered if the constable had been lonely, or was so resigned to solitude that it was no more a consideration than taking the next breath.

Ambrose pressed PLAY and the spinning descent of the camera resumed. He saw images of darkness and moisture, dripping mud and sharp rock.

"There," he said, bedsprings creaking as he leaned forward. Clumsily he rewound the tape and replayed the section in question. "I—" he began before repeating the process with the tape, until he was certain he was seeing a freshly denuded ribcage.

His head fell into his hands and he held still for several moments before looking at the TV screen again and letting the tape continue. He paused the VCR again, rewinding so he could watch the moment. A long, white bone amidst wet mulch. The brightness of the object, set amongst the shattered skeletons of so many small pigs, marked it as new.

As human.

"Help me, Father," Ambrose whispered as he allowed the tape to play until the camera had struck the ground. It was tilted on an extreme angle and the flashlight splashed a bright cone across a cavern wall.

"Oh!" Ambrose exclaimed and pulled back from the TV screen. For a third time he replayed a section of tape, staring intently at the light spread across the subterranean wall.

A shadow. Low. Crawling. Something was alive down there.

"I've failed," Ambrose whispered.

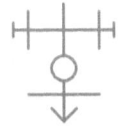

TWENTY-EIGHT

- 1 -

At half past eight Bone sat downstairs at Fenn's eating a bowl of chowder he was too tired to taste. A piece of bread dipped earlier and forgotten had grown into a swollen growth atop the liquid.

Bone had sealed off Hazel Milk's house, the constable's spartan dwelling and his office, and said as much to everyone he saw on the street so they would spread the word. Not that he expected much help with that.

Even Fenn had cooled noticeably, and Bone had to ask for coffee three times before the tavernkeep brought it over.

"He let a dead man escape him," a muffled voice said, and schoolgirl titters raced around the room, all the uglier coming from old men.

Bone glanced around at the muted hostility. Some met his eyes, others glanced at the gun in his holster.

"Mr. Bone," a thin voice said, and Bone looked up to see Wallis, the town selectman who had discovered the constable's bloody disappearance. "Camera saw fresh bones down in that hole. Didn't look like pig bones."

Even though it was expected, the news of another killing was a shock. "Everyone stays away from that hole. Crime scene techs will get anything out that needs to come out."

"We should talk," the older man said, a tall person shrunken, unable to fill out his frame.

"Take a seat." Bone pushed out the chair on the other side of the table with his foot. "Who stole Slocum?"

Wallis' eyebrows rose in genuine surprise and he froze halfway to sitting. "It wasn't us."

"Who's us?"

"I—"

The door banged open, silencing him.

"Wallis," Increase Mather said with false heartiness. "It's been a grim day. Let me buy 'e a drink."

Wallis forced a smile as he straightened and strode over to Mather. "'E saved me from the need to show Christian hospitality, Mather." Even Bone could hear the lie in his voice.

Us. It wasn't us. The selectmen? But he believed Eldred Smith when the grizzled fisherman had said they wanted him gone. He was working on the quiet assumption that the constable had a hand in Slocum's death. But the constable was dead.

Did the constable have help in killing Slocum? That person could have eliminated the constable to dry up the trail until Bone left. Everyone knew he was returning to the mainland with Slocum's body, but the theft of that body didn't make any sense. It kept him on the Isle.

In a small community, two major crimes were likely to be related. A major robbery followed by a murder were likely connected. An arson followed by a kidnapping were likely connected.

Why would someone want me to stay here, blundering around like a bull in a china shop? Shit, I don't even want me to stay here.

It was easier to think about than Burden Ipswich's tale of murder and secret books in an abandoned town that was accursed. *Accursed?* The story was a Robert E. Howard novel printed on cheap pulp with a lurid cover. A tower by the sea with a beautiful woman standing on the top, watching the approaching wanderer.

"Balls," he said to the idea. This was some local thing that probably went back deep. Or someone just lost it, stopped imagining the flow of blood and set about to make it really happen. There just wasn't enough of him, alone, to chase everything down at once.

"None of this was happening before you got here."

Bone glanced up but saw no one looking his way. The implication and the cowardly sniping pissed him off.

"Bullshit," he said, leaning back until his chair creaked. He closed his eyes but let his voice project. "It happened to Richard Slocum."

He opened his eyes and not a man was looking his way. He caught his own reflection in the mirror behind the bar. Unshaven and greasy, white scars lurid against the dark stubble on his cheek, flickering orange in the lantern light.

He rubbed a hand across the sandpaper planes of his chin and cheeks and became aware of the stink from his day's work. The mossy taste of his mouth and grit in the corner of his eyes. Emotions colored in violet were beginning their dance, filling his belly with lead and tightening his chest. The siren call of fear brought the anger in response. Not on a white charger, no Lone Ranger this. It rode a black beast covered in a patchwork of pale scars.

Bands around his chest tightened and some small voice said, *Hold on.*

He knew what it was. He had learned it sitting in group settings on folding metal chairs as his ass and mind grew numb from the droning voices. But the black horse rode through the group, scattering wounded men and cheap chairs alike.

"God, I want a fucking drink." He hoped he hadn't said it out loud. Then he said it louder and more clearly. "Fenn. Whiskey."

The glass landed on his table with a *thunk,* and Eaton Fenn poured him a liberal dose, leaving without a word.

Bone downed the drink, easily a double, nearly choking on the hot poison as it sizzled down his gullet.

Nine o'clock came and went on the big clock over the bar, and no one else spoke to Bone. The feel of the whiskey was writhing into his consciousness and calling for more. He rose abruptly with his coat in hand and walked to the door. He turned back to survey the room, ready for the comment, the crack, the insult and its implied threat.

Not a soul looked at him, and the room had gone so quiet that the banging of pots and pans in the kitchen were the only sound.

He backed into the door and shoved it open with his shoulder blades.

- 2 -

Bone didn't notice Burden Ipswich until he had passed the wheelbarrow and rain barrel. The man's shape and size were wrong enough that it didn't trigger the instinctive alarm that someone waited in the dark. Bone's first awareness of the dwarf might as well have been the frozen spike of a knife in his kidney.

"Marshal Bone, I'm sorry," the little man said quietly as the shadows produced him. "I couldn't be seen in there talking to you. I think I'm already in trouble."

Bone barked a laugh. A loud gunshot of mirth split the night, and he didn't care who heard him.

"Trouble? You're in trouble all right."

- 3 -

Burden saw something terrible in the lawman's eyes and his guts filled with ice water. The foolish humor of the morning and cleverness of the afternoon vanished.

"Mr. Bone, please listen to me for sixty seconds. And if you don't agree with what I'm saying, I will do exactly as you ask. Please."

"Talk fast."

Burden Ipswich looked up at the lawman and saw Reverend Ezekial Healy stepping alive and on fire straight from the pages of the damnable book. He prayed that Bone was not as merciless as that hellhound of God and plunged straight on without embellishment.

"I have discovered things I don't understand, but I believe they are behind the killings, and I believe there will be more. I do not know who the killers are, but I think I know why. I am not an investigator but you are, and you may be able to use what I know to stop this thing. I have come to you because I am terribly afraid that in the days to come I will find my death, as will others."

"Tell me, right here and now," Bone said, his voice tight.

"I need to show you—"

Bone tried to interrupt but, incredibly, stopped at Burden's raised hand. "Please, listen to one question." Burden took Bone's silence for assent. "How did you sleep last night? What did you dream?"

It was impossible to see in the night, but he had the sense that Bone went pale, his scars lighter against his unshaven face. The lawman's shoulders dropped an inch.

"The quilt on your bed, who gave it to you?" Burden asked.

"What does that have to do—"

Burden felt the momentum and seized it, a fishing line grown taught with a running catch. "It is called a curse quilt and it was made here on the Isle. It is very old. You can see the stitched curse written among the designs around the edges. Whoever gave it to you did not want you to sleep easily. Does not want you here."

"Curses are bullshit."

"I know that and you know that," Burden said, his words slowing from their previous headlong rush. "But there are folks here that believe in curses and act on that belief."

"That's insane."

"What did you dream?"

"Stop asking about my dreams." Bone snatched a handful of Burden's lapel. "Where the fuck are you taking me? Will it tell me who killed the constable? Nutter? Slocum?"

He released Burden and the little man stumbled backwards, arms windmilling until he sat down hard.

"What the hell do you want to show me?" Bone asked.

"I want to show you my grave."

TWENTY-NINE

- 1 -

"Bone is not to see the tape," Increase Mather said.

"Do 'e think the constable is down there with Nutter?" John Wallis asked.

Mather, Wallis and Eldred Smith were clustered at a wooden table in the public house, elbows planted amidst a graveyard of empty glasses.

"What did the reverend say?" Wallis asked.

"He has said nothing since he watched the videotape," Smith said. "'E isn't at the church."

"The marshal is thinking our murderer is a madman," Mather said.

"So we give him a madman," Smith said.

Wallis studied his knuckles. "What did the reverend see in the tape that we didn't?"

"We put the lawman on a boat, *White Sailor* maybe, get him into radio range of the coast," Mather said, ignoring Wallis.

"But *Leviathan*—" Wallis began.

Eldred Smith chopped the edge of his hand down hard and the glasses on the table jumped. Mather just shook his head and said, "*Leviathan* has nothing to do with anything now."

The few patrons remaining in the public house quietly cleared out.

"They feel the black clouds gathering," Mather said.

"Forget about them, it's Bone 'e need to focus your thinking on," Smith said. "His fingers are 'neath the damned lid and ready to pry it off."

"The Isle will be crawling with mainlanders—"

Mather cut him off with an upraised hand. "Not if we send him back like Slocum."

"He has a gun now," Wallis said.

Smith grunted. "We can put three men or more in a boat hold. *Fisher Cat* is a better vessel for that."

"But—" Wallis said, flinching at another bang of Smith's hand against the wood. A glass landed on its side where it rolled to the edge and fell but did not break.

"John Wallis, do 'e want to wave our shame like a flag for all to judge?" Smith said.

Mather calmly leaned over and picked up the glass, righting it on the table. "Do 'e want digging and sniffing mainlanders in your house? In mine? Do 'e want to teach the Littles of the Isle or have them learn it from the twisted tongues of people who know nothing? NOTHING!"

Wallis shook his head and mouthed the word "No."

"The lawman must go," Mather said.

"The lawman must go," Smith said.

John Wallis looked into the sullen eyes of his fellow selectmen and finally nodded. "The lawman must go."

- 2 -

John Wallis knew how important his role was to the Isle and would do nigh on anything to protect it, but still felt dirty as he pulled the sacking down over his head and adjusted the eyeholes, his nose filled with the scent of old potatoes.

Increase Mather finished cutting eyeholes in his sacking and pulled it over his own head. He felt grim determination.

Eldred Smith was filled with excitement.

They left by the back door of Smith's house to remain unseen, burdened with coils of rope, flashlights and worn axe handles. Eldred Smith had a fishing net wrapped crosswise around his torso like a bandolier and a big knife on his hip, "For cutting the rope," he said.

It was a clear night, painted blue in the moonlight and just the right amount of cold. They trailed a stream of mist from their mouths and, in exchange, the Isle gave them the clean scent of wet leaves and dry branches freshly broken. The forest sounds were like struck crystal in the autumn air.

Only Wallis glanced back at the warm lights of the house as they trudged into the trees.

"What's that smell?" Wallis asked.

Smith looked back, teeth flashing in a white grin. "Littles."

He tapped the object hanging by a rope and set it swaying, giving new life to the animal as Wallis marched beneath the branch from which it dangled. It was the third hanging cat they had seen in the woods, and he knew they were close.

"They're getting bold," Mather commented with a note of approval. The other dead felines had been desiccated husks and farther away from their goal.

"I've heard not a howl," Wallis said.

"Means the crazy bastard should be asleep inside," Mather said.

"Quiet now, we're close," Smith said, though quiet was a relative term as they trampled through brush in their approach to the house to which no trail led.

"Turn off the lights," Mather whispered, holding up a branch under which they filed, reaching the lip of a hollow.

Down below, as if it had slid to the bottom of a bowl, was a very odd house that appeared blue and grey in the moonlight. It seemed too small to be two-storied with three peaked roofs, yet somehow it managed both. It had the squeezed feel of three drunks leaning on each other for support, the flaking peaks like heads pressing together, the boards on either flank snapped and sprung free like spinning limbs frozen in time. The tendency of the house to curve down in the middle and up at either end gave it the appearance of the forest's secret expression, an enormous disembodied grin.

The men had been to it before, as most on the Isle had, but were still appalled by the squalor, the piles of grotesque compost arranged in no discernable pattern, the wooden outhouse that had been tipped on its side for years, exposing the revolting hole to the world.

Smith covered his nose but grinned beneath his hand. He loathed Annie Weeks and reveled in her deserved situation.

"Smoke from the chimney," Wallis whispered. "And food cooking."

"How can 'e tell?" Smith asked and fought down a cackle.

"C'mon you two," Mather said. "Quick and fast, and don't let the madman run."

They filed down the slope behind him, taking great strides as gravity pulled them into a trot. Wallis slipped on something and he cursed as he scrambled after his axe handle.

Smith picked up speed and Mather let him pass. This was work for a man like Eldred Smith.

Breaking into a sprint, Smith lifted his axe handle like a tomahawk, but slowed at the last second before he reached the door and reared back to lift a boot. With a shout he stomped the portal to flinders and rushed inside with Mather on his heels.

Wallis heard the voice of Increase Mather, "Gentle Annie, you tell us where he is!" Then a terrible sound that was one of the many voices of Eldred Smith.

Wallis stopped his charge with one hand on the door frame and doubled over. The run, booze and idea of what they were doing created a spasm in his gut, and yellow bile splashed over his feet.

- 4 -

Annie Weeks was not merely fat, she was huge. When she stood, which was not often, great drabs of suet hung from the back of her arms past her elbows. Of late she wore only dresses she made herself, cobbling together smaller bits of clothing into patched circus tents that fit her frame.

They had netted her and tried to hoist her up to the ceiling, but the beam had fallen instead so that it slanted down across the room.

"Good God, woman, what are these things made of?" Eldred Smith asked.

Annie Weeks craned her neck against the press of the net, the cords cutting into her skin to mark her with a red hatching of welts.

Floating in a glass jar were the false teeth made by her genius son, Enoch, in one of his clear headed moments. They were big and blocky things of hard plastic polished into shape and rooted firmly into the pink gums of her previous false teeth. Where most adults have thirty-two teeth, Enoch had only presented her with six atop and six below, giving her a horsey look when she wore them. They were foolish, she knew, but she so rarely saw other people that it didn't matter much, and Enoch said they would work, and they did.

"Where is he, Annie?" Increase Mather asked, crouching down with a grimace of effort. In her kitchen, Eldred Smith swatted the jar with an axe handle and it shattered in a spray of wet glass, her teeth sliding free like something used to bait hooks.

Annie whimpered in despair through a mouth that had collapsed inward like a sinkhole, as if she were being sucked inside out by a force that caught hold of her lips.

"With Samuel," she tried to say. But poor education, too much solitude and the lack of her blocky teeth made it sound like "Wooh Samooh."

Mather rose with a grunt of disgust and went to look out the open door, so Annie returned to praying.

She never once, during the ninety-seven minutes that Eldred Smith and Increase Mather were in her house, prayed for herself.

Never once did she pray for vengeance upon the men who had beat her up and wrapped her in a net and hung her from an overhead beam.

She only prayed that her genius son who was so often frightened would not come home. But she was afraid that prayers would not be enough. It had been several days since she last saw Enoch, though she had heard his singing in the woods at night. She knew he was forgetful and wouldn't eat enough and soon would think to come home so she could make him supper, or lunch or breakfast, whichever he wanted.

Eldred grunted and straightened from his inspection of a lumpy seat covered in red and pink stripes. "What did you stuff this with, pig shit?"

Annie looked away as much as she could, her nose catching on the net and leaving a wet smear. The chair was stuffed with leaves gathered in the woods, and even if it was mildewed she liked the colors.

Please baby boy, don't come home now.

Eldred suddenly sprinted to her and began pounding the ground in time with his words. "Where is that crazy son?"

She closed her eyes, trying to pull back into herself like a turtle.

"Christ above, 'e are as dumb as he is," Smith said, spinning away to kick apart one of Enoch's half-finished projects. When he was feeling better, Enoch built things, sometimes even completing them before he had to go outside for a few days again. Eldred smashed another and another, the precious relics of Enoch's sanity and good heart. Annie sobbed.

"Hah! 'E place doesn't look any worse for my work," Eldred said, spitting on her floor. And to an outsider maybe it wouldn't. The walls slanted and yellowed paper rolled free from them in gooey sheets, revealing rings of mold in myriad sizes. The furniture was patched and too plentiful, and the carpet was eaten away, presenting large patches, and smelled terrible.

But her Enoch would come home when he was hungry, and her boy Samuel would bring her things from the mainland, even if they weren't always as new as he said they were. And she never left food out and always washed the dishes and stacked them after eating.

Eldred stormed outside, and she heard raised voices, so she squirmed and twisted like a hill-sized slug on the floor, heaving and rolling over before settling back, defeated, netted like the prize catch of the day.

Please don't be Enoch, please, please.

But it was Increase Mather who came inside.

"He's been hurting people," Mather said.

"No," she shouted back through wobbling lips.

"The boy's been killing people."

"No," she refuted him, a wall of denial miles high.

Mather approached with an axe handle dangling from his hand and a rope coiled on his shoulder.

"I know you can call him home."

Annie shook her head, but the net held her skin and hair fast so all she did was shimmy her skull.

There was the sound of pounding feet and Mather spun around, but it was Eldred Smith trotting back inside with a bundle in his arms.

"What—" Mather said when Smith shouted, "Hah!" and hurled several mummified cats at her.

Annie couldn't help herself. She hated the dead cats, *hated* them. She wailed out loud.

"What are you trying to do, Eldred Smi—" Increase began then stopped, and Annie saw the color not drain, but flee from his face.

An animal howl rolled from somewhere outside and in through the door.

Oh no, Annie thought.

Eldred grinned. "The madman's here."

- 5 -

John Wallis aimed his flashlight beam in zigs and zags along the top of the slope. It was on a zag, swinging back to his right, that he caught movement. He whipped the light down to catch the thing that was running, leaping, tumbling straight for him in utter disregard of balance, pain or self-preservation, anything that would dull its speed.

"It's him!" he shouted and dropped his light, bringing up the axe handle in both hands and swinging wildly with all the grace of a Little Leaguer in his first at-bat.

Enoch Weeks came in low, and the wood *spanged* off his shoulder, swatting him off line so that he slammed face first into the wall beside the open door instead of crushing John Wallis with his charge. Wallis came up off one knee and lifted the axe handle over the falling madman, freezing at the sight of him, all wild white eyes and fresh red blood on a face below an eagle's nest of hair and sticks.

Enoch grabbed Wallis's ankle, yanking hard so the much taller man fell backwards, landing on his shoulder blades, his air blasted from his lungs with a violent *whoosh*. The madman swarmed up his body and squatted on his chest, rearing back to raise both fists overhead and bring them down once, together.

Dynamite went off behind Wallis's eyes and he felt his nose crush like a piece of fruit, hot wetness spraying across his cheeks. He squinted up through the blood and crossed his arms over his face.

"No, please!" he shouted as Enoch reared back again and lifted his terrible fists...

A woman's cry rang inside the house and Enoch turned, John Wallis forgotten just that fast.

- 6 -

Eldred Smith drew back his boot to deliver another kick when a dark and shrieking shape appeared as if conjured whole and furious on the spot and the doorway was a portal to Hell. The madman leapt and grabbed the mantle over the door, broken wood crumbling in his grip as he used it to vault into the room with single-minded purpose.

Eldred Smith had only begun to turn towards the threat when Enoch Weeks crashed into him and they fell to the floor amidst broken furniture and the shattered projects. Enoch raked and pounded, and Eldred screamed as he felt a fingernail drag across one eye, but he bucked the smaller man off of him and jerked himself up to one knee, ripping the big knife from his hip where it gleamed in the light of the lanterns, long and oiled and deadly as a snake's fang. Enoch bounced off the wall, reversed his momentum and charged, the pitch of his howl rising abruptly as the sharp blade dug into his hip and his head slammed into Smith's nose.

Both men rolled away spurting blood and noise.

Increase Mather, frozen at the sudden ferocity, a violence he had not been truly prepared for, took one giant step with his long legs and swung his axe handle in a flat arc that made a wet smack as it impacted with Enoch's ribcage. Enoch staggered sideways over a toppled table, dropping so abruptly out of sight he seemed to vanish.

"Kill him," Eldred Smith growled in a spray of blood, his dripping knife slashing the air.

"Eeeeenoch!" Annie Weeks screamed, her son's name the last sound she made on Earth as Eldred kicked her in the head.

Enoch rose from behind the furniture with a table leg in his hand and bellowed at them, cords in his neck straining, ropes of spit and blood streaming from his mouth.

"Spread out," Mather said, drawing Enoch's eyes and immediately his rush, as the madman ran partway up the beam and used it to leap, his jump sending it spinning into the back wall. Mather swung and struck Enoch in mid-air, but this time momentum carried the smaller man into the larger and they both went down in a rolling tangle, punching and swinging their weapons of wood. Eldred Smith rushed in to find an opening, only to catch Mather's elbow flush in the teeth. Smith sat down hard, his knife a glittering pinwheel as it flew from his grasp.

At that very moment John Wallis stepped through the doorway, mouth hanging open at the violent tableau. Enoch Weeks, catching movement at the periphery of his vision, spun off Mathers with simian speed and batted Wallis's jaw off its hinge so that it jutted to the side, tearing an ugly red fissure in the flesh of his face. Wallis toppled backward as if pole-axed, his eyes whirling.

Enoch leapt onto his chest, a mirror image of their pose outside the house, this time raising a length of wood overhead.

"Stop!" Eldred Smith shouted through a spray of blood.

Enoch brought the length of wood down once. Twice. Then dropped the club and ran to the netted form of his mother, the noise dying in his throat as he knelt and touched her head, feeling the dent left by the toe of Eldred Smith's boot.

He croaked a sound meant to be a word in the moment before the blade arced down and slashed across his shoulder. He spun and jerked away from the gory visage of Increase Mather clutching the axe handle in one white-knuckled fist and Smith's knife in the other.

Enoch Weeks stood slowly with his mother's body between them as Mather collapsed to one knee, then pushed himself back upright with the axe handle, the knife dripping as it jerked erratically back and forth.

"'E murdered him," Smith said, kneeling at the side of John Wallis.

Tears streamed down Enoch's face, creating riverbeds through grime and grue as his mind came into focus and he accepted, at least in a surface context, the death of his mother. The horrible knife wounds in his hip and shoulder wove together with the sharp ache of jagged bone in his ribs to send a symphonic message of agony to his brain. But Enoch Weeks knew pain beyond that in his daily life, pain which dwarfed the physical.

"I'll kill you," Mather said as he again fell to one knee, a bubble of blood exploding ludicrously from one nostril.

Enoch regarded him and did not care because he had recently discovered a pain that did not merely dwarf that of his normal life, it towered over it. It was moon-sized, planet-sized. And though he was covered in layer upon layer of filth and stank of himself, and Increase Mather was a man clothed in responsibility, a respected leader in the community, the madman's lips twisted with contempt.

"Pathetic man," Enoch said.

"I'll kill you," Mather said again. Warning. Pleading.

Enoch, temporarily himself, limped to the door and left the house that was no longer anything resembling his home.

- 7 -

Increase Mather sat against the wall, dabbing uselessly at the blood on his face. He was missing teeth and could feel the swell of blackening eyes. He kept his focus on the open door, but did not really believe the madman would return. He knew what he had seen in the other man's eyes, and it wasn't insanity. He had understood the man's words and knew them for truth.

Mather wasn't entirely certain where Eldred Smith had gone, but John Wallis lay dead not two feet from his outstretched boot, the front of his skull pushed in. He was beginning to stink, having befouled himself when his skull was crushed.

There were things to be done, adjustments to be made to the plan. He was still first selectman and had his responsibilities. But the air was fat with guilt, and Mather, weighed down with his part of it, was temporarily unable to rise.

THIRTY

- 1 -

Head wreathed in a mist of breath silvered by the full moon's light, Bone felt as if he were walking through a fiction.

"We go without lights, the way it was," Burden said as they set out into the woods. But who needed lights with a moon of such size and brilliance overhead?

Bone dragged a hand over his face and fought to clear his mind. A flashlight or lantern, as artificial as their light might be, would cast things back into the spectrum of the normal. The moonlight had a different quality than the light of day. It edged tree branches in silver and gave the leaves a faint glow. It drained colors into a spectrum of blue and rendered his companion's eyes into dark holes punched through the canvas of his face. It was as if reality had been given a small nudge, enhancing it, making things more real.

"Here," Burden said, and Bone snapped out of his reverie, looking at the long-handled shovel Burden was offering.

"Where'd you get that?"

"It was my mother's," Burden said, expression twisted. "Take it."

"Why?"

"Because I'm only three and a half feet tall," Burden said. "And because I can't stand to touch the thing."

Bone had the sense that to ask the obvious question would be to break some thin membrane of trust that existed between them. It was an instinct born of years in law enforcement. Burden was ready to talk. Needed to talk.

Bone followed as his guide moved on, Burden somehow managing to avoid twigs that popped and crackled under Bone's own feet, ducking beneath branches and avoiding bushes that Bone blundered through. He felt wooden fingers scraping his sides and poking at his hair, more than once plucking the hat from his head. Examining him.

Burden marched through a small sea of silver-tipped grass as the woods opened up into a clearing, and Bone glanced about warily, unconsciously holding the shovel at port arms as slithering sounds circled them. The distant screech of feral cats ripped the fabric of the night and just as abruptly ceased.

Bone felt the cold march of fear up his spine. He was struck by the absurdity of the moment. The sheer bizarreness that had nothing to do with normal life, even a life gone as far off the rails as his. There was no room to worry about career-ending hearings or the banal embarrassment of being a cuckold.

"Did you ever meet a census taker named Tate?" Bone asked.

"Yes," Burden said, shifting his feet, impatient.

"What happened to him?"

Burden's glance spoke volumes.

Bone looked up at a high-pitched sound as bats flew overhead in an eruption of leathery flapping. "This isn't the way to the cemetery," he said. When Burden failed to respond, the marshal caught up to him with a long stride and put a hand on his shoulder. "Where the hell are you taking me?"

"Back."

"Back? What does that mean?"

"You need to see what used to happen, so I'm taking you back."

"I don't have time—"

Burden stepped close and jabbed a thick finger into his middle. "You. Don't. Listen. You still think you're investigating a murder."

"Wait a minute—"

The little man rode over him on a tide of long-suppressed emotion. "You blunder around this way and that like your badge means something and people call you marshal to string you along," he said through gritted teeth. "You are not on the mainland, lawman. You are on the Isle, and this is its own place. Its *own* place. Do you understand me?"

Bone stepped back under the force of Burden's anger.

"Everything that happens here is for old reasons," Burden said. "You won't read the damned book, so this is how I'll show you."

"You're frightened."

"You bet I am."

"Why?"

"Because something that was withered and gone has come back, and I think it's worse this time."

"I don't understand."

"You will."

- 2 -

The trouble with grabbing a tiger by the tail is that sooner or later you have to let go. Burden looked back warily at the scarecrow stalking behind him and fought down a tide of unease. He thought that if he had composed the bit about tails and tigers he would have added an addendum. Only fools and heroes try to hang on.

Burden Ipswich was no hero, but he had plenty of evidence of foolishness.

Bone seemed strangely bemused and introverted. *Bemused* was the wrong term. *Fey*, perhaps. "Marked by an apprehension of calamity," as his dictionary might say. The simmering anger Bone displayed earlier had subsided and in its place was a weird awareness. Looking at him sheathed in moonlight caused Burden to shiver, seeing all too clearly the spectral return of Healy the Puritan.

Burden stopped to wipe tears from his eyes, irritated from whipping branches. His ear in particular was on fire and he kept touching it to check if it was bleeding.

"I need to rest a moment," he said, scrunching his feet inside his boots to ease the ache.

"Okay," Bone said.

Burden placed a hand against a moss-covered tree trunk and grimaced as his palm smeared through a row of mushrooms. He felt he was alternately hanging onto the tiger and cajoling it forward, a fool of a ringmaster with nothing but a kitchen chair between his naked throat and its yellow fangs.

"Goddammit," Bone swore behind him, and Burden heard the wet crunch of broken branches as the mainlander tripped.

The little man was surprised that he had managed to summon the force to override the marshal moments ago. He was still trembling from the rush of adrenaline. It would have been so much easier if the lawman would just read the damned book, make his discoveries and take Burden back to the mainland in the aftermath.

He wondered at the effect the Isle was having on the mainlander. Teasing some instability out into the open.

"What's that?" Bone asked.

"Water," Burden said back over his shoulder. "The stream we're looking for."

Bone stumbled and fell to one knee behind him, a branch knocking the hat from his head. As Burden looked back at the lawman fumbling on the dark ground to locate the hat, his inner monologue ground to a halt, and for a moment he saw what was, not what he *thought* it was.

Bone was no tiger to be grabbed or led.

He was a man alone and far from home and Burden was leading him into danger. Because he, Burden Ipswich, wanted to leave the Isle and was too cowardly to set off for distant shores alone. His *quid pro quo* was this: "I'll offer you terror and maybe death in return for a ticket to the mainland."

Burden's lips twisted in a sneer as the familiar cloak of self-loathing draped itself across his shoulders. Bone looked up at him, openly surprised at the little man's face.

"I tripped," Bone said.

"I am a fool and a coward." Burden snatched the hat from a bush and handed it back to the lawman. "But I like to think that I am no cad."

"What the hell are you talking about?" Bone grunted as he stood, wiping the knees of his pants.

"We're turning back."

"The hell we are."

"You should leave the Isle as soon as you can," Burden said as invisible ice fissured beneath his feet.

"What happened? Why are you saying this?"

Burden's grin was ripe with self-loathing.

"I had a moment of perfect clarity, Marshal Bone. I try to avoid them, but occasionally they sneak up behind me."

Bone glanced around, peering into the underbrush as if expecting a trap.

"I think you might still be able to leave," Burden said. "I think if you made a big enough stink, you could get someone to ride you out into radio range of the mainland."

"Why are you saying this?"

"Guilt."

"You'll get over it."

"No one wants you to see this. None of them."

"None of who? The selectmen?"

Burden shook his head in frustration. "I'm saying you might not be allowed to leave after this."

"You really are frightened."

The whites of Burden's eyes caught the moonlight. "I'm terrified."

Bone's hand unconsciously rested on the butt of the revolver.

"You might as well point that at the ground and pull the trigger for all the good it will do," Burden said.

"I have back-up coming," Bone said with finality.

Burden turned away in frustration, unable to undo his earlier salesmanship. Bone was committed and would not leave.

What if the Isle doesn't want him to leave?

Burden led the mainlander towards the sound of running water, carefully parting bushes with his hands. He heard Bone moving up behind him.

"Burden—"

"Shhh. Listen."

"Listen for what?" Bone asked, his long coat dragging along the ground as he crept up beside the dwarf, the shovel held out to one side like a bushman's spear. Burden crossed his lips with a finger.

"Imagine there's a sound—"

"What?"

"*Listen.* Imagine there's something everyone on the Isle can hear except you. We can hear it. It's real."

"What the hell are you talking about?" Bone asked, and even in the dim light Burden could read Bone's expression. But after a moment something changed in the marshal's posture. "What can you hear?"

"The trees are screaming, Marshal Bone," Burden said. "They haven't screamed since before my birth, but they're screaming again and people are dying."

"That's…" Bone trailed off when Burden held up his hand.

"Now, as you listen to the trees, I'll tell you a story," Burden whispered.

- 3 -

The boy stumbles, unable to catch himself because one wrist is trapped in his mother's iron grip. A fang of wood thrust hungrily up from the forest floor stabs his knee, and he hears the rip of his pants even as a live current of pain shoots through his body and fills his eyes with hot tears.

The boy is only four, but he does not cry. He has learned not to cry.

His father was crying as his mother dragged the boy out of the cramped warmth of their house into the cold night, but he did not ask why.

"Get up. Get up, you," his mother hisses, yanking upward so he scrambles to regain his clumsy footing.

He shivers, wet snot blocking his nostrils. His mother did not dress him in his coat, his hat or his scarf.

"Come, boy," his mother says, eyes glinting as she looks down at him with her mouth twisting into a smile more frightening than her previous anger. "Come see your new room."

Branches whip and roots trip. His mother has not brought a torch or flashlight, not even a lantern. The man in the moon does what he can to light their way, but the boy's mother leads them on pathways of shadow, avoiding the icy glow.

An owl hoots. A rat rustles through the underbrush. The boy has a desperate need to pee but does not release his bladder. He is four and has learned many things because, as the old reverend once said within his earshot, "He is frighteningly intelligent."

The rushing sound of water over rocks tells the boy where he is. A forbidden place where children do not play, but they tell stories of it, even to one such as he.

For the first time he balks, digging the worn heels of his shoes into the slippery loam.

"Not the bridge," his tiny voice cries. "Don't put me under the bridge!"

- 4 -

"I can't," Burden said, eyes fixated on the flowing quicksilver. "I can't until we pass the bridge."

"Where?"

Burden pointed at what the boy saw so many years ago. Ice ran down his spine as he watched Bone survey the ominous hulk of the bridge. The deadfall of branches and thorns crowned it in a burlesque of madman's hair, and the arch below yawned like a gaping, black mouth to inhale the stream's innocence. He had the strangest sense of *déjà vu* and knew he had seen it somewhere before.

"Your mother dragged you through that?"

Burden nodded. "I'm sorry, I need a moment," he said, eyes averted.

"If you can't go—"

Burden flapped a hand at him. "The answers you need are on the other side."

The little man still refused to look at the bridge, but he did look up at Bone's pallid countenance, noting the fixed stare, the tongue wetting dry lips.

"You're beginning to understand."

"What?" Bone said distractedly.

"The Isle is its own place."

"Through there?"

"Yes."

And then Bone did something that surprised Burden. He held out his hand.

"We can do it."

Burden reached up.

- 5 -

How to describe their passage under the bridge? The awful wet and stink of moldering stone that had never and would never see the light of the sun. The fleshy slime coating the rocks that he and Burden stumbled and slid across, both of them going under at one point. Bone's fear was enormous, and he could barely fathom the greater terror that the little man experienced as the water crested his belt.

Dank things hung from the low arch above and caressed their cheeks with rotting fingers even as sharp claws raked and jabbed at them, the wooden branches cracking like bones as Bone kicked his way through.

He was uncertain where his own labored breathing left off and Burden's began, but the Under Bridge gave it back to them in wet, whimpering echoes. The Under Bridge had a voice, a tubercular awfulness that urged them to go back, and Bone realized he had succumbed to the reality of the Isle's otherness.

Emerging into the moonlight was to be transported to a sun-drenched beach in the Caribbean. Bone looked back at the way they had come and was shocked to make out a silver glimmer on the far side of the passage. Such a short distance.

He looked down at his small companion still holding tight to his hand. Burden's eyes were wide and white, wary, as the man and boy existed simultaneously.

"We have a ways to go," Burden said, disengaging his hand. "I'll talk as we walk."

- 6 -

"Come!" the boy's mother urges, dragging him, his uneven legs churning awkwardly and his lungs straining in the torqued confines of his chest to produce oxygen enough to keep him moving. Her face is the white of a dead thing, and the jagged line of blood across her cheek is painted black. The boy's shirt is torn and his pants are sodden with water. His icy feet squelch in wet shoes. Pain and terror are beginning to transport him.

Time loses its meaning and, unbidden, tears flow down the boy's cheeks. A new knowledge is pressing inward on him, lighting his nerve endings with more sorrow than fear.

Then he is skidding on his belly, coating himself in a mess of dirt and pine needles. His mother is doubled over, one hand braced on her skirted knee and the other clutching the haft of a shovel which has been planted in the earth like a marker. Her breath wheezes, loud in the night, and almost obscures the man's voice.

Through the smear of tears, the boy looks up to see a massive, round shape detaching itself from a tree, a wild, white corona of hair surrounding its head. The boy feels a familiar chill as the moon glints off the cross hanging around the man's thick neck.

"Bless us, oh, bless us," his mother gasps.

The answer is a fierce whisper. "Speed, woman. We must be swift."

She turns to the boy, and he recoils at the twisted grotesquerie of her face. Taut and tear-streaked, her eyes bulge from the intensity of her emotion.

The boy scrambles backward but the round figure is quick. A black cane lashes out and knocks him to the ground. Before he can react, a fat hand, slimed with sweat, catches at his collar and pulls him forward. The voice is a hiss, and it will be many years before the boy understands the meaning of the word he hears: "Abomination."

"Mother," the boy cries.

"Obey the reverend," his mother responds, glancing away in shame.

"We have made a new room for you, child, a wonderful room in the forest," the reverend says, his wheedling voice full of false cheer. The boy would no sooner believe a sugar-coated sea anchor was candy than believe the voice of the fat man in black.

And then he stands on the precipice of his new room, of the hole dug in the forest floor. A blanket lines it, one the boy recognizes from his own bed. And his toys litter the floor, scattered around a dim lantern.

The boy turns in the reverend's grip and looks at his mother. A horrible, powerful, unbearable new knowledge deciphered in his frighteningly intelligent four-year-old mind.

"Go to your room, Burden," his mother says. The boy's eyes fixed on her white-knuckled hand on the haft of the shovel. "Get down in your room."

Lip quivering, he obeys, sitting on the edge of the hole and sliding down until he lands, scattering his toys. He looks back up and sees his mother standing with a shovel full of dirt above him.

"It must be done," the reverend says.

"Mother?" The boy coughs, spitting dirt from his mouth, crying openly at the grit in his eyes. He can hear her harsh sobbing, but it does not stop the next shovelful from scattering down into the hole. The figures above him go dark as the faint light vanishes, the moon hiding its face.

The boy shrieks, clutching the warmth of the lantern to his belly, afraid of the night. Dirt rains down, pebbles sliding into the collar of his shirt, bouncing off his hair. He squints through his lashes to behold the incomprehensible sight of his crossed legs covered in earth and feels the caress of what will become his lifelong companion, a concept beyond most four-year-olds.

Despair.

When the shouting happens and the lights cut through the night, he barely registers the interruption. Powerful hands hoist him free from the pull of the earth and he rises, trailing dirt into the thunder of adult argument, but he feels no sense of relief. No presence of hope.

Despair has touched him, and he knows it will be back.

- 7 -

"It was Hazel Milk's father," Burden whispered. "My own had gone to the public house to cry in his beer."

Burden trailed off as Bone worked, digging down into the packed earth that had once tried to swallow a child. An enormous maple tree loomed over them both.

"But the Isle was hungry and not to be denied," Burden continued. "My father rowed out to sea with a bottle one month later. He never returned."

Waist deep in the hole, Bone regarded the shovel in his hands. A blister had formed and burst on his right palm. "I saw this in your...in the lighthouse."

Burden squatted like a gargoyle at the edge of the hole, expression unreadable. He nodded.

"This is the same shovel? You kept it?"

Burden's eyes were unblinking white pools in the night.

"Jesus," Bone said, flinging the tool away to clatter against unseen trees. "Feels like its crawling with worms."

Burden pointed down with one thick finger. "Dig that up."

Bone squatted and scraped dirt and a slick of mold away from a small, metal box. It was badly dented and left a dark residue of rust on his hands. He handed it to Burden, who stared at it with what might have been horror. Or fury.

"I hated this fucking thing," he snarled. "It made me cry when I was a boy." He began turning a crank on the side and gravelly, off-tune carousel music filled the night. Bone shivered as tension gathered in the air. His foot nudged the edge of a rotted blanket sticking up from the dirt as he cast his gaze about the small clearing.

"Stop," Bone said as the music gained speed.

"She knew it. She knew it, and she was going to trap me down in that hole with it forever."

Burden cranked the handle faster and the music picked up tempo.

Bone was gripped with a sudden and unreasoning certainty. "I don't want to see what's inside."

Burden looked up and turned the handle one final time. And the music stopped.

"Neither do I," he said, setting it down beside him. He offered his hand to Bone, helping him emerge from the hole. Bone couldn't pull his gaze from the black pit and missed the silver streaks of Burden's tears.

"Why would your mother have done this?"

Burden spread his arms wide and cocked his foot in a jester's pose. "I am an abomination."

"Bullshit."

"Such pretty words will turn my head."

"Burden, this…what does this have to do with the murders?"

Burden moved past Bone and ran his hands along the trunk of the maple tree, tracing something Bone couldn't see. "Put your hands where mine are," he said.

Bone leaned across the hole and ran his hands along the trunk, feeling the distinct lines and grooves, curving up and across and around. "What is this?" he asked.

Burden gently traced spots on the trunk. "Eyes. Nose. Mouth." He fumbled in a pocket and pulled out a box of matches. "Now, light."

Bone pulled back as the acrid stink of sulfur stung his nostrils, but followed the bright flame with his eyes as Burden traced a distorted oval on the maple, weirdly elongated on the vertical plane. The features were similarly stretched but having been named, were recognizable. But it was the mouth that Burden lingered over with the flame, the widened curve of a grin at the top descending into an impossibly dropped bottom lip easily a foot lower, pulling the mouth painfully wide.

"A child might think the face was laughing," Burden said.

At that moment the distant howl of Enoch Weeks carried to them on the night wind. The two men looked at each other, startled, before Burden produced the stub of a fat candle from inside his coat. He lit it and ground the match into the mulch.

Bone followed as Burden led him deeper into the trees, stopping periodically to hold the candle close to a trunk. It was difficult to understand what he was seeing at first, some of the features had distorted over many decades. But by the third tree, Bone could see the quiver of a wide mouth in the flickering light, the hideous dance of eyes gaping with the horror of eternity.

"They are called the Screaming Trees," Burden said.

"Screaming?"

At one point something cracked beneath his shoe and he became aware of the scattering of lobster shells on the forest floor.

"These are all graves?" Bone asked.

Burden nodded.

"Why aren't they in the cemetery?"

"Because they are…" He stopped, searching for the word. "Rebellion."

"Graves of children?"

"Yes."

"Like you?"

Burden shrugged. "Not like me. These souls were never given a chance to grow into abominations."

Bone heard a rushing in his ears and struggled to find a coherent question. The enormity of what he was seeing was such that he didn't know where to begin. His gaze lingered on a swaying something hanging from a tree. He approached it, extending a single finger to prod it. The lobsterman swung on a loop of rusted wire. A tooth rattled in its belly.

"Why?" It was a plaintive sound. Small. Everything.

"Because we are cursed we live in isolation. Because we live in isolation our blood grows thin. When the curse manifests in a newborn child…" Burden swept his arm out, and Bone pivoted slowly on his heel, the pressure of carven eyes palpable.

"How many?" Bone asked.

"A forest. Decades before me," Burden answered, his tears starting afresh. "Longer."

"My God."

"You don't want to meet the God of this place." Burden's smile was hideous. "But, my, look at how strong and true the trees have grown!"

A gobbet of spit was flung from Burden's lips, and Bone watched as the little man closed his eyes and regained control through sheer force of will.

"This way."

Accompanied by another distant howl from the tormented Enoch Weeks, Burden led Bone to a small clearing under the guard of a young tree. The ground was newly disturbed. Bone could make out a freshly carved face on the tree bole. The speckled shell of the lobsterman hanging from a branch still gleamed with recent memories of the sea.

"Pruitt," Burden said.

Bone struggled to ask a meaningful question. "These babies were still-born?" He struggled to hold Burden's wet stare.

"They survived birth. Our children are given back to the curse as soon as it manifests, even if that moment is the child's first breath," Burden whispered. "It is the unspoken center of our belief. Those children are never seen again."

"But I thought the parents buried them here."

"These graves hold only the broken hope of what might have been."

"Where are the bodies?"

Burden waved his arm vaguely again. "With the curse."

"Who did this?"

Burden's eyes gleamed. "Ask yourself, *who is dying?*"

"The constable and—" Bone caught himself. "The leadership. The leadership is dying." Bone paused. "Burden, who is doing the killing?"

"Ask yourself, who is hurting?"

"This isn't a serial killer, is it?"

"No."

"Did Richard Slocum know about this? Is that why he was killed?"

"Yes and yes."

"And he would have used it," Bone said, and Burden nodded. "Do you know who, specifically, killed the constable?"

"No. Maybe."

"More than one person?" Bone didn't wait for the answer as he walked to the tree and touched it, fingers scraping audibly down the smooth bark, imagining what he would feel if a child were taken from him to feed some morbid belief. The breath left him in a whoosh and his head swam as realization struck.

"This isn't murder. This is civil war." Bone looked at Burden and waited for him to nod. "Who is at the center of this?"

"You know," Burden said.

Bone pictured the kind figure of the reverend bending over him, caring for him. The reverend surrounded by the selectmen, so hostile to Bone's presence.

"The church looms over the entire town," Bone said, not realizing he had done so until Burden responded.

"The church casts its shadow over everything on the Isle," Burden said.

Bone wandered away, bracing his hand against a tree. "The bodies of the children are gone," he paused, making the connection. "What about the bodies of the recent victims? Same place?"

"Given to the curse, I suspect."

"The fuck does that actually mean? Out in the water?"

"Yes, but, I think I may know where they are given to the sea."

"Specifically?"

"Specifically."

"Shit. That book, it details what's been happening with the children?"

"More than a century of infanticide."

"I don't know when *Leviathan* will return with help. We need to get that book to the mainland," Bone said. "Tonight."

Burden shook his head at Bone as if at a slow pupil. "You don't know if *Leviathan* will return with help."

The obviousness of Burden's statement thundered through Bone.

"We need to get the book to the mainland, and us too," Burden said.

"If I leave, will this thing break open?" Bone asked.

"It already has."

"They'll kill the reverend, maybe others. Mather."

"Not if we bring back help. You can't stop this by yourself." Burden pointed at the star on the marshal's chest. "They've been shining you on and as long as you stayed dumb, they were content to do that. As soon as everyone realizes you understand what's happening…" He shook his head.

Bone cursed under his breath. "First things first, I need to see that book. I'll think while we walk." He started off but stopped abruptly. "This curse, it's real?"

Burden shrugged. "People think it is. Maybe on the Isle, it is."

"Why are you cursed?"

"Oh, that," Burden said, lifting the candle flame to light his face from below. "Our ancestors were cannibals."

- 8 -

Bone blundered beneath the bridge in Burden's wake, impervious to the stinging whip of branches. He caught up with him on the far side.

As Burden picked his way up the bank, Bone looked back down the flow and saw the bridge in the clear moonlight. He felt the frisson of connection and scrambled up after Burden.

"Hazel took a photo of this place," he said. "She knows about the Screaming Trees."

"Everyone knows."

THIRTY-ONE

- 1 -

The Isle folk called it a night shadow, when the sky was clear enough and the moon bright enough to throw the church steeple's shade across their rooftops. A weary terror gripped the town as it crouched in the night shadow, beneath the greater dark of the church, the Isle folk one and all were haunted by expectation.

- 2 -

Honor Pruitt's drawn face was a study in shifting shadows, a Halloween mask of orange and black, the planes of her face lit from below by the burning logs in the fireplace. Her eyes hid in the dark hollows of their sockets, the eyes of a jack-o'-lantern with no fire inside, ignoring the bustle of shapes in the dark room as she watched a single, yellow gobbet of fat swirling atop the bubbling liquid in the path of her great, wooden spoon.

"And the rosemary." Picked from the Isle.

"And the salt." Gathered from the shore.

"And the mushrooms." Harvested among the trees.

The other women took turns approaching the enormous, black cauldron, left to Honor by her grandmother and used every year since its forging to prepare stew enough to feed the entire community.

"And the sage." Grown in every woman's garden.

"And the wild onions." Dug from the western slope.

"And the chives." Cut by each of them.

Each woman released a pinch into the pot as Honor continued stirring, blending the flavors together. The wooden spoon scraped around the pot's great rim, blackened and pitted with age. The flames below licked directly against the round metal as they had done for near on to a century. Finally Honor lifted her head and looked at the gathered women in the dark kitchen.

"And the meat," Honor said.

Feet scuffed and skirts rustled as each of the women reached into a great, wooden bowl and drew forth a dripping fistful of meat, approaching to drop the slimy mass into the pot accompanied by plops and splashes.

"And the meat."

"And the meat."

"And the meat."

Potatoes would be added later. As would carrots and turnips. The bubbling stew would simmer through the night as Honor stirred it round and round. It would be the prize of the feast. It would be special.

Honor flinched when the spoon struck a small, metal object buried beneath the burbling surface. Soon, however, the muted clink became a natural part of the evening and ceased to have meaning.

- 3 -

The men had gathered in the public house and kept Eaton Fenn busy behind the bar as young and old listened to an exhausted Increase Mather inveigh against the madman. "Finally gone murderous and with his own ma'am." The stature and wounds of Mather and Smith were enough to convince many of the men, who were eager to reimagine Gentle Annie as a victim to be avenged instead of the sordid outcast and mother of grotesquery that she was.

Beneath a growing cloud of cigarette smoke, the younger men were centered around Jeremiah Pruitt with his bandaged ankle propped on a chair. Big Jon Tuttle made a joke about witch's brews and Jeremiah took a good-natured swipe at him, almost toppling from his chair while the rest of them laughed. They were drinking heavily and seemed less concerned about the death of Gentle Annie than their elders. Their merriment drew a glare from the fearsomely battered countenance of Eldred Smith, but they shrugged it off with an attitude more appropriate to juvenile delinquents than seasoned Isle men in their twenties and thirties.

- 4 -

Feeling the noise from the common room through her bare feet, Hazel Milk stood naked in the bathroom, studying herself in the mirror. Her breasts were pleasingly firm, she thought, and her belly unmarked by pregnancy. Vague thoughts stirred by the arrival of the marshal were gathering into something like resolve. She suspected if he returned to the inn before she went to sleep, she would join him in his room. What would come from that was a fog-shrouded sea.

Goosebumps pebbled her pale skin and tightened her nipples at the thought, but she worried about the attraction, worried that it had more to do with his scarring, both visible and not, and the gaping loneliness she thought she could fill. It was better to think about this, to focus on why she should not be drawn to him. Because to be drawn to him might mean...

Leaving the Isle. And there her thinking ran into a grey wall that extended into the sky as high as she could see and to the horizons both east and west.

"Virgil," she said aloud, and cracks spread across the great barrier. She shivered physically in reaction, glancing behind her reflection to see if anyone had witnessed the blasphemy in her heart as she allowed herself the fantasy of sailing back to the mainland to embark on a new life. To leave the Isle. To leave them all.

- 5 -

Ambrose Tinker stifled a yawn and sat with Reliance, the wife of the late John Wallis, offering what comfort and explanation he could, but mostly listening. Comfort was like that, he had learned. It was being present until the clouds of sorrow parted and the sufferer could see they were not alone. The lighting was intentionally dim, and he thought it was not flattering to the other women that had gathered, washing out what color was left to their hair and drawing attention to wrinkles and wattles alike. They spent a good deal of time talking and sniping, and to the reverend it sounded like a nest of birds squawking over each other in an effort to be fed.

- 6 -

Mary Nutter crept out of bed and past the sleeping form of Hedde Smith, her movements masked by the older woman's robust snoring.

Barefoot and in her nightgown, Mary picked her way to a narrow stretch of cliff a good half hour from her home.

The foaming surf struck the cliff, vibrating in her shins like tuning forks.

She breathed deeply, expanding her ribcage, enjoying the wakening effect of the crisp air. She held the breath, feeling the cold over her whole body, a complete awareness. Upon exhaling, she said, "It's all right," and threw herself into the sea.

THIRTY-TWO

- 1 -

The tower thrummed from the crashing waves as Bone read by candle-light, the words slithering on the page as if attempting to free themselves of their paper bondage. The whistling sea wind slipped through cracks in the lighthouse windows and tried to pluck the pages from his fingers, furthering the illusion of escape.

"I don't like touching it," Bone said. "I know that sounds weird."

Burden's mouth curved into a humorless smile. "And you're wondering if it's the spine of moldering lobster shells or is it the thing itself."

Bone, who had once held the snapshot work of a pedophile in his hands, said, "Both."

"Some of it is written so…" he trailed off, looking at Burden for help.

"Lovingly?"

"Yes. But how?"

"You're reading from Reverend Wallace," Burden said, picturing the fat man standing over his young self as the dirt poured down. "He was a different sort than Reverend Tinker."

Somewhere in the dark lighthouse below a cat howled as Bone flipped carefully forward and scanned the text, the illustrations. "I can't read the Latin, but even Tinker's writing—shit, I can't believe Tinker…" He caught himself again and shook away his disbelief. "I'm not sure what I'm trying to say."

"Just say it," Burden said.

Bone looked at the shadows dancing on the stone walls. "There's so much detail, it's almost like they love it. I mean, they're capturing ev-erything. Shining a fucking spotlight on it. There's no attempt to cover over… Cannibalism? Infanticide? I mean, Jesus fucking Christ."

"I take it you haven't talked to many priests?" Burden asked.

Bone leaned back and the wooden chair creaked as he shook his head. He was staring out the windows at the starry night over the black nothing below. It was cold and both men still wore their coats. Burden had not lit a fire, only the few candles.

"I have intimate acquaintance with two, Wallace and Tinker. And priests, reverends, whatever you want to call them, live in a very different place from us, immersed in belief, perpetuating belief. It's their reason for being," Burden said.

"But even if that guy Wallace was a complete bastard, Tinker seems…" Bone imagined the man caring for him. "He was very kind, very helpful."

Burden paced the length of the tower room, nudging a stack of books aside with his foot. Now he was the one looking for a path to expression. "But if the belief, the reason for being is rooted in something bad…no… something evil, what will happen to a man who consorts with it so completely, so intimately?" He stopped and pointed at Bone. "You read about the original event in there."

"Most of it was in Latin," Bone said.

"Fine, but Reverend Tinker also told you some of that story, didn't he? Why would he tell that to you? A lawman?"

"I don't know."

"To frighten you away?" Burden asked, shaking his head. "He wanted you to understand because he is caretaker of the community *and* its curse."

"And then I dreamed about it."

Burden nodded. "And then you understood it."

"But what did he think I'd do?"

"What can you do?"

Bone tipped the book shut with a loud clap. "We can't let this continue. You grew up here. What we do will… Burden, it will change everything."

"Marshal Bone," Burden said and moved in his sliding way to place one gnarled hand on the book's cover. "This is my history, but I would burn this thing right now if I thought it was the right way to smash this." He waved a hand inland. "Smash it all."

Burden wondered at the sense of purpose that rode on the night wind. Nothing like he had felt when contemplating his flight from the Isle. The sordid excitement of his dealing with Slocum. He stumped over to the mirror and regarded his own hated face. "It twisted me from birth in a way everyone can see." He made a horrible face at his own reflection and looked at Bone. "The guilt of it has twisted everyone here."

The words, which might have struck Bone like a blow only days before, instead rang true. He understood guilt, or was at least on a path towards understanding. The wind gusted and howled and he saw Burden cock his head to one side, his expression abruptly quizzical.

"The wind?" Bone said.

Burden shook his head. "Enoch Weeks. But he never comes down here. He's afraid of the old village."

Bone rose and the candle flames waved inward at him as he stretched aching bones. He crossed to the windows and braced his hands on the stones, sensing a telegraph tapping against the tower.

A black crow fluttered in the open window, pin feathers flared and furious. It fixed him with an ugly, yellow eye and flew back out with a scream.

"Burden?"

"Yes?"

"I want you to bring a boat back to the tower. Something that will at least get us out into radio range of the fishing traffic."

"I can do that," Burden said, thinking of the boat he would steal. "What about the book?"

"Take it with you on the boat. Keep it there."

"What about you?"

Bone did a slow push up against the wall, nose touching the shivering glass window. "I'm going up to the public house to get Hazel."

Burden's rush of emotion at her name was interrupted by another, piercing howl from below.

"Burden?"

"Yes?"

"There are lights coming this way."

Burden hurried to the wall and peered inland. Bobbing fireflies were pouring down the dark hill.

"They're in the old village." He squinted. "I think they're chasing some-one."

The identical thought struck both men, but only Burden whispered the name.

"I think things just broke out into the open," Bone said.

Bone swept back his coat and drew the revolver, spinning it in his hand to offer the butt to Burden. "Take this with you. Use it if you have to. Leave if I don't come back, but get that goddamned book to the mainland. The book is the priority."

"How long should I wait for you?"

"Your call."

"What about you?" Burden asked, sliding the pistol barrel through his belt.

Bone touched the star on his coat.

- 2 -

Burden pounded awkwardly along the shoreline, dodging inland where the tide had come in to swallow the beach. He crested a dune, pushing through sharp grass high enough to slash at his cheeks, stopping at its crest only when the pain in his legs became unbearable and he doubled over, panting, one hand pressed against his side as if to staunch a bleeding wound, unable to quench the burning stitch.

Gradually the pain lessened and his breath slowed. He opened his eyes, tear-blurred vision transforming the scuttling night crabs into a movement of the dune itself. White ghost crabs, spirits of the pale sand. He stood, pulling the pistol from its uncomfortable position in his belt and stuffing it into a deep coat pocket.

"Take the gun back," Burden had said as they stood on the beach with his tower looming behind them and separation before them. The water boomed, an old man's wordless bellow.

"You take it," the marshal had said.

"You'll need it."

"*You'll* need it."

Bone had placed a hand on Burden's shoulder and looked down in a way so lacking in condescension that Burden was shocked by its novelty.

"If this won't work," Bone had said, patting his golden star. "Then six bullets won't be enough to help me, but they might help you."

"I can't go to the mainland alone," Burden had said. "No one will listen to me."

"You're a compelling witness and they will listen to you, Burden. Now go."

Bone had turned away but Burden called him back.

"Without your gun, they'll kill you," Burden had said, voice raising in anger. "Why are you doing this?"

Bone's teeth were a flash of white, there and then gone.

"Because you told me that Enoch Weeks was too frightened to hurt anyone," Bone had said. "And *I* listened to you."

On the dune, Burden touched the pistol and looked back down the beach to the dark spire of his tower, the lights put out before they descended the circling iron stairs. Nothing moved but the wind-sheared grass around him and the glowing white roll of the surf as it destroyed itself on the shore. He wished the marshal had carried the gun so he could have heard the shots and know who won. There were no more shouts, no more of Enoch's howls. Whatever had happened in the old village had happened already, and it was not his to know.

- 3 -

The roar of the sea flattened into a steady background noise as Bone sprinted over the bed of shells towards the old village. His breath whistled between his parted teeth, and his coat caught the wind, flapping behind him like great wings.

A shifting patch of blackness flapped over his head and cawed lustily as he passed the waist-high foundations of what had once been gibbets. The hat blew from his head and he let it tumble behind him, not his, never his. A scream pierced the night and Bone could hear the pain in it. The terror. He heard as well the muttering undercurrent of the hunting men, channeled through mausoleum streets and amplified by them, as if the crumbling place was eager for what was to come.

Bone passed below vacant bedroom windows empty in their ignorance and want. The ground rippled before him as vermin scattered. Denizens of corners and holes crouched at his intrusion.

He slipped once, down to one knee and up again with burning palms slapped down to catch his fall. An ankle like fire. Eyes watering from the caress of cold air.

Running.

The shouting grew louder, almost words now. He began to see flashes of illumination. He flew through a black-and-white film, the kind shown late at night when the airtime was cheap and it mattered not a bit if the old special effects looked real. The castle-like tower was a set. The villagers carrying torches were extras. He was only an actor.

Everything that is happening is really happening. The thought clear enough he said it aloud. "Everything that is happening is really happening." The words spit out between breaths. Necessary. Focusing.

The space before him opened up, and he took in the round hump of the ancient well and the crumpled form at its base. He skidded to a stop in a spray of shells. He knelt and the sharp stab of a clamshell refocused him into the moment. The madman was curled in on himself, an animal protecting its wounds. Blood as dark and thick as motor oil gleamed, and Bone placed his hand on a shivering bare shoulder. Enoch went taut and Bone spoke quickly, the first words that came to mind.

"I'm here."

The curled form seemed to flow through itself, it turned so quickly. Pipe-stem arms wrapped around his middle with alarming strength, and the madman pressed his matted horror of hair and branches into Bone's coat. "Help me."

Bone stood with Enoch Weeks in his arms, the body no more than a bundle of sticks. So slight. So light.

Glowing flames surged into the square, the men beneath a chaotic array of goggling eyes and bared teeth, shouts a meaningless tumult of bestial rage.

Flashlights converged on him from front and back, white beams stabbing like searchlights, roaming across his body and the wounded man in his arms. His marshal's star flared and they homed in on his face, beam after beam to blind him. Bone remembered the first night in the graveyard, the constable aiming his flashlight into his eyes. The contest of it.

Everything that was happening was really happening. Bone felt the heat in his chest from tortured lungs, his legs aching from the hard run and his ankle gone from fire to icy agony. His shoes crunched as he turned in place, and he could feel a slick of blood draining into his hands and running down his wrists, inside the sleeves of his coat. The black harbinger cawed overhead, and the wind screamed, pulling at his hair. Bone's awareness had never been so huge.

"Give him to us."

"No."

THIRTY-THREE

- 1 -

Hazel sat upright, startled at unfamiliar surroundings lit by a dancing candle flame in a glass lantern.

The door shook again in its frame, and she registered the heavy tread of someone beyond it. A man's tread.

She threw back the blankets and slid her feet to the floor, wincing at the touch of cold wood, rubbing sleep from her eyes as she hurried to the door, taking a moment to consider and disregard the wild fly of her hair, her blouse untucked from her wrinkled skirt.

She unfastened the latch and pulled open the door.

"Virg—" She stopped mid-word as she took in the sight of Jeremiah Pruitt leaning heavily on a cane. "What is it?" A roaring filled her ears with certain knowledge.

"There's been some trouble," Jeremiah began, rubbing one hand compulsively over his whiskered chin.

"Is it Virgil? Marshal Bone?"

Jeremiah held up his hand, and she caught herself. "Enoch Weeks went crazy is what 'e are saying. Killed several people including 'is ma."

"Gentle Annie?"

Jeremiah nodded. "'E were chased and caught in the old village," Jeremiah paused and shivered. "Nets, 'e see? Several men became tangled... Oh, Hazel, they tumbled into the old well."

"Virgil?"

Jeremiah nodded. "Honor said she knew 'e had been close and would want to know."

Hazel felt the rush of blood warming her brain and seemed to rise above herself, her own words emitted by a distant imposter.

"We need to get ropes and a pulley. They may be injured—"

Jeremiah shook his head. "The tide came in," he said. "It came in before anything could be done, according to Increase Mather."

The name struck her like a slap and clarity returned in a cold rush.

"And Burden?" Hazel asked.

Confusion danced across the fisherman's open features. "'E wasn't mentioned."

"Of course not," Hazel said, turning to sit on her bed and pull on her wool socks and boots.

"There are injured men up at the church bein' tended to by the reverend," Jeremiah offered.

Hazel rose and clomped across the boards to brush past Jeremiah. She descended the stairs heavily, one hand on the wall as if drunk, entering the common room to find a subdued crowd of older men drinking somberly. They were rough and filthy, reeking of drying sweat. The familiar smells of beer and stale grease filled her with nausea and the room tilted.

"Where is Increase Mather?" she asked to the room where the men gaped at her with mixed surprise and hostility.

"Up at the church bein' tended," Arn Corn finally responded, perched on a stool near her elbow.

"The marshal fell into the well and you men couldn't lower a rope? Is that so?" Hazel asked as a log shifted in the fireplace with an explosion of sparks. She was met by black muttering.

Hazel recoiled as Arn Corn leaned closer, his powerful breath laced with whiskey. "'E wasn't the only one, 'e precious lawman. Eldred Smith fell—" He stopped with a scream, clutching the red furrows in his cheek even as he toppled backwards off the stool.

Hazel loomed over the fallen drunkard, her hand hooked in a claw. "Don't you mention his name in the same sentence, in the same hour—"

Rough hands grabbed her and pulled her back with a rip of fabric. She whirled and swung wildly, the smack of her palm across Otter Tindle's wrinkled face like wood against wood. He reeled back clutching the red imprint on his cheek, tearing her blouse along the shoulder seam.

"You..." she hissed, words failing to express the growing ball of fire in her guts. Chairs skidded back and several men stood, surrounding the slit-eyed, wild-haired woman.

"You're not men enough," she snarled, a bright speck of spittle clinging to her lip.

"Hey!" Jeremiah bellowed from the stairs where he stood with the cane clutched in both white-knuckled fists like a woodsman's axe.

Hazel met Jeremiah's gaze and stood, brushing back her hair with her fingers, allowing the torn blouse to fall open enough to reveal the strap of her bra and the pale swelling of one breast. She let the men drink it in before she spit on the muddy floorboards. She banged out the door, leaving it open behind her. Cold air swept inside and napkins blew off of tables as the bell over the door jangled.

"Harpy!" Arn Corn shrieked, holding out his blood-smeared palm.

Jeremiah made his painful way across the room after her, cane tocking in counterpoint to his boot heels, and paused in the doorway. "Isn't enough drink for what ails you men," he said, pulling the door closed behind him.

- 2 -

One end of the room basked in the orange glow from the fireplace, the rest of it an indeterminate space filled with fragrant steam, rendering the women into indistinct shapes that left eddies in their wake.

They regarded Hazel's disheveled state, but no one offered her a hand or asked after her well-being. It was not a night for well-being.

Hazel stared at her old friend seated by the fireplace in timeless repose, sheathed in luminous steam as if she had transcended her station. No longer a woman but an icon. A painting. A purpose.

It was old, this thing they did, and words were not needed.

Hazel held out her hand to one side, never seeing the woman who placed something into her palm. She squeezed her fist and held it to her nose, then walked towards the warm fire and the steaming cauldron.

"And the mint," Hazel said, feeling the heat and condensation gathering on her wrist as she opened her palm and let the crushed mint leaves fall into the broth.

Honor Pruitt stared up at her and stirred the pot.

"And the meat," Honor said.

Hazel nodded. "And the meat."

THIRTY-FOUR

- 1 -

The man's eyes bulged—Bone remembered his name was Woody. He remembered accepting a handheld cigarette from him in return for a lurid story. Woody's eyes bulged as Bone's slim stiletto punched into his belly. Bone heard the sound—the sharp pop of bubble wrap—and felt the weird shock of it up his arm as hot, alcoholic breath splashed across his face.

It was a memorable sensation, stabbing a man.

The nets had been flying, men trying to pry Enoch Weeks from Bone's arms. Bone screaming. Everybody screaming. Blows thudding off his numb shoulders and head. His ear sang with hot agony, and he remembered the still-burning torch swung like a club.

On his knees tangled in fishing nets and men, Enoch Weeks bound to him by the same idiot savages trying to pull him away, the blade leapt into his hand of its own volition. The metal fang snapped free and struck out, slashing, stabbing, until angry shouts transformed into bellows of pain.

Then the force of them moved Bone and Enoch in the midst of a rugby scrum, the stone lip of the well striking the back of Bone's legs as he over-balanced, clutching desperately as a tangled tumble of men went down.

But that had already happened.

Bone opened his eyes and registered faint shapes below him and an immense pressure in his head. A small circle of light showed two pairs of boots stretched out, presumably connected to men in repose. He sipped air in shallow breaths, choking on the stink of rotting seaweed and long-dead fish.

A crawling sensation. Something in his hair. Pain erupted in his arm when he tried to brush the spidery crawler away. He offered a feeble moan and might have said, "There are hooks in my arm."

Pressure in his head.

Blackness.

- 2 -

In his dream he had been telling Julia about it all. The absurdity. The Treasure Island bullshit of dangling upside down in an abandoned well that stank of forgotten seas and buried treasure.

Julia.

He awoke.

The pain was incredible, the pressure in his head such that he felt it would burst like an overripe grape. He fought back a moan as he registered the tangle of netting, shifting and bouncing against the side of the well, gritty with salt crystals. His coat pulled against the hooks and he began to jerk and twist, bouncing harder against the salty stones, this insult so minor he ignored it even when his head exploded with stars.

It was several seconds—minutes perhaps—before he noticed the sandbar rising out of shallow water below him.

Fresh boot prints marred the sand.

Panic punched him in the adrenal glands and he thrashed, shouting wildly, the jabbing pull of the hooks only amplifying his unreasoning fear.

He heard the hollow boom of a drum and a spray of Atlantic water coated him, carrying with it his wife's name. His wife's voice.

"This is happening," she said, and he caught the ragged hem of his emotions and pulled it to his chest. *Boom.* Wetness.

The tide.

He felt a tickle inside his cuff and scrabbled at it, batting away something hard and many legged. Desperation powered him as the crawling sensation grew, so much more terrifying than the pain of the hooks, and he patted his pockets with his free hand but his flashlight was missing. There, a lump. He fished it free.

Julia's phone.

A thumb slimed with something unidentifiable slipped across the button until he concentrated and pressed it, the faint glow from the screen near to a sunrise for the lift in spirits it brought. Quickly he panned the light over his chest and up towards his tangled legs.

Hundreds—no, *thousands*—of black, scuttling things moving across his body and the strands of netting like spiderwebs, he the fly. He shrieked, twisted and tore, only by some miracle keeping hold of the phone as his body jackknifed free, and the wail of terror became a scream of bright pain.

His feet punctured the soft sand and a puss-like eruption of crabs burst forth. He fell back against the jagged rock wall, brushing frantically at his hair and clothes, scattering the hungry crabs from him. Ocean sounds filled his hearing, as if he was inside the world's largest conch shell. He struggled to slow his breath and his panic subsided, his emotions too exhausted to operate at a fever pitch.

A sea cave was where he found himself. The well emptied into a sea cave where the tide swept the bodies out to the eager embrace of Old Man Atlantic.

It really was Treasure fucking Isl—

A sound cut against the natural rhythm.

Bone lifted the phone like a talisman and thumbed the button in time to see the predatory grin of Eldred Smith, knife blade held between his teeth, the eyes above it seething with blue hate as the fisherman crept towards him. Eldred's bloodied face twisted in rage as the light bathed him, and he rumbled into a charge, water geysering as he splashed through a glimmering subterranean tide pool.

No gun. No knife. Bone reached up and grabbed the dangling bit of fish net, letting the pain of the hooks fuel him as he lifted his knees and dropped his weight suddenly. The net came free from whatever protuberance had caught it and Bone landed hard on his backside, teeth clicking together as the net piled in his lap and a length of wood slammed painfully into his collarbone.

He rolled sideways in a clumsy tumble, splashing down a shallow bank into water and darkness even as Eldred's boots punched into the wet sand and he stumbled. Bone reared up onto his knees and tossed the net, which flew against Eldred's trousers, hooks catching, wrapping his legs until the big fisherman toppled into the cave wall.

Bone knew he had only moments before the powerful Isle man recovered and he overrode his pain, bursting from the water to drive his shoulder into Eldred Smith's back, piling the older man face-first into the rocks. Smith sagged to his knees and clutched at his face even as Bone kicked him hard in the kidney.

The fight was clumsy and brutal. Bone straddled the other man, raining wild blows, leaning close to slam his right elbow down, hearing the crunch of Eldred Smith's nose in the moment before the fisherman's probing knife reached through his coat and scored his ribs. Bone leaned back and the bigger man heaved, arching his back, rolling the marshal from atop him.

Bone rocked up to his feet, teeth bared and hands hooked in animal fury.

Smith was gone.

Bone held his breath and listened, heard the splashing footsteps of his opponent fleeing through shallow water, swallowed by the darkness of a cave mouth.

Exhaustion swamped him and Bone reeled back, catching himself against the rough, stone wall.

"Fuck, oh, fuck…"

His lungs burned with exertion and he pressed the heels of his palms against his temples until the black circle stopped compressing his vision.

"Help!" he shouted up the well shaft, not sure what he expected. Several more cries elicited no response.

Julia's phone was lost and the dim light from the well above was nearly useless. Bone dropped to his knees and patted the sand with his hands, jerking back when he touched the moving shape of a crab. There. Wood. He felt along it and lifted the unlit torch, muttering wordless thanks that it was dry enough to catch when he put flame to it. After a minute of carefully averting his breath, the tip of the torch licked with a small, blue fire. A shifting, untrustworthy light, but so much better than no light at all.

He lifted the torch into the well shaft and quickly determined there was no way he would be able to climb out without assistance.

Water shifted across his shoes and he turned away from the shaft to figure out exactly where he was.

He was standing on what appeared to be a sandbar. Sea caves swallowed his torchlight to the left and to the right, and he quickly ruled out the latter when he saw a foaming rise of water belch forth from it to wash across the sandbar. He wondered how long he had until high tide.

Eldred Smith had gone in the other direction, perhaps a way out. Bone lowered the torch and studied the sand, noting the drag marks visible next to Smith's deep boot prints.

As if someone had dragged a body.

Bone knelt, lowering his face and the light to make out faint traces of yet another set of footprints. A person traveling barefoot.

"Enoch?" Bone called out, hearing only the swirl of water and slap of waves in response.

Bone waded into the ankle-deep water after Smith, pausing once when his foot came down on something brittle that snapped beneath it. He crouched, reaching into the water with his free hand to lift the tiny ribcage free.

He replaced the gleaming white array of infant bones and was surprised when his eyes prickled with tears. He decided to offer the nameless child a moment of silence, some form of communion was required in this wet Hell, when a sudden movement beneath the surface startled him and he sat down hard in the water, only realizing after the fact it was a small lobster scooting away with its weird, backwards propulsion.

He rose and shook himself off before moving farther into the cave.

- 3 -

Bone crouched in the water and held his torch next to the seated man, still leaking from the removal of nose, eyes and feet.

Woody.

The corpse was seated in a stony pool that came up to his belt, and Bone had the sensation of small shapes fleeing when he splashed up to it. Forced himself not to look at the walls which crawled with movement in the uneven firelight.

He turned away, covering his mouth, and froze.

A high-pitched sound. Damp and chirping.

Wavelets splashed across the surface of the pool and Bone caught movement from the corner of his eye, spinning with a great disturbance of water to see Woody shifting against the wall.

"Woody?"

But he was dead, so clearly dead and…

A gleaming blackness twisted within the open wound in his gut, something too hard to be an organ.

"Oh, Christ." Bone staggered away.

He splashed water on his face and into his mouth with his free hand, spitting away the taste before he lifted his torch overhead and moved on, the water churning quietly in his wake.

- 4 -

Bone crouched at the edge of a great pool, watching the shifting surface of the water, hoping to catch sight of it again. Hoping he was wrong, that fear and suggestion were playing tricks on him. It was the third great cave, near the entrance, the scope of it ballooning open before him, foul green light reflecting back from his weak torch.

The air in the cave tasted bad and he sipped shallow breaths, battling back a creeping paranoia that insisted he was slowly suffocating.

There! He saw the black, swaying object break the surface some twenty feet away as if waving at him. An object impossible to identify unless you knew what you were looking at already.

A claw.

A low moan of naked emotion leaked from him. The lobsters were getting larger.

He spun, torch thrust at the cave mouth behind him, at the swaying strands of seaweed so like hag's hair, the odd, breathing quality of the shifting breeze. Shadows twitched and took on the shape of letters, and Bone closed his eyes, unwilling to read them. He fought the urge to understand them, to comprehend his surroundings. Insanity.

"Stop it, you jackass." His voice elicited a wet chirp in response from somewhere unseen.

Another warbling bird sound, reminding Bone of water whistles they had played with as children. Wavelets slapped at the subterranean beach. God how he hurt.

Eventually he acknowledged his dwindling torch and followed Smith's footprints towards the cavern wall where he stepped gingerly through the shallows, one hand on the slimy stone, the other holding his flame out over the liquid surface as he hunted for movement.

Unchallenged and grown huge, aggressive, cannibalistic.

He had seen and stepped on countless shells, driving jagged bits of lobster armor into the sand. Crushing it underfoot on seaweed-slick rocks.

He made out the serpentine shape of a deliberate current in the center of the small lake and wondered what caused it. A spring? A change in salination? He beheld the scattering of bone fragments only partially unearthed on a subterranean beach. A bleached human skull quite identifiable, as was the mostly intact jawbone of a shark, lined with needle-sharp teeth. Bits of driftwood, polished smooth by decades. Jungle-like falls of seaweed from wall and ceiling. He pushed through it while tiny shapes fell into his hair and clung.

A line of foam raced across the water and Bone heard the hollow boom of the surf. The tide was coming for him. He reached the far shore and another arched opening in time to see not only boot prints, but a single, barefoot impression in the sand before the lake behind him overflowed and surged past his sodden shoes, washing into the winding passage forward.

Bone looked over his shoulder and saw a pair of claws break the surface, lowering his torch to make out a black, breadbox-sized shape that crawled towards his left foot.

He turned and splashed beneath the jagged archway, ignoring the ominous clacking sound behind him. He ran the fingers of one hand along the wall for guidance, discovering a smooth surface like the inside of a clamshell. Bone felt as if he were moving through the digestive system of a great creature, larger than anything living in all of history. A series of stomachs sloshing with juices.

He stepped carefully downslope, resisting the miniature waterfall that tried to sweep him into the shallow body of water spreading out before him. He fought the notion that he descended great stone stairs, their pitted levels washed clean of sand by the incoming flood.

A hard shape banged against his heel and he jerked aside in panic as a lobster tumbled past, a revolving animal turret in green and black that splashed into the lake.

Another surge struck and Bone leapt out of the waterfall to land on a sandy bank to one side, nearly dropping his torch. As in the other caves, the pearly walls reflected back and amplified his torchlight with the decaying taint of Jenny Green Teeth, seen only a few days and a lifetime ago.

So caught up was Bone with his observation of the space itself, a great domed cavern even larger than the others, that he failed to notice the drama taking place in the center of the shallow water until a bellow of outrage drew his attention.

Bone looked up to see the impossible, the crazed form of Enoch Weeks charging from a small sandbar dead center in the lake. The water seethed around him, claws breaching the surface clacking in anger. Bone's ears were assaulted by the maddened chirping of a thousand drowning birds. Enoch went under the water as if something pulled him, but was up in an instant, a flailing dervish of motion until he sprang onto a beach across the cavern some fifty yards from Bone. Wild-eyed and keening, Enoch pressed his back against the wall and began edging around the pool, eyes fixed on the turbulent water.

"You bastard!"

Eldred Smith remained behind on the sandbar, isolated in the middle of the lake.

The Isle man saw Bone's torchlight and fixed him with desperate eyes. "Marshal, for the love of God, 'e must help!"

Bone was frozen in horrified wonder as he saw the burbling tumult in the water around Eldred Smith's island. Unable to stop himself he cried out, "Run!"

"I can't!" Smith wailed. "The madman has left his blood in the water and they awaken!"

"This way!" Bone's head jerked around as if on strings to see Enoch Weeks waving desperately. "Come! Come!"

Bone shook himself as another wave surged in from the previous cavern and rolled down the worn, stone steps.

How can there be steps—

Something grabbed ahold of his pant cuff and he screamed in revulsion, kicking hard against the stone wall until the clinging lobster exploded in a burst of white meat and liquid.

"Come!" Enoch repeated.

Bone's paralysis broke and he ran around the edge of the subterranean lake, high-stepping, splashing through knee-deep water with reckless speed, too fast for the crustaceans to react to his passage. The incredible, furious clicking sound was deafening now, and he looked across the water, gripped with icy horror at the sight of dozens of claws breaking the surface and clacking together.

And it happened. His shoe struck a hard but yielding form, a lobster several feet in length. He was flung headlong, torch sailing like a comet over the water until it splashed beneath the surface.

But strong fingers grabbed his coat and hauled him up onto a pile of sand and shells.

"Come, come!" Enoch pulled Bone but he resisted, looking back as Eldred Smith's wavering form straightened in a futile attempt to get further away from the rising water.

"Oh, my God!" Eldred Smith cried out as a wave washed past his shins. "Don't leave me!"

Bone fled as a burbling whistle drowned out the last scream of Eldred Smith. Then a wave caught the lawman behind the knees and he slipped in the current. He struggled to scream and choked on saltwater as he jolted down the first of another wide series of steps.

"No! No!" Enoch grabbed his shoulder in a vise-like grip and leaned into the cave wall while pulling Bone into a bear hug. Scabbed lips whispered in Bone's ear and he struggled to decipher the terrified warning, convinced that the madman said, "It gets bigger."

He couldn't possibly have said, "*They* get bigger."

"Up, up!" Hand tangled in the collar of Bone's coat, Enoch clambered up onto a rocky shelf and wriggled into a narrow shaft. Bone shed his coat and thrust his arms into the shaft, writhing up and inside, struck with the profound relief at not witnessing the next, larger cave and struggling to suppress the thought there might be still more great spaces beyond. Larger. Deeper. Full of horrors.

Piercing whistles goaded him like a whip and he struggled up after Enoch Weeks.

- 5 -

Bone crawled and was pulled up through an esophageal tube of rock and mud, crawling through an unending graveyard of bloody bones until he was expelled, gasping, into the mud and shit of the surface.

He slapped down into the filth beside the slime-covered form of Enoch

Weeks, both of them with ribcages heaving, drinking in the air of the world above.

Bone gradually became aware of the swaying branches and their rasping, twiggy whispers, narrow finger bones of wood backlit by the sun.

"It's daytime," he said, coughing and turning his head to spit out a clump of something unnamable. Enoch lay beside him, bony chest expanding and compressing, eyes wide, barely present.

Bone rolled over onto his belly, unheeding of the muck, and pushed himself to his hands and knees. He recognized the broken fencing of the pigpen. The house.

"Inside," he said, reaching down to help Enoch to his feet, but the wild man was unable to do more than twist in place. Too exhausted to lift him, Bone grasped Enoch by both wrists and dragged him through the mud, ignoring the white agony of his ankle until he backed into a door.

He dragged Enoch as far as the kitchen before he fell down beside his charge. He had vague thoughts of cleaning their mud-caked wounds, worries about infection, but directed action was beyond him at the moment.

And so Virgil Bone and Enoch Weeks sank into unconsciousness, having emerged from the halls of Old Man Atlantic to sleep surrounded by the bloody graffiti of Mad Mary Nutter. The house providing the two wounded men a moment of peace and security it never offered her.

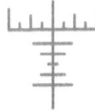

THIRTY-FIVE

Bone woke with a start, but an all-consuming pain squeezed him in its fist and he sagged back.

The light streaming in through the windows was different, but he could still read the writing on the walls.

DADDY IS IN HELL

He let gravity roll his dirt-encrusted head to the right, wincing as his cheekbone slapped the plank wood floor. Clumps of dirt and debris. He suspected if he looked at it from above, from a hot-air balloon, he would see it was in the shape of a man.

He said Enoch's name but it came out as a weak croak. His eyes wanted to close again but he fought them. He had been dreaming already—

Enough with this island and the fucking dreaming.

—and remembered snatches of conversation as Enoch washed himself in the kitchen sink and ate a bowl of something.

"I make them when I'm not feeling…" Enoch fluttered his hand to describe his madness. "Tiny coffins so the children will be safe underground. But the trees scream at me when I try to bury them, so now I just make them and pile them in the woods."

Snatches of conversation Bone felt might have made sense in a dream but were disconnected in the real world.

"Hospital and doctors." Bone was saying. "There is medicine that can help you stay you."

Enoch weeping quietly and rocking, holding himself. "I won't make it to 'e boat by myself," Enoch saying. "I'm slipping."

The words a mush coming from that tangle of rotting teeth and black gums. Why had Bone unpinned his marshal's star? Dream logic. "Carry this to the boat, follow it to the boat," Bone said.

Enoch cradling it with desperate gratitude, the way a Catholic might hold his cross the night he learns vampires are real.

Bone was sitting up and then standing, his mind busy cataloguing too many hurts. The colored wheel spinning. Buffering. He looked around the place as his vision steadied and heard tendons in his neck creak like cables.

There was a bowl on the counter, some sort of mush in the bottom. The sink. He crossed the Sahara Desert in seven steps and leaned his hands on it. Slick with mud, filled with dirty water. Bone splashed it on his face and scalp until clods of dirt slipped free and he could finger-comb his hair back.

Not a dream. Guess that really happened too.

He felt half-human again, power bar hovering around fifty percent. He had given away his star because he no longer needed its power. Enoch Weeks needed it. But by God did he still wish he had his own talisman. Her phone.

He shuffled across the floor until he found Hatevil Nutter's spartan bedroom. Took a hooded fisherman's coat from the closet. It stank of the other man but Bone didn't care. He was in a "fuck it" state of mind.

Hazel and Enoch to the boat and then with Burden get everyone to the mainland. Get everyone home even if it kills—

"No ifs."

Bone paused to rifle the kitchen and take a little something he concealed point-first in a deep coat pocket.

The door was open and he walked out, left it open behind him. A fuck it state of mind and stuff to do.

THIRTY-SIX

- 1 -

It was a gleaming cobalt disk against an azure sky blown clear of clouds by steady Isle winds. It was a two o'clock sun, just to the west of the great church steeple and bathing both the ancient frontage and gathered folk below in nothing short of perfect light. In such a light, every platter on the long communal tables glittered like genuine silver. Every cut of meat and every pot of stew reflected an enticing gleam, the orange and brown autumnal vegetables no longer shabby cousins of the summer harvest, but earthy and glorious and rich with vitality they were happy to pass on to the facing rows of seated townsfolk. Steam curled visibly in this light, bestowing warm, wet kisses on the wrists and hands of the women setting the food at appropriate intervals. You could *see* the aroma, see it with your eyes, in the day's light. Rolls were fatter. Breads were crustier. The slabs of butter bigger.

In the two o'clock light.

A gathering of Littles performed with the dressed lobstermen they had made with Miss Nutter the week before, re-enacting the first settlement of their beloved Isle in 1680. It was awkward and silly, as it was every year. It was enthusiastic as well, lobstermen shaking like rattles and the youngest of the Littles, named Gyles, unable to contain his giggling. All those adult faces watching patiently understood the excitement of the Littles to be the focus of attention. Each had done it his or herself when they were younger.

In the two o'clock light.

Then why the muted conversation, the lessened applause? Why did gazes slide past each other instead of meeting? It could have been the bandages that a number of older men wore, or the pounding heads near every man felt after too much drink the night before. It could have been the empty seats scattered here and there, no names mentioned aloud, but each name screamed silently by someone.

The slap on the back of Arn Corn's hand when he tried to sneak a roll was loud in the afternoon and brought a moment of levity, snickers and some laughter, some of it too loud. People tried to bridge the invisible restraints just then, pushing back the feeling that something needed to be done by each of them, even if they didn't know what.

Eaton Fenn rolled out his great cask of beer and spiked it, earning a laughing cheer as men greedily held out mugs for medicinal hair of the dog. Gazes slipped past each other with less speed as the frothy beer was sipped and shoulders relaxed all along the tables.

Then Jeremiah Pruitt stood—with the aid of big Jon Tuttle—and clapped as the Littles bowed and scattered, Honor's retinue timed perfectly to wheel in the great cauldron of stew, women marching alongside with ladles like an honor guard. The other competitors followed, bringing their chowders and soups and smiling retainers. Bowls would soon be filled and the contents judged, wagers of money and gear and work-time paid off. Arn Corn would work Increase Mather's boat again, as he never picked a winner. Not much of a victory for Mather as Arn wasn't much of a fisherman. But it was the way things were done, and had been done, since every one of them could remember. Honor Pruitt would most likely win again unless Matty Weaver's mixed shellfish soup, which was rumored to be quite good, could unseat Honor's stew. The best part of all was that, as the rules stated, no dish could be entered unless there was enough for everyone to taste, and after the three judges made their selections and a winner was announced, the Isle folk would scrape the cauldrons clean, complaining to the judges about their choices. Everyone remembered the year young Jon Tuttle, not yet big, had climbed into one great metal container with a loaf of bread to sop up the leavings and fallen asleep inside it with a full belly.

New stories would be added to old stories and the Isle folk's true wealth—that of tales—would be increased for another season, to be told and retold and argued about at the public house and during quiet mornings as the fishing fleet set out to sea.

Men stood and clapped, some whistling in appreciation. And those women preparing the tables suppressed the automatic stab of jealousy the great cauldrons always elicited. This too was normal, however, and the tension diminished even more, unable to stand against the memories of feasts past and the anticipation of favorite dishes.

Reverend Tinker stood as well from his traditional seat at one end of the chain of tables, his expression softening even as his palms slapped each other red. There had been talk of canceling the celebration in light of recent events, but Ambrose Tinker knew the Isle folk needed a reminder of the good, a reminder of each other. The ancient celebration of who they were and where they came from was his singular chance to knit this torn flock back together, to seep the conflict free from their souls as poison is drawn from a wound.

He pushed back his chair and stepped away, gathering up his bowl and spoon and stuffing a still-warm roll in one pocket. He nodded at Increase Mather, who nodded back with a confused but relieved expression, gathering implements like the reverend, though he chose a piece of cornbread for sopping. Tinker frowned and tried not to show it as he glanced quickly to the empty seats of John Wallis, Hatevil Nutter and Eldred Smith.

He felt the warm tingle of inspiration and raised his voice to cut through the din. "Jon Tuttle! It's time you did your solemn duty, and we all know you like soup!"

The gathered folk within earshot laughed and passed the reverend's command down to those who couldn't hear, engulfing the assemblage in merriment and good-natured ribbing as the big man was shoved away from his seat. He held up his hands, suspenders straining to cross his wide shoulders. The crowd quieted.

"Good friends—"

Tuttle was interrupted by Arn Corn crying out, "'E's too big to fit in 'e great kettle this year!"

The crowd roared, drowning Tuttle out while his face turned red. Gamely he trotted to the reverend's side and leaned down to whisper in the older man's ear, who nodded decisively.

"Everyone!" Reverend Tinker raised his hands as Tuttle had and the crowd quieted a bit more quickly. "Good Jon, while able and willing even if he must sit outside the cauldrons and use a spoon like the rest of us..." Tinker paused to let the laughter roll past like a morning breaker. "Jon has informed me that he, in fact, provided the meat for Honor Pruitt's stew and cannot stand as an impartial judge."

Before the crowd could erupt in dismay, Jeremiah Pruitt caught Arn Corn's shoulders and shoved him up to the table. "Arn Corn! I nominate Arn Corn!"

This broke up the gathering completely as Arn Corn spilled beer down his front. Reverend Tinker was so pleased to see Jeremiah Pruitt engaged in good-natured revelry after the past night's events that he waved the old drunk to the steps of the church and sat down as someone pressed bowl, spoon and buttered bread into Arn Corn's hands, the beer having been snatched deftly by a Little who darted away with it before anyone could stop him.

The three judges sat in a row on the church steps, their implements of judgment ready, and Tinker called out over the din. "It's time we learned what mysterious ingredients have gone into Matty Weaver's pot!" He had the good nature to blush even as a laughing Matty Weaver used her ladle to fill the three waiting bowls.

"Begin!" Matty cried, waving the dripping ladle overhead like a cavalry saber signaling a charge.

In unison, the three old men placed their sopper of choice on their right knee and lowered spoons into bowls.

- 2 -

Torn and broken bodies littering the street. Houses with their doors kicked in, thatched roofs ablaze. Imagery informed by the Middle East. Bosnia. The smell of soot. The sound of screams.

Despite his expectations, Bone saw none of this as he made his way up the dirt track towards the public house beneath a cheery blue sky. Smelled none of it. Heard none of it. In fact, he heard nothing beyond his own ragged breathing. As if, during his time below, the entire town had packed up and left *en masse*, swept away by a fleet of hot-air balloons. He suspected that if he peered through windows into quiet kitchens, he would still see plates set for the midday meal and steam rising from cups of hearty tea.

Bone didn't remember when he started shaking, but he remembered when he *noticed* it, having stopped without meaning to, one hand on somebody's weathered fence post. Whatever weird vitality had propelled him through the underworld had remained below, spitting him back into the world above with only the diminished reserves of a battered man far from home, with miles of hard road before him.

The shakes passed but his shoes dragged long scuffs in the dirt. He reached over his shoulder and dragged the raincoat's hood over his head, which mainly succeeded in cutting down his field of vision. That was fine by him, as long as it blocked the vacant, junkie staring of the houses as he passed.

He remembered the nights when drinking had been at its worst. When little white piles were cut into lines with a credit card. Didn't let himself go too far down memory lane. He had stuff to do right here and now, but he tapped that period in his life for strength. Thought about half a bottle of Cutty roiling in his gut and the coke making every sneeze bloody. About how he'd focus, walking straight, even driving when he needed too, reminding himself every five seconds to focus, focus.

The bell rang overhead as he pushed his way into the public house and he cursed, having lost a little time just like he'd do on a whiskey fueled drive back home. He was struck by the mundane smells of sour beer and dried ketchup, the underlying stink of fish. Smells so normal he was tempted to sit and wallow in them. Instead he clomped up the stairs, leaning on the handrail.

"Hazel," he said with a knock, tapping against a drained keg from the sound. He opened the door and stepped inside to see the neatly made bed but no Hazel, though he lifted his face and scented her, faint and soap-like.

He paused outside his own door and decided not to bother. There was nothing of him in the room. All he had left was in and on him. It was a melancholy notion, and his steps were heavier descending the stairs.

Bone was walking down the main street, having lost a few more minutes. "Fuck." It was the terrifying feeling of being dropped onstage in mid-scene. He stumbled and nearly went to his knees, hair rasping against his hood as his head swiveled wildly to take in the false fronts of the houses where nothing lived or ever had lived.

Focus. Breathe.

He collapsed back onto his haunches and sucked in great, heaving breaths, thoughts swirling in the grip of a fearsome tide, the tiny boat of his rationality suddenly swamped beneath a wave of certainty that *he had not made it out of the caves.* That even now he was a white and bloated thing bobbing in the seawater, drowned and consumed by some prehistoric horde as alien to the world of men as a being from another planet.

Clack-clack. His skin felt translucent, wide open to memories of those damnable claws in their dozens and hundreds. When a line of singing children bounded and skipped around the corner from the main street, Bone blinked at the sight of them. He fought the urge to flee from the rattle and clack of their lobstermen—

Black claws waving above the surface.

—and struggled to make out their high-pitched words—

A bubbling whistle that pierced his ears.

—when the lead child skidded to a halt and the others piled into him. A dozen faces regarded him, mouths like round holes and eyes wide with fear.

Bone raised a hand in a stop gesture, and several of the children shrieked at the hooded man. "Wait," he croaked, but they scattered.

He planted his hands on his knees and pushed himself erect, reaching up to slide his hood back. He closed his eyes and tilted his head, listening, catching a susurrus of noise that made little sense out of context because he was too far from the shore to be hearing the murmur of the surf.

His wits made a guest appearance, and he decided that whomever the kids brought back to investigate, he wanted to be elsewhere.

He opened the nearest gate and quickly moved around to the back of the house, where low fences separated yards with clothes lines and fallow truck gardens. Unable to suppress an involuntary groan, he clambered over the first fence and crunched over dead grass through the backyard, ducking beneath a row of white T-shirts drying on the line. He moved over the next fence and promptly tripped over a hoe that had been leaning against the rail. "Shit." He rose and continued on in that fashion through several more backyards before pausing again to tilt his head and listen.

Crowd sounds. Talking and cheering.

Bone pressed forward between two stone cottages set catty-corner and faced a low row of trees. He lifted his hands and parted several branches, slipping through until he emerged onto the main street, taking in the long row of tables laden with platters of food and steaming bowls of soup. The smell staggered him, and his stomach pinched as an enormous hunger gripped him. He looked up the length of tables towards the looming church and adjusted his hood to conceal his features.

"What the hell?" he muttered.

Hundreds of bodies shifted around the church steps where, as best he could tell, some sort of eating contest was going on. It looked like something from the Food Network, if the Food Network had existed in the nineteenth century.

"Delicious!" The reverend's head emerged above the crowd in a prairie dog's motion as the noise swelled and diminished. Bone rested his hand against the fitted stone of the nearest cottage to catch his breath.

Somehow he was already in the crowd. His eyes darted back and forth, unable to reconcile the faces around him with the dark knowledge he carried in his heart. Did they all know?

Bone was slipping between people, eyes scanning from the cave of his hood for Hazel Milk.

He concentrated on not making bodily contact, of sliding sideways against a current, swimming against the riptide to get out. The smell of humanity and beer was prevalent. Words around him were just chopped bits of sound, a mixed vegetable medley of meaningless pieces, except for the clear, trained voice of Reverend Tinker over it all as he called, "Honor Pruitt."

Bone clapped when everyone else did. He was the guy in church mouthing along half a beat behind while the rest of the congregation sang.

He staggered at a hearty slap between the shoulder blades and heard, "Francis!" in his ear, turning on instinct, feeling the electric moment of eye contact and seeing the confusion in the man's blurry eyes as he recognized Bone.

- 3 -

"Honor Pruitt!" Reverend Tinker called out over the throng, drinking in the smiles and laughter, the chatter and changing bets.

"Oh, Matty's stew were a good one," Arn Corn cried out after a belch, and folks in the front row laughed, turning to pass back what happened to those behind. Tinker watched the mirth work its way through the crowd in a wave and basked in the warmth of it. The normalcy of it. His consciousness, cast suddenly outside himself, saw that he was smiling openly for the first time since—

Must not think it.

And that his people were similarly engaged in the moment.

Tinker sat as Honor Pruitt and her friends wheeled forward the pitted, black bulk of her aged cauldron, and he was struck by the moist scent rising on waves of visible steam from within.

"If that tastes as good as it smells," Increase Mather said, leaning over towards the reverend to be heard over the noise. "'E will win again for sure, the longest record I can recall."

"We must keep an open mind," Tinker said, stifling a belch with his hand. "But if Honor wins again, we will have to think of some special way to commemorate it."

Ease of mind, so long absent, seemed to light his nerve endings with excitement. It was that feeling of wellness on the first morning after a fever has broken. You think, *This is how I normally feel. I must remember how good it feels to be well.* And though the sheer pleasure of normal well-being fades—it always does—Reverend Ambrose Tinker celebrated it silently.

"Bowls, gentlemen," Honor Pruitt said.

Someone behind her remarked, "Aye, aye, Captain Pruitt."

Laughter erupted when she wheeled about, hawk eyes seeking, but even Honor Pruitt was smiling when she turned back to face the judges and filled each bowl carefully with her big spoon, chunks of green vegetables and brown meat, bright orange carrots and russet potatoes cascading down in a wash of glistening broth.

"Go get 'em, Honor," Jeremiah Pruitt called out to his wife, waving his hat in the air.

"Have 'e got 'e soppers?" Katie Fenn asked, holding up a basket of bread and rolls.

Arn Corn reached forward and snagged a roll with a quick hand and a, "Thank 'e."

Katie Fenn stepped back with the other women in Honor's retinue, all of them save Hazel Milk watching with bright eyes and flushed cheeks. Hazel was frowning back into the crowd, but Reverend Tinker decided the problem of Hazel Milk could wait for another day. Today was about knitting the torn fabric of their community whole once again.

"Are 'e ready?" Arn Corn asked, and Increase smacked his shoulder with a spoon.

"Ain't a race, 'e daft idiot," Mather said.

"That's right, Arn Corn," Honor said, shaking her spoon at the grinning old drunk. "You eat every last bite. I'm not losing to Matty because you ate mine too fast."

Shouts of "Matty!" and "Honor!" rose in volume, and Reverend Tinker lowered his nose over the bowl, inhaling the incredible fragrance even as he tried to ignore a disturbance deep within the crowd. He watched Hazel turn and abruptly push back through the gathered throng and caught Honor's frown, but forced the distractions away with an effort.

Honor clasped her hands, and his smile was filled with warmth as he held her gaze with his own and lowered his spoon into the bowl, snagging chunks of potato and meat by feel as he lifted the steaming mouthful to his lips and slurped loudly, his eyes closing in reflex as the crowd noise rose, and a rolling eruption of seasonings and roasted meat saturated his tongue. He chewed and rolled the mouthful around like a wine taster, eyes still closed to aid concentration. He swallowed and spoke, "Dear Lord, Honor Pruitt, you've done something different this year and outdone even your own stew from last year."

Tinker glanced over at Mather and Corn and saw both men nodding at him, even as they spooned more of the incredible stew into their mouths.

"What's the difference this year?" Mather shouted with a full mouth, and Tinker glanced up as a freak eddy of people parted the crowd.

He choked.

Eyes seemed to glow from the depths of the man's hood, whites like the foam atop a breaking wave and the centers dark as a storm-tossed sea. Dread superstition poured over him in a cascade of ice as Reverend Tinker stared into the unforgiving and all-knowing eyes of Old Man Atlantic himself, until the crowd once more blocked his view and Tinker knew he had seen a dead man.

"Reverend?" Honor slapped his back and he coughed a chunk of gristle into his mouth, turning to spit it out. He forced a grin, trying to muffle his own coughing. Mather and Corn watching but too busy eating to offer help.

"Take a small sip of the broth then," Honor said.

"No—" The reverend begged off.

"Don't you 'No' me. Ask Jeremiah how well that works if you want to know, or just take a sip and sooth your throat the way I ask."

Increase laughed as Jeremiah and Jon Tuttle crowded in. "Best do as 'e says," Jeremiah said. "For all our sakes."

"All right, all right," Tinker said.

"Honor, really, it's the meat, ain't it?" Arn Corn said. "Jon, what is it?"

Reverend Tinker lifted the bowl to his lips and sipped the broth, juice running from the corners of his mouth as Honor leaned in and looked at each man in turn.

"The long pork," she said, smiling fiercely.

Reverend Tinker pulled back, spilling broth on his shirt, too distracted by the abrupt electrical charge of her expression to immediately take in her words. When her statement unraveled its meaning, Tinker lowered his bowl and looked into it with dawning horror as the wonderful walls of his reality came crashing down.

"What have you done?" Reverend Tinker asked.

"Long pork?" Mather asked. "Something special brought in on *Leviathan*?"

"You did not do this." Tinker said, unsure if he whispered or shouted. Honor's eyes took on a furious glow, and Reverend Tinker knew it was true.

She stirred the pot until she heard a clink and lifted the ladle. The constable's badge swam in broth.

"Big Eats wouldn't be the same without the good constable present, now would it, Reverend Tinker," Jon Tuttle said.

Tinker surged to his feet and hurled his bowl aside, stabbing with his finger and opening his mouth to deliver a thunderous volley. The words died unspoken in his throat as Jeremiah Pruitt swung his cane, crying out in a voice full of anguish and fury. "His name was Nathaniel!"

Reverend Tinker's face exploded in pain as the cane crushed his nose, the sound of cartilage sickeningly audible *inside* the reverend's skull. He fell back into his seat and tumbled over backwards. The breath was driven from his lungs as his back struck the unforgiving steps of the church, and he lifted his hands away from his face, seeing the awful red paint of his own blood on them, throat burning with the need for air.

Mather was on his feet and moving with the speed of an able seaman in bad weather, but Jon Tuttle caught the side of his neck with one ham-like fist and the first selectman fell hard. Before he could recover, Tuttle delivered a mighty kick to his belly, and Mather curled around himself in pain.

- 4 -

Bone blinked and thought for a split second that he had lost time again, so quickly had the throng shifted from revelers at a country fair to tooth and claw.

Mere seconds had passed.

Young men throughout the crowd produced short-hafted clubs and boathooks from beneath coats, and Bone saw the design of the thing. Punching and wrestling escalated into clubbing and hooking.

Screams split the air.

The person who had recognized Bone earlier made a clumsy reach for him, and Bone snapped out a stiff left jab, rocking his head back. Before he could recover, a young Isle man brought his club down on the older man's head, and Bone's opponent didn't so much fall as leap forward onto his face, cheek bouncing off the dirt. Wild eyes sought out Bone's own and the young fisherman lifted his club, leaping over his victim. Bone backpedaled and ripped the carving knife he had stolen from Nutter's kitchen free from his pocket, planting his feet and stabbing forward in an awkward stop thrust. But it was enough to back off the club wielder, who dodged into the swirling mosh pit of the crowd.

Not even a minute gone, and bodies lay curled and writhing on the dirt, groups of younger adults, men and women alike, kicking and hurling insults down at their fallen foes. A skull-faced young woman bent an older lady backwards over a chair, both hands buried in gray hair while another young woman smashed the matron with a ceramic mug. A queer shriek drew his attention and Bone saw a man dragged along the ground, a boathook through the stretching skin of his face.

The rage of centuries had been released and it demanded blood.

A hand clutched at his ankle and Bone looked down to see Arn Corn hiding behind him. Blood ran in a red starburst from his ruined mouth, and the words bubbling from him amounted to one thing, "Help."

Even as Bone was bending to offer a hand, a shrieking harridan landed on his back. He shook the woman off and swung his knife wildly. The steel parted the fabric of a dress and then the skin beneath, drawing a red smile across Katie Fenn's thigh.

Bone tripped over Corn, who had curled into a wailing ball. He pushed himself to his feet, fighting a wave of dizziness. "Hazel!" he shouted.

His head swiveled, but he could not make out her features among the snarling mouths and berserk eyes of the combatants. He charged recklessly through the crowd, bulling people aside, screaming her name. "Hazel!"

When he was caught within a scrum, the entire group crashing to the earth like a crowd of drunks, he fought his way free, swinging and spitting as savagely as any of them.

"Hazel!"

He swung his arm overhead and brought the haft of his kitchen knife down on a man's skull, striking him behind the ear. The man tripped over the woman he had been stomping with his boots, and Bone thought he made out the swollen features of Reliance Wallis beneath the blood and dirt.

Amidst all the frenzy, a sight of monstrous violence arrested him, and he stopped his headlong charge, powerless to do anything but watch it unfold. Big Jon Tuttle, cords in his forearms and neck bulging like cables, was shoving Increase Mather headfirst into the hot cauldron of Honor Pruitt's prize-winning stew. Bone could see the smoke rising where the older man had braced his bare palms on the hot rim, skin peeling as he shifted his grip, pushing back, teeth bared in a rictus of pain, eyes clenched shut with the effort. Another big man, a powerful man, but no longer the match of the broad-shouldered Tuttle, who lifted his right fist and smashed Mather's braced arm, chopping away at the support, while his left squeezed the back of the first selectman's neck and pressed downward, an irresistible tonnage.

"Eat it! Eat it! Eat it!" Jon Tuttle demanded until, with a moan of utter despair, Mather's head splashed down into the deep well of stew. Tuttle fed more of him into the pot until the older man's shoulders were submerged and his feet, no longer touching the ground, kicked wildly.

And then as crowds do, an avenue clear of bodies opened up and Bone beheld the reverend, blood smeared across his cheeks. His back was pressed against the church doors and he was swinging his chair from side to side, momentarily holding his attackers at bay.

"Marshal!" Reverend Tinker cried, blood spraying from his mouth. He straightened and threw his chair down on the steps. "Marshal, stop this madness!"

The fighting seemed to pause, taking a deep breath, as if the violent group consciousness that gripped them had cocked an ear to listen.

Bone shifted, squaring himself with the reverend and, he realized, directly with the church itself, the steeple towering above him. The light was of perfect quality and Bone was gifted with the ability to regard the tableau in near infinite detail, from the grain of wood on the ancient church doors to the brightly shining bubbles of blood popping beneath the wounded reverend's nose. He saw the uneven splotches in Honor Pruitt's cheeks and could make out white beads of spittle on the lips of her husband Jeremiah.

The crowd was watching, heads swiveling between Reverend Tinker and the hooded lawman like spectators at a tennis match, and with the absurd perception Bone momentarily enjoyed, he realized they were watching a struggle between two moral poles. He felt the sudden urge to break the silence with laughter, to watch their shocked faces as the moment shattered like glass.

Virgil pushed back his hood, sweaty hair catching the light as he smiled not in humor, but in recognition. "I have read the book, Reverend," he said, not in a cop voice, but a full-bodied speaking voice that carried to each ear. Whispers rippled across the crowd in tiny wavelets and he waited for them to subside. "I've been to the trees and heard them scream. I've been below. I have seen what it is, and I've come back."

Reverend Tinker shook his head and held out a hand. "You don't understand."

Bone slashed the air with his empty hand and the reverend flinched as if struck. "I do understand."

"What do you understand?" Tinker's voice was tiny, but his lips shaped the words clearly.

Bone felt the wind toss his hair and cool the runnels of perspiration on his cheeks. He was struck by the clear intellect in the reverend's eyes and his acceptance of the verdict to come.

"We pay for what we do," Bone said. "It may take a while, but we always pay for what we do."

A sigh emanated from the audience, and in that brief moment Bone considered steering the ship towards a new course. But before he could finish the thought...

The sound expanded quickly, forceful, sudden, an explosion from every direction.

Honor Pruitt was screaming. Bone watched the whites of her eyes roll back under the force of her mania, a streamer of spit extending from her upper teeth, vibrating in the wind of her raw emotion. It could not have been more than a few seconds, but for Bone the noise grew and grew and extended across lifetimes to underscore his words.

Heads tilted back and mouths opened around him as the Isle folk wailed in maddening unison, a chorus all the more frightening because Bone knew it was unrehearsed.

The world would have its payment.

A strong hand grabbed the shoulder of his raincoat and spun him around even as he brought up the knife to slash—

"Come with me," Hazel Milk said. Her eyes were focused and clear, unlike those around her, but her hair was a tangled mess and a welt marked one cheek. "Quickly now."

And like that the spell was broken. Hazel took his hand and led him from the wailing choir, slipping and dodging like an eel to avoid the rigid bodies of her kinfolk. For they were all of them kin, connected by ever-narrowing rivers of blood.

She led Bone between two of the long tables and he resisted for a moment, turning to look back at the stiffly upright pillars of vibrating flesh that had been human beings, transformed into something alien by the immense pressures of time and pain.

"Virgil." Hazel grabbed his lapel with her free hand and jerked him off balance. "We go now, or we don't go at all!"

Clods of dirt flew from the soles of their feet as Bone and Hazel fled down the street.

THIRTY-SEVEN

- 1 -

A tiny point of light through which a pinhole camera photographs the world. Expanding, the walls of a narrow cylinder pushing back as gold and orange washed through autumn leaves to bathe his hands. Burning hands. Abraded hands clawing the dirt.

"Virgil? Virgil, are you all right?"

The voice competing with an under sound. A gossamer touch along every inch of exposed skin.

"The trees are screaming," Bone said.

"You said there was a boat. Where is the boat?"

"What?"

"Who has the boat?"

"Burden," he said, closing his eyes, feeling the sharp pain of a root digging into one knee. Nausea twisted his guts and he realized he had a concussion. So he shared that.

"We have to keep moving. Where do we meet Burden?"

"Lighthouse."

Bone opened his eyes and sat back on his haunches, two images of Hazel's round face sliding across each other until they stabilized.

"What happened back there?" he asked.

"We have to—"

"What happened?" The near shout made his head swim dizzyingly.

Hazel crouched beside him and lowered her voice, as if afraid the woods might hear her. "They've spent so long giving voice to the children, to the trees," she said. "Now they're taking it back."

"I don't understand."

"Understand this. What you heard, what you saw, was only the beginning of decades, of centuries, of screaming that has been given back to the people of the Isle. There will be no mercy. There is only pain and fear folded over and compressed a thousand times and it demands expiation."

Bone leaned heavily on her as she helped him to his feet.

"Did you know?" he asked.

Hazel met his eyes unflinchingly. "Everyone knew."

- 2 -

Reverend Tinker staggered amidst the mob, his arms bound behind him, led by a noose around his neck. On either side the sea wind whistled through the empty windows of the old village, and the houses mocked, hollow laughter booming from open doorways.

People he knew, had raised since they were Littles, ran ahead and posted themselves along the march, heads back and mouths open to offer their ululating cries. They ran into houses and up stairs, screaming hatred down from above. It had the horrid precision of a ritual known well and celebrated often, but he knew that was not the case.

The curse had taken over their souls. It had damned them on earth. And God above had turned his face away from the unholy abomination of his people.

He fell and was dragged by the neck across rough cobblestones until Jeremiah Pruitt jerked him to his feet so roughly his shoulder dislocated. He wailed past the shards of his teeth and felt a strong fist in his hair, turning his head until he saw the women around the well and the bloody parcels they threw down into its black and hungry throat. His vision swam, and his knees went weak when he recognized the eyes and fat tongue bulging from the severed head of Increase Mather.

"We call them to awaken for 'e," Honor Pruitt said, at some point having drawn stripes of blood along her cheeks, dried flaky and brown. She went rigid and straight, pressing her palms down at her sides even as her head snapped back and she howled at the sky.

The rope around his neck tightened and Tinker stumbled past the well. At the edge of the village, where human habitation met sand, were the foundations of six gallows.

He saw that one foundation was now occupied by a new tenant of rough-hewn wood, hastily erected.

And it was just for him.

- 3 -

"Get down," Hazel said and pressed Bone bodily to the shell-strewn sand behind a dune, the tide sliding up to lick his shoes, tickling the soles of his feet.

He felt sick and lightheaded, weaker than he remembered ever having felt. And yet he was keenly aware of the warmth of the sunlight washing down with no cloud to mute it. Of the smell of sea and sand and Hazel pressed atop him.

"Burden's not here," she said.

Shrieking carried to them, answered by the roar of a crashing wave.

"What are they doing?" Bone asked, feeling the sand in the back of his hair, inside his collar.

It occurred to him that under other circumstances, being trapped beneath Hazel Milk on the beach might not be such a terrible thing. He tried to gather steam to offer the observation when she said, "They're hanging Reverend Tinker."

Bone shoved Hazel to the side and sat up as the world titled beneath him. He felt his stomach spasm and fought back the urge to retch.

"Get down," she said.

Propped on one arm, Bone could just see over the rill of sand and spied the dancing figures around some kind of pole. A rope dangled from it, and he understood what he saw. He looked away and made out a dark smudge rising over the waves, even as he heard the mechanical chuffing of an engine.

"There," he said, pointing. "*Leviathan.*"

THIRTY-EIGHT

- 1 -

Up ahead the lighthouse gleamed, graced with a patina of white by a for-giving sun. Burden realized this was the first time he was seeing his tower at the edge of everything from the seaward side, and he was confused by a pang of regret. If the next few minutes went according to plan, he would never see it again.

"Get below, Enoch," Burden said, leaning out of the pilot house. The madman had taken a position in the bow and the fierce sea breeze swirled his hair into a mane. "Enoch!"

Enoch turned and showed his blackened teeth. "I see 'em on the beach."

The pitch of the engine changed beneath Burden's feet, and the dan-gling lobstermen clacked together. He braced himself as *Leviathan* slowed its approach to the Isle, the cries of the gulls overhead increasing in fervor.

"This is as far as 'e dare take *Leviathan* or we risk running aground," Samuel Weeks said. "'E need to drop anchor."

Burden smiled up at the ugly fisherman and rotated the cylinder in the constable's revolver.

"Quickly now," Samuel said, eyeing the heavily armed dwarf.

Burden slipped out of the pilot house and made his way forward, not placing the pistol in his pocket until he had released the anchor and heard the splash, watching as the chain uncoiled and soon stopped. He braced one hand on the rail and shaded his eyes with the other, a jolt of fear run-ning through him when he saw the cavorting madness around the gallows.

"No—"

He bit back his words as two figures moved quickly near the waterline.

"They're here," he shouted, running back to the pilot house and draw-ing the revolver again. "Go get them."

"What?" Samuel asked.

"Take the skiff and go get them," Burden ordered, gripping the pistol in both hands and thumbing back the hammer.

"All right, all right," the pilot said, raising his hands.

Burden backed him to the skiff and watched him lower it over the side, tossing in both oars.

"Beach the boat and give it to Marshal Bone," Burden said. "You're staying on the Isle."

Samuel shaded his own eyes with a hand and went pale. "Oh, Lord, what are 'e doing?"

"Looks like a hanging," Burden said.

"'E must take me with you, to look after my brother—"

Burden jammed the barrel of the weapon into the pilot's soft stomach, just above the belt.

"If you had gone to the mainland and brought back lawmen, this wouldn't be happening, you sonofabitch."

"But Mather and them told me—"

Burden pointed with his free hand towards the distant gallows. "They're not telling anyone any more. Now move before I shoot you dead."

Samuel Weeks hastily scrambled over the side of the boat, which rocked precariously on the waves. Burden flinched back from the sea spray, and when he looked again the pilot had locked the oars and was rowing hard, hate-filled eyes fixed on Burden.

- 2 -

The noise was deafening, a cacophony of wild shouts and screams unlike anything Reverend Tinker had ever heard. He tried to compose his thoughts, to think of the martyrdom of Jesus Christ, but the pagan wildness—pagan being the only word he could conjure to fit the moment—of the gnashing teeth and rolling eyes surrounding him swamped his rational mind under a tide of fear.

The women continued going rigid, palms pressing down as if they sought to push away from gravity itself, consumed by the need to release ear-piercing shrieks.

Honor Pruitt jabbered in his face and he felt the spray of her saliva.

She seemed to have lost command of the English language, yet the Isle folk obeyed this high priestess as she gesticulated, and the end of the rope around Reverend Tinker's neck was thrown over the gallows.

Tears streamed freely and Reverend Tinker strained to hear beyond the horrid howling to the soothing rumble of the sea, but it was denied him. Second only to his mortal terror was the incredible sensation of failure. The curse they lived under had overwhelmed them and he had forsaken his duty to protect his people.

Still unable to fathom their words, Reverend Tinker yet heard a change in tone and wanted to shout, "Wait!" but the noose tightened with unbelievable force around his neck. His voice and wind were choked off, and the pain was immense, increasing tenfold as the weight of the men on the other end of the line prevailed and he was jerked roughly from his feet, aware of the hot wash of his bladder failing even as he felt a stabbing, white pain from the vertebrae in his neck. He kicked and spun as the Isle folk danced below him, cheering as his cheeks bulged and his face purpled.

His spinning took him quickly past a nonsensical view of the sea and a boat at anchor, then revolved him past a glimpse of the old village.

He sought to offer a small prayer that he would be killed before he was thrown to that which lived below, but the pain unhinged his thinking, and his last conscious thought before the black swirled through his mind was terror at the idea of being eaten alive.

- 3 -

Hazel stood at the stern of the skiff as Bone fought to get in, struggling against the bobbing caused by the incoming waves. He staggered along the side until frigid seawater rose to his thighs and pushed down on the edge of the boat, rolling himself over the gunwale.

"Take the oars!" Hazel shouted. Shocked into lucidity by the cold water, Bone scrambled onto the bench, faced inland and grabbed the oars. He could see Reverend Tinker dangling from the gallows and heads turning their way.

"Get in!" he cried out. "They're coming."

"I have to push off," she said, grunting and pressing hard against the stern, fighting to get the rising and falling boat out past the surf. "Row, dammit! Row!"

Bone leaned forward and dipped the oars, digging in as he leaned back and swept them through the water. The boat immediately straightened and breasted the wave trying to swamp it.

"Hazel!"

Bone froze, not comprehending why Hazel wasn't following, until he realized she was backing up towards shore. A wave caught the boat and began to turn it when he saw the first of the Isle men splash into the water. He dug in with the oars, heaving hard against the Atlantic's urge to smash him on the beach. Spray from the waves hurtled against the shore and cast rainbows through the air.

More and more people splashed into the surf, and he feared for Hazel until he saw Katie Fenn lead her off the beach.

As Bone pulled for *Leviathan*, Honor Pruitt, her hair a medusa's nest in the wild wind, waded waist-deep into the sea and pointed at him.

- 4 -

Burden's mouth was compressed into a thin line as he watched Hazel turn back for shore, a final and unexpected insult to his heart.

"Bone!" he cried out as the lawman clumsily angled the small craft. Isle folk were entering the water, and while he knew none were so foolish as to swim in such accursed seas, there was every possibility that Bone would be carried back into their reach by a strong wave.

Burden drew the revolver from his pocket and rested both elbows on the railing as the boat rolled up on the starboard side. He thumbed back the hammer and *Leviathan* prepared to deliver a broadside.

- 5 -

Bone saw the flash at the end of Honor Pruitt's arm before he registered the high-velocity crack of the gunshot and saw the Isle woman absorb the recoil. He had just enough time to realize he was being shot at with his own pistol when a deeper gunshot sounded behind him. Several people on the shoreline looked over Bone to *Leviathan*, shock writ large on their features. A second shot from *Leviathan* sent them diving to the sand and even into the surf, but by then Honor Pruitt had taken aim again.

- 6 -

"What is that?" Katie Fenn asked as she and Hazel hugged the dune. Hazel scrambled around and looked seaward past Virgil Bone's struggling rowboat, unable to fight back a fierce grin.

"It's Burden Ipswich," she said, prideful fire sweeping through her breast.

- 7 -

Bone was beyond the roughest surf, into the sea proper and parallel to the lighthouse. He looked back over one shoulder and aimed the rowboat for *Leviathan*, capturing a quick glimpse of Burden sighting carefully over the railing as a puff of smoke and sharp report signaled another shot fired.

Honor Pruitt had more ammunition in the Glock, and if this turned into a sea chase, with the Isle folk pursuing in another vessel, that could prove an important factor. But so far Honor had demonstrated little skill.

There was an immense kick in the shoulder and his body slapped sideways against the gunwale. He had no sensation for a single breath before pain exploded throughout his body and he slumped over the rail, his limp right arm and the tips of his hair dangling in the sea. He told himself to move, to right himself, distantly aware of Burden shouting, of how close he was to *Leviathan* even as another portion of his brain calculated the damage caused by a bullet that had failed to pass through, had instead lodged in the heavy bone of his shoulder, shattering it, a crippling blow.

Burden's shouting grew faint, and Bone felt his will to move slipping free along with the hot blood pumping from the wound.

The boat shifted and turned sideways against the waves, spray striking Bone in the face. He found himself lying on the hood of his car as the rain pounded down. He was staring back through the broken windshield into his wife's eyes as life leaked from her.

Julia silently mouthed a last word that Bone could not hear as the car's hood rocked beneath him, and Bone slid from the rowboat into the sea.

The crashing sound of the world above faded to the pervasive sound of bubbles as he sank, trailing a shimmering stream. He felt an awful pang of longing at the thought of her, and the water grew darker around him, enveloping him in a deep cold.

The final bubble left his lips and he pressed them together, hoping only to buy a few moments as he sought to decipher his wife's last word.

As the darkness rolled below him he looked away from it, towards the distant glimmer of light above and the decreasing rumble of *Leviathan*'s engine, resisting the urge to face the thing that gripped his calf, at first gently and then with increasing pressure until finally he beheld the horrible enormity beneath him. He was unable to fight the urge, and his mouth snapped open to issue a silent scream.

There was a moment of brilliant sensation as impossible fire lit his wounded shoulder and he was abruptly rising, thrashing against the pull, hands grabbing the wooden shaft of the long boathook sunk into his flesh.

He broke the surface in an explosion of foam and blood, sucking in a great *whoop* of air even as the cruel pull of the boathook dragged him against *Leviathan*'s barnacled side and he slapped his palms against the hull. Steel grated against bone and he screamed as a fist buried itself in his hair, and then he was rising with the howling effort of Burden and Enoch as they pulled him from the sea.

END

MORE DARK FICTION FROM
GREY MATTER PRESS

"Grey Matter Press has managed to establish itself as one of the premiere purveyors of horror fiction currently in existence via both a series of killer anthologies — *SPLATTERLANDS, OMINOUS REALITIES, EQUILIBRIUM OVERTURNED* — and John F.D. Taff's harrowing novella collection *THE END IN ALL BEGINNINGS*."

- FANGORIA Magazine

GREY MATTER
P R E S S

A DARK THRILLER

MISTER

WHITE

THE NOVEL

DO
NOT
SPEAK
HIS
NAME

JOHN C.
FOSTER

MISTER WHITE
BY JOHN C. FOSTER

In the shadowy world of international espionage and governmental black ops, when a group of American spies go bad and inadvertently unleash an ancient malevolent force that feeds on the fears of mankind, a young family finds themselves in the crosshairs of a frantic supernatural mystery of global proportions with only one man to turn to for their salvation.

Combine the intricate, plot-driven stylings of suspense masters Tom Clancy and Robert Ludlum, add a healthy dose of Clive Barker's dark and brooding occult horror themes, and you get a glimpse into the supernatural world of international espionage that the chilling new horror novel *Mister White* is about to reveal.

John C. Foster's *Mister White* is a terrifying genre-busting suspense shocker that, once and for all, answer the question you dare not ask: "Who is Mister White?"

"*Mister White* is a potent and hypnotic brew that blends horror, espionage and mystery. Foster has written the kind of book that keeps the genre fresh and alive and will make fans cheer. Books like this are the reason I love horror fiction." – Ray Garton, Grand Master of Horror and Bram Stoker Award®-nominated author of *Live Girls* and *Scissors*

"*Mister White* is like Stephen King's *The Stand* meets Ian Fleming's James Bond with Graham Masterton's *The Manitou* thrown in for good measure. It's frenetically paced, spectacularly gory and eerie as hell. Highly recommended!" – John F.D. Taff, Bram Stoker Award®-nominated author of *The End in All Beginnings*

GREY MATTER
P R E S S

greymatterpress.com

MANIFEST RECALL

ALAN BAXTER

"GRABS YOU BY THE NECK AND NEVER LETS GO."
— JOHN F.D. TAFF, BRAM STOKER AWARD-NOMINATED AUTHOR OF
THE END IN ALL BEGINNINGS

MANIFEST RECALL
BY ALAN BAXTER

Following a psychotic break, Eli Carver finds himself on the run, behind the wheel of a car that's not his own, and in the company of a terrified woman he doesn't know. As layers of ugly truth are peeled back and dark secrets are revealed, the duo find themselves in a struggle for survival when they unravel a mystery that pits them against the most dangerous forces in their lives.

A contemporary southern gothic thriller with frightening supernatural overtones, Alan Baxter's *Manifest Recall* explores the tragic life of a hitman who finds himself on the wrong side of his criminal syndicate. Baxter's adrenaline-fueled approach to storytelling draws readers into Eli Carver's downward spiral of psychosis and through the darkest realms of lost memories, human guilt and the insurmountable quest for personal redemption.

"If you like crime/noir horror hybrids, check out Alan Baxter's *Manifest Recall*. It's a fast, gritty, mind-f*ck." — Paul Tremblay, Bram Stoker Award-winning author of *A Head Full of Ghosts*

"Alan Baxter's fiction is dark, disturbing, hard-hitting and heart-breakingly honest. He reflects on worlds known and unknown with compassion, and demonstrates an almost second-sight into human behaviour." — Kaaron Warren, Shirley Jackson Award-winning author of *The Grief Hole*

"Alan Baxter is an accomplished storyteller who ably evokes magic and menace." — Laird Barron, author of *Swift to Chase*

GREY MATTER
P R E S S

greymatterpress.com

"A POWERFUL TALE OF CRIME AND DEATH,
CLEVERLY CRAFTED AND FLAWLESSLY EXECUTED."
JAMES A. MOORE, AUTHOR OF *SEVEN FORGES*

DEVOURING DARK

ALAN BAXTER

DEVOURING DARK
BY ALAN BAXTER

Matt McLeod is a man plagued since childhood by a malevolent darkness that threatens to consume him. Following a lifetime spent wrestling for control over this lethal onslaught, he's learned to wield his mysterious paranormal skill to achieve an odious goal: retribution as a supernatural vigilante.

When one such hit goes bad, McLeod finds himself ensnared in a multi-tentacled criminal enterprise caught between a corrupt cop and a brutal mobster. His only promise of salvation may be a bewitching young woman who shares his dark talent but has murderous designs of her own.

Devouring Dark is a genre-smashing supernatural thriller that masterfully blends elements of crime and horror in an adrenaline-fueled, life-or-death rollercoaster ride that's emblematic of the fiction from award-winning author Alan Baxter.

"*Devouring Dark* is a thrilling mix of crime and horror, a book that somehow defies either description yet embraces both. It moves like a juggernaut, thundering towards an intense, emotional conclusion. " — Gary McMahon, author of *Pretty Little Dead Things*

"*Devouring Dark* is a powerful tale of crime and death, cleverly crafted and flawlessly executed. I'm a fan of Alan Baxter and *Devouring Dark* is a perfect example of why." — James A. Moore, author of *Seven Forges* and the *Serenity Falls* Trilogy

"Action-packed yet emotionally resonant, Devouring Dark held me to the last page." — Kaaron Warren, Shirley Jackson Award-winning author of *Tide of Stone*

GREY MATTER
P R E S S

greymatterpress.com

AVAILABLE NOW
FROM GREY MATTER PRESS

Before — Paul Kane

The Bell Witch — John F.D. Taff

The Devil's Trill: The Ladies Bristol Occult Adventures #1 — Rhoads Brazos

Dark Visions I — eds. Anthony Rivera & Sharon Lawson

Dark Visions II — eds. Anthony Rivera & Sharon Lawson

Death's Realm — eds. Anthony Rivera & Sharon Lawson

Devouring Dark — Alan Baxter

Dread — eds. Anthony Rivera & Sharon Lawson

The End in All Beginnings — John F.D. Taff

Equilibrium Overturned — eds. Anthony Rivera & Sharon Lawson

The Fearing — John F.D. Taff

I Can Taste the Blood — eds. John F.D. Taff & Anthony Rivera

The Isle — John C. Foster

Kill-Off — John F.D. Taff

Little Black Spots — John F.D. Taff

Little Deaths: 5th Anniversary Edition — John F.D. Taff

Manifest Recall — Alan Baxter

Mister White: The Novel — John C. Foster

The Night Marchers and Other Strange Tales — Daniel Braum

Ominous Realities — eds. Anthony Rivera & Sharon Lawson

Peel Back the Skin — eds. Anthony Rivera & Sharon Lawson

Savage Beasts — eds. Anthony Rivera & Sharon Lawson

Secrets of the Weird — Chad Stroup

Seeing Double — Karen Runge

Splatterlands — eds. Anthony Rivera & Sharon Lawson

Suspended in Dusk II: Anthology of Horror — ed. Simon Dewar

www.ingramcontent.com/pod-product-compliance
Lightning Source LLC
Chambersburg PA
CBHW020603260626
47157CB00003B/846